LOOK BEFORE YOU LEAP

TWELFTH BOOK IN THE BRIGANDSHAW CHRONICLES

PETER RIMMER

ALSO BY PETER RIMMER

∿

∿

∿

Each to His Own (Book 2)

❧

❧

First published in Great Britain in June 2021 by

KAMBA PUBLISHING, United Kingdom

10 9 8 7 6 5 4 3 2 1

Peter Rimmer asserts the moral right to be identified as the author of this work.

PART 1

MAY 1988 — "DOWN BY THE RIVER"

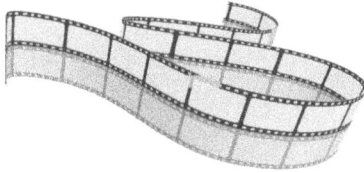

1

Randall Crookshank woke to the cry of a fish eagle. The campfire was out, a thin spiral of white smoke rising straight up to the morning sky from the ashes. All night, Randall had piled wood on the fire to protect himself from the wild animals. Still in his sleeping bag under the tree that rose seventy feet above him, Randall watched the big bird as it came down the river. The bird dropped its talons in front of Randall, fifty yards offshore, pulled a Zambezi bream out of the water and planed away towards the opposite shore, the fish too heavy for it to pull up into the sky. On the opposite bank of the big river, the fish writhing in its grip, the fish eagle ripped at its prey with its hooked beak. On and off for five minutes, through the German binoculars he had borrowed on the farm from his father, Randall watched the big eagle eat its breakfast. When the bird flew up into a tree to settle comfortably on its perch, the satisfied eyes searching the bush, Randall got up from the ground to make himself tea.

Under the riverine trees where the leaves had fallen the previous winter the ground was comparatively soft, the groundsheet he had placed over them keeping the bugs off Randall where he had slept. At the fire he stirred open the ashes, placing the kettle directly on the hot coals. Within a minute steam was pouring from the old tin spout. He made the tea in a mug with a teabag and sat on a fallen log. Even without his father's binoculars Randall could see the bird on the far side of the river, the flotsam floating down with the slow flow of the water. He was alone, happy and free of alcohol for the first time in months, England far away but close in his memory. Stirring the tea bag with a spoon Randall remembered the last time he had seen James Oliver. He had gone for a walk in Holland Park to get over his morning hangover. His son had just turned one year old. Amanda was sitting on a park bench talking to an old man, Randall's son in the pushchair in front of her. She had left him for a woman, taking his son

Randall pulled the tea bag out of the mug with the spoon and flipped it onto the embers of last night's fire. With a teaspoon of dried milk stirred into the tea, he put down the mug to cool. He was hungry. Picking up the binoculars, Randall looked again at the fish eagle. The bird, with telescopic eyes that could see a mouse in the grass from high up in the sky, was watching him. Randall smiled. He was at home. In his favourite place on earth, the Zambezi Valley. For three weeks, since leaving the farm and driving the farm Land Rover from World's View through the Centenary block and past his mother's grave before descending the escarpment into the valley, Randall had neither seen nor spoken to a soul. He was drying out, his days of drinking alcohol to forget Amanda and James Oliver behind him. During his alcoholic haze, the woman she had gone off with had paid Amanda's lawyers to divorce him. The woman, older than Amanda, was rich, and they were now even richer with Amanda's own inheritance. With a rented room in a boarding house in Notting Hill Gate and a job as a temporary waiter, there was no way he was going to get custody of his son. He had signed the papers hoping for a better future, a future for him with money that would bring back his son. His life had collapsed: his career, his marriage, even the country he had once called Rhodesia, all gone. Amanda had not seen him in the park. She had looked happy talking away. He had gone home to his room, packed his bags, paid Mrs Salter a month's rent in lieu of notice, which she had refused, borrowed the airfare from Oliver Manningford and James Tomlin, his old friends splitting the loan between them, and booked his flight back home to Zimbabwe. They had seen him right to the gate of the terminal at Heathrow Airport.

"I'll pay you back."

"You paid us back many years ago. Old friends, Randall. You'll come right again. Life will pick up. We've all been through it. Have a good flight home. And never, ever, stop writing books. You'll see. One day you'll get a literary break."

"I'll miss you two. Keep an eye on James Oliver. You are his godparents even if he hasn't been christened."

"We'll write to you at World's View. Life's a bugger."

"Stay well, old friends."

"Don't look so morbid, Randall. Our friendship isn't over. It'll only be over when we're dead."

"I'm going down into the Zambezi Valley to dry out and get my head straight."

"We'll be thinking of you. Have a safe flight."

Randall sipped his tea, the thought of friendship making him happy. The bird was still up in its tree, no other birds or animals to be seen, a moment of hush hanging over the Zambezi Valley. Later, when the sun was up, it would get hot. Randall finished his first cup of tea and took off his pants, walking down the steep bank to the water. Camping high on the slope made it safe from the hippo, the big animals unable to charge up such a steep incline. All through drinking his tea Randall had watched for crocodiles. Between the tall reeds there was a patch of clear water. Carefully, his mind on the crocodiles, Randall walked into the water. The water was cool. With only his head above the surface, sitting on the bottom of the small cove that pushed up to the riverbank, Randall kept watch around him. A small bird with a yellow breast and black beak was hanging on the side of a reed ten yards away, both of them comfortable with each other's company. The bird was eating something from the side of the reed making Randall remember he was hungry. As he stood up, water cascading from his body made the bird fly away. Across the river, the fish eagle had gone. Scrambling up the slope, Randall felt happy. One day, when his books had made a fortune, he would show his son the big river. The woman had had the money, the woman who had twice stolen his wife and now stolen his son. With money, that would change. Money changed everything. Money made a person powerful. All Randall required was a publisher who believed in his books. A publisher that would spend large amounts of money on publicity.

Back at last night's fire, Randall poured a mugful of water into the old tin kettle and put it back on the embers of the fire. When the water boiled he poured it into the mug on top of a fresh tea bag. Picking up his fishing rod and bait box Randall went back down to the water. The best fishing spot was next to the reeds. With the hook baited with a mopane worm, Randall cast his line. High up above the river, rising on the thermals, he could see the fish eagle, its great wings spread to give it lift. Randall slowly wound in the line, keeping the hook and bait just above the bottom of the river. High up, above the eagle, were a few fluffy white clouds. It would not rain again for months. The dry season they called it in Zimbabwe, the place of his birth... Randall felt the tug of a fish, waited and struck, winding the fish into shore. It was a Zambezi bream, the same size as the one caught by the eagle. Randall took his catch out of the water. With his sheath knife he gutted the fish, throwing the entrails up onto the bank so as not to attract the crocodiles. Then he washed the fish in the river.

Back at the fire, Randall put on more wood. The fish eagle called from high up on the thermals. Downriver, hidden by the riverine trees, another fish eagle called back. They were lovers. When Randall put his fish over the hot coals of the fire, the birds had circled together. Randall smiled. Life in the bush was so beautiful.

The cooked fish was bigger than the tin plate. Randall, as he ate, told himself there was nothing in the whole wide world better to eat than fresh river bream. The birds were still circling high up in the sky, the powder-blue of the sky highlighting the black of the wheeling birds as they circled each other. Once again one of the birds called, quickly answered by the other. Hungrily, Randall ate his fish, the white flesh peeling perfectly from the clean bone. Down at the river the weaver bird had come back with some of his friends, the reeds bending as the small birds pulled for their food. Before Randall had eaten his fish the flock of birds flew away. The fish eagles had flown out of sight. As Randall cleaned the remnants on his plate into the fire he heard the birds call from far away.

The sun was getting hot. Randall walked to the Land Rover. In the back was his writing table. Next to the table was a wooden box with blank paper and pens. For the first time since Amanda had gone off with his son to join Evelina, sending Randall to soak himself in drink, he was going to write. For all the weeks by the river, he had neither seen nor heard any trace of man, the therapy working. He had told the family he would go back to World's View when he ran out of food. With the rifle and shotgun Randall hoped to stay alone and write for the rest of the dry season. As he had come into the valley down the sparsely used road from the farm, the back way into the private hunting concessions and the Mana Pools national park, no one had noticed him. Surrounded by the thick riverine trees and so far into the wilderness, it was unlikely anyone would find him or hear the report of his gun. Small buck and guinea fowl were plentiful. With the bags of dried fruit from the farm and the sacks of rice, he would have total peace for months.

With the table erected next to his sleeping spot under the trees, the folding chair placed close to it, Randall took out a wad of clean foolscap paper, put it on the table and tried to write. Nothing came. Nothing happened. Randall daydreamed as the sun grew hotter. He smiled. There was all the peace and time in the world for his story to flow. Some said the first book was the most difficult. Some said the second. Some the third. This one would be the fourth he would finish. Oliver Manningford and James Tomlin were actors. They had all lived at the top of Mrs Salter's boarding house for so many years. Randall wanted to be a writer despite his degree in economics. Amanda had wanted him to be in business where there was money. For five years, Randall had worked for his Uncle Paul while going to night school. Amanda had lost their first baby, the pregnancy that had made him look at life more seriously: with women and family, life was all about money... Then the words began and Randall walked into his other world, the world of his characters, the lives of his characters where he could be and do as he wished. Two hours went by without Randall being conscious of his physical surroundings. His writing hand ached. Getting up from the chair, he walked to the fire, searched the ash with a stick to find the hot coals underneath, put a mug of water in the old tin kettle and made himself a mug of tea. He had never been happier. His new book had begun. It was the day he had first met Amanda. It was their story. He was now thirty. Then he had been twenty-one, a virgin just out of Africa, a whole new world away from terrorist attacks in front of him; in the book his fictional character was young, naïve and full of hope.

With his rifle over his left shoulder Randall went for a walk. The story was quickly moving from fact into fiction, his characters taking on a life and momentum of their own. The best stories of people were always an amalgam of Randall's experiences. The walks, plot walks as he liked to call them, freed up his mind for the story to talk and grow in his head. He even thought at night when he was asleep the plot was still talking to his subconscious. Past the riverine trees was the savannah, the great, lonely wild of Africa. The .375 was loaded, not to kill, but for protection. A mile away next to a clump of acacia trees was a giraffe, only the long neck and head visible. The animal was browsing the top of a tree. With the binoculars Randall could see the small knuckled horns on top of the animal's head. Far away behind the giraffe was a small group of elephants. With the long, dry grass of the savannah that came up to Randall's waist, it was difficult to see the smaller animals. At evening time they came down to the river to drink. Dusk was the time to see more of them. The sun was hot, the big bush hat protecting his face and shoulders. Randall switched the rifle to his right shoulder to make his walk more comfortable. The book had gone from his head. He was thinking of himself. If the book did not sell he would have to look for work to make himself a living. Africa was so beautiful but had no future for a white man. Robert Mugabe, the president of Zimbabwe, was seeing to that, the flywheel of the white man's economic engine going round in freewheel eight years after the black man rightfully took back his country from the British colonials sending them flying all over the world. Thanks to Amanda he had his degree. In a few years the flywheel would stop and with it the country's economy.

"They can take away your money, Randall,' his father had said when he met him at the airport. "Take away your property. But they can't take away your brains unless they kill you. That degree is vital to your future. You were wise to work so hard. Farming in Africa for us is a passing story."

"Thanks, Dad. I was hoping to go back to farming."

"When the story of the British is looked at from the long distance of history people won't know the British as a people, the same way we don't know the Romans. We were the last gasp of the British who came from England, Scotland, Ireland and Wales to a place we arrogantly called Rhodesia after Cecil John Rhodes. But it's gone. We and the empire have gone. Your future lies in England, or America. We Rhodesians don't exist anymore. Enjoy your solitude down in the valley. Write yourself a book.

Get your head right. But don't think of coming back to live on World's View. The farm is an anachronism. As are we. And in your future keep off the booze. Alcohol is a killer. Physically and mentally."

"I was just drowning my sorrows."

"What so many of the farmers here did during the bush war. Did none of us any good."

"Do you regret having come out to Africa from England?"

"Of course not. I've had a life. Many people in suburban England don't have the chance of real life. They sit in front of the television and die of boredom."

"It's not that bad."

"So what are you doing here, son?"

"Running away. The snag is, you can't run away from yourself. Why do we always think that going somewhere else will solve our problems?"

"Human nature. The quest for excitement. We have one life, Randall. Make the most of it. What went wrong in America?"

"A woman. We worked together at BLG Inc. Then Amanda pitched up again with Oliver Manningford and James Oliver. They were on their way to Hollywood for auditions. Amanda said she had left Evelina but looking back I'm not so sure. They wanted a child and now they've got one. When I got back to England Uncle Paul disowned me for being disloyal for joining the American company. Then the property market crashed and I had to sell our flat at Westcastle. After paying back the mortgage we had nothing. Amanda went back to Evelina. The good news is I don't owe any money other than to Oliver and James who paid for my air ticket. I've been screwed, Dad, well and truly screwed. Uncle Paul won't give me a reference. And no one wants to promote my books about the good old days of colonialism. *Masters of Vanity* was about the world of finance and even that didn't work... How's my stepmother and the rest of the family?"

"Bergit is fine. As are your brothers and sister. You can take the Land Rover and anything else you need. You want me to pay back your friends?"

"I'll handle it. We've always helped each other over the years."

"You're lucky to have good friends. Treasure them. They're worth more than any amount of money. Put your bags in the boot and we'll drive back to the farm."

"How was last year's crop?"

"Not too bad. It's the future that worries me. They're talking of designating all the white-owned farms for black settlement. Good luck to them. It will kill agriculture. You can't run anything without proper management. They must have taught you that at the London School of Economics. How is my brother Paul?"

"I haven't seen him since he told me to get out of his office. Grandmother sends her love... What are you going to do if Mugabe takes away World's View?"

"Go back to England I suppose."

"You're lucky to have invested in that Chelsea block of flats."

"You have to think ahead in life. Always have a way out... Is the weather still as bad in England?"

"It's terrible. You get used to it."

"You want to drive, Randall?"

"Do we ever learn from our mistakes?"

"Throughout history man has never learnt from his mistakes. Wars follow wars. Man-made disasters follow man-made disasters. Most of it's greed. We're all a greedy bunch of bastards. If we haven't got it we try and steal it. Most of us think we are righteous but none of us are. Politics and religion. We're a lovely species. One day we'll self-destruct."

"You make life sound pointless."

"When you get to my age you begin to wonder."

"Have you enjoyed your life, Dad?"

"Almost every minute of it. And I'm especially enjoying it now. Good to have you home again, son. You'll get through your problems. With a bit of help from your family and friends."

THE BOOK BEGAN TO FLOW, destroying the picture of his father at the airport. Always looking down for snakes in the grass, Randall walked on mulling his story, his mind drifting in different directions: there were many false starts and dead ends in the process of writing a story. The first three books had taught him a lot... Breaking out of the long grass to where it had been flattened Randall found the remnants of the kill. A family of impala had been attacked by lions. Usually the female lion made the kill. What he saw in front of him brought back the memory of his mother. Soon after he was born his mother had been attacked by a pride of lions. What the lions hadn't eaten was buried at the top of the escarpment. On his way through Randall had placed a red rose on her grave. The wooden cross that his father had made on the farm had fallen down and rotted. It had been difficult to find the grave. His mother had been an alcoholic, and drunk, alone, had driven away from the farm into the bush. He would have to be careful of alcohol. All through his life he had missed his mother. He blamed the booze, not the lions... There were flies on the carcase of the buck. From the other side of the small clearing made by the savagery of the lions Randall heard something. He was still attuned to every sound in the bush despite his years in London: a sound, a spoor, a broken twig caught his attention. Randall walked across and back into the elephant grass that came up to his waist. The gun was cocked and at the ready. There was no smell of lions. Randall picked up a handful of dust and let it trickle through his fingers to find the direction of the wind. The wind was coming from the direction of the sound. Whatever it was, the animal was in pain. Fifty yards into the long grass Randall found the buck. The animal's eyes pleaded with him. Its back legs had been mauled by the lions, and it had crawled away from the clearing on its stomach. Quickly, cleanly, Randall shot the buck. The pain went out of the impala's eyes. For a long moment Randall stood in silence. Then he picked up the carcase and threw it over his shoulder, pleased the lions had made it necessary for him to kill his supper. The carcase was a good fifty pounds, food for more than a week.

"Life, Randall. One dies, another lives."

By the time he reached the campsite, what he carried on his right shoulder he thought of as venison. Randall hated killing the animals. Down by the river he skinned and gutted the lion's kill, as he preferred to think of it. What he couldn't eat he carried up with the carcase and put near the fire. The skinned and gutted carcase, minus one of the haunches, he hung in a tree. He had seen no baboons down by the river. If they came, attracted to the smell of the carcase, he would hear them. Vervet monkeys were the same. When he made the fire to cook the venison Randall threw what wasn't edible on the flames. Every evening he would need to wash the carcase in the river to get rid of the eggs laid by the flies, before they turned into maggots and ate his meat. When the sun went down in the evening, sitting comfortably in a camp chair, he watched the haunch of meat cook over the coals of the fire. Next to his camp chair stood a fifty-pound gas bottle. From it there rose a long, thin metal cylinder connected to a lamp. For the umpteenth time Randall settled down to read Hemingway's *Fiesta*. The gas light spread up into the trees as the dusk faded into night, the meat cooking, Randall turning the meat as it cooked on the improvised spit he had made out of wood from a branch of the trees. The idea of a drink came into his head and was sadly rejected. The sound of frogs and cicadas had reached their peak with the night. His world was the campfire and as far as the gas light went up into the trees. He was happy. When he ate the meat with a bowl of rice he had boiled over the fire, he thought of Amanda and his one-year-old son. Maybe he still loved her. He wasn't sure. Later, replete, the mosquito net hanging round him from a branch up in the tree, the fire well stacked with wood to burn into the night, Randall got into his sleeping bag that rested on a groundsheet laid over last year's dry leaves and went to sleep. Twice he woke in the night and stoked the fire, taking his gun that he kept loaded next to his bed, each time quickly going back to sleep. He had spent the years up until he was twenty in the African bush. He was at home. Content and feeling safe. With everything around him familiar, he had never felt less alone.

The birds woke him with the dawn, the light just paling the sky. Instead of getting up, Randall put his hands behind his head and lay back. He was thinking of how life could change. One minute he was an executive of BLG Ltd in London, running the Westcastle project, turning an old warehouse by the Thames into an upmarket block of flats. They were lucky. They had finished and sold the flats before the property crash that, when he sold his own flat, had taken away his hard-earned savings. And now he was under a tree. Had she gone for him for who he was or for his financial potential? Or was it just sex? Had she been a lesbian before they met in the pub? He was young, had got what he wanted and not asked any questions. Only when Amanda fell pregnant did he take the relationship seriously. Nothing had been planned; ever since losing his virginity to Amanda, each event had simply followed the other. Like the big river in front of him they went with the flow. Their first baby was stillborn and six months later Amanda had gone off to live with the woman. Looking back Randall wondered what it had all been about. The years at BLG had gone on without Amanda asking for a divorce. There had been no point. She couldn't marry a woman.

Randall got up and went down to the river. The air was still cool from the night. Naked, he walked into the water. Behind him, against the bank, he had left his gun. The water was cool. Refreshed, happy and content, he walked back to his campsite and put on the kettle. The remains of the haunch of venison were in the Land Rover. He went across and cut himself some of the meat. The kettle had quickly boiled. His day had begun. He took the tea to his writing table under the tree. He sat down, read through what he had written the previous day, and began to write.

After writing all day, his mind tired from so much concentration, he packed up the materials on his desk and put the written pages and the clean pages in a small suitcase with his pen. He felt good. Writing always made him feel good when it went well. Randall walked away from the water and out of the riverine trees, the tall trees that all year round fed off the river through their roots that spread out under the water. Behind the trees was a small mopane forest that kept the line of the river. In the trees were the mopane worms, fat, hairy things he used as bait. Years earlier as a boy he had seen one of the villagers in Botswana fry mopane worms in a pan over the fire. He was going to try them. The worms on the leaves of the tree were easy to find. Back through the trees, Randall put the bag with the worms next to his camp chair near to last night's fire. There were still thin lines of smoke rising up into the air from the white ashes. Under the ashes the fire was still hot. The mound of wood he had collected was still enough to last a few more nights. Sleeping without a good fire was dangerous. With the frying pan he took from the Land Rover and the bottle of vegetable oil, Randall began to prepare for the first course of his supper. Under the white ash nearest to the chair the coals were just right. The pan with the oil was quickly hot. Randall added a handful of worms from the brown paper bag. The worms writhed and then sizzled. When he thought they were cooked he spooned out a few onto a plate to let them cool down. All the hair on the worms had disappeared. Testing for heat with his finger, he waited. The villager had said they were good to eat. Randall was not so sure. Eyes closed, he picked up a worm and put it in his mouth. Then he chewed. The worm was delicious to eat. Just like shrimp. Better than shrimp.

Randall laughed at himself for all those years he had wasted. By the time he had cooked and eaten the bag of worms he wished he had gathered more. There was so much in the African bush to eat that he did not know about.

Too lazy to get up and go to the Land Rover for some of the cooked meat, Randall sat back in his chair. Out in the stream he could see a family of hippo, just their heads in the water and the bulging eyes. They were far away. The day was going, the sun setting, the first cool breeze of the night coming across from the river. Remembering the raw meat hanging in the tree, Randall went to fetch the carcase, took it down to the river and washed it. There were no flies or maggots on the meat. Back at the tree, Randall covered the meat with the gauze and put it back up in the tree to hang. The venison was best after it had hung a few days. Like a good pheasant, the time to eat was just before the meat went rotten. Or so his grandmother had once told him. Like the delicious mopane worms, life was full of new experiences. His grandmother had said her mother hung the pheasants up by their heads and when the body of the bird fell away from the head she knew the meat was ripe. Randall was going to try the trick with a guinea fowl. Above in the trees the birds were singing. The perfect sounds weaving in and out of each other reminded him of a symphony orchestra, different birds playing different instruments. When he turned round, the red glow of the setting sun was reflected in the slow stream of the flowing river. The picture was so beautiful it made his heart sing with happiness, the symphony orchestra playing, the perfect picture made by nature in front of him. In a moment of joy Randall held both of his arms up to heaven.

Dusk came quickly. Half an hour after the sun set it was dark. The birds had stopped singing. Randall put kindling on the fire and it burst into flames. Only then did he put on big pieces of fallen trees he had humped into his store of firewood. Three big logs he pointed to the centre of the fire to come to a point. It was easy to push the logs in further to keep the fire burning. Where the burning logs met was the place to cook. A splash from the river made Randall stop what he was doing. He listened. The bush had gone quiet, only the frogs and cicadas taking no notice. Randall lit his reading lamp, the gas making its distinctive hissing sound. There were no more splashes from the river. With Hemingway in his hand Randall sat down to read. The girl in the book had been screwed by all the men; it was set in Spain over sixty years earlier. Nothing had changed. One American beat up a nineteen-year-old matador for screwing the girl, the American's thirty-four-year-old former girlfriend. Nothing had changed except the men didn't go off with the men and the women with the women. Or if they did Hemingway didn't write about it. Homosexuality had been taboo in those days. The single roar of a lion not far away brought Randall instantly out of the book. Getting up and leaving the book on the chair, Randall put small wood on the fire to bring up the flames. Again the splash in the river. Hungry, Randall went to the Land Rover, finding the piece of cooked venison. Back at the chair, the book on his lap, Randall began to gnaw at the haunch of venison. Again the roar of the lion but further away. Randall relaxed. The meat tasted good. They were all animals. Throwing the clean bone on the fire he went back to the book. The firelight was high up in the trees. The lion had seen the flames. Why he had gone away. The .375 was close by, resting against the table. Lost in the book, Randall forgot his surroundings.

The book finished, he made himself a cup of tea. He was tired. With the gaslight out, Randall walked with his mug of tea towards the river, away from the light of the fire. Only then did he look up at the night sky. There were three distinct layers of stars, the Milky Way in the middle. The moon had not yet come up. Out in the great expanse of river the stars were reflected. The slow, powerful flow of the starlit river was silent. Randall sipped his hot tea. He was comfortable being with himself. Away from all the people. Away from the booze. Nothing around him now was artificial. His body was recovering, no longer craving alcohol. Or craving the company of people. Briefly he thought of his one-year-old son seven thousand miles away in that other part of the world. For the moment there was nothing he could do for his son. His mind wandered away in many directions. Then the moon came up. A sickle moon, thin and beautiful. So far as his son was concerned he might as well have been on the moon. Randall finished his tea and walked back to the fire. The night temperature had dropped considerably. After piling wood on the fire and picking up his gun, he went to his bed. Under the mosquito netting he climbed into his sleeping bag. The gun was just outside the bottom of the net, lying alongside him. Within a minute he was fast asleep.

2

The crashing noise woke him out of his sleep, his heart pumping, his mind on full alert. With the loaded rifle now gripped in his right hand, Randall waited. By the sound of it the animal was settling down for the night. Randall got up and put a pile of dry wood on the fire, the flames coming up, the light of the fire spreading further into the trees. Not wanting to move too far from the protection of the fire there was nothing he could see, the underneath of the further trees pitch-dark. Again Randall waited, every nerve in his body alert. Outside of the constant whirr of the cicadas and croaking of the frogs everything was silent, the African frogs seeming to say 'fuck me, thank you, fuck me'. Smiling as the tension in his body seeped out of him he remembered his brother Phillip's words: 'They're the randiest, sexiest frogs in the world, and the girls are all so polite.' Randall went back to his bed, climbing under the net and into his sleeping bag, the gun back on the ground in easy reach next to him. The fire was burning bright. An owl called from far away. From further away it was answered by its mate. The moon had gone down behind the trees, making the stars in the heaven that much more bright, the river flowing through the reflection of the stars. His eyelids grew heavy. The next thing Randall knew he was awake and the morning light was coming up, the early birds beginning to sing to each other. Well rested, Randall got up. Walking away into the trees, Randall completed his morning ablution by relieving himself into a bush. Behind the bush, not fifty feet from where Randall had been peacefully sleeping, the grass had been flattened. A big animal had slept close to him during the night. By the extent of the flattened grass it could only have been an elephant lying on its side. Vaguely remembering another time this had happened, he made a mental note to ask his brother if elephants ever lay down.

"I'll be buggered. That's one for the book." Hands on his hips, Randall stared at the flattened grass.

With nothing to eat and just a mug of tea Randall set up his table to write. Soon he was back in his book, the characters taking on a life of their own, their stories consuming him... The book grew, days following days of solitary writing, weeks flowed into each other. At the end of July, with the book nearly complete, Randall heard the strangest of sounds coming from far upriver. Happily, he thought, at last the bush had made him lose his mind. Putting down his pen, Randall listened. It sounded like 'Randall'. Up in the tree a Cape turtle dove was calling 'How's Father', the translation of the call quite normal, the words listed in Randall's book of African birds. The 'Randall' call, intermittent, seemed to get closer. Randall got up from his desk and walked down to the river. Everything else sounded perfectly normal. Everything except the distant call that sounded just like 'Randall'.

"You've gone nuts, old boy. Must have been all that booze you drank in England. Withdrawal symptoms."

Randall shook his head to bring his mind back to normal. Still the call came, the sound that said 'Randall'.

"If I wasn't in the middle of bloody nowhere I'd say that sound is getting closer."

In time, Randall heard the sound of an engine. He was not going nuts after all. There was a boat somewhere on the river, upriver but coming closer. Within an hour, Randall was certain. Upriver, someone was calling his name. Even in the distant land of primal Africa he could not get away from people. Hoping he had imagined the word was 'Randall' he waited, the loaded gun back in his hand. His heart was thumping in his chest. The late sun was no longer so hot. The bush around Randall had gone deadly quiet. Not a sound. Not a sign of a bird or an animal on either side of the big river. Above in the blue sky a few white clouds hung motionless. The chugging noise of the approaching boat drew closer. Randall walked down the bank to the water, positioning himself behind the reeds. To anyone passing he was invisible.

"Whoever it is will see the bloody Land Rover," he told himself.

Randall held his breath. It was most probably illegal for him to be camped in a private game reserve. The boat came opposite to where he was hiding, out in the middle of the river. He still couldn't see the boat. The sound of the boat's engine changed. Whoever it was had turned towards the shore, towards the small estuary between the reeds where Randall swam and fished. Through the reeds Randall could now see the boat, the type of ski-boat used by tourists. On the front of the boat a black man was standing. Randall recognised him and stepped out from the cover of the reeds. The man was old, his short curly black hair now turned almost white.

"Silas! What are you doing out on the river?" Only then did the head of Randall's brother pop up from inside the boat.

"Ah, there you are. Good afternoon, Randall. It would be nice if you looked pleased to see us."

The boat rode into the shallows and stuck in the mud, Silas jumping down onto the ground. In his hand was a long piece of rope. He was grinning all over his face. Phillip jumped down next. At the wheel another employee of World's View was still standing in the cabin. The boat's engine went silent.

"What's happened, Phillip?"

"We thought by now you were dead." Phillip was smiling all over his face. "The idea is for Silas and Willard to drive the Land Rover back to the farm and for you to come with me on the boat. My truck's at Mana Pools. How are you, Randall? Father got worried though that's not the reason I am here. Villiers Publishing have accepted *Masters of Vanity* for publication. A fifty thousand-dollar advance in royalty and your airfare to America. Business class I might add. You're about to become famous, brother. All your wishes are about to come true... What the hell have you been eating the last three months? By now you must have run out of what you took with you from the farm."

"Venison, fish and guinea fowl. And rice. The rice has lasted. You are of course pulling my leg. How the hell did Villiers get hold of the manuscript?"

"You gave a copy to Harry Wakefield, the famous journalist and our dear stepmother's brother. It's not what you know but who you know. That old thread of Harry Brigandshaw has struck again in the family. I'd have brought a bottle of champagne but you are not allowed to drink. They want you on the next plane to New York."

"I can't leave here without finishing my new book. The characters will disappear from my head if I'm interrupted. Were you calling my name upriver? It sounded so weird."

"Don't I get a hug?"

"How are you, Silas?"

Instead of hugging his brother Randall first shook Silas by the hand, Silas who had worked for his father since the first year his father moved onto World's View long before Randall was born.

"You like venison, Silas. We'll roast a buck over the fire tonight."

"You got petrol for the Land Rover? Willard's going to drive."

"There's plenty in the cans to get you back to the farm. Good to see you."

While Silas and Willard walked up the slope carrying bags from the boat, Randall turned to his brother.

"Good to see you, old bugger."

Then they hugged. Both of them had tears in their eyes.

"After so many weeks and you didn't come back I thought the lions had got you. Just like Mother."

"You mind if I finish the book before we go? Take me another three or four days. At night we can sit round the campfire and catch up with our lives. We'll enjoy ourselves. The Crookshank brothers on safari."

"Wasn't that Carruthers?"

"You're right. Carruthers in India. There was an old boy in the club. Been in the Indian Civil before he came to Rhodesia. Specialised in those old colonial Carruthers jokes. So for three or four days we'll be Carruthers brothers on safari."

"I'll enjoy that."

"So will I... I put a rose on Mother's grave for both of us. The cross has fallen over."

"We'll go together one day and put up a new one."

"The site of her grave is so lonely."

"She lives in our minds. What she would have wanted."

"Life's a bugger."

"You can say that again."

Silas was coming back with a wooden stake he had found which he hammered into the bank of the river. Over his shoulder Randall watched him secure the boat.

"Where did you get that boat from?"

"Mana Pools. One of the tour operators owed me a favour. Tourism is booming since the end of the white man's rule and the end of sanctions."

"Didn't some writer call it the white man's burden?... You got a girlfriend yet, Phillip?"

"Where does a man like me find a good-looking girl in Zimbabwe? They've all pushed off."

"What about the tourists that go on your safaris?"

"Mostly one-night stands. Satisfying but temporary."

"And a lot less complicated."

"What's the book about?"

"A lesbian who goes for a man to get herself pregnant. Or that's how it started. Turned out to be the story of a young couple's life."

"How does it end?"

"Haven't finished yet. The end is going to be as much a surprise to me as the reader."

"I was really asking about *Masters of Vanity*. According to the letter from Harry, they are going to pay you ten per cent of sales. When that exceeds fifty thousand dollars you'll get more money. The letter to you was addressed care of Bergit. In London they think you disappeared off the map."

"Employees of banks gambling with depositors' money to make themselves big bonuses without any personal risk. All to boost their vanity. Rich people are as vain as peacocks. Like to show everything off... Why do they want me in New York?"

"Publicity tour and getting you on television. The fact you lost every penny of your money in the property crash makes a good story. You'll be doing a tour around the States signing books in all the bookshops. Appears writing a book is only a small part of the story. And that's a horrible pun. Villiers want to make you into a celebrity. In his letter to Bergit, Harry said a good publicist is more important than a good writer.

They're going to turn you into a commodity... Don't you have an ex-girlfriend in New York? She'll love a famous author."

"She won't need me to boost her ego. Hayley's got enough conceit for both of us. She's quite a bit older than me. Rich with a powerful job all thanks to her daddy... Do I have to go to America?"

"It's part of your contract. By the sound of it, for fifty thousand dollars and counting they've bought you as well as your book. Should be fun. All that money and fame."

"They want to buy my soul?" Randall looked out over the river. The birds were again singing. On the far bank a male kudu had come down to drink.

"Something like that... You got anything to eat? I'm hungry."

"Didn't you bring any food? Just kidding. I promised Silas we'd spit-roast a buck. You and I are going hunting. I only shoot when I eat. Good to see you, Phillip."

"You got over all the booze?"

"Had the shakes for a while but that's all gone... Does Willard know the way back to the farm?... In *Masters of Vanity* my heroes are all a greedy bunch of bastards. The thought of great wealth appeals to most of us. But there's a price. There's always a price. Even in writing books by the sound of it. Mugabe thinks us whites are also a greedy bunch of bastards who couldn't afford the price of land in England. Four thousand whites, mostly 'old family' Englishmen down on their luck who through owning six-thousand-acre farms in Rhodesia turned themselves back into feudal barons. Maybe he was right. But there's a catch. Like with the young bankers in *Masters of Vanity* the white farmers are indispensable. You need money to set up as entrepreneurs, to get new business going, to make wealth in the world and drag people out of poverty. And that's what Mugabe is going to miss if he kicks the white man off their farms. Not only did they create the best agricultural economy in Africa, they provided work and food for the people. Sure, the comparison of a rich tobacco farmer in his Mercedes Benz against the black labourer is appalling. But without the white man's capital he brought into the country, and without his expertise in farming and running a business, the land that Mugabe likes to talk about so much as belonging to him would still be lying fallow, grazed only by wild animals. The poor sods who lost out are the wild animals, not the indigenous people. The whites took a big risk coming out to Africa. The bankers in *Masters of Vanity* say they take risks. You can argue any problem from either direction, depending on which side of the fence you are sitting. Everything that goes around comes around, as the old saying goes. Who's right and who's wrong will be told only by history. But blaming bankers for the property crash, for lending money indiscriminately, is as good in a book as criticising the white farmers for getting rich from the sweat of the black man's brow. Mostly in history one lot of predators are replaced by another. The only question for history to answer in Zimbabwe is whether us whites have been predators or providers."

"So Dad was wrong to come to Africa?"

"Many will say so. They'll only find out the truth when Dad is thrown off the farm."

"You think that will happen?"

"He thinks it will. Who knows? It'll mostly depend on how Mugabe wants to run the country. What suits him and his ZANU party. But don't get me onto politics. I leave that to the characters in my books... Fifty thousand US dollars? I'm rich. I can pay back my friends for lending me the airfare to come home."

"Do you still think of Zimbabwe as your home?"

"Of course I do. Don't you?... 'New York, New York.' Here we come again."

"You don't have to sing."

"Of course I do. My cycle of life has begun again."

"Is the new book any good?"

"I have no idea. The writer never knows. That's up to the reader... You want some tea? I'll put on the kettle... Life comes and goes in strange ways. One minute I was sitting here thinking I was finished, with no way of making a living, and the next minute everything has changed... I'll miss this river. I've enjoyed writing the book. Being alone can be comforting. You don't have to put up with other people. Other people who most of the time are wanting something from you... Does an elephant sleep on its side at night? I seem to remember asking you before."

"I'm not sure."

"Neither am I... Tea, and then we'll go hunting. Got to feed everybody."

"So the tea lasted?"

"Of course it did. A man's got to have his tea. Did you know tea is a Chinese word?... Will Silas and Willard be all right while we go hunting?"

LATER THAT NIGHT, when they had all eaten their fill round the fire, Silas and Willard went down to the boat to sleep. All through supper the four of them had spoken to each other in Shona. To Randall it felt like family, a lifelong kinship.

"We can both sleep under the mosquito net. There's enough room on the groundsheet for both of us."

"Do you miss your son and your ex-wife?"

"I try not to think of them. A man should think forward, never back."

"How does it feel to be about to publish a book?"

"Hasn't sunk in yet. I'm still physically in Africa and mentally in my new book. That was a good long shot that took out that impala. Glad you made the kill. I hate killing anything. I'm tired, Phillip. Been writing since the sun came up. The story is still so much part of me. More real than myself. You mind if I go to bed?"

"I'll leave you alone under your tree. I've taken my antimalarial pill and I have some spray for my skin. I'll sleep round the fire. Keep it stoked during the night. When did you last start the engine of the Land Rover?"

"Three days ago. I start up the engine every week. If you don't stay alert in this life it'll kill you. It's really good to see you, my brother. How did the tobacco crop sell on the auction floors?"

"Dad had a good season. The prices were good."

"But he doesn't think it will last."

"The Lancaster House Agreement between Smith and Mugabe gave the two sides a transition period of ten years, while Mugabe and his friends took control of the country. Then it's 'willing seller', 'willing buyer' or meant to be for the farms."

"What will you do if Mugabe kicks out the whites? He's had a go at the Matabele."

"Who knows? I take life as it comes. We've all got British passports in the Crookshank family. Go back to England I suppose... What's New York like?"

"Big, powerful, exciting and dangerous. So different from my life here on the big river the mind boggles. A whole different world... Won't tourists always need safari guides?"

"I hope so. I'd hate to leave Africa. It's my home. Where I live. Who I am. I could never live in a great metropolis. I'd be lost."

"So they are going to publish my book. I can't believe it. My world is again being stood on its head. Sleep well, brother. Keep your gun next to you. Oh, that really is stupid. You're the safari operator."

"See you in the morning."

Randall woke twice during the night. Both times the fire was blazing. He could see his brother lying on the ground next to the fire, a blanket half over his body. Phillip had not taken off his clothes. The second time, Randall lay awake listening to the African night. It was difficult to keep his eyes open and not fall back into sleep. There was no sound coming from the boat. Upriver, where they would be going when he had finished the book, he heard splashes. Then silence. A buck barked, the one short bark so different to a dog's. Randall drifted back into sleep and his dreams.

When he woke with the dawn Phillip was kneeling next to the fire, looking into the old tin kettle to see if the water had boiled. He burned his hand moving the lid and sucked his finger. Randall put his hands behind his head and lay where he was under the mosquito net. It was going to be tea brought to him in bed. When Phillip made the tea, Willard came up from the boat. He was carrying a fish. Together the two of them made four mugs of tea. Silas, the old retainer, joined them. They were speaking in Shona. Silas was also carrying a large fish, which was still wriggling on the end of the boat hook he had used to haul it out of the water. The fish was a vundu that looked like it weighed over fifty pounds. There was going to be plenty of fresh fish for breakfast. Randall smiled. He tried to bring the story of the book into his mind and failed. He would have to wait until Silas and Willard drove away in the Land Rover and everything quietened down again. Writing a book required his full concentration.

"Don't you ever get out of bed? Here's your tea."

"Thanks, Phillip. You sleep well? Thanks for stoking the fire during the night... When are they going?"

"After we've all had breakfast. You see that fish? Then I'm going down to the boat to read my book so you can get on. Can you finish in three days?"

"What day is it?"

"Wednesday. All day. On the first day of September, the first day of spring, by the time I take you back to the farm Dad will have started the dry planting. The new tobacco season will have started. Let's hope we have a good rainy season."

"Thanks again for the tea."

"My pleasure... You want to go for a swim? Willard can stand on the bank with the gun. This river is infested with crocodiles. The trick is to bang a couple of shots in the water before you go for a dip. I'm sure you know that one."

"Let me finish my tea. I'll get to my desk when they've gone. Now I've got a deadline I won't muck around."

"This is the most beautiful place in the world."

"Don't tell me."

An hour later, with the sound of the farm Land Rover receding into the distance, Randall went to the folding table that served as his desk. He read back the previous day's writing. Instead of the story flowing, nothing happened. There were too many new thoughts in his mind. Instead of staying in his book he was back in New York, thinking of Hayley and his life in business. Struggling to concentrate, his mug of tea cold in front of him, he got up and went for a walk. Soon he was back in his story, all thought of his affair with Hayley forgotten. Quickening his pace he went back to his desk, straight into the story, the real world forgotten. Randall wrote all day, the story flying towards its climax. As the sun was dropping behind the trees it was over. This time the lovers had parted forever. Exhausted, Randall put down his pen. He felt terrible. Everything had gone. All the people who had kept him company had gone. Despite his brother he was alone. Lonely, he got up and walked away through the trees. He would never be with them again. He had lost his friends. From now on they would belong to his readers. Depressed and despondent, what he needed was a drink. Trying to overcome his feeling of sadness, he walked back to camp. He packed all the papers on the table away. Phillip was sitting on the front of his boat, down below on the bank of the river. The birds were calling to each other, telling their mates which tree they would be roosting in for the night. Randall put more wood on the fire, stirring the ashes. The new wood burst into flames. There was enough of last night's impala for their supper. Plenty of cold fish. The feeling of sadness at having finished his book would not go away. He had never been good at happy endings. Life rarely ended happily. There were just the happy moments as it went along.

Phillip came up from the boat.

"What the hell's the matter with you, Randall?"

"You don't by any chance have a bottle of whisky on board that boat? I've finished the book."

"That was quicker than you thought."

"Happens that way. We can pack up and leave tomorrow. Not much to take on the boat. Just me and the book, the table and chair and the bedding. The rest went in the Land Rover."

"You really think you should drink?"

"The Carruthers brothers on safari, don't forget."

"I've got a case of good South African wine on board."

"That'll do."

"Are you happy with the book?"

"I'm miserable. Postnatal depression. Worse than having a baby. About the same as Amanda suffered after she lost our first baby. Oh God, was she depressed. Trouble was I didn't help enough... We don't have to cook. There's plenty of cold venison and fish. And I need a drink."

"Why not? You only live once. What the hell. Most of us are alcoholics. We just won't admit to it. I'll get the case of wine, the corkscrew and the wine glasses."

"That's the stuff, Carruthers."

"We don't have to go tomorrow. Tonight the brothers will get drunk. Tomorrow we will recover. The next day we'll go upriver... How was the ending?"

"Sad. Very sad. Like most people's lives."

"Will it sell?"

"Oh, there's lots of fun in the middle. Readers like to recognise themselves. They'll have plenty to recognise. Reading a book is lonely. You do it by yourself. Lots of people cry when they finish a book. Come on. I'll help you by carrying the wine glasses... You know, Phillip, I wonder if I'll ever see the big river again? My life is about to change. I just hope it changes for the better. But you have to be an optimist."

Randall stood on the high bank for a moment looking around. He knew it was an important moment, a moment of memory for him to carry with him for the rest of his life. There were tears in his eyes blurring the picture. He had lost the book forever and with it Amanda. He had based the lady in the book on his wife. James Oliver, one year old, was too young to have come into the book. Maybe later, when he was a famous and rich novelist, his son would want to come into his life. Most of the people he had met in England and America liked to mix with the rich and famous. There was nothing better than a bestselling book to make a person popular. The thought of having to buy his son's attention made him sick. The light was beginning to fade as the sun slipped away. The few clouds in the sky coloured up red. He could see the rich crimson red of the clouds reflected in the river. The river flowed on and on forever. Another day in the bush had almost gone. His eyes pricked, the tears coming again. A brief wind came up and stopped. The birds were all singing. His brother walked up the steep bank of the river carrying the case of wine. On top of the case were two tall wine glasses and a shiny metal corkscrew. The glow of the setting sun reflected on one side of the wine glasses. Their eyes met. Neither spoke. Both of them knew. What they were about to enjoy would never be repeated. They were making a memory.

"That should be enough wine," said Randall trying to smile. "The past is the past. Only the future has any relevance."

"Unless you learn from the past."

"Don't be stupid. Never once in the history of man have we ever learnt from our mistakes. Looking back turns us all into pessimists."

"You think you should drink?"

"No."

"But you're going to?"

"Yes... You know, Phillip, there is nothing more pathetic in a man's life than feeling sorry for himself. When Amanda left me for Evelina I drank myself into oblivion, trying to forget. I'd lost my wife to a lesbian, my house to a crash in the market. I couldn't get a job because my employer, our esteemed Uncle Paul, wouldn't give me a reference. And drunk I wasn't much good waiting tables. Which came first, the booze or the depression, is anyone's guess. I got right down to the bottom and I ain't going there again. Winston Churchill said he could use booze to his benefit. They say he drank seventeen tots of brandy every day. And he did all right. Won the war and went down in British history forever. Not as a drunk but a national hero. Let's hope this time I can control my drinking. It's all mind over matter. With my books I have a purpose again. And thanks to Villiers Publishing it looks as though I can make a living out of my writing. So tonight, round the campfire, let the brothers enjoy themselves. The ultimate in sibling bonding. And just look at that. Nederburg Cabernet. My very favourite."

"You want to take the glasses before they fall off? Lead on, Carruthers. We have a night to spend."

"Thanks for being my brother."

"She would have liked to have watched us tonight."

"Maybe she is. Her bones are buried on the top of the great escarpment. Maybe her soul floats over the valley."

"We'll drink to our mother. That's what we'll do. She liked a good bottle of wine, according to father. It's so strange to go through life not having known your mother. If there is a God, we'll meet her in heaven. Tonight, while we sit round the fire, let us hope she is watching over us and smiling. Come on. Let's pop the cork."

"You think they'll get the Land Rover back to the farm?"

"Of course they will. There's only one road up the escarpment."

Randall took the glasses and the corkscrew off the top of the case of wine. He was smiling. There was no point in going back to the boat for one bottle at a time. Certainly not when they were drunk and couldn't see where they were going. Last night's cold venison and the rest of the vundu were hanging in the tree, protected by the gauze netting. Randall brought the supper out of the tree and put it on the table he had moved next to the fire with his chair. The three folding chairs from the boat were still where they had left them the previous night. Phillip popped the cork, moved one of the chairs next to the table, poured a small amount of the wine into a glass and handed the glass to Randall to taste. Randall first smelt the wine before taking a sip.

"Nectar of the gods. The perfect wine. Heaven in a bottle. To your health, to hell with your wealth. Fill up the glasses. The party has begun... You want a chunk of meat or I can break off a piece of fish? What the hell. Help yourself."

Phillip poured out the wine, held his glass up to the quickly fading light, the last of the red sun blending into the red of the wine, making it glow. They raised their glasses to each other. Neither said a word. Both of them drank, both of them smiling. The last forked rays of the sun slipped away to shine on another continent. The day had gone, the firelight spreading with the dark up into the tall riverine trees. The birds had gone silent. There was a faint reflection on the flowing river where the tiny waves caught the first light from the stars. The moon had not yet come up. Despite finishing his book, Randall was happy. Over the years growing up together they had had their arguments but none of it had mattered. Neither had ever borne any malice, their arguments quickly forgotten. Best of all they were friends. His brother, his only full sibling, was his best friend. Losing their mother had bonded them together from an early age, giving each other the comfort they would have got from her. In comfortable silence they let the night envelop them, their world shrinking to the small patch of light from the fire. A piece of wood broke off and fell back into the heat of the fire sending a shower of sparks up towards the heavens. In among the dark of the trees Randall could see a firefly glowing in the blackness. The wine he was drinking tasted delicious, the alcohol, after so long an abstinence, going straight to his head. He was content. To increase the taste of the red wine he cut himself a chunk of venison off the impala carcase and happily began to chew. After each mouthful of meat he sipped his wine.

"What are you going to call it?" asked Phillip.

"The Woman Who Stole My Wife."

"Should catch the eye in the shops."

"That's the whole idea."

"You want to tell me more about it?"

"Not really... You ever think of wanting to have kids?"

"Of course I do. If you don't leave children behind you leave nothing."

"Have you been in love with a woman?"

"Not yet. But I live in hope... A lot of women are materialistic. A white safari operator, a washed-up-on-the-shore relic of despised colonialism, isn't exactly a long-term catch. The women I have met were happy to have fun and move on. Women all want a future whether they say so or not. For themselves and their children. And why not? It's built into human nature. A woman wants a man who will give her children a comfortable and permanent nest. I don't fit into that picture unless I find a Zimbabwean girl who can't get residence in a country outside Zimbabwe and wants a ticket out of the mess. It's called self-preservation. Not love. So here I am in my thirties and still single. And until I bloody well have to, I don't want to leave Africa. Just look at this place. It exists nowhere else in the world. I can't willingly change this for an overcrowded England. How did you manage it?"

"You get used to anything. And there are compensations. Lots of them. Running a highly successful development project for Uncle Paul was a rush. You've never seen so much money created from nothing. An old warehouse by the River Thames torn down and converted into a thriving block of modern flats. The front ones with a view of the river sold for a fortune... America had its moments. Many moments. The last one with Hayley not as good as the first."

"I'm afraid of change. Too long in the bush. You get bush-happy."

"Most of us hate change."

"Cut me a slice of meat."

"My pleasure. Goes well with the wine... Are you happy, Phillip?"

"I don't know. I think so. I hope so. Whoever knows if they are really happy?"

The other world, the brutal world of other people permanently screaming to get what they want, had gone. There was just the two of them and nature. They were both totally in the present. They drank slowly, no need to get drunk. No need to forget the past or not think of the future. They were just there, the two of them, the only humans left in the world. Looking up, Randall saw the heavens. The stars, the planets twinkling. There was no evil up among the stars. The Milky Way was as if the gods had sprayed a jug of milk across the heavens. The stars made no sound. All they did was twinkle. The pain at losing his book was going away. Like the Milky Way he had splashed out something that could live forever. His people would live forever. There had been some strange purpose in his life, all the turmoil having a meaning. He was getting himself drunk and making up another story. The book was only a story. An entertainment. In the very old days before words could be written, the storyteller sat round the fire telling stories to entertain. The storyteller was an important part of people's lives. He was the only source of entertainment in the long, cold winter nights of Randall's ancestors. In the north, where the Vikings had come from to conquer England, the winters were mostly night. Maybe, Randall thought, some of his ancestors had been storytellers, the reason why his need to write was so intense. Writing the book had contained his alcoholism, not stopped his drinking. His brother Phillip was just as much of a storyteller, one of the reasons his clients came back. Like now, they wanted to sit round the fire and be told stories of Africa, stories they would always remember when the picture in their minds of Africa had faded.

"You're very silent, Randall. You are letting me do all the talking."

"I love your stories of the bush. You have experienced so much. For me it's so much wonderful material."

"I'm looking forward to reading one of your books."

"I hope so. I hope I don't disappoint you."

Randall got up from the comfortable canvas chair he had been sitting in, leaving his empty glass on the ground, and fed fallen tree branches onto the fire. He stood looking into the fire as the flames grew and with it the spreading light. The fire, and its protection from wild animals, was comforting. The wine and the fire made him feel relaxed.

"I'm sure it was an elephant that slept on its side not far away. I heard it go down for the night. The next day all I found was flattened grass."

"You sure it was an elephant?"

"What else could it have been? There's something rather nice in imagining sleeping away the night next to a wild elephant."

"A friend of mine was killed by a hippo. He had a small, ramshackle houseboat moored close to Kariba Breezes, one of my favourite pubs. Clarence had got drunk as usual and was walking down to his boat. You weren't meant to sleep on your boat without a permit from the owner of the surrounding campsite. It was pitch-dark away from the hotel. The hippo snapped him in half with its big mouth, apparently protecting its calf. My friend would never have known what happened. He was broke, out of a job and starting to get old. Some said it was a blessing."

"Poor man."

"There was only Clarence. No wife or children. His only love was the bush. After the funeral and the cremation we scattered his ashes out on the lake. Then we all went to the pub at Kariba Breezes and got ourselves drunk."

"When did it happen?"

"Couple of years ago. I'll always remember Clarence... You want me to open another bottle? It's going down rather well, Carruthers."

"Why not?"

For a long while they were silent.

"Did you love her?"

"I'm not sure. I think I loved Amanda. I hope so."

"One day I want to meet my nephew. James Oliver. Two names in one. Isn't that a little strange?"

"I have two friends in England. Both are actors. Quite often out-of-work actors. One is James. The other is Oliver. Didn't want to choose."

"Makes sense."

"They are James Oliver's godparents. Except he hasn't been christened."

"They are still his godparents."

"Exactly... I'll open the wine. Just look at the heavens. It's all so beautiful. I'll miss Africa more than anything."

"So would I. I try not to think of it. I think I'd shoot myself in preference to leaving Africa."

"Please don't do that."

"I've never lived anywhere else."

"You could always try. The English countryside is very beautiful. The wild flowers. Bluebells in the woods. You'd get used to it."

"You think so?"

"I'm sure of it... If he was broke, who bought Clarence the drinks?"

"We all did. He was a great storyteller. There's nothing to watch on Zimbabwe television. Most of it's Mugabe's propaganda... Are there many lions in this area? I didn't hear them last night."

"There are plenty of lions. They don't like the light from the fire."

"You sleep with a gun?"

"Every night. In life, you have to keep your wits about you... Is there anything more beautiful than the sound of a cork popping out of a wine bottle?"

"You let me pour."

"Thanks, Phillip. Good to be with you. Chin-chin."

They clinked glasses, the firelight showing Randall the happiness reflected in his brother's eyes.

"We're lucky."

"I know we are... Want some more meat?"

"Was Clarence born in Rhodesia?"

"I don't think so. Came out from England after the war someone said. He had a bit of a Rhodesian accent. There weren't many jobs in England after the war. It was not until the sixties the economy built up. Some of the chaps who came out then said in retrospect they would have been better off financially if they had stayed in England. But whoever knows what's coming in the future? You do what looks good at the time and hope for the best. For centuries man has roamed the world looking for a better opportunity. We're never content. Some say it's all part of the process of evolution. Who we now are, you and I, came out of Africa in the first place. Lucy, who the scientists say is one of our ancestors, roamed the African forest over three million years ago. Makes you think."

"So Africa was our original home?"

"If you believe all the anthropologists. Was it creation or evolution? You believe what you want. What you think is good for you. I like to believe God created man six thousand years ago as it says in the Old Testament. Gives life a point. Without God we are just a link in an ongoing chain. Maybe we shouldn't take every word in the bible literally, including the seven days of the creation. Maybe God took a lot longer to make us."

"Do you think a lot?"

"I try not to. Too much thinking muddles the brain. Until we die we're not going to find out but I like to hold onto my faith in the Christian religion."

"I envy you."

"Don't you have faith, Randall?"

"Not really. I think when we are dead we're much like that carcase hanging in the tree. So much dead meat."

"How awful... You hear that? That's a lion. Far away. Nature is God, Randall. Believe me."

"If nature is God, I'm the most religious man in the world. Nature is beautiful. You're right. Who else but God could have created something so beautiful?"

"She can see us now. I can feel it. I can sense our mother's smile."

Randall fell silent. For him the night was themselves and the lion, however much he tried to feel his mother's presence. He drank down his wine and filled up his glass, refilling Phillip's too. The moon was coming up from behind the trees, the love cries of the frogs in full flight. An owl called and was answered by its mate. The night was alive. They sat and drank. Filling their glasses, the wine taking over control of Randall's mind. After they drank the third bottle of wine they went to their beds. Randall had forgotten his gun. He got under the netting that hung from the tree, climbed into the sleeping bag and went to sleep. Somewhere between being awake and being asleep he heard his brother wishing him a good night. He didn't dream. The wine had seen to that. When he woke with the light of day he remembered nothing from the night. They ate cold meat and moved everything down to the boat. By the time the sun was over the trees they were on their way. They both had slight hangovers but nothing serious. The Carruthers brothers had left the campsite, both of them knowing they would never return together. In the boat, with the engine running at full throttle, neither of them spoke. They both looked sad. As if they had lost something. They were out of the present and travelling into their future, neither of them sure where they were going.

The boat cut a wake through the heart of the river, like a dagger thrust into its soul, sending a V-shaped turbulence towards both banks. Phillip cut back the throttle to save petrol. Two hours into their journey they saw the first thatched huts by the side of the river. A small boy, quite naked, waved at the boat. Randall and Phillip waved back. They were all smiling. Earlier, they had eaten the last of the meat, the bones of the fish thrown into the water. All through their journey they saw wild animals on both sides of the river. Only near the African huts had there been any cattle, the big-horned cattle as skinny as rakes. Only the wild animals looked fat and healthy.

"Those cows don't look good."

"They don't like to graze them too far from the huts for fear of wild animals. Not enough grass."

"How much further is it?"

"Have patience, brother."

"Now I've made up my mind to go I don't want to stay around."

"I know the feeling. We'll stay one night with my friend who lent me the boat and then drive up to the farm. I'll phone Dad from Mana Pools. He was getting really worried about you. Myra and Craig are in Harare. We can say hello to them on the way through."

"What are they going to do with the rest of their lives?"

"You can ask them."

"If our mother hadn't been killed by lions they would never have been born. Bergit wouldn't have married Dad."

"And her brother Harry would not have found you a publisher."

"Life is one big chance."

"Makes it exciting."

"Not for our mother. And if Livy Johnston had wanted to stay in Africa she would have married our father and neither of us would have been born."

"And the family wouldn't have the security of that block of flats in Chelsea that Dad still owns with Livy."

"Life is indeed strange."

"You want to drive the boat for a while?"

"Why not?"

"When are you flying to America?"

"As soon as possible once they send me the ticket. The money they can pay into my London bank account."

"You still have a bank account?"

"Nothing in it."

"You can call them in New York from the farm."

"You know, I envy that kid living his life on the bank of the river. Some would call it living in poverty. I would call it living in peace. The world of aeroplanes and telephones, of bank accounts and hordes of people is sucking me back and I don't much like the feeling."

"Don't you want to be a famous novelist?"

"I'll find out what it's like when it happens."

3

There were tents among the trees down the side of the river, Randall back among people, having to remember what to say. It was important among people to be nice to them. Phillip had taken back the wheel of the boat and was steering them into shore. Behind the tents, Randall could see trucks and cars. Someone was playing a radio. A girl, a beautiful girl, waved. It wasn't all bad. Randall smiled at the girl who seemed to know Phillip. Up front in the bows, holding the rope, Randall waited for the bump. Then he jumped off the boat. Behind him, Phillip turned off the engine. Randall tied up the boat. Everything was organised. Everything in its place.

"This is Alison. Alison, meet my brother Randall."

"So you found him?"

"Took a while. Alison is the boat owner's girlfriend."

"What were you doing all on your own?"

"Writing a book."

"Is it finished?"

"Every word of it."

"Phillip says you're going to be famous."

"Who knows? At least I have found a publisher."

"Congratulations. How long are you staying?"

"Just tonight. I have to fly to New York."

"Sounds so exciting. Beats the life of a tour guide. What's in that bag you're clutching?"

"My new book. Don't want to lose it. At the moment there is only one copy... Where's your car, Phillip?"

They walked to the parked cars and Phillip opened the boot of the Toyota Land Cruiser. Randall put the small case in the boot. The girl had gone.

"The car looks new. Must be making money."

"People like to go on safari with professionals. They pay big money."

"She's very pretty."

"Down, boy. She belongs to my friend."

"No one belongs to anyone... It all looks so commercial."

"Making money. That's what life is all about. You got to have money."

They emptied the boat, putting most of the stuff in the Land Cruiser. A few bits went into the tent, a square frame tent Phillip had erected the night he borrowed the boat. The tent next to them belonged to his friend. The day was coming to an end, the cooking fires started, people bringing out the drinks. The girl came back again, this time with her friend. Phillip gave him back the keys to the boat.

"I owe you one."

"Just bring me customers when you're overbooked."

They were all introduced, all of them polite to each other. Randall was back in civilisation, and despite the pretty girl, not sure if he liked it. It would take time getting back. Being what people liked to call normal. The man, like the girl, was impressed with him being a writer. Before he had found a publisher no one had been interested. Later, when they sat round the fire drinking another bottle of Phillip's red wine, the girl kept looking at him. The girl was very pretty. Randall was flattered, despite his scepticism. It was like his days at BLG when he had had a big salary and all the girls were interested. He was back in the world of people, voices everywhere, and the sound of a radio. He could still hear the frogs and the cicadas but they were secondary, man with all his games and frolics more important than nature. It made Randall sad.

The next day they drove away from the national park with the dawn, through the security gate, the man in the guard-room recognising Phillip and raising the boom. Ten minutes later they turned onto the tarred main road, to the right Zambia, to the left Harare, the dust trail no longer billowing out behind them. They were both feeling flat.

"She never comes on to me like that. Poor Godfrey. Right in front of him. I must write a book. She's good with the tourists. Pretty girls usually are."

"She was just being polite."

"Don't talk bloody nonsense."

"She was interested in hearing about me as a writer, not in me. Something different to talk about."

They reached Harare before lunch, stopping at Meikles Hotel. The restaurant in the hotel was the best in Harare. Their half-sister Myra would be working in the bank so they had time to kill. After lunch, expensive and paid for by Phillip, Phillip went off to do a promotional tour of the travel agents, trying to drum up business for his safari operation. He and his partner Jacques owned two safari buses. Phillip had gone off looking quite the man of business. They didn't know when Craig would be out of university where he was finishing his degree in Social Science. Sitting in the corner of the lounge, no one took any notice of him. The book, he hoped, was still safe in the boot of the Toyota, parked in the hotel garage. After half an hour of twiddling his thumbs Randall left the hotel and went outside for a walk in what used to be called Cecil Square, the square that had been named after Cecil John Rhodes, the founder of colonial Rhodesia. Idly, Randall wondered if Robert Mugabe, the man who had toppled colonialism, knew the park had been named after Rhodes. Or the Centenary, where his father farmed, which had been founded on the hundredth anniversary of Rhodes's birth. The small park with its fountain and wooden benches was quiet. He could hear the call of the doves. The doves that called 'how's Father' reminded Randall of his son James Oliver who by now should have spoken his first words. There were a few blacks lying on the grass taking naps. One of them woke, saw Randall on his bench, and smiled. Randall gave him a smile. Again, the thought of leaving Africa made him sick. Comfortable, hands on his lap, he nodded off. When he woke the man had gone, the patch of well-kept grass empty. Probably, the man had gone back to work. At five o'clock, as arranged, he walked back into the lobby of the hotel. Phillip was waiting at reception. They drove to Baker Avenue and the small flat shared by their half-brother and half-sister. Myra opened the door. She looked as pretty as paint. Even more beautiful. Craig was standing behind her. All of them hugged, all of them talking ten to the dozen, all of them trying to get in a word.

"After a month, when you didn't go back to the farm, we thought you had died."

"No such luck, Myra."

"This time I'm coming with you to England. There's no future for us in Zimbabwe."

"I'm going to America."

"Then I'll come to America. I'm sick of being a teller in a bank. Craig wants to come too. Don't tell Mum and Dad. They'll think they're being abandoned. Harare is so parochial. I want some excitement. I'm twenty-one. There's got to be more to life. When are you going?"

"When they send me a ticket and give me some money."

"Good. I can't wait. Look happy for me, Randall. I'm about to get a life. Come in. The place is in a mess. But who cares? Oh, it's so wonderful to have a famous brother."

"I'm not famous yet."

"But you will be. Oh, you will be. Isn't it wonderful? Are you going to visit your famous grandfather in America? Ben Crossley, the actor. So amazing to now have two famous people in the family. Even if he is not my own grandfather."

"Your own grandfather, like your uncle, was a famous journalist."

"There's a bit more to fame being an actor or a writer."

"Is fame so important, Myra?"

"Of course it is. Fame is the most important thing in the world. Fame and money. All famous people get rich one way or the other."

"You won't be able to work in America. You'd better wait for me to go back to England."

"Oh, good, you're not going to live in Zimbabwe."

"I doubt my publishers will let me. A writer, to promote the sale of his books, has to be in the limelight. You have to make a noise. Catch the attention of the media. You can't do that living far away in the African bush... What are you going to do in England? You'd better make us some tea. I'm not meant to drink alcohol. And Craig, what are you going to do now you are about to graduate?"

Randall followed his sister into the small kitchen. No one had done the washing up. She was right. The flat was a mess. Craig, understandably, had avoided his question.

"So, little sister, who is no longer so little, what are you going to do in England?"

"Oh, I don't know. Maybe I could become a model like Amanda suggested. Get some photographs taken. Meet a rich nice young man and get married. No, I'm too young to get married. I want to have some fun, Randall. See the lights. Find some excitement. You knew you were going to have fun in England or else you wouldn't have gone."

"I was scared off by a terrorist's bullet that killed my cat."

"You poor thing. I remember that cat. You loved that cat. Always slept on the windowsill."

"Don't you ever clean this place?"

"It's not like the farm. We don't have servants. I've been saving every penny so I can get out of Africa before the whole place collapses."

"It's not going to collapse."

"They hate us. When Mugabe gets full control of the police and the army he's going to kick us whites out of the country. There's no future for a white girl in Zimbabwe. Or a white boy. And certainly not for our children. We'll be the odd white dot in one big black puddle."

"Who tells you this?"

"My friends. Most of them have gone already... How much is fifty thousand American dollars in Zimbabwean currency?"

"It will help pay for your airfare."

"You're such a darling."

"What are brothers for? Give me the milk. I like to pour. After dried milk for three months I want to get it just right... Give me another hug. After the tea we are on our way. Dad's expecting us. Phillip phoned him from Meikles Hotel. They're expecting us on the farm in time for supper."

"Why does everything have to be so quick?"

"We'll make a plan for both of you when I get back to England. Has Craig made up his mind what he wants to do?"

"He hasn't a clue. He likes being the eternal student. Not a bad life. Everything he wants is paid for by our father. Okay, so the rent of this flat is paid for so I don't have to pay rent. Who's complaining?"

The drive up to the Centenary took them an hour and a half. When they got to the farm the dogs went crazy. Phillip got out of the car and opened the security gate. There was a key to the gate on his car ring. The four Alsatians jumped all over them before tearing off round the garden. The floodlights had come on when Phillip stopped at the gate, the light shining over the well-kept grass and the trees, the trees ringed by flowerbeds. Behind the trees was a fenced-in swimming pool with a *braai*. The two brothers walked up to the sprawling single-storey house at the top of the hill that gave all the windows in the house a view as far as the eye could see. Why the farm was called World's View. In daylight, far away in a purple haze, were a range of distant mountains, to Randall the most spectacular view in the world.

"At least you're alive. Frightened the shit out of me. How did you find him? Anyway, you're home. Congratulations on the publisher. Did you do any work? Supper's ready. Go and say hello to your stepmother. She's in the kitchen."

As they all trooped into the house the floodlights, that had been installed at the start of the bush war for protection, went out. The dogs ran back into the house. In the lounge, as Randall passed on his way to the kitchen to see Bergit, were three of the cats asleep on the chairs. Without a word Randall hugged his stepmother. Then he whispered 'thank you' into her ear.

"Wouldn't have helped if the book wasn't any good."

"You can write the best book in the world but it isn't any good unless you get someone with clout to read it. Your brother has done me the greatest favour of my life."

"That's what families are for."

They ate supper in the dining room. No one had had a drink. Despite the wine in the Toyota there was no wine on the table. No one mentioned Randall's drinking. The drinking that had nearly destroyed him. As was the habit on a working farm, they went to bed early. In the early days without electricity the farmers went to bed soon after the sun went down and got up with the dawn. A working day on a farm was a long one.

The following morning, Randall had booked a call to America for later that afternoon. The editor who had written the publisher's offer answered his own phone. His name was Henry Stone. The conversation was quick and business-like after the man's first words of congratulation.

"We're going to sell a million copies. You can bet on that. We don't take books that won't sell. Okay. So I've got your bank account details and you know where to pick up your ticket. What would we do without international travel agents? See you in New York. You look after yourself, Randall. What you been doing in Zimbabwe for God's sake? We couldn't find you. Harry Wakefield. That's a big name in the media business. On both sides of the pond. Now you look after yourself, Randall."

"Thank you, Mr Stone. I was writing a book."

"Call me Henry. You finish what you were writing?"

"All of it. I'll bring it with me."

"You do that, Randall. Have a nice day."

Before Randall could thank him again the man had put down his phone. The call had barely lasted five minutes. The Americans were efficient. When Randall walked down to the pool, where the family were preparing a *braai*, he was smiling. He was in good hands. No doubt about it.

"There's a direct flight from Johannesburg to New York the day after tomorrow. I fly to South Africa tomorrow."

"How did he know when you could fly?"

"He'd found out the three weekly flights to New York before I even phoned him. Uncle Harry told him they had found me on the farm. Those Americans are on the ball. They don't muck around. So that's it. I'm out of here. They are talking of selling a million copies."

"You want a glass of wine, son? Phillip explained his opening of the case of wine."

"I thought you'd never offer, I'm back in control. I'll never again go down the slippery slope of alcohol and depression. I have a new life ahead of me."

His father looked sad. So did Bergit. Myra was right. Everything was so damn quick, a man barely had time to think. With only the light from the fire, mostly hot coals now cooking the meat, Randall could see the full might of the heavens, the three layers of stars that no one on earth knew anything about. Randall wondered if the world looked as small from the other direction, just a twinkle in the vastness of the heavens. He would miss the sight of the night sky. In New York there was too much light on the ground and too much man-made pollution up in the sky. He could smell the meat cooking over the *braai*, everything a man could wish for. Lamb chops, steaks the size of a plate and the best sausage, *boerewors*, in the world. His father still looked sad. So did Bergit and Phillip.

"We hoped you would stay a while longer."

"Sorry, Dad. That's the Americans. Nothing stops when it comes to business. Henry Stone wants me there when he does the editing. Makes it quicker to sort out any problems as he finds them. They want the book out in the spring and ready for the Frankfurt international book fair in Germany. Apparently it's the biggest book fair in the world. Everything's a rush. There's a whole different world outside of Zimbabwe. Here, on the farm, we're still in the old world of British colonialism, an era long past for the rest of the world. Elsewhere it's money, money, money."

"You're young. You'll survive. Keep in touch, son. Let us know what's happening in your brave new world."

"You don't envy me do you?"

"Not in the slightest... The steaks are ready. Light the gas lamp. Let's all eat. Who knows when next we'll all be together on World's View? Pity Myra and Craig aren't here. At least they are only in Harare. Not halfway round the world."

Randall kept quiet. Bergit had taken his father's hand. They probably knew. His whole family, in the end, were going to leave Zimbabwe, the farm an anachronism, something left in the past. He wondered if Myra with all her excitement had thought of her mother and father. Like Myra, when he had first run away to England he had only been thinking of himself. Life was like that. People were inherently selfish, something they never admitted, not even to themselves. Randall sipped his wine. Savouring the memory. A memory, like the one on the banks of the Zambezi River that would likely never be repeated. For the first time in his life he realised how much he loved his father, the kind of emotion the colonial English would never think of mentioning. Randall tried but the words did not come out. Then they ate supper up at the table under the gaslight. Soon after they all went to bed.

He was back in his old bedroom, back in his old bed. For a long while Randall did not sleep. The next thing he heard was the call of the pigeons. The new day had begun. His journey as a novelist was about to begin. He got out of bed. He was on his way. Instead of dressing he walked to the window in his underpants. In front of the fly screen the window was open. The new day was beautiful, colourful birds in the green of the trees. In Zimbabwe the trees were always green. There were so many birds flitting among the trees it was difficult to count them. Silas, who had come up from the compound, was collecting the dirty dishes from last night's *braai*. Silas and Willard had driven the Land Rover back to the farm safely. Randall watched Silas walk away with the loaded tray to the kitchen, a separate building at the back of the house. Silas had not seen him standing in the window. If Silas was up at the house there would soon be breakfast. Randall was hungry. The farm breakfast was the best meal of the day. They were always the same: bacon and eggs, sausage, fried tomatoes, lashings of freshly made toast, homemade marmalade and coffee, the Zimbabwean coffee from the Vumba, the best in the world. In his imagination, Randall could smell the coffee. He put on his clothes. There was plenty of time to get organised. Phillip was going to drive him to the airport outside Harare for the two-hour flight to Johannesburg. He would stay in a hotel at Jan Smuts Airport the night before his direct flight to New York. He was going to say goodbye to his father on the farm. The dry planting season was about to get under way. He put his hand on the small case that contained his manuscript to make contact again with the book. The book that had been his sole companion for three months on his own by the river. The touch again connected him with his characters, making Randall smile. When he walked through from the bedroom he could really smell the coffee. A cat was sitting on his chair at the family table in the alcove off the lounge. Phillip was waiting to be served his breakfast, a cup of coffee in front of him.

"Dad has gone down to check the seed beds. Silas just brought in the coffee."

From the hob, Randall picked up the pot of coffee and poured himself a cup. The coffee smelt really good.

"It's impossible to imagine, standing here in a room I've had breakfast in since I could sit in a chair, that in two days' time I'll be in the rush and tumble of America."

Gently, Randall picked the cat up from his chair and put it on the ground. Through the lounge he could see the window the terrorist had fired a shot through that had killed his cat. The cat had been asleep on the windowsill and was killed by a shard of glass. It was all about to go, the farmhouse and all the memories, the good and the bad. The pain pricked behind his eyes. He sat down at the table with his coffee, neither of them speaking. Then Silas brought in their breakfast, his timing always perfect.

"Life marches on, Phillip, life marches on. Never stops. I'll miss the farm. It's my one true home. Thanks again for coming to find me."

"To happy days. Who knows? One day the Carruthers brothers may meet up in America."

"Who indeed knows? My God this breakfast looks good."

Then they tucked in, the two of them, the Carruthers brothers at the final end of their safari.

PART 2

SEPTEMBER 1988 TO APRIL 1989 — "THE
LAST COLONIAL"

1

---

*R*andall waited patiently in the queue before handing the man his British passport. Kennedy Airport was teeming with people, the rush and noise a world of organised chaos. The man flipped through the pages before looking up at Randall. He wasn't smiling. Like Randall the man looked tired. Harassed and tired.

"The multiple visa from my last visit to America is still valid. I checked with the travel agent."

"Where are you staying, Mr Crookshank?"

"I'm not sure."

"You've come all the way from Africa to America and you're not sure?"

"No, sir. I'm not sure. I'm being met at the airport. I'm a writer. My book has been accepted by one of your publishers. Villiers Publishing, if you've heard of them, one of the biggest in the world. If not the biggest. They paid for my ticket."

"Did they now? Welcome to America. Have a nice visit."

The man from immigration stamped his passport and gave it back to Randall. The man was smiling. Randall walked through to wait for his luggage, the small case of hand luggage with the new manuscript clutched under his arm. He waited five minutes. The luggage conveyor belt began to move. Others from the flight were also waiting. Randall recognised the man who had sat next to him on the plane and smiled. The man did not see him, more concerned with finding his own luggage. Randall saw his case, checked the label and walked out of the terminal into the concourse. The place was crowded. Bewildered, not knowing what to do next, he put the bigger case down next to him and looked around. There had to be a place he could go to announce his arrival on the loudspeaker. He had no idea where to go or who to ask. It was all so overwhelming. He was lost and a little frightened. Behind the crowd, near to a wall, a board was held up above the heads of the people. When the board turned round to face him Randall read his name. Relief flooded over him. Picking up the heavy case he pushed his way through the packed crowd. A young man, not much older than a boy, was holding up the board.

"I'm Randall Crookshank from Rhodesia."

"Johnny Stiglitz. I'm Henry Stone's junior assistant. Is that all your luggage? Good. You're booked into the Plaza. Not a suite, I'm afraid. Just a room. Later, when you're famous, they'll book you a suite. First we go to the office in downtown Manhattan. Did you get any sleep on the plane? Henry wants to get started right away. He's like that. Exhausting. He never slows down. I liked your book."

"Did you read it?"

"That's my job. Henry likes a cross section of opinions. The young and the old, men and women. A book that's going to sell has to appeal to everyone. Let's get a trolley. There's a bit of a walk to the cab rank. Or taxis as you British call them."

"I'm from Zimbabwe."

"Thought you said from Rhodesia?"

"They're the same place."

"Where the hell's Zimbabwe?"

"In southern Africa."

"You live there?"

"Grew up on a farm. Travel on a British passport. No, don't take this case. It's my new book. Only one copy. Until it's copied I won't let it out of my sight."

"We've made a mock-up of the cover. You'll like it. Covers are very important. They do judge a book by its cover. Has to make them put out their hand and pick it up off the shelf. Once you've got that far you're halfway home. Marketing. Henry's always talking about marketing. Without good marketing you can't sell a book. This one will do. Shove the cases in the boot. The airport was busy. Always is. I was worried I wouldn't find you."

"So was I."

They both laughed and settled back.

"You want a cigarette, Randall?"

"I don't smoke. But you go ahead. My father is a tobacco farmer. Once we calculated at a party in the club that World's View produces enough tobacco every year to fill a billion cigarettes. We were drunk, so don't hold me to the number. We were stripping packets of cigarettes and weighing the tobacco on a pair of scales we found in the kitchen. Anyway, we grow a lot of tobacco. Rhodesia and tobacco farming is quite a story."

"You should write a book about it."

"I did. Called it *The White Saviour*. A past and future book. A bit too pro the colonial British. The publishers weren't interested. They only wanted books about the heroes of the struggle. People like our new president Robert Mugabe."

"Maybe you should."

"Who knows? Maybe I will."

"You got to write what sells."

Henry Stone, when Randall met him in his smart office, was the last thing he expected. Randall had imagined a business executive in a dark suit. Instead the man reminded him of a professor in economics at the London School of Economics when Randall was taking his degree. Like the professor, Henry wore a bow tie and glasses, the glasses on the end of his nose to look at the papers in front of him. But there the resemblance ended. Over the glasses Henry Stone stared at Randall appraising him. Not a word. Then he smiled. Johnny Stiglitz had been sent off on an errand. They were alone. The door was closed. The windows closed. The room quiet. Randall sat still, waiting. Henry, the glasses back up his nose, opened the file in front of him, pulled out a sheet, turned it round and pushed it across the desk towards Randall. To Randall it looked like the cover of a book, his own book except for the name of the author. The title, *Masters of Vanity*, was bold. A man who looked like the typical bond trader was sitting in a Ferrari, next to him a well-dressed woman. In the background was a country mansion. In the front a townhouse, a park in front of the building. The picture exuded affluence. The American dream.

"Who's Randall Holiday, Mr Stone?"

"As I said on the phone, call me Henry."

"Who's Randall Holiday, Henry?"

"That's you, Randall. We took ourselves a liberty. The word crook in a name has a wrong ring to it. Shank is the cheap cut of the meat. No offence to you or your ancestors. My job is to sell books. My bonus depends on it and my wife is very expensive. My third wife. She's much younger than me. Used to work in the office."

"You changed my name?"

"Yes we did. It's all in the contract we sent you."

"That I haven't seen."

"Yes. Of course. We sent it to Mr Wakefield. He's going to give us a pile of publicity. Wonderful news. Get the media on your side, Randall. What it's all about. He's your stepmother's brother so not a blood relative of the Crookshanks."

"I rather like my name."

"Don't be difficult, Randall. What do you think of your cover?"

"Very rich."

"That's the point. *Masters of Vanity.* Brilliant title. You'll be in the office next to me during your stay. You and young Johnny. We have a tight schedule. I want this book put to bed as quickly as possible. Time is money. Now here's the first chapter and these are my editorial notes. You'll probably want to argue. Don't. But if you do I will listen. You have a good flight? You look a bit tired."

"The time is all different. And I haven't slept since I left Johannesburg. Never could sleep on an aeroplane."

"Well, off you go."

At the door Randall turned round.

"Why Holiday?"

"It has a warm ring to it. Everyone likes a holiday."

Henry was smiling broadly, a twinkle in his eye. Randall smiled.

"Randall Holiday. You're right. You get used to your own name and never think about it. I'll have this back to you as soon as possible."

"Do you have any friends in New York?"

"As a matter of fact I do. Though I doubt the lady will give me the time of day. My maternal grandfather lives in Los Angeles. You may have heard of him. He's the character actor, Ben Crossley."

"Will he help promote your book?"

"I'll have to ask him."

"Oh, and while you are with us you will enjoy an expense account. Johnny has made the arrangements."

His head swimming, and feeling light-headed from lack of sleep, Randall walked through to the adjacent office carrying the edited first chapter of *Masters of Vanity* in one hand and his small case in the other, the Zambezi River as far away as the moon. Johnny handed him an American Express credit card and took the case from under his arm. The credit card was in the name of Crookshank.

"I'll get it copied straight away."

"I'll come with you wherever you are going."

"Relax, Randall. This is Villiers Publishing. No one is going to steal your book. You won't believe it but Holiday was my idea. You don't even want to know the other names we bandied about. The amount on that card is unlimited but don't go crazy. Villiers have a habit of testing people. After work we'll book you into the hotel and you can take me out to dinner. You want me to bring a couple of girls? All part of the service. No, they're not hookers, stupid. Friends of mine. Every girl in New York wants to meet a published author. The girls use me more than I use them. Just kidding. What's wrong with a night out? We're young and single. Going out with girls is what life is all about. Take a seat, Randall. Back in five minutes."

"That quick?"

"This is America."

There was a couch against the one wall of the small office. Randall sat himself down. Next to the couch stood his big suitcase with his clothes. He was so tired his bones were aching. His eyelids shut. The office was surprisingly quiet. Randall fell asleep.

"Better not let Henry catch you sleeping in the office. Here is your book. I thought by now you'd have finished reading that first chapter."

"I couldn't concentrate if my life depended on it. I must have nodded off."

"MaryJane has started the typing. She doesn't like the title. It's too long and could be construed as being rude to lesbians. She's coming with us to dinner."

"Please, Johnny, take me to the Plaza. Let me sleep. Tomorrow I'll do some work... What day is it? You've changed my name in the first book so you can do what you like with the title."

"It's Thursday."

"Good. We'll do the dinner bit tomorrow."

"You won't tell Henry?"

"Not if you don't."

With the original copy of *The Woman Who Stole My Wife* safely back under his arm they left the office, Johnny carrying the other case. It was all a dream. None of it was really happening. Outside Johnny's office was a sea of cubicles full of busy people, heads down, all of them working. The main door to Henry Stone's office was still closed. Half an hour later Randall was lying alone in a strange bed, a strange room, a strange hotel. Only when he slept did he find himself back in the Zambezi Valley, next to a sleeping elephant.

Randall woke during the night, fear gripping him. He had no idea where he was. The place was dark and claustrophobic. He put out his hand for his gun. Faraway he could hear the sound of voices. Then he was awake, recollection coming back to him. Beside the bed was a clock that said half past three. Not sure with the heavy curtains closed tight if the time was day or night, he went back to sleep. He was back in the Zambezi Valley, alone, the escarpment far away, the sun shining. A giraffe was looking at him while it chewed the leaves of the tree it had been browsing. The giraffe's expression was one of curiosity, fellow animals in the great wide expanse of Africa. Randall woke to a knock on the door. A girl had brought him a pot of coffee on a tray. The hotel room was full of light, artificial light from the hidden strip-light around the walls of the room. The young girl smiled and put the tray down next to him.

"You asked to be called at six in the morning. Have a nice day."

Not remembering asking for anything, Randall poured himself a cup of coffee. In America they drank coffee in the morning, never tea. Johnny Stiglitz must have asked them to wake him. He got up, bathed, shaved and put on the crumpled clothes he pulled out of his case. It was a working day. He was back in business. Back in the corporate world.

Outside in the busy street it was a day like so many he remembered from his days at BLG in London. Everyone with a single purpose. The purpose of making money. The man in hotel livery at the swivel door called him a yellow cab. Randall got in the back and told the driver where he wanted to go.

"You got a funny accent, bud. Where you from?" The man was trying to be friendly.

"Zimbabwe."

"Where the hell's that?"

"A country in southern Africa."

"Never heard of it. You could have walked. With all this morning traffic it would have been quicker to walk with the rest of them."

"I'll remember that when I'm a little more orientated."

"You got business in New York? Everyone's got business in New York. I love New York. Best place in the world." For a while they drove in silence. "You see what I mean? That's the building you want to go to, on the other side of the street. Mind out for the traffic. Have a nice day. Where you say you were from again?"

"Zimbabwe. Am I really there?"

"Right across the street."

"I'm only five or six blocks from my hotel."

"You got it, bud. Seventeen dollars."

Randall gave the man a twenty and told him to keep the change. Along with the credit card, Johnny had given him five twenties. Remembering to look left and not right, Randall crossed the street. Johnny was already in his office. Well slept, his mind alert, Randall got down to work.

That night they went out to dinner, the four of them. MaryJane talked mostly of books, her one ambition in life to write her own and get it published. Instead of having a step-uncle big in the media business she was working for a publisher, building her contacts. Randall was thinking of Hayley. Their affair had been short, sharp and at the end not very sweet. Hayley was old enough to be MaryJane's mother. At the end of the evening MaryJane came on to him, Randall not taking the bait, the golden rule never to mix business with pleasure. He had done it once with Hayley and he wasn't going to do it again. He had kept his drinking to a minimum so as not to lose his control.

Johnny went off with the other girl as Randall hailed a cab for MaryJane.

"I'm glad you're typing my book."

"You don't want me to come back to your hotel?"

"Of course I do. But it wouldn't be right. We're working together. Tell the cab driver where you want to go."

Still standing on the pavement he asked the driver how much the fare for MaryJane would be. He gave him two of the twenties. The dinner he'd paid for with the card. Alone in the great metropolis Randall walked the two blocks to his hotel.

The night came and went without incident. There was no coffee tray in the morning. After a good American breakfast of waffles, followed by a choice cut of steak, Randall went back to his room to phone his grandfather in Los Angeles. The old man's cancer had been in remission. Randall expected the worst. Instead, the phone was immediately picked up and answered.

"Randall! What you phoning for?"

"Thank you, Grandfather, for such a happy reaction to the sound of my voice." Randall was smiling. "I've found a publisher for *Masters of Vanity*. I'm in New York. At the Plaza. Villiers Publishing. Phillip sends his best. I came in Thursday from Zimbabwe. How are you?"

"Slow down. Still got my problem but I'm still working. When you coming for a visit?"

"We're doing the editing. They don't play around in New York. When I've finished with the editor I'll be free to travel. They've paid me fifty thousand dollars in advance. Going to sell a million copies."

"How's my great-grandson?"

"I'm not in touch with them. When Amanda went off with the woman, the woman paid some fancy lawyers to get Amanda her divorce. I'd gone off the rails. Drinking. He's a year old. If I sell a million copies I'll have the money to get him back again. You feeling well?"

"As good as can be expected for an old man. Good to hear from you. I may be coming to New York. There's a new movie. My agent's working on it."

"I still don't have an agent."

"You always need an agent in America. I'll talk to him."

"Does he do writers?"

"He does anyone who is making money. Have you signed the contract?"

"Not yet. It's a long story. I've been in the bush on my own for the last three months. The contract is still in England."

"Good. Don't sign it until we've had a look at it along with my lawyer. Everything is done with a lawyer in this country if you don't want to get screwed. Artists are a prime target for producers and publishers. When the big boys have got what they want they use the fine print to maximise their own profit. It's called good business. I'm not much good at chit-chat on the telephone. If they try any tricks give me a ring."

"Why would they want to trick me?"

"Copyright. Tying you up for the future so they can decide what they want. It's one big nasty money-grabbing minefield. I've been through it. You're lucky to have a grandfather in a similar business. Someone you can trust. Keep in touch, Randall. And I am happy to hear your voice. My whole spirit lifted. Doesn't happen too often to an old man. I'm seventy-eight. Can you believe it? What was the little bugger's name again?"

"James Oliver."

"Just kidding. I may be old but I haven't lost my mind."

After putting down the phone Randall sat thinking. The room was quiet. It was good to have a grandfather, a man he knew would always be on his side.

THE ARGUMENT with Henry Stone on the Monday began just before lunch. The sandwich-man was due. Randall did not mind his editor changing a word or putting in a semicolon or a comma. But when it came to altering the story Randall was adamant.

"Don't forget I know far more about books than you do, Randall."

"Then why are you still an editor and not an author of your own books? If you are going to change my story I'm out of here."

"You've got to be kidding. We flew you to America and paid fifty thousand dollars into your London bank account."

"But I haven't signed a contract. And you can take out half those new punctuation marks when I come to think of it. A sentence must flow. Language must flow. You don't need a million little stops and starts. Simple, short, understandable sentences."

"Then you sign a copy of your contract today or we're finished. And you can forget about the sandwiches."

"Why are you grinning?"

"You have a passion for your work, Randall. I like it. And you're right. If you asked me to dream up the story for a good novel I'd burst my brain."

"I'm getting an agent."

"I thought you would... So I can't change the plot?"

"No you can't."

"And what about the punctuation?"

"We can compromise. You're allowed one semicolon every third page."

"You got to be kidding. You know what. Better I take you out to lunch."

"So you're not going to change the plot?"

"Who've you been talking to?"

"My grandfather."

"I thought as much. Am I going to meet him?"

"Probably. His agent's working on a new movie with people in New York."

"Are you close to him?"

"Only met him a couple of years ago. When my mother was killed by a pride of lions, he had already drifted off to America and lost touch. Things can happen like that in families. Why is life so strange? So many of us just drift through life thinking only of ourselves. I think he feels guilty. Old people quite often feel guilty about things they did in the long-lost past. At the time he said leaving a wife and losing touch with my mother when she married my father and went to live in the bush of Africa wasn't so important. A petty argument with a wife can lead to such big and lasting repercussions. I think we all do it. I'll only understand myself when I'm a whole lot older. I've been told a few times by people who think they knew that I'd never write a worthwhile book until I was forty. Until I've been through the ups and downs."

"Not always true. Some writers write their best when they are young. They communicate with young readers. Often they write just the one book. Makes them a celebrity and they never write anything worth reading again."

"Who knows? You can argue anything from both ways... When are you going to finish the editing?"

"If I don't have to rewrite any of the story, fairly soon. Good. We understand each other. Let me buy you lunch. I want to get the first print run much sooner than anticipated into the bookshops."

For Randall, the excitement of finding a publisher was beginning to ebb. It all reminded him of being back in his old office at BLG, the only important item on the agenda that of making money. His grandfather was right. If he'd signed the contract before seeing the editing he would have been screwed.

A week later *Masters of Vanity* was finished. The next day it was sent to the printers and Randall was introduced to Nora, his publicist... The real job of marketing his book had begun. For the first time in his life Randall was interviewed by a newspaper reporter. The man was interested more in Randall than he was in Randall's book. The reporter wanted a story. Rhodesia, Zimbabwe, the death of his cat, it all came out. Another man from the same paper took his photograph. Within three days Randall was defending the whites in Zimbabwe under a barrage of media attention. He was quickly a celebrity, constantly pumped up by the publicist. In pursuit of publicity they had used his colonial background to make him interesting. Henry Stone was smiling as the pre-launch orders from the booksellers mounted. He was billed as the last of the British colonials, the last of the soon to be forgotten British Empire that had given way to American hegemony. Mostly, they were laughing at him but to the publicist that was all part of the game to get Randall Holiday's name known to the public. Randall had to smile. The woman was good. It was all free publicity. By the time he did his rounds of the bookshops they would be lining up for him at the door. Everyone liked a celebrity. Everyone liked to own a piece of a celebrity, especially his signature on a book. According to Nora, they would all want to meet Randall Holiday, the last colonial, the new celebrity everyone was reading about who had happened to write a book about people climbing the corporate ladder to satisfy their vanity. It was all about selling books. By the time Randall went out with MaryJane on their first date at the end of October, Randall was not sure if he wanted to go where his book was taking him – to fame and fortune at the expense of his privacy, at the expense of what he hoped was a good book. He wanted his book to be read, not for him to be famous. Randall wanted to be a writer, not a media chewed-up celebrity. He missed the bush, the peace of being alone by the side of the Zambezi River, an animal among all the other animals. Most of all he was no longer sure whether becoming a successful author was going to be worth it. When he complained to Nora Stewart, the independent publicist appointed by his publisher, Nora put it simply.

"You can't have it both ways, Randall. The publisher is out to make money. You are part of that process. Unknown authors don't sell books. Enjoy yourself. What's wrong with being in the limelight? It's what everyone wants. To be rich and famous. Henry is delighted."

They were all happy. All except Randall. But Nora was right. There was a price to pay for everything. His mother had paid a price for her drinking and been killed by a pride of lions. James Oliver was paying a price for his mother's sexuality. And when Robert Mugabe took World's View from his father, his father would have to pay the price of going to Rhodesia. Being worked over by the media for being one of the last of the British colonials was going to sell his book. The fact he interviewed well and, according to Nora Stewart, looked good on television, the deep suntan from the Zambezi Valley still not having faded, also had something to do with it. Henry Stone, realising the attention span of the media was shorter than a gnat's, had pushed forward the date of the launch to coincide with the printing, the distributors ready, everyone on full alert. Randall was impressed.

The restaurant was small, cosy and intimate. Both of them were excited. It was Randall's last day at Villiers Publishing, his job in the office finished. He and MaryJane were no longer business colleagues.

"In your days in business you never took out a girl from the office?"

"Once. It was a disaster. Cost me my job and my business career."

"You British are funny."

"I'm not British. I'm one of those bad colonials."

"You never believe what they say in the press."

"I hate it. Now I've got to go round signing books and smiling at strangers. I want to be back in the Zambezi Valley, away from all this attention."

"Has Henry read the book I typed?"

"Not yet. He wants to wait. See what happens to *Masters of Vanity*.

He's holding it over me so I sign the contract which I've promised to do tomorrow. My grandfather's agent, together with his lawyer, have been through it with a fine-tooth comb. Henry's legal department are due to come back to him tomorrow. If they agree to the changes, I will sign."

"I love your books."

"Thank you, MaryJane."

MaryJane put her hand out across the table, the small table lamp showing Randall the delicacy of her small hand. It was the first time they had touched each other.

"Are we going to make love tonight, Randall?"

"I think so."

"That's good... I'll have the trout for starters."

They were both laughing. Both of them comfortable.

"Was the book based on your wife?"

"Some of it."

"You must have loved her deeply. How horrible to go off and leave you for a woman. I don't understand lesbians."

"Neither do I."

"What are you going to do after the book tour?"

"Go back to England I suppose. Find somewhere to live. Probably in the country so I can write. Who knows? Maybe I'll go walkabout and look for another story."

"You're a writer now, Randall."

"So they tell me. Why are the best things that happen to us always so short? We could go walkabout together."

For a long moment MaryJane looked into his eyes, her face gently smiling. "Not really, Randall. There has to be more to life than walkabout. There has to be permanence. Something solid. Something that will last."

"Nothing ever lasts. Not even our lives. It's how it works... Thank you, Miles," he said to the waiter who had come back to their table. "We'll start with the trout. Both of us." When the man had gone, Randall again took hold of her hand. "It's nice in America. Everyone uses their first names. Makes everything more friendly."

"You could stay in America."

"I couldn't. I don't have a work permit. What you call a green card. Just a temporary visa... How's the wine?"

"Perfect. Just perfect."

It was a date like so many of the others. Ships passing in the night. They would make love and go on their way. Another brief, happy episode that made up the sum of his life. Nothing, thought Randall as he enjoyed his evening, had any lasting purpose. It was all pleasure. Hedonism. Call it what you will. By the end of the second bottle of wine they had both had too much to drink. The slippery slide had begun. Miles smiled when, to impress MaryJane, Randall gave him a big tip. They went to her apartment in a cab, both of them laughing, both of them in the moment. They had sex, a frenzy of lust people called making love. They went to sleep. In the middle of the night they woke and did it again. MaryJane went to sleep. Randall stayed awake, his mind going back to the five years of rock and roll in his life when he was separated from his wife. Most of those girls he could barely remember. Many were one-night stands. He took them out, paid the bill and they had sex. Wine, women and song. That's all it was... Still feeling the effect of all the wine, Randall went back to sleep. In the morning they went about their daily lives as if nothing had happened. Maybe it hadn't.

"Whenever I read one of your books in the future I'll remember I made love to the author. Are we going to do it again?"

"I hope so. It was a wonderful evening."

"Yes it was. One to be remembered. Good luck with signing your contract."

"We could run away and live in the African bush."

"Don't be ridiculous... You want some coffee?"

"That would be nice."

The hype reached its climax on the night of the launch. Nora Stewart had borrowed a stuffed lion from a local natural history museum and put it on display in the main function room at the Plaza Hotel. When Randall gave his brief speech of appreciation the yellow glass eyes of the lion were staring at him. Sounding more like a nervous award-winner, Randall thanked everyone for coming. Only then did he read a piece from his book. The room was full of the media and representatives from the retailers. The food was of the best. There was wine, cocktails, whatever they wanted. Randall, to stop making a fool of himself, drank glasses of lemonade. MaryJane smiled at him. Henry Stone shook his hand. The media were all over him the more they had to drink. Nora Stewart guided him round the room, introducing him to important people. His grandfather had refused to come to the launch.

"It's your night, Randall. I'll leave you alone to bask in the glory. When the party is over you and I, alone, will go out to dinner."

All round the room on separate tables were piles of his book. He kept signing copies of the book. Two hundred thousand copies had been shipped that morning to the shops. Nora Stewart introduced Randall to every book critic who had come to the party. He did as he was told and said how honoured he was to meet them. Randall preferred to call it arse-creeping. Nora said it usually worked: Nora, who was going to be with him every step of his upcoming tour of the country to promote the book.

The quiet dinner with his grandfather was more pleasant. MaryJane had gone home by herself, Randall not sure if she believed he was dining alone with his grandfather. It would have been better for both of them if they had not made love.

"Do you feel any different, grandson?"

"The word dirty springs to mind. Do you know, if there hadn't been a war and they hadn't killed my cat, I'd have become a Rhodesian tobacco grower?"

"You are what happens, Randall. We all have to prostitute ourselves in pursuit of fame. You stand on your hind legs and bark like a dog until you get their attention."

"Why don't people just buy a book that's good to read?"

"Why do they go to a movie? Mostly because advertising tells them to. The modern world of commercialism is one big constant advertisement wherever you look. Whatever you turn on. Branding. Getting a name. Becoming familiar. Then like lemmings they will buy you, everyone buying the same product, their brains numbed into submission. The power of advertising herds everyone."

"But if the film or book is lousy?"

"People read what they are told to read. Of course a book has to be professionally edited and easy to read. My lines have to be convincing. But without the likes of Nora Stewart I would never be asked to play a new part and your book would end up in the dump."

"Maybe the critics will pan it."

"You'll soon find out. At least the critics have been primed in your favour... Why aren't you drinking tonight?"

"It doesn't do me any good. I took advantage of a very nice girl because both of us were drunk."

"Takes two to tango."

"She wanted more than a one-night stand."

"Did she want Randall Holiday or Randall Crookshank?"

"I'm not really sure."

"Be careful. You'll get lots more of that."

"Are you going to do the new movie?"

"I think so. They want me to co-produce. They know I have money. It's a good script and a good director so I don't mind. If the film goes like my last one I'll make money both ways. From acting and producing."

"What are you going to do with all the money?"

"Leave it to you and Phillip. In reality I'll be working for my grandchildren. In practice it gives me something to do. A man has to work or there is no point in living."

"I much prefer your company to your money."

"Thank you, Randall. Now, let's eat. I don't stay out late. A good meal and one glass of brandy and it's me off to bed... When do you start the rounds of the bookshops?"

"The day after tomorrow. With Nora. She's sweet. Hard-bitten but sweet."

"How old is this Nora?"

"About fifty."

"I'll be watching the newspapers. I'll have my fingers crossed. A few good crits in the leading papers could make all the difference. Despite what we might think from the barrage of advertising people do prefer to read a good book. Have you signed your contract?"

"We have a meeting tomorrow. In the boardroom. Their team and mine. Thanks, Grandfather. Without Manfred Lewis and your lawyer they would have walked all over me."

"Just sit back and let the others do the arguing. Now, enough of your book. Tell me all about Phillip."

2

$\mathcal{T}$he contract was signed the following morning, a three-book contract instead of the one, and an upfront royalty payment for the two hundred thousand copies already shipped to the bookshops. Every month the agent was to receive a statement of sales. If there was a dispute Manfred would be entitled to send in an independent firm of auditors. If the auditors found any discrepancies the cost of the auditing would fall on the publishers. The verbal fight had lasted all morning, right up to the signing. With a cheque in his agent's pocket for half a million dollars the arguments turned into smiles. Of his royalty payment Manfred took ten per cent, the same as the lawyer. It was how it worked in the world of money. A file, full of paper clippings, was put in front of Randall by Henry Stone.

"You'll mostly like what you read, Randall. The reviews are good right across the country. These are just the New York papers. Have a good book tour. Oh, and I read your latest book. I like it. Very much. It's a story that will resonate with people. Like MaryJane I don't like the title. Leave it to us. You're going to be big, Randall. Very big."

"Thank you, Henry. Sorry about the earlier arguments."

"That's just business. How it should be. In the end both sides have to respect each other. When are you going to start another book?"

"When I return to England. I'm going to look for a place in the country now I can afford to buy myself a house. Ten acres. Next to a forest. A river. 'The Tawny Wilderness.'"

"You don't think of living back in Zimbabwe?"

"I do. All the time. But the Zimbabwe dollar is a mousetrap currency. Once you take your money in you can't get it out again. To give me peace of mind into the future I want a strong financial base and I want to own my own property. The most difficult thing in life is not to make the money but to hold onto it. I tanked once. Not again. Whatever I buy will not have a mortgage. I'm never buying anything again on credit... You want to look at my earlier books?"

"We've got enough to go on. Writers have to write. I want to see your next one... Gentleman, this meeting is over."

Everyone went around shaking hands. As he walked through the main office MaryJane was watching. She looked sad. Randall's smile was not reciprocated. Feeling guilty he followed the two men who had secured his financial future out of the office, wondering when he would come back again. They were going to have lunch to celebrate.

RANDALL'S GRANDFATHER was waiting for them in the restaurant. Manfred showed him the cheque.

"That's better than a slap in the belly with a wet fish."

The agent and the lawyer talked about his grandfather's new film leaving Randall time to look around the room. There was a bar at the side of the restaurant. A young girl caught Randall's eye. She turned and talked to the man she was sitting with, the man trying to look at Randall. The man seemed to recognise Randall and smiled. Randall looked behind at the next table. He had never seen the man or girl before in his life.

"You can expect more of that in the future." Manfred had watched where Randall was looking. "Your picture in the morning newspapers. We're in the heart of New York's literary and advertising world. Relax. It's only just started. Look out, she's coming over."

"Mr Crossley, may I have your autograph? I've so loved all your movies."

"This is my grandson, the novelist. His name is Randall Holiday.

You'll be hearing more about Randall than you ever heard about me. He wrote *Masters of Vanity*."

"That's what my boyfriend must have been talking about. I thought he wanted me to get your autograph, Mr Crossley. Can I have them both on the same piece of paper?"

When the girl got back to her seat at the bar she turned again and smiled at Randall.

"That was a bit of a balls-up," said Ben Crossley, smiling. "I've got competition. How does it feel to be famous, Randall?"

Before Randall could put the words together to explain his uncomfortable feeling the three men were back talking about the contract for the new movie. They were talking about the money. Not wishing to look around the room, Randall looked down at his plate. That comfortable feeling of anonymity had gone. Being recognised by a perfect stranger made Randall want to run away. To go far away. Back into the bush. Back to the peace and certainty of the African forest. His world had changed and not for the better. When he wrote, his books belonged to him, the story and all the characters who lived in his book. Now they had gone from him. They belonged to the public like the stranger sitting up at the bar. It was like losing a best friend. From now on he was going to have to share his life with millions of people. In real life you shared your days with your friends. As a celebrity you were obliged to share them with everyone. To Randall it was the loss of the one thing he cherished most in his life. As a published, bestselling author he had lost his privacy. Probably forever.

Daniel Garcia, the lawyer, gave Ben Crossley a brief outline of the movie contract. The deal was going to be signed. Randall wondered if at his grandfather's ripe old age he would want to make another movie. His grandfather was smiling, happy with the deal. The man and the girl up at the bar had gone to sit at a table. Tired, unhappy, and by no means elated as he had hoped he would be, he followed his grandfather out of the restaurant. To Randall's amusement and surprise the lawyer had picked up the tab for the lunch.

"Keep in touch, Randall. I'll pay the balance of the cheque into your London bank account. You'll need an accountant to do your British tax return. Don't lose any of your expense chits as what you spend of your own money on the road will be deductible. Nice doing business with both of you. A couple of good days' work don't you think, Daniel?"

In the end it was all about money. The book, the movie didn't matter. His grandfather was flying back that night to his home in Los Angeles. They all shook hands outside the restaurant and parted, each of them going their own way. Tired, Randall took a cab back to the Plaza. He had never felt more alone in his life. There was his father and Phillip in Rhodesia. James Oliver in England. His grandmother Crookshank in London with his Uncle Paul. His grandfather Crossley on his way home. And he was alone in New York. He was friendless, without his family and without a permanent home. And his book belonged to everyone.

Back in the quiet of his room, Randall got into bed. Within minutes he was sleeping. In his dream he was back in the Zambezi Valley, on his own but not feeling lonely. When he woke in the early hours of the morning Randall felt better. It was not all bad as his friend Oliver Manningford would say. At ten o'clock, dressed to look just a little arty, Randall went to his first signing. Nora Stewart was waiting for him at the bookshop. So were a crowd of people. His first day of smiling at strangers and shaking their hands had begun. His book was flying off the shelves. By lunchtime Nora said he had signed over two hundred copies of *Masters of Vanity*. They had a quick sandwich in the office at the back of the bookshop, thanked and said goodbye to the manager, and took a cab to the afternoon signing. For ten long days Randall signed his books in New York, everything swirling around him. Only then did he book out of the Plaza Hotel. For three long months Randall toured America. Another three hundred thousand of his books had been shipped. He had talked and smiled his way around the country, pushed on by the zeal of his publicist. The promotion had nothing to do with writing books. It was all business. All about making money. And as the cheques kept coming through to his agent Randall had no idea what he was going to do with all the money. As he said to himself, a man could only eat one meal at a time, sleep in one bed at a time. He was awash with money. Instead of becoming a writer he had become a machine for making money, most of it for other people.

· · ·

RANDALL ARRIVED BACK in London on a freezing day at the end of February, Nora still sitting next to him. They had flown first class, compliments of Villiers Publishing. Villiers's London manager was waiting for them at Heathrow Airport. The publicity game was about to start all over again in England. Randall shook the woman's hand and smiled. Her name was Brenda Foster, a woman much the same age as Nora. The two women talked ten to the dozen, Brenda excited. The launch in London was to be in the Savoy Hotel after the new publicity campaign that Brenda had already started organising. Randall felt more like a marketing tool than a writer. Never once did Brenda mention the story in *Masters of Vanity*, not one comment on the writing. All she wanted to know was how many books they had sold in America. The book tour in England was scheduled to last for a month. Until then Randall belonged to his publishers.

"I've booked you into the Savoy," Brenda said finally.

"Oh, no. I want to be close to my friends. I lived in London for ten years. I started off in Notting Hill Gate. I had a room in a boarding house. You may have heard of Oliver Manningford the actor. Stage and screen."

"Not quite the address for a famous novelist."

"I haven't changed, Mrs Foster."

"We'll have to see about that. First we go to the office in Old Bond Street. Now that's a good address. I will show you your schedule, Mr Holiday."

"My name is Randall Crookshank. Holiday is my pen name."

"Is it now? Anyway, I will call you Randall Holiday. You'll be staying at the Savoy. Can't have someone from the *Times* or the *Telegraph* slumming it in Notting Hill Gate."

Worn out and tired from the flight Randall did what he was told. They owned him, lock, stock and barrel. When he had a moment he would escape and go visit Oliver Manningford and James Tomlin and say hello to Mrs Salter, his old landlady. He had missed them. He had had no idea until now how much he had missed them. Later he would phone Amanda and ask her if he could see his son James Oliver.

"Can children walk at two years old, Mrs Foster?"

"Actually it's Miss Foster. I was married once. Terrible. Went back to my maiden name. Never had any children, so I have no idea."

"It's my son's second birthday tomorrow... My wife went off with a woman."

"Lucky girl... Taxi!... There we are. Luggage in the front compartment."

"Why is the weather so lousy in England? Are you going to promote me in England as the last of the colonials? The Americans thought it was amusing. But not for me or my family. I lost what I thought was my country."

"Oh, we won't need any of that in England. You're famous, Randall Holiday. All we want is press interviews. Radio talk shows. Interviews on television. We want your photograph and book splashed all across the media. Isn't that right, Nora? Of course it is. Tonight we will all be having dinner in the Savoy Grill with some of my media friends. I want to sell a million copies of your book in England and the Commonwealth."

"Have you read my book, Miss Foster?"

"My job is to sell books not to read them."

"Don't you read your authors' books before you accept them for publication?"

"This is different. The Americans have done that part of the job."

"And if your friends in the media want to know what the book is about, what do you tell them?"

"That's your job if they ask. Normally they don't. They want to know about the publicity campaign. How much advertising they are going to get. We all feed each other. The more we spend, the more they will write and talk about you. This time with your huge success in America I want a frenzy, a real top-class media frenzy. That's what sells books. We're going to have the rich and famous at the launch of your book. People who have come up in the world by making their fortune like to be seen at a literary function. There's an old saying in the north of England: where there's muck there's brass. With all their money some of the new rich find it difficult to be accepted in society. They'll be delighted to shake your hand, the media taking photographs... So your wife went off with a woman? How interesting. The gay community have a lot of clout when it comes to publicity. Why so many of the artists have been coming out of the closet. Would you mind my mentioning it to my gay friends in the media? The gay community is very close. They help each other. Why so many of them are now so well accepted and applauded."

"My wife is a lesbian, Miss Foster. I just love women. No, please don't embarrass the mother of my son."

"She won't be embarrassed. She'll love it."

"But I won't."

"Oh, well, these things have a habit of getting out. You have to explore all the avenues when you are promoting an author. I hope your politics are left wing. You did support the struggle in Rhodesia I hope? Robert Mugabe is an icon of the liberation struggle. Wonderful man. Freed his people from colonialism. Colonialism is so dead. You must have found that out in America. We all need to be the champions of democracy. Never forget that, Randall. I may call you Randall? I call all my authors by their first names."

"Winston Churchill said democracy was a dreadful way to govern. The only problem, he said, was he couldn't think of a better one. No, Miss Foster, I am not a champion of gay rights. Any more than I am a champion of Robert Mugabe. Did you know, in his determination to cement his one-party state he killed twenty thousand Matabele who opposed his Shona government?"

"No I didn't. But so what? They must have done something wrong."

"They did. They opposed Mugabe until he beat them and their leader, Joshua Nkomo, into submission. Nkomo, the leader of the Matabele in the struggle to overthrow Ian Smith, is now touted to be a vice president, meek and mild. At least he's still alive, which is more than can be said for twenty thousand of his tribesman. No, I don't think Mr Mugabe is a wonderful future for Zimbabwe. But a little like Churchill I don't know what is."

"You promise not to blab that off to the press?"

"You can rest assured. I will do exactly as I am told." Randall was not smiling. Nora put her hand on his knee and gave it a rub. For the rest of the journey all three of them were silent. For Randall, a month with Brenda Foster was going to be a long time. She was doing her job. She was going to sell his books. What he thought inside his head did not matter. He was forgetting. He was being foolish. It was all about the money. And nothing else.

In the big oval entrance to the Savoy Hotel Randall stepped out of the taxi first and walked round to the other side, opening the door for the woman who was going to be his boss for the next month.

"I'm sorry. I wasn't thinking. They killed my cat."

"Don't think any more about it. And I have an idea. I'm going to read your book. I have an idea I'm going to enjoy it."

They were all smiling as they walked into the foyer of the hotel, a hotel employee following with Randall's luggage. The place was crowded. He was back among people. Everyone going about their business.

The dinner in the Savoy Grill went off like all the rest of them, Randall being polite to strangers, everyone wanting a piece of him. Who they were as individuals Randall had no idea. One of the girls was young and pretty, Randall not sure if her flirting was to find personal material for her paper or because she was interested in Randall. Randall politely kept her at bay, not wishing to mix business with pleasure. Nora was watching him and so was Brenda. Tired at the end of a long day and evening he took the room keys from the receptionist and went up to his room. When the door closed at last he was alone. Nora too had gone to bed. Brenda had gone home to her flat. It was always difficult for Randall to sleep in a strange bed. All night he tossed and turned.

When Nora knocked on his door the next morning to start the day Randall was exhausted.

"You look about as tired as me."

"Can't sleep in strange beds."

"Join the club. Can you give me ten minutes? Then I'll join you at breakfast. It's my son's second birthday. I've been winding myself up to phone my ex-wife ever since I got up this morning."

"Don't be long. We have a busy schedule. Brenda Foster is certainly organised. It's all go."

First, Randall sat back on the side of the bed. The phrase 'tense as a turkey on Christmas Eve' came into his mind. Then he picked up the phone, asked for an outside line and dialled the number of Evelina, the woman who had stolen his son. It was half past seven in the morning, before people went to work. The phone rang and rang. Relieved, Randall was about to put down the phone and go to join Nora at breakfast when he heard Amanda's voice, a voice that was so familiar. Luckily, the other woman had not picked up the phone. The sound of her voice brought back a flood of good memories.

"It's me," he said and waited. There was a long pause.

"This is a surprise, Randall."

"Not really. It's our son's birthday today and I want to see him."

"Oh, you can't do that. The divorce court didn't make provision for a drunk to see his son."

"I'm not drinking so much."

"What all the drunks say."

"I'm not a drunk."

"You are. We had a private investigator look into your life prior to the divorce."

"It's me, Randall, Amanda. The other half of the laid-back couple."

"Being laid-back and irresponsible is fine when you are not a parent. Evelina will never allow you to see her son."

"He's my son."

"Only biologically."

"I'll fight you in the courts."

"Cost you a fortune and, if you remember, you don't have a job other than that of an itinerant waiter. And you don't have any money."

"We'll see about that."

"Oh, go to hell."

The phone went dead.

Downstairs in the dining-room Nora was waiting at a table. She had not yet ordered breakfast.

"How did it go, Randall? You look mad as hell."

"How do people become so completely different? I loved that girl. Now she hates me."

"Why I'm single. What do you want for breakfast? Breakfast in England is so different to America. All you get is bacon and eggs."

"What I need is a drink."

"That you are not going to have. We have a big day."

"She won't even let me see my son on his birthday."

"You want to tell me what happened to your marriage? I'll be happy to listen."

"Not really. What I need is a good lawyer."

"You have one in America. I'm sure Brenda can find you one in England. We're due in the office at nine o'clock. Eat some breakfast. It'll calm you down."

"Can I have the day off on Sunday?"

"Of course you can. You want to see your old friends. I can do with some time on my own. These book tours take it out of the publicist as much as the author."

"I'm sorry. I was only thinking of myself."

"We all do, Randall. It's human nature... So, she doesn't know you are famous? When those people last night get to work on you and your book she'll change her mind."

"You think so?"

"I'm sure so. It's called the power of fame and money... What are you having?"

"Bacon and eggs."

They both laughed, Randall not so easily.

"Why is life always a struggle, Nora?"

"By the time you get to my age you get used to it... Thank you, waiter. We'll both have the bacon and eggs. Coffee for me. Tea for my friend."

For a long while they were both silent.

"It all collapsed one after the other. I lost my new job in America because of the behaviour of the woman I was dating when my wife came back to me. I couldn't get my old job back in England as my uncle said I had been disloyal to him for joining the American branch of our company. The property market crashed and without a job I was forced to sell my flat to cover the mortgage which I only managed by selling every one of my moveable assets. I sent copies of *Masters of Vanity* to ten publishers, including Villiers Publishing. They all rejected. I was penniless with a pregnant wife living in my old boarding house waiting tables. And then she left me. Now, out of the blue, thanks to Harry Wakefield who took the time to read the book, I am rich and getting famous. How can life change so quickly, Nora? One minute up, not a care in the world, next minute penniless. One minute happy and alone on the bank of an African river and now all this. What's life all about? Why does it happen? What's the point in doing what we do? Did she only like me when I had money? Did she come back to me from her lesbian lover just to get pregnant? I don't understand. I don't know what life is all about. I met her in a pub. A perfect stranger. That night we became lovers. It's all so haphazard. Choosing a wife is the most important decision a man has to make. And yet it's all so casual. Chance. Luck. Where you happen to be. And in the end do we really know what our lover is thinking? Is it money? Sex? Or just convenience? It's all so trivial and it shouldn't be. Now half of all the marriages end in divorce. Single parents. Two women as parents! Do we ever know what's right and what's wrong? There's no trust. No loyalty. Just a headlong rush to enjoy ourselves... I'm sorry, Nora. Other people's problems are boring... Thank you, waiter. Just as I like it. Bacon and eggs, sausage and fried tomatoes... What a day. What a life. Makes you wonder what's coming next. Now I've got to get myself an expensive lawyer if I want to see my own son. Where the hell have we all come to? Makes you think, Nora. Makes you think."

Feeling sad in the depth of his being, Randall set about eating his breakfast. When he looked up Nora was looking at him, her expression a mixture of sympathy and sorrow.

"You've been through it too, Nora?"

"Yes I have. Most of us do. It's life, the good and the bad... We'd better go. Don't want to be late."

"What do I do?"

"Put it in your books. Share it with people so they don't think they're the only ones that get hurt."

"I don't even know what he looks like."

"You'll get to know him. Time heals all wounds. People mellow. Including your ex-wife. The boy will grow up and have his own life. Much the same as yours. And mine... Come on. We've got a book to promote."

The money chase went on right up to Saturday evening. The promotion went well, the media happy to take advantage of a bestselling author in order to promote their own interests. The wolves were good at feeding each other. For the first time since leaving America Randall slept properly. He did not go down to breakfast, wanting to spend the day in a world of his own. He took the Tube to Notting Hill Gate. Before leaving the Savoy Hotel he had cashed a cheque with the help of the receptionist, the poor girl obsequious to a hotel guest, just doing her job. It was ten o'clock in the morning when Randall rang the bell. He rang three times. It was Sunday morning. The church bells were ringing. Randall, excited to see his real friends, stood on the top step in front of the door and waited. In Mrs Salter's basement flat the curtains were drawn. It was cold standing out on the step, and Randall put his hands under his armpits to keep them warm. After the fourth ring the curtain in the well beside the front-door steps opened. A familiar face was smiling at him.

"Randall! Is that you? Oh, how wonderful. Where have you been? Have you lost your key? Hang on. I'm coming up. What's going on?"

"I gave the key back to you when I left, if you remember. I sold my book."

"Oh, how wonderful. I'm getting old. Forget things. Are you coming back to live with us?"

"I'm going to buy myself a place in the country. I've come to see you all. Are they home? James and Oliver?... Someone inside is running down the stairs. Sounds like Oliver."

"Go and see your friends and then come and have a cup of tea. How are you, Randall?"

"Better. I stopped all the heavy drinking."

"That's wonderful. Everything in moderation."

"How are you, Mrs Salter?"

"Getting old. It's so wonderful to see you. You three boys are my only family."

"Not boys anymore. We're all over thirty."

"You are to me. You are to me, Randall."

The front door burst open. It was Oliver.

"Good Lord, it's Randall. How are you, old boy? We'd better wake up James. What's going on?"

"I sold the book."

"I'll be buggered. Why didn't you tell us?"

"I wasn't sure if the book would sell."

"But it did?"

"So far nearly two million copies just in America."

"You'd better come in. Why does England have such a lousy climate? You see, Randall, it's not all bad. I've been telling you that for years."

They were both smiling as Randall walked into the house. Mrs Salter had closed her basement window and redrawn the curtain. The church bells were still pealing. Randall was home.

"I brought you both some money."

"Don't be ridiculous. We gave you your airfare to Zimbabwe. It was meant as a gift. What are you doing in London? Where are you staying?"

"At the Savoy."

"I'll be buggered."

"I wanted to come back to Notting Hill Gate. See if Mrs Salter had a room for a month. My publishers wouldn't let me. They thought it wouldn't look right. The money world is all about appearances."

"Have you seen Amanda?"

"She put the phone down on me."

"Women! Love them and hate them. But without them we wouldn't have any fun. And my godson?"

"She won't even let me see him."

"Oh, dear. She's still with Evelina? Life really can get complicated. Come up to my room and tell me all about your book."

"Are you in a play?"

"Resting at the moment. We call it resting when we're out of work. The life of an actor comes and goes. One minute you are popular. The next they don't want to know you. Bit of a down spot at the moment... James! It's Randall. Get out of bed, you old bugger... Never did understand the gays and lesbians. Frankly I don't think I understand anyone other than you and James. Tea. I'll make some tea. We can all have a tea party."

The years fell away from Randall as if they had never been. He was twenty years old again. Just arrived from Rhodesia. His whole life an exciting question mark. Passing the door to his old room brought back all the memories. He was back at the top of his favourite flight of stairs. The door to his old room was closed. James Tomlin opened the door to the next room, grinning all over his face. Nothing had changed in ten years.

"Randall Crookshank. What a sight for sore eyes."

"How are you, James?"

"As well as can be expected. What are you up to?"

"I sold my book. Is someone living in my old room?"

"Mrs Salter finally let it to an old pensioner. Nice old boy."

"I'm making tea. We're going to have a tea party. Be a good chap and go down and tell Mrs Salter. Mrs Salter's troopers are back together."

Randall watched Oliver, as tall and lanky as ever, put on the kettle. They had all headed into his room, the place a shambles as usual. Randall took out his wallet and counted out the money into two equal amounts. He gave them each a small pile of ten pound notes.

"You loaned me money for my airfare to Zimbabwe. When I was a penniless drunk. I owe you both far more than money. You can't repay a friendship with money. Anyway, this is the best I can do. If either of you ever need any more just let me know."

"It's far more than we loaned you."

"So what? I've now got more money than I know what to do with. It's embarrassing. Takes the fun out of it. And James, are you in a play?"

"For the moment. Acting is pretty much one job at a time. The future is never guaranteed. I'll go down and get Mrs Salter. Where are you staying?"

"The Savoy."

"I'll be buggered."

"Just what I said." Oliver was smiling while he prepared the tea.

They laughed, all together. Oliver put the teacups on an old tray. When the kettle boiled he made the tea. Mrs Salter joined them. Old friends, comfortable together. Randall smiled. He was home. The banter went on all morning.

"I thought I would take you all to the pub for lunch."

"Lead on, Macduff." Mrs Salter declined the lunch invitation, smiled and left the room.

Randall was happy. Something he had not been for a very long time. He'd been content alone in the Zambezi Valley. But not completely happy. Friends, he told himself as they walked together down to the pub. That was what it was all about.

The Leg of Mutton and Cauliflower was the same as it always was. The place he had met Amanda. The memories, all of them good, came flooding back again.

"Are you drinking, Randall?"

"I'm allowed two beers. No more. I never, ever want to lose it again."

"The prodigal son returns. A toast. To Randall Crookshank and his book."

"Actually, Oliver, it's Randall Holiday. They changed my name. Like everything else in my life."

All through lunch Randall kept looking around the pub expecting to see Amanda. She wasn't there. Only her smiling face in his mind from the time when both of them were happy. Before the days of responsibility. Before the days when it wasn't about money, but having fun, enjoying each other's company. Being young... As he looked round the familiar bar he recognised no one. The people, like Randall, had changed. They'd all gone their separate ways. It was probably why Mrs Salter never came to the pub. Too many memories.

"So, what are you going to do with all your money, Randall Holiday?"

"I have no idea Oliver Manningford. But I expect someone in the future will find a use for it. Money attracts people. Mostly the wrong kind of people. The ones after your money."

"Often it's better not to be too rich or too famous."

"That's what worries me. You want something so badly and when you get it, it isn't what you thought it was. The only thing that matters is the book itself. Not the money that comes with it."

"Most people would disagree with you."

"We all think money will solve our problems. It was so good when we all had nothing. Seems silly to say so. But it's true. But life goes on. You take it as it comes."

"You going on television?"

"Tomorrow. Give Amanda a surprise. If she's watching."

"What time?"

"Ten o'clock on the talk show. I've done it plenty of times before in America. All part of the hype."

"I'll tell her."

"Who?"

"Amanda. He's my godson even if he hasn't yet been christened. Or if she did christen him she didn't tell me. Evelina still got the same phone number?"

"Same one. Amanda will tell you, like me, to go to hell. To mind your own business."

"But she'll watch you on television. I'd like to be a fly on the wall to see her expression. You'll get to see James Oliver. How it works. Fame will do more for you than any lawyers. And however much you may wish to change the mother of your son, you can't. So we have to make the best of it... Two years old? Time flies... You want a third one?"

"No thank you."

"Mind if I have one?"

Randall paid the bill with his credit card up at the bar.

"Look, I've got to love and leave you. Dinner at the hotel with Harry

Wakefield, the Fleet Street journalist. Works for the *Daily Mirror*. He's my stepmother's brother. He got me my publisher. Just the two of us. I want to thank him and talk about writing. Nora thinks he will promote the book. You never know if you are genuinely thanking someone for a favour or trying to get something else out of them. What looks like the right thing from my side of the table looks like a promotion to everyone else. You two stay and enjoy yourselves. I put a couple of extra rounds on the bill. Real good to be with friends again."

"Don't let them swallow you."

"I'll try not to, Oliver. I'll keep in touch."

"Good luck with finding a place in the country. I always like sitting in front of a roaring log fire. So, when shall we three meet again? In thunder, lightning, or in rain? Shakespeare. Now, there was a writer. Will Shakespeare."

Feeling flat, Randall left them in the pub. If he had stayed he would have started drinking. Outside in the cold he pulled up his collar. Hands deep in his overcoat pocket he walked to the Tube station. All the way, with the east wind blowing in his face making his eyes water and his face grow numb, he tried to think of Zimbabwe and the farm, the memory of sunshine his only comfort.

3

---

*L*ike so many other times when it came to understanding human nature, Oliver Manningford was proved right. The afternoon following his first British television broadcast there was a message from Amanda waiting for him at the Savoy Hotel when he returned from a lunch with Nora and two of her handpicked journalists she had found with the help of Brenda Foster. The lunch had gone well, helped by the previous night's talk show. Interest fed interest, the two men wanting their piece of the pie, their piece of Randall Holiday... The message was simple, 'Give me a ring'. From his upstairs room in the hotel, Randall dialled his ex-wife's number. The phone was picked up immediately, as if she had been waiting by the phone.

"Two million copies, Randall! I couldn't believe it. How much money have they paid you? It must be a fortune. Villiers Publishing. Aren't they the biggest publisher in the world? James Oliver's daddy on television. I couldn't believe my eyes. Sorry I was a bit abrupt when you phoned me. I was having a bad day. When are you coming to see your son? You're published, Randall. It's so wonderful. And you're staying at the Savoy."

"Would you like to bring my son to the hotel?"

"Of course I would, Randall. When would it be convenient?"

"Right now."

"I'm on my way."

The surprise was not the boy's resemblance to Randall's father but the size of his mother. Amanda had put on so much weight, Randall barely recognised her from the slim, pretty girl that had been his wife. The boy was shy, holding his mother's hand, sucking his thumb and keeping close to his mother's skirt. Even Amanda's face was fat, skin sagging under her chin.

"The last time I saw you, Randall, you were waiting tables. I've never before been in a bedroom at the Savoy Hotel. Very posh. A famous writer. So the launch party is here on Friday? Can I come?"

Randall picked up his son and had a look at him face to face.

"I'm your father, James Oliver. Soon, you're going to come and see me in the country and you're going to play with the rabbits. Bunny rabbits."

The boy wriggled and Randall put him down. The thumb went back in the mouth, the boy staring up at him.

"He's a bit shy. This is all a surprise."

"I'll bet it is. Did you tell him who I am?"

"It's a bit difficult... Rabbits. What have rabbits got to do with it?"

"When I have my place in the countryside I want to have him for a while. Get to know each other. Let him get to know who I am. We need some time together, father and son."

"My father left me a fortune. Both my parents are dead, I'm afraid. Bit ironical, don't you think? You wouldn't have had to wait tables after all."

"How's Evelina?"

"She's fine. She loves this little boy just as much as I do... So, am I coming to your fancy book launch? I'll bet there'll be lots of famous people. I can't wait."

"I'll ask Brenda Foster to put you on the invitation list. Would you like me to include Evelina?"

"That's very civil of you, Randall. Very modern."

"We all have to be modern, Amanda."

"Are you being sarcastic?"

"Just a little... There's a resemblance to my father when he looks at me. No doubt I'm his father. Just look at him. My son!"

"Why are you putting on your coat? Where are we going?"

"Sorry, got to run. If I don't leave now they'll wonder what's happened to me. Another promotion. Never stops. Will you have someone to look after him when you come to Friday's party?"

"We have a live-in maid. It's nice being rich."

"Thank you for bringing him. Duty calls. We can all go down together in the lift. Does he talk?"

"Not with his thumb in his mouth... Say 'hello Daddy'."

Randall watched, a small, frozen moment in time, as James Oliver took his thumb out of his mouth. The boy stared, saying nothing.

"Hello, son. I'm your father. We're going to be friends... How did you get here, Amanda?"

"By taxi. There's a taxi rank outside the front door of the hotel."

"Everything is such a rush."

"The price of being famous. I always wanted to be rich and famous. Now I'm just rich. Inherited money. It's not the same. Apart from James Oliver I haven't produced anything in my life."

Randall saw them into the taxi, the boy still not connecting. Standing out on the pavement he watched the taxi drive away.

Friday came, and with it Amanda and her live-in lover, Evelina. The woman looked so old Randall wondered what it was all about. What life was all about. The brief moment of introduction was like any other. Randall moved on to shake the next person's hand. The function room was full of chattering people, most of them standing with a drink in their hand. Waiters passed between them with trays full of drinks and snacks. Copies of his book were stacked on the centre table, a big blow-up of the cover and a large photograph of Randall standing on either side of the table. It reminded Randall of a newspaper-seller's stand. Selling books, selling newspapers was all much the same. When Harry Wakefield passed down the line Randall thanked him again.

"You're the guest of honour, Mr Wakefield. Without you none of this would have happened."

"Call me Harry."

"Of course. I owe you more than I could ever repay."

"But you can repay me, Randall. By writing more good books. Books with more than fluff in them are difficult to find at the end of the twentieth century. I'd like you to meet Jocelyn Graham. She's my intern at the paper. Waiting to take up her place at Oxford. She's been with us at the *Daily Mirror* for nearly six months, isn't that right, Jocelyn? She saw you on television and wanted to come to the launch. She's also read

Masters of Vanity. I said I'm sort of your uncle. She's going to read literature at Oxford and then become a journalist."

The girl had put out her hand, Randall taking it. They looked at each other, both of them feeling the power of the silent bite. Randall smiled. With her middle finger the girl scratched the palm of his hand, giving Randall an instant erection. As if the girl knew, she smiled at him. A sweet smile of 'we'll meet again'.

"I can't remember being more absorbed by a book."

The girl was good at flattery as well as smiling. The girl looked down, gave a knowing smile in the direction of his trousers, took a glass of wine from the tray of the hovering waiter and passed on down the line before looking back at Randall and again catching his eye. The girl mouthed 'give me a ring' before turning round. Randall, doing his duty, went on shaking strangers hands as the room filled up to capacity. Right at the end came Oliver and James, both of them looking surprisingly smart... When Randall gave his speech he thanked Harry for finding him his publisher and thanked the famous actors, Oliver Manningford and James Tomlin, for giving him the help and inspiration to write, making sure after the short reading from the book that the photographers included Oliver and James. As he had told them before the launch party, there was nothing better than free publicity. Soon after the photographs, Amanda and Evelina left the party. Amanda said she felt out of it, no one giving her any attention.

"I'm sorry. You see, I'm working. Thank you both for coming. Enjoy the rest of your evening together."

Both of them were holding signed copies of his book. Even though Evelina made her living as a successful dress designer no one at the party had been interested in either of them. As they left, Randall felt sorry for them, a strange feeling.

"Who was that, Randall?" The girl had come up to him, that same knowing smile on her face.

"My ex-wife and her lady lover. They're lesbians. She was a lot thinner when we were married."

"Harry's leaving. Are you going to take me out to dinner?"

"Why not? The work's over. I'll say goodbye to Nora and Brenda and then we'll make a duck. It's Friday night. The night is young. Apart from going round the country signing books in the shops I'm finished. By the end of next month I'll be my own master."

"Do you enjoy being the centre of attention?"

"I hate it. You have no idea how much I hate it."

"What are you going to do?"

"Disappear. Find a place in the country right out of the way. I'm not even going to have a telephone."

"They won't leave you alone."

"Then I'll go back to Africa."

"They'll find you. People who have read your book will think they own part of you. You see, I know you Randall, just from reading your book. Far better than if we'd already been out to dinner or whatever else you and I get up to tonight. Oh, they'll never leave you alone. Like your friends, the actors, you're public property, Randall Holiday."

"My real name is Crookshank."

"I know... Where are we going?"

"Three times round the block and back to the hotel."

"Sounds good to me."

"Seriously, we're going to a jazz club I know in Soho. Gerrard Street. You'll like the atmosphere. In a smoky basement no one will know or care who the hell I am. You like jazz? Trad jazz. Another one of my quirks."

"Will we be able to hear ourselves think?"

"Probably not. Sometimes it's nice not to have to think."

Randall did his goodbye rounds. Harry Wakefield had gone. So had James and Oliver. The pile of books on the table had disappeared, not a book left, just the poster of the cover and Randall's photograph standing alone. People were leaving. The party was over. Looking across the emptying room Randall could see her waiting by the door. She was young, very young, but who the hell cared? Life was a constant flow, one thing leading to another. Happy, smiling, Randall strode from the room, poking his photograph with his finger and knocking it flat on its back.

"What you do that for?"

"You mind if I hold your hand? I want to make a friend tonight. I'm sick of being polite to strangers."

"Friends! You want us to be friends!"

"It's always best to start as friends. To get to know each other. I'm sick of one-night stands. You want a hamburger? In Soho they sell buns not caviar. Too much conspicuous consumption makes me sick. A good old pint of beer and a bun."

"This is going to be a whole lot more fun than I imagined."

"I hope so. For both of us. Let's walk to the Tube station and get off at Piccadilly Circus. Tonight I'm going to be Randall Crookshank on a first date."

Smiling, they walked out of the hotel and down the street. She had taken his hand, the hand warm and soft. People on the street took no notice of them. They were normal people, a man and a girl, holding hands as they walked down the street.

They found a hamburger place off Piccadilly Circus, the statue of Eros still visible through the window. They took their food to one of the tables and sat down to eat. Having eaten few of the snacks at the party, both of them were hungry.

"What time do they stop playing jazz?"

"Eddie Blake is playing tonight. In the days before I was born he played the clarinet in Benjie Appleton's band. My father has all their old records. Benjie Appleton went to Eton."

"What's that got to do with it?"

"In those days it wasn't quite the thing for an old Etonian to be in a jazz band. A string quartet playing Mozart would have been considered more appropriate. How times have changed. I hope racism goes the same way as class. We all look the same under a bus… A good old American style hamburger. What more could a man want?"

"I want to write a book. How do I start?"

"At the beginning. Find a story and start at the beginning. Can we talk about something else? I've had my fill of books for the moment."

"You grew up in Africa. What's it like?"

"The most beautiful and exciting place in the world. Africa is real. Most of urban life in Europe is artificial. Man-made entertainment. You're always having to spend money to keep yourself amused. In the Zambezi Valley I hunted and fished for my food. Months of paradise all to myself. Lions and elephant and a glorious multiplicity of birds. There you belong to nature. Here we're just part of an ever greedier economy with everyone chasing money."

"I've never been out of Europe. I'd be frightened of snakes and lions."

They ate the food, drank the coffee and walked back into the street. Randall had asked the girl who had served them up at the counter the way to Gerrard Street. They found the jazz club easily, Randall paying the small entrance fee. They walked down a flight of stairs into the basement, surrounded by ever increasing noise from the band. For Randall, not having to talk came as a blessing. It was nice to listen to music instead of the voices of people.

"New Orleans jazz. Dad said it was the best." Randall didn't think she had heard him. They danced, the two of them feeling each other's bodies. Outside, when it was over, they took a taxi back to Randall's hotel. Like the book tour it was all a rush. With the lights still on they made love. Like Amanda, they met and became lovers. Lying awake, with the girl asleep next to him, the hum of distant traffic still permeating the room, Randall hoped all would be well. The girl was so young and innocent. He hoped he had not used his book to take advantage of Jocelyn. Then he fell asleep. Once he woke in the night, a brief flash of fear not knowing where he was or who was sleeping in the bed next to him. Then he remembered the girl who had tickled the palm of his hand. Smiling, Randall went back to sleep. When he woke in the morning the girl still had her arm round him.

"Good morning, lover. How'd you sleep?"

"Just fine, Jocelyn."

"You want to make love?"

"Are you on the pill?"

"Of course I am, silly. Bit late to ask. In this day and age a girl has to look after herself."

"Yes, I suppose she does."

Like so many times before, when he was working for his uncle at BLG with a top executive's salary, he knew nothing about her mind, only what he saw of her body. All he knew was the pretty girl next to him naked.

For ten long, deeply satisfying minutes they made love with their bodies, no thought in their minds other than their primal need. When it was over they lay on their backs looking up at the fancy ceiling.

"We're animals, Jocelyn."

"What's wrong with that?"

"Can you imagine if someone in the year ten thousand eleven

hundred and four BC had said, 'not tonight darling', none of this would have happened. One or both of us wouldn't be here."

"How do you know the exact year?"

"Law of averages. With all our ancestors in our genealogy one of them had to be playing around in the year ten thousand eleven hundred and four BC. I'm glad he or she did. I enjoy my life."

"You think we're related?"

"Have to be. The whole world's related... If we were in Africa we could go for a walk in the bush. All we can do now is call room service and get them to bring up some breakfast. For all its swank, we're stuck in a room."

"Will you take me to Africa, Randall?"

"That depends if we become friends. Find we have more in common than sex... What can you do in London at the end of February other than spend money on entertainment?"

"We could go to an art gallery."

"We could."

"We could take a nap. Or we could talk. Tell each other our story."

"Did you like the jazz last night? You write your story in a book, Jocelyn. That's how it works."

"I liked you, Randall. That was what was more important. What do your family do in Zimbabwe?"

"We're tobacco growers. A six-thousand-acre farm for the moment. Mugabe accuses us of being feudal barons and wants the land back again."

"Will he get it?"

"Probably. No one likes a feudal baron, no matter how much good they are doing by employing and looking after them. They are given houses, running water and the new houses have electricity."

"It's nice and warm in bed. You're so lucky to be a writer. You can go where you will and do what you want, never having to worry about money. My father is always worrying about money."

"Sometimes it's better not to have money and then you don't have to worry about it. Sadly, that's not how it works. If you don't have money you're screwed."

"How many books have you sold?"

"A couple of million and counting."

"Wow, that's a lot of readers. And with every copy in print being read by ten or more readers, just think of all those people's heads you've got into. The mind boggles."

"I'll order up some tea."

"Would you? You may have a funny accent but if you drink tea you must be English. Do you like cucumber sandwiches?"

"Of course I do. And bacon and eggs for breakfast."

"You're kidding."

They were both giggling. They were going to be friends as well as lovers... Randall picked up the phone and ordered up some tea.

"Will you come and visit me at Oxford?"

"Of course I will. Will you visit me in the country?"

"Are you kidding?"

Later, after eating breakfast in the room, Jocelyn went home, saying she had other commitments. They had promised to see each other soon but Randall wondered. It had all happened so many times before with equally lovely girls. They had both got what they wanted. Did it have any meaning? Was it a roll in the hay? One of life's pleasures and amusements? It made Randall sad. Did people just use each other and pass on their separate ways? Did she want him or the fame of his book so years into the future when she read another of his books she could say she had slept with the author, a small break in the humdrum of her life? Or would they meet again? All the thinking made Randall feel lonely. He had nothing to do. All that money and nothing to do.

Instead of feeling sorry for himself Randall took a bath, got dressed and left the hotel. He was going to surprise his grandmother in his Uncle Paul's townhouse in Hyde Park. It was time to make amends.

As so often happened in life there was nobody in. The doorbell rang and rang. Wet, cold and with nothing to do Randall walked the London streets, the drizzle dripping down his face, people hurrying past him in both directions. The shops on either side of the street were full of people. After all the acclaim of the launch party, he should have been elated. He felt flat, empty, without any purpose. Randall walked to the Odeon theatre and bought himself a ticket. It was dark inside the theatre, the movie halfway through. He took off his wet overcoat and put it over his knees. The theatre was warm, the seat comfortable. Within a few minutes Randall fell asleep.

· · ·

THE FOLLOWING MORNING WAS SUNDAY, the day of reckoning, the day of
the reviews. Randall went out to buy himself the newspapers. Jocelyn
had not given him her home phone number. He would have to wait to
phone her at the *Daily Mirror*. Anyway, she probably had a boyfriend.
The sun was shining, the east wind cold, his overcoat keeping him warm.
He found a newsagent and bought all the Sunday papers. Back at the
hotel, alone in his room, fear fluttered in the pit of his stomach. To
Randall the reviews were all that mattered. He spread the newspapers on
the bed and looked for the literary sections. In all the papers his name
and the name of his book leapt out at him. He had forgotten to order up
tea. Sitting on the edge of the bed, Randall picked up the *Sunday Times*
and began to read the review. Halfway through he found what he was
looking for.

> *Mark Fletcher wanted fame, recognition and permanent
> attention. He used his new-found wealth to buy what he
> craved. The trophy wives came and went, useful for as long
> as they brought him publicity. They were either rich, very
> beautiful or appeared on the stage. He built an office block in
> the heart of the City of London, a beacon on the London
> skyline. He courted famous singers. Famous actors. Politicians
> who needed his money. Nobel Laureates and priests to help
> them with their good causes. Mark Fletcher craved public
> attention like a drug addict craved his fix and an alcoholic
> craved his drink. The fact the man was a cheat, a financial
> manipulator, what in a smaller man would have been called
> a thief, didn't disturb him or those he used. Fletcher is the
> rotten, corrupt core of the worldwide capitalist system. He
> created wealth out of nothing making financial products for
> greedy investors. He made money out of other people's money,
> never taking the risk himself. He only had one aim in life and
> that was to feed his vanity. Mark Fletcher, in Randall
> Holiday's novel, is the master of vanity among all the other
> masters of vanity, the people who one day will beggar the
> world. If we want to understand the meaning of living in a*

fool's paradise we should all read this book. It may call itself fiction but one day, through the greed of men like Mark Fletcher, it may all come true leaving us floundering in a city world with nothing and nowhere to turn. When the financial institutions that span the world, all interlinked and dependent, come crashing down it will be the end of civilisation, the end of life as we know it. All the glitter will fade. The lights will go out. And as one of the ordinary folk in this heart-pulsing book points out: 'you can't grow potatoes in the pavement'.... Let's just hope it doesn't happen. But don't hold your breath, folks. A world that had two billion people when Mark Fletcher was born now has five billion and counting. Enjoy the book. Like me, it will make you think. We're going to hear a lot more of Randall Holiday. And the likes of Mark Fletcher. Masters of Vanity. *Now that's a good book.*

For a long while Randall sat still. The room was quiet, Randall's mind full of mixed emotions. Did his book have that much significance? Even if the financial world collapsed wouldn't people pick up the pieces? And who was he, Randall Holiday or whatever else they wanted to call him, to say the world had reached its Armageddon? Man had survived so far in far more perilous circumstances... One by one Randall read the rest of the reviews. All of them were good, making Randall wonder if the work of Brenda Foster might have had something to do with it.

"You're good, Brenda, you and your publicity machine."

Randall picked up the phone and asked for Nora Stewart's room.

"Can I come down and see you?"

"You've read the reviews."

"I want to thank you, Nora. The book without you, Henry Stone and Brenda would have come to nothing."

"We all do our jobs, Randall. All those links in a chain. And when the chain is perfect you give it a pull. Tomorrow we go on the road to yank that chain."

"Is it just about money?"

"In this lovely world you've got to have money."

"Thanks, Nora. You've made me famous."

"I hope you don't find it a curse. What are you going to do with all that money?"

"Give it away, I suppose."

Nora chuckled. She sounded happy. A job well done. Without saying another word she put down the phone.

Lying back on the bed Randall looked out of the window. Outside it had begun to rain. Inside on the wall was a picture of the Queen of England as a young girl wearing a dark blue robe. Below the photograph, the minibar stood waiting, small dinky bottles of spirits at prices that blew Randall's brain. Everything in the room was expensive. Everything polished and clean. But however Randall looked at it he was still caught between four walls. He got up off the bed and looked at one of the paintings. Modern art and no doubt very expensive. To Randall it looked like some kind of artist's joke, a painting of nothing, a bit like Mark Fletcher's financial derivatives. Would it last like a Renoir? Randall doubted it. No doubt the man was famous with a good publicist... Under his feet the carpet was thick, his bare feet warmed by the wool. The curtains by the window, the outside of the window now splattered with rain, were dark and rich and perfectly hung. The applause ringing in his head from the reviews began sounding hollow. There was nothing in it for Randall any more than there was in the room. The Zambezi Valley flooded back into his mind, a place he had lived in for months costing him nothing. The call of his name downriver seemed like a lifetime away, the call that had brought him all this glamour and acclaim. It made Randall laugh. He was worse off now than then. The minibar kept on looking at him, the old drunk in Randall wanting a fix, snapping the picture in his mind of the Zambezi River. Going to the bar he picked up one of the miniatures and put it back again. He had nothing to do. Everything had now been done. He was bored. The worst thing in life was to get where you wanted to go. To arrive. To have nowhere else to go. No more challenge. No more hope for excitement. He had arrived at the Savoy Hotel, arguably the most iconic hotel in the world, but it was still four walls, a large, warm, well-decorated and mind-bendingly expensive box made of concrete and bricks. Instead of being able to put the kettle on the fire he had to phone room service to get himself a cup of tea. He had to talk to people. With all the money in the world he was not his own master. But he wanted a cup of tea so he rang down and sat back on the bed and waited, the newspapers splashed all round him. He got up, picked up the papers and dumped them in a wastepaper basket that sat under the dressing table. As he got up from bending he looked into the mirror and saw himself, something in the valley he had not been able to do. He was not sure he liked what he saw. The man was old, far too old for Jocelyn... There was a knock on the door. He stopped looking at himself. Tripping over the shoes he had taken off and left by the bed he went to the door and took the tea-tray from the waiter. There were small cakes on the tray with the tea. The man expected a tip. Outside it was raining harder. He was trapped. Trapped in the most expensive shoebox on the planet. Sighing, Randall poured himself a cup of tea and added the milk. The man had left with a pound tip. Randall never took sugar in his tea. When the tea cooled it didn't taste the same as a cup of tea made from the water from the Zambezi River. There was a metallic taste, as if the water was slightly tainted.

"You're an ungrateful bastard. The world is your oyster. Pull your finger out and go and enjoy your new-found wealth. Most people would kill to have what you've got... And stop talking to yourself. It's the first sign of insanity."

The second cup of tea was better. The tea finished, Randall lay back on the bed. He was smiling at a comment made by his father when Randall was growing up.

'According to Dagwood, the character in my favourite cartoon, the best thing in life is a nap between naps.'

Later, when Randall woke from his snooze, he was feeling a whole lot better.

FOR A MONTH they yanked the chain, one bookshop looking much like the other. It was all about cashing in on Randall's celebrity. From town to town they went like itinerant minstrels singing their song, the public lapping it up, people awed by a man they had seen on television. The local press were fêted in exchange for their articles in the provincial newspapers. *Masters of Vanity* sold like hot cakes. With Randall in tow they went as far as Edinburgh and back again. By the end of the book tour Nora looked exhausted.

"You're going home, Nora. It's over."

"I'll miss you. If I'd been twenty years younger you wouldn't have stood a chance."

"Did you want me as a lover?" He was smiling gently at Nora.

"We all still hope even when we're past it. What happened to Jocelyn?"

"She had a boyfriend. They're going up to Oxford together."

"Poor Randall. Are you taking me to the airport? When are you coming back to America?"

"I never asked, but were you ever married? And yes, I'm taking you to the airport."

"Once. Long ago. I was Jocelyn's age. My first lover. Both of us young. Both of us desperately in love. Or so we thought. I got pregnant. We got married. We were kids, really. Two months later I had a miscarriage. There's something wrong inside me. I had two more miscarriages. I was working as a secretary in an advertising agency. So was Ralph. How we had met. We were together ten years before he moved on. By then he was making a lot of money. I learned a lot from Ralph. About life. About the temporary nature of everything. He wanted kids. Something to leave behind. I don't blame him. I wanted kids more than anything in the world... That first boy would have been your age by now. They were all boys. Some older women seduce young men but I couldn't do it to you. For these last months you've been that son that died. Looking back I see my life died with the boys."

"Did Ralph remarry?"

"Three times in ten years."

"Do you talk to him?"

"When love dies between two people it's better to leave it alone. Thank you for the company. I hope you write many more books. Good ones. Don't think about the average reader. You've got enough money to last you a lifetime. You don't have to write just to make money."

"If I don't give it away."

"Always keep a nest egg to fall back on. Then you can write what you want. I'd love to have been a writer."

"You're crying, Nora."

"I'm a silly, middle-aged old woman. My flat in New York is going to seem so cold when I get home. So empty. You can have all the material things the world can offer but if you're on your own you have nothing.

You have to be able to share with someone. Share those little bits of excitement. Why don't we say goodbye to each other here and I'll catch a cab to Heathrow? Or I'm going to make a fool of myself in public. Goodbye, Randall. Have a good life. At least I'll be able to visit you every time you bring out a new book. Look after yourself."

"You know my real mother was eaten by a pride of lions. In the years to come we should see a lot more of each other."

"You look at me as a mother?"

"You look at me as a son. That's better. You're laughing. And no, you are not going to the airport on your own. And you don't look middle-aged. Not by a long shot. We're going to first have a last good lunch. Talk about Ralph and talk about my mother."

"Now I really am going to cry."

"She was an alcoholic. I have that in me too. She drove into the wilds of Rhodesia away from World's View, ran out of petrol and tried to walk home. My brother and I have missed her ever since. You mind if I have a couple of drinks with my lunch? Break the rules. Drink to the lifelong friendship of Nora and Randall. Friendship lasts a lot longer than love. I'll always be friends with Oliver Manningford and James Tomlin. And now I'm always going to be friends with Nora Stewart. Is Stewart your name or his?"

"Mine. I changed back to my maiden name when Ralph remarried. There couldn't be two Mrs Grangers."

"Do you miss him?"

"All the time. You don't stop loving just because you are no longer loved."

"There must have been other men."

"Plenty of them. Even now. You see I'm rich. I work for myself on commission from the publishers and anyone else who needs a publicist. Modern life is all about getting recognition. Branding. My job is to brainwash the public."

"It's all so mercenary."

"Welcome to the end of the twentieth century. I hate to think what the next one is going to look like with all the new technology. All these computers. Perhaps we'll be able to hunt down every last customer."

"I don't want to think. I hoped my book would sell because people liked it. But it's not like that. The public move in unison like a shoal of fish, following the leader. And you, Nora, were the leader. All those links in the chain so you can pull them all together. The world is going to be a very sad place. Big Brother will be the power of advertising. We won't have minds of our own."

"It made us both rich. Should we complain? And if we do, it won't make any difference... Let's go and have that lunch."

Randall noticed something had changed. They were both looking at each other differently.

In the restaurant Randall ordered himself a whisky. Nora took a glass of wine. The whisky tasted good, warming the cockles of Randall's heart. They sat and smiled at each other. When the food arrived Randall ordered a bottle of wine.

"You can sleep on the plane. There's nothing much else to do. I hate flying. Stuck in the same seat hour after hour."

"How old were you when your mother died?"

"I don't really remember her I was so young. Phillip and I became close. Then Bergit came along. She tried her best. There was something missing. Blood."

"Her brother found you a publisher."

"Life turns in strange ways... How's the fish?"

"Perfect... What are you going to write about next?"

"I'm not sure. I see a place in the country far from the noise of people. Spring is on its way. I'll go for long walks on my own and think. I'll find another book to write. If I don't, I'm finished. There's nothing else I want to do."

"You could go on your travels and look for a story. Books are about people. Have you changed the title of *The Woman Who Stole My Wife*? MaryJane was right. The title is not right."

"I'll think of a new one. Or leave it to you and Brenda Foster. Maybe Henry will come up with a good one."

"You want to leave it to us?"

"Why not? I don't understand marketing despite my degree from the London School of Economics."

"What will Amanda think of the book?"

"We'll have to find out. There's one thing for sure. James Oliver isn't going to be allowed to read that book until he's a whole lot older."

Nora looked at her watch. It was time to go. They finished the fish and Randall called for the bill. The bottle of wine was still half-full. When they got outside the restaurant the taxi was waiting. In the cab they sat close to each other, neither of them saying anything. The driver dropped them right outside the terminal. They were back in the world of other people, everyone in a hurry. They stood looking at each other for a long moment, Nora's luggage on a trolley. They moved towards each other and kissed. Not the kiss of mother and son. Her mouth was soft and welcoming. They stood back and looked at each other, the taste of her lips in Randall's mouth. Nora turned, took hold of the trolley and pushed it towards check-in. She had gone. She looked back once and waved. There was a bar across to Randall's right. When he was sure she had gone, he walked towards the bar. He ordered a double whisky. The slippery slide had begun. He was still booked into the Savoy Hotel for two more nights. After three stiff whiskies Randall took a taxi back to the hotel. It was always best to get drunk close to home. If she hadn't gone back to America they would have become lovers. In the back of the taxi, Randall felt the tears well up behind his eyes. He felt so lonely. He felt so damn lonely it made him cry.

PART 3

APRIL TO MAY 1989 — "BROKEN LIVES"

1

———

While Randall was sitting alone in a downstairs bar at the Savoy Hotel Nora Stewart was looking out of the small round window of the plane. All she could think of was Randall. The man next to Nora was fat as a pig, his bulging left side encroaching on Nora's seat. She was cramped into the window. She had let down the small table in preparation for supper the stewardess was pushing down the aisle. Despite her money Nora always travelled economy when on her own. Old habits die hard. The man next to her, sexually quite repulsive, had tried to come on to her. They were both of a similar age. On the man's fat finger on his left hand was a wedding ring almost lost in the bulging flesh. The stewardess asked if she wanted the chicken or beef. The small tray was passed to Nora, the fat man trying to help and getting in the way. For something to do, Nora picked at the food. There was no one meeting her at the airport. No one in her apartment, an expensive three rooms in Manhattan to be close to all the action. She was due to see Henry Stone first thing in the morning, the time difference between London and New York giving her plenty of time to sleep. Had she been a fool by not trying to seduce him? By the reaction to her kiss on his mouth she was sure it would have worked. And why not? Many old men seduced young women. Married them. Had children with them. Why should it be any different for women, except the older women couldn't have children.

Was that the reason? Was love between a man and a woman only about procreation? So many times in her past she had thought of the other person, never enough of herself.

"You having a drink with that chicken, lady?"

The fat man had squirmed round in his seat to look at Nora as he chewed on his steak. His eyelids were hooded, hiding his lecherous smile. He was an American, probably from the Bronx.

"We've got another four hours to waste. You too live in New York?"

"Manhattan."

"That's swell. Must be rich. Why you flying economy? Never mind. Let's each have a small bottle of wine. My name is Ted. Sorry I'm so fat. They don't make plane seats big enough these days. Back in the good old days of the 707 you had room to move. We used to go to the back of the plane, near the galley, and turn it into a bar. I'm a travelling salesman. Plastics. Toys for kids. Made in Hong Kong. I've spent most of my life visiting shops. We got the worldwide agency. It's all in the marketing. You do good advertising and follow it up. Make it personal with the store buyers. What you do, lady? Hope I'm not boring you. Myself, I get bored on planes. Make a point of talking to the people next to me. You'd be amazed how many friends I make on the planes."

"I'm a publicist. Nora Stewart. I work for myself."

"Who do you publicise?"

"Artists, mostly."

"Anyone I know?"

"A writer. Randall Holiday. Why I was in London."

"I've heard of him, Nora. You want that wine? The bar trolley is right next to us... Steward, two bottles of red. If she don't drink it I'll have both of them. Them bottles are small."

"Why not, Ted?"

"Make it four. A little wine and a good old chat, we'll make New York come a whole lot quicker."

"Have you really heard of Randall Holiday?"

"Probably not. Last time I read a book I was at school. A whole long time ago. Wasn't he on television?"

"He was. It's all about marketing... How many kids have you got?"

"Three. Second wife. The first one ran out on me."

Apart from the squash it wasn't so bad. The fat man talked on and on, some of it amusing. It took Nora's mind off Randall, the kiss still lingering. The wine helped her to relax. It was better entertainment than listening to music through earphones. Ted drank down his red wine like water, every morsel of food on his tray having gone. The young man in the aisle seat had ignored Ted, so Nora had his full attention. The young man was leaning out into the aisle to find himself some space. The 747 flew on. After the wine, Nora made herself comfortable against the small window, the wing visible out into space. She began to drift off. Ted kept on talking. A monologue. All of it about himself. His voice merged into a dream. She was making love to Randall. In the dream she was young, the same age as Jocelyn. When she woke from the dream, Ted was still talking. Nora smiled at him. There were two more small bottles on the small table that rested on his belly.

"You're a good listener, Nora."

"Thank you, Ted... You mind if I take a nap?"

"You go ahead."

Ted tried again with the young man next to him, gave up and stared straight ahead. Ted was unhappy. Nora felt sorry for him. Wine and sadness never went well together. When Nora woke the second time it was dark out of the window. She pulled down the flap. Ted was asleep, stuck like a toad in a trap. The young man was still leaning towards the aisle, the earplugs stuck in his ears. He was smiling. With the help of Ted's monologue and her sleeping she was halfway home. She began thinking of Randall. She couldn't get him out of her mind or her dreams. It made her feel twenty years younger. In the past she had a future. In the present she had little. But life went on.

"You're smiling, Nora. What you thinking about?"

Ted had woken and was looking at her. The lecherous look had gone. He had the look of a friend.

"Randall Holiday. And I shouldn't be. I'm old enough to be his mother."

"We all dream, Nora. Nothing wrong with dreaming. Sometimes all we have left is our dreams. Not the big ones. Little ones that get us from day to day. Place to place. London to New York. My boss will be pleased with the sales figures. All he ever asks about... Did he sell a lot of books?"

"A whole lot of books."

"That's good. It'll make a lot of people happy. The more I sell the more the money goes round. Everyone is happy. What life's about. Selling. Maybe dreaming. I always dream I'm going to sell more than I do. Pushes me on. Makes me want to sell harder. Is he married?"

"His wife left him for a woman. What Randall's new book is all about."

"I'll have to read that one. What's the title?"

"We don't know yet."

"How about *My Best Fantasy*. I've always liked the idea of my wife going with a woman. Both of them. Both of them together. Now that's a fantasy."

"That's pornography, Ted."

"We all have our dreams."

"It wasn't a fantasy for Randall. He has a son. The woman took his son. In the book they planned it."

"Did they?"

"Randall's not sure."

"The modern world, Nora. The modern world."

"How much longer have we got?"

"Couple of hours. Then I'll be able to listen to all my wife's moans. The kids are teenagers. Always arguing. Life at home can be hell."

"You're lucky to have a family. I wish I had a family... You mind if I go back to sleep?"

"You do what you want, Nora. You either sit or sleep on a plane."

"Do they argue all the time?"

"All the time."

Nora's daydream went in a different direction. She was thinking of two-year-old James Oliver. With Randall rich enough to support his son and no longer binge drinking he would be able to fight the lesbians in the court for custody of his son. Nora was smiling. In her fantasy they were lovers, James Oliver her son. She still had plenty of life to bring up the boy. The dream played on. They were living in the country far away from people, Nora no longer a publicist. She was a writer, writing her own books, all three of them happy. They had everything. A small farm in the hills with a big fireplace for winter. A river for summer at the bottom of the farm. Long walks together full of happy silence while both of them worked out the future plot of their books. James Oliver was a darling. She and Randall were friends as much as lovers, the difference in their age not mattering. They were happy. All three of them content and happy. Cats and dogs. Horses to ride. The perfect life.

"You have that thousand-yard stare, Nora."

"Is it that obvious? I was playing out my own fantasy."

"I hope it was good."

By now, Ted was getting a little drunk, his voice wistful. Nora knew he wanted to talk.

"Tell me more about your life, Ted. Where did you grow up?"

Like a water tank with the plug pulled out he was off again, his life gushing. If nothing else it stopped Nora romanticising. Being ridiculous. Putting ideas into her head, none of which were possible. The reality of life was a lot more horrible. Affairs started and just as quickly ended. The rest was a whole lot of dreams. There was no place in the country, no perfect ending. Life was where you were, in a plane, listening to a sad fat man telling his story, trying to make something out of his past. Nora thought of writing a book about people's sadness which she quickly discarded. She was a publicist. No one wanted to read about sadness. They wanted a book to take them out of their misery. A good book was a place to escape. A place to run away to and escape the real world. The hard, harsh, materialistic world where people drove their own agendas, with little real concern for others. Ted went rambling on between the sips of his wine, the empty bottles now tucked into the pocket under the flap table. The stewardess had brought him two more bottles of wine. She had smiled, saying they were the last. That maybe Ted should drink a cup of coffee. The young man in the aisle seat, like most of the others on the plane, had gone to sleep. The lights over the seats had mostly gone out. The plane went on into the night, no one thinking of the pilots. The monologue stopped, making Nora turn to look at Ted. Ted was asleep. Gently, Nora took the empty glass and wine bottle from his table and tucked them into the pocket in front of her knees. Ted's head had flopped over, resting on her shoulder. Nora made herself as comfortable as possible. She hoped he was dreaming pleasant dreams.

An hour later, Ted still asleep, Nora having pushed his head gently away from her shoulder, Nora having got the cramps, the plane began to descend. The lights in the aisle came back on again. The pilot spoke over the loudspeaker. She was nearly home, the thought of home making her feel happy. She would take a cab direct from Kennedy to her apartment. She would sleep in her own bed. That friend of Randall's whose name she could not remember had it right: 'it wasn't all bad.'

"Are you going to be all right, Ted?"

"Now or later?"

"I was thinking of the wine. You drank a lot of wine."

"You get used to it. When duty calls, you sober up. I've gone from drunk to sober in a minute. You snap out of it. Thanks for the company. The one part of my life as a travelling salesman I hate is the travelling. Don't make no sense really but a man got to make a living. We all got to make a living, Nora. Here we go. My quiet friend on my right is going to be the first off the plane. Once the seat lights went out he was off like a bullet. Don't expect you and I will meet again. I'll look out for Randall Holiday. Easy name to remember."

"Are your family waiting for you at the airport?"

"Don't be ridiculous. I'm the banker, Nora. The provider. All they want from me is money. Well, it's better than living a life on your own. I hate my own company. She'll ask how much I sold. How much commission I made. And then have an attack of the gimmies: Gimmy this, gimmy that. If she gets what she wants we have sex... Have a nice life, Nora."

"You too, Ted."

The plane emptied, Nora one of the last to leave her seat. The luggage came off the same for everyone. With his hand luggage hung over his shoulder, Ted had disappeared. Once more she was alone in a sea of people. She passed through immigration, found her suitcase, marched through the 'nothing to declare' pushing her trolley and quickly found herself a taxi. She had once caught sight of Ted as the luggage wound out on the conveyor belt. Ted had not waved. Nora gave the driver the address of her apartment. The man had got out to help her with her luggage: she would have to give him a good tip. Life was all about money. The man dropped her on the pavement outside her apartment building. She had paid and tipped the man inside the cab. It was raining, the noise of the streets of New York a happy welcoming home. The uniformed man at the door greeted Nora, and picked up her bags.

"Thanks, Josh."

"Pleasure, Nora. You have yourself a good trip? April showers. Summer's on its way."

When the lift came, Josh put her luggage inside, holding the door. Then he went back outside to do his job. Upstairs she let herself into her apartment and turned on the lights. Everything was familiar. She was home. She put the cases in her bedroom and went back to the lounge. She turned on the television. The silence was broken. She had company. With a whisky from her cocktail cabinet and a packet of crisps from the small kitchen, she sat down to watch the news. She was smiling. Happy to be home. She would unpack tomorrow. The long journey with Randall's book was over. She would report back to Henry Stone in the morning, discuss a title for Randall's latest book, and think about finding a new client. She had many old clients who would be clamouring for her attention: a publicist's job of keeping a client in the news never stopped. Downstairs in the lobby her mailbox would be full. Her answering machine would be jammed with messages. She would do it all tomorrow. First a couple of whiskies to make her sleep and then down in her bed, her own familiar bed.

"Here's to you, Randall."

She was smiling. Still not sure if she had done the right thing by keeping her hands off of him. Time would tell... The news was still the same old rubbish. Politicians pushing their agenda. A disaster in Indonesia. A famous actor who had died. When the weather forecast came on she made herself a sandwich. After three drinks she went off to bed. With the sheets pulled up to her chin she fell asleep.

For the first time in weeks she was sure where she was when she woke in the morning. The bed was the same bed in which she had slept next to Ralph for ten years. The thought made Nora think of sex. For the first year of marriage to Ralph they made love last thing at night and first thing in the morning. Nora was randy. She hadn't had sex for years. The men of her age were mostly overweight and half of them balding. Nora liked young men. Young men like Randall Holiday. There was another way. Some of her rich and single female friends found themselves toy boys. Young men to play with. Young men without money happy to service a middle-aged woman who had lost her looks. Nora could not do it. Could not buy friendship, let alone sex. The young men didn't seem to mind. They were going nowhere. All they had was their youthful good looks and the prospect of marrying an old, rich woman. Randall was different. Randall was rich and famous. If Randall had made love to her it would have been because he wanted to. Not because he was being paid.

Frustrated, Nora got out of her bed, the bed she had insisted taking with her at the end of her marriage. She didn't want Ralph using it with other women. The first job in the morning was to do her exercises. She had a strict regimen. First a one-mile run on the treadmill she kept in the corner of her bedroom. There were stretches and bends in a sequence that followed, Nora always counting, making sure she wasn't cheating herself. She had slept well. Her mind was clear. The exercises had made it clearer. Like a mind, a body needed exercise. And so did her sexual organs. The fact she had gone through her menopause didn't make any difference. Regular sex was a need. A way of keeping the body healthy. Use it or lose it... Nora took a shower and got herself dressed. There was nothing in her fridge to eat, the milk having gone off. She wasn't sure about the eggs but didn't want to eat them. She made coffee with dried milk, ate a stale piece of brown bread with margarine. In her bedroom she touched up her make-up and looked at herself in the long mirror. Her body was still good. Her eyes still had the twinkle. What was that man's name? He was an actor.

"Anyway, whoever you are, it isn't all bad. You don't look a day over forty."

Downstairs Josh was still on the door. He called her a cab. The one thing Nora enjoyed about being rich was being able to afford a taxi. She gave the cab driver the address of Villiers Publishing and sat back in the seat. The traffic was heavy. Maybe one day she would change her old habit of flying economy.

Henry Stone, as was his habit with people who made him money, did not keep her waiting. The more books Randall Holiday sold, the bigger his bonus.

"This cheque's for you, Nora. How does that look?"

"You sold that many books?"

"You got that right. Here are the sales sheets. We're working on his book about the lesbian. I don't like the title. Sit down, Nora. You've done a good job, looking at the book sales. Give me everything you've got. When you've finished your report I'll take you out to lunch. To celebrate

Randall Holiday. Now, give me the details. Success is in the details. What have you done to yourself, Nora? You look chirpy. You somehow look younger."

"Stop it, you old flatterer. You want me to find you another Randall Holiday? Remember you found him, not me. And how's your wife?"

"Which one? The first one hates me, Nora. After twenty-five years she still hates me. You're so lucky being divorced... Now, where were we?"

Henry, his signature bow tie making him look different, got down to business. Randall had said Henry looked more like a university professor than a business executive. Henry's third wife wasn't much older than Henry's daughter. Everyone's life was a mess. She hoped Henry had signed a pre-nuptial contract. Young wives were predators when it came to money, much like young men. Was there ever a better solution? Marriage? Divorce? Living alone? Was Ted's life better than hers? Was Henry's?

"You mind if I take a rain check on that lunch? I've had my fill of restaurants. Let me know when you want to start promoting Randall's new book."

"When's he coming back to America?"

"He's not. He wants to live in England. Money isn't safe in Zimbabwe. He wants to become a hermit and live in the country."

"Get him back to America, Nora. We have to keep pushing him forward. A writer's job only begins when his book is published. You must find him a cause to champion. Find him a charity to support in full view of the public. We don't want the media to take their eye off of him. Try and get him made a roving ambassador for the United Nations. Make him a champion of the underdog. Don't stop working on him, Nora. I want you to earn more of those fat cheques. The more you get, the more I get. My wife's expensive. So are my other two marriages. Kids! You can't believe the money it takes to satisfy kids. You're lucky, Nora. You just don't know how lucky."

"Can we get a writer a green card?"

"There's always a way. Work on it."

"He wants to write another book."

"He can write in New York."

"He says he can't write surrounded by people."

"He can find a place upstate. Get him back here. Don't let him get away from you."

Back at her apartment Nora sat at her desk in her office, the third room in the flat. She needed an assistant. It was all getting too big. The pile of letters she had collected from her mailbox spilled over her desk. She listened to the messages on the answering machine, making notes. She hoped she had not made a mistake by not going out to lunch. Later in the week when she had caught up with all the paperwork, she would give Henry a ring. Make him her guest for an expensive lunch. It was all expenses to be claimed from the taxman. She hated doing her accounts. She looked at the cheque and smiled. She could afford an assistant. For years she had stayed a one-woman band. Employing people took on their problems. They had to be watched. Told what to do. She would need an office. She couldn't have an assistant working in her apartment. There were always problems... One by one she returned the calls on the answering machine. Opened the mail. Took out her cheque book and paid the bills. By late afternoon she was finished. Tired and finished. She would bank Henry's cheque and post the mail in the morning. There was no doubt about it. She needed an assistant. Only when the work was done did she realise she still hadn't eaten. Now she was starving. She picked up the phone and ordered a take-away. She was too tired to go out. Too tired to do the shopping. She needed an assistant. No doubt about it. She went into the lounge and poured herself a drink. They all drank too much. Why lunch with Henry would have been a problem. Drinking at lunchtime was the worst. Afterwards, Nora wanted to sleep. Which ruined her night's sleep. There was always a problem. Again she looked at the cheque. It really was a big one. Nora was smiling, thinking of Randall. A nice hideaway in the country sounded good.

When the delivery man brought her the bucket of fried chicken and a covered bowl of salad, she was on her second whisky. She paid the young boy, gave him a good tip and closed the door. There were three locks on the door. You had to be careful. Hungrily, she ate the food out of the bucket. Opened a bottle of wine. The fried chicken and red wine together tasted good. She turned on the streaming music channel on the television. The music was classical. She always kept the channel on symphony music. It was playing a Mozart piano concerto. The chicken and wine tasted even better. It was nice to be on her own. In her own apartment. Away from people. Randall had written a book called *The Tawny Wilderness*. She understood. The music changed to a Tchaikovsky symphony. For the first time in weeks Nora was content. Chicken and Tchaikovsky. What more could a girl want? Before taking herself off to bed she again looked at the cheque. Just to make sure. It was the biggest cheque she had ever been given.

"Now, that's a lot of money, Randall." She was smiling. If she had had his phone number she would have given him a ring. It was the wine. She was always more confident after a few glasses of wine.

In the morning, after a trouble-free sleep, Nora went to her desk. It was work, work, work. She had a plan to bring Randall back to America. For herself as much as for Villiers Publishing. In the social swirl of New York she had met film directors of note. One of her rules was to write down worthwhile information in a way that was easy to find. Nora called it her contact system. Like the exercises, there were many systems in Nora's life. She always told herself a girl had to be organised.

"It's all in the detail, Henry."

By lunchtime she had spoken to or left messages for every film director or film producer on her list. She had kept Felix Kranskie until last. Once, years ago, at a party, he had come on to Nora. They had become casual friends. The receptionist asked who she was, a way of saying 'what do you want'.

"I'm the publicist of Randall Holiday. The author of the bestselling novel *Masters of Vanity*. Three million sales and counting. Please ask him to phone me."

Not sure whether it would work, Nora put down her phone. She was still waiting for most of the others to return her call. Important people were always too busy. Nora got up from her desk to stretch her back. It was part of her daily exercises. When she reached her twenty stretches the phone rang on her desk.

"Nora Stewart speaking."

"Nora! What a pleasant surprise. Felix Kranskie. Can we meet? I finished reading *Masters of Vanity* at my beach house over the weekend. Can you fly to California? Are you in a position to offer me the film rights? Who's his agent? Do you have the inside?"

"The author is a personal friend. We've been together for three months promoting his book."

"Naughty Nora. Can we write the script? Do you want me to get a scriptwriter?"

"You want to make the movie?"

"I never joke, Nora. How are you? Long time no see. If you fly into LA on Friday I'll have one of my people pick you up at the airport and drive you to the beach. See you Friday, Nora. Good talking to you. Have a nice day."

When they wanted something they came back to you quickly. It was always the same. A phone call to her travel agent booked her a flight to Los Angeles early on Friday afternoon. She phoned Felix's office and gave them the details. It was all part of the system: a girl had to be organised. Having had enough of business for the day she went to the gym. Florence was there as usual. They had been friends since college. Old friends were so important.

"Well, if it isn't the travelling girl. How was England, Nora?"

"Frustrating. I fell for my client."

"What's wrong with that?"

"He's twenty years my junior. Anyway, you should never mix business with pleasure. Even if something did happen between us it would never last."

"Nothing lasts forever. You should know that."

"That's it, Florrie! That's it!"

"What is?"

"The title. The title of Randall's last book. *Nothing Lasts Forever.*"

The chit-chat went on for an hour while they did their exercises. The gym was as much of a club as a place to exercise. It was easier for a woman to go to the gym on her own than visit a bar. Half the men were gay but it didn't seem to matter.

"How's the new lover, Florrie?"

"It's finished. The older you get, the shorter it lasts. He was a lousy lover. I think there was something wrong with him. Men have more problems than women."

"How old was he?"

"Sixty something. They never tell you exactly. It was probably my fault. After a couple of goes I didn't turn him on."

"That's what worries me with Randall... Do you think we've had our lives when it comes to men? What are we going to do with all those years ahead of us? All the money in the world can't buy back your youth... How are the kids?"

"Doing their own thing. They have their own lives now. I'm no longer of any use to them."

"Don't be silly,"

"You have to be realistic. Once you've brought them up you've done your job. Why in the old days women had so many children. To keep them company in their old age. And these days they don't even give you grandchildren. All three of them are miles away. They phone me and that's something. Whatever would we do without a telephone?... You want to go for a drink? Go drown our sorrows. Has he got any children?"

"A two-year-old son. His wife went off with a woman."

"That's nasty."

"And took his son."

"What a bitch. I've never tried a woman. Have you?"

"Don't be ridiculous."

"You never know till you try. There must be something in it. Just look at this place. The men come to meet men. Not to meet women. How's business?"

"Never been better."

"One part of me wants to be in a relationship. The other part doesn't want to lose its freedom. What's his new book about?"

"Two lesbians deliberately setting up a man so they can have a son."

"Sounds like a bestseller."

"Felix Kranskie is going to make *Masters of Vanity* into a movie. I'm flying over on Friday. Staying at his beach house."

"Didn't he fancy you when you were married?"

"Now it's strictly business. I'm going to persuade Randall to come back to America and write the script."

"And then you're going to seduce him."

"Nothing lasts forever."

For ten minutes they worked the treadmill watching the pedometer. Both of them built up a sweat. They went to the bar and had a drink. Nora was pleasantly tired. They parted, both of them comfortable in their friendship. A good old friend. It was probably all both of them would have in their future.

Back at the flat, thankful she had made so many friends in her life, she switched on the music channel. The music was Mozart. So much of the music on the symphony channel was Mozart. He was one of Nora's favourites. Sitting comfortably in her chair, happy on her own, Nora listened to the beautiful music. When it finished, Nora took a glass of water from the small kitchen and went to her bedroom and took off her clothes. The long mirror came into focus, Nora looking at herself.

"How can one man touch so many millions of people with his music, centuries after he is dead? Thank you, Wolfgang Amadeus Mozart. That was the perfect end to a pleasant evening."

Nora got into bed and turned out the light. She always slept in her panties ever since her marriage to Ralph. It had made the foreplay that much easier. She lay back in the dark and thought of Ralph. If only she had had three children like Florrie. She wouldn't feel so alone. For a while the memories flowed through her mind, the past so much better than the future. The last thing she thought of before falling asleep was her title for the book: *Nothing Lasts Forever*. In her dreams Ralph became Randall. There were children, everyone happy. Nora woke once in the night, drank from her glass of water without turning on the light, and cuddled her pillow. She could still hear Mozart in her mind. The traffic outside was distant. New York never slept. Nora drifted back into her dreams.

2

---

*B*ack at her work desk in the morning, Nora gave Randall's editor, Henry Stone, a ring.

"I think I've got it, Henry. *Nothing Lasts Forever.*"

"What are you talking about?"

"The title of Randall's book about the lesbians. You want to have lunch with me tomorrow? I'm flying to LA on Friday. Felix Kranskie wants to buy the movie rights to *Masters of Vanity*. What's my commission?"

"Ten per cent as usual. That's wonderful. He's big. How did you do it?"

"He's an old friend of mine. It's not what you know but who you know. It may be a cliché but it works. How much do you want for the movie?"

"As much as you can get. Negotiate between us. How you get the best price. Where you want to lunch?"

"The usual. What's that restaurant in the building next to your office?"

"The Writers and Artists."

"However could I forget? See you there at one o'clock. Do you know how to contact Randall?"

"Don't you?"

"Not at the moment. He's off scouring the English countryside for somewhere to write. He said he would contact us when he was settled."

"Get him back to America, Nora."

"I'm trying. Why I phoned Felix."

"Were you lovers?"

"Not exactly. More like a couple of one-night stands."

"Weren't you married?"

"We all make mistakes. No one is perfect."

"Did Ralph find out?"

"I don't think so. But I still got my comeuppance. You do bad things and bad things happen. I thought then Ralph was infertile. The things we do when we are desperate."

"Nothing lasts forever."

"You can say that again."

"I like it."

"One o'clock."

"See you there. I'll be in the bar."

It was all go. From one client's problem to the next. No sooner had she talked on the phone than it rang again, switching to the answering machine more of a time-waster than letting it ring. Despite Nora's rule to be five minutes early for an appointment she was five minutes late the next day. It annoyed Nora. Other people's time was valuable. The guilt at sleeping with Felix to get herself pregnant was still riding with her. She was no better morally than Randall's Amanda. But it had solved her problem. Afterwards, she had gone to her doctor for tests. She was the one who was infertile, the one stopping Ralph from having his children.

Henry Stone was up at the bar, sitting between MaryJane and Johnny Stiglitz, the typist and the assistant. MaryJane had been out to dinner with Randall, making Nora jealous, a jealousy Nora had been careful to hide.

"Sorry I'm late, I hate people to be late for their appointments. Hello, MaryJane. Hello, Johnny. What's this, a Villiers Publishing conference?"

"It's important to get the opinion of youth when choosing a title. MaryJane typed *Nothing Lasts Forever*. They like the new title. Why I brought them to lunch."

"I thought I was paying."

"For the girl who is finding us a film contract I think the company can afford to pay for the lunch. Can you imagine what a blockbuster movie by the famous Felix Kranskie will do to the book sales? All that lovely publicity. So, he just vanished?"

"Into thin air. You had to find him the first time on the banks of the Zambezi River in the heart of Africa. England should be easier. If we don't hear from Randall in a month I'll phone his father in Zimbabwe. He's close to his family. Do they have phones on a farm in Zimbabwe?"

"I tried to find the place on the map but couldn't," said Johnny Stiglitz. When Nora came up to the bar, Johnny had stood up and offered Nora his seat next to Henry.

"Probably an old map. Look under Rhodesia."

"Oh, so that's what it was called. Is he going to write a book about Africa?"

"He's written one. It's called *The Tawny Wilderness*. Needs some editing."

They drank, ate food and discussed book titles and the upcoming movie. All the talk about the movie made Nora nervous. She had not yet completed the deal.

"Oh, if he read the book in one weekend and phoned you back in minutes, he'll buy the movie rights."

"How much?"

"Five million. In his contract, Randall gets half of the movie rights after our expenses. That man is getting richer by the minute. You know he was stony broke when his brother found him beside the river. How fortunes can change. Now he needs accountants and investment managers. The tax man is going to have a field day. Well done, Nora. You've got the title and you've sold the film rights. Randall will be pleased. Just get him back to America. So, are we all agreed? Good. The new title sticks. Back to the office. You've got my home phone number when Felix wants to negotiate. If needs be I'll fly to LA. It's been a good day."

"I hope he comes back soon," said MaryJane.

"What's that look for, Nora?" asked Henry.

"I was just thinking about Felix."

"What would we do without Nora?"

All afternoon Nora fulfilled her appointments, going by taxi from office to office. Not once was she late. She was still annoyed at the look on MaryJane's face at the idea of Randall coming back soon. Just to think she, Nora, had a chance with Randall was a waste of time. At the end of the day she went home. She wasn't hungry. There was nothing on television. Instead of sifting through the messages on her answering machine she poured herself a drink. When she was bored, with nothing she wanted to do, she was inclined to drink. Her doctor had told her to keep it down to three drinks a day, which was a laugh. She'd had three up at the bar of the Writers and Artists; a glass of French wine with her lunch; all of it part of doing business. Now the drink was for her. Her liver would have been in a better condition if she had stayed a secretary at the advertising agency she had joined after leaving college, instead of climbing the corporate ladder, as much to impress Ralph as to prove herself. At the age of thirty, still apparently happily married to Ralph, they had made her an account executive. One of the agency's clients was a company that made soup and sold it in well-advertised cans, the sales of the company in direct proportion to their advertising budget. The more they advertised the more they sold. It was all about television advertising. An unknown artist made a painting of line after line of the client's cans of soup and distributed prints. The soup company considered suing the artist for unlawful use of a registered trade name, Nora happy with the idea of the press getting on the side of the impoverished artist being pilloried by a major industrial corporation. The case stretched out, both the soup company and the artist getting priceless advertising for nothing. The artist won, as much to the benefit of the soup company's agenda as the artist's. The painting of the soup cans went on to sell for millions. The artist became famous, the rich buyers of modern art competing with each other at auction to own a painting that was famous. As far as art was concerned, to Nora the painting was no different to the latest publicity stunt by a conceptual artist who had stuffed a pig, soaked the dead animal in formaldehyde, put it in a glass case the size of half a room, and called it art. But it worked. Both artists became famous and rich. When her marriage came apart soon after, Nora left the advertising agency and set herself up as a publicist. It was all about making the client famous. Randall Holiday, 'the last colonial from the British Empire'. Like the soup-can saga the press had picked up the story, as much to cock a snook at the end of the British who had once ruled America. Nora's job was to find the hook on which to hang up her client for public scrutiny, the soup cans and the artist never forgotten. Without the potential court case and all the publicity Nora doubted the painting would have sold for more than a thousand dollars. Who wanted soup cans on the wall in the lounge? They were bad enough in a cupboard in the kitchen. The print of the soup can painting in the restaurant at lunchtime had brought it all back to Nora. She sighed, got up from the couch and poured herself another drink. At her age, all the fame and fortune made no difference. She was alone. Would stay on her own with a social life that started and finished at the gym. She missed having a man.

"You're lucky to have money. A lot of women at your age have no man, no prospects and no money. Be thankful for what you've got. Cheers, Randall," she said raising her glass. "Here's to Friday and another half million. I wonder if Felix will still want to have sex with me?"

With the new drink in her hand, Nora turned on the television, sat back on the couch and relaxed. It was a sitcom. It made her laugh. It made her comfortable with herself. To hell with men. If she sold the film rights to Felix she would find herself a toy boy.

THE BEACH HOUSE reminded Nora of Mark Fletcher, the vainglorious main character in Randall's *Masters of Vanity*. The place screamed of being rich. Up on the cliff with a panoramic view of the ocean over a swimming pool the size of a tennis court, the bungalow-house spread over an acre, telling the whole world Felix Kranskie was rich. A limousine with a uniformed driver had met Nora off the plane and driven her to the coast. When Nora was shown through the house by a manservant, her small suitcase taken she knew not where, Felix was sitting in his swimming costume next to the pool. He got up on seeing Nora, smiling his trademark smile. There wasn't an ounce of fat on his body. His face still looked young. Nora, inwardly smiling at a man of over sixty without one grey hair, suspected his face had had surgery, the skin was so neat and tight under his chin. His hair, no doubt, was dyed. Nora received the ubiquitous kiss on both cheeks. A man with a drinks tray was hovering. The Pacific Ocean looked perfect, not a breath of wind. Nora, feeling overdressed, sat down. If she was going to pull Randall or find herself a toy boy she would have to follow suit and find herself a plastic surgeon. She ordered a drink. The pleasantries followed. On the white, wrought-iron table was a copy of *Masters of Vanity*. No wonder the book had struck such a chord with Felix. He was one of the masters of vanity, missing the entire point of the book. Nora kept it to herself.

"How much do you want, Nora?"

"Five million and two per cent of the gross."

"Make it one per cent."

"Done."

"Don't you want to check with the publishers?"

"I'll have them confirm in a telex. You want me to phone?"

"Have a drink. Good flight?"

"The usual."

"You want to put on your bathing costume?"

"After a drink."

"You haven't changed, Nora."

"Neither have you, Felix."

"Nice to do business with you."

"Nice to do business with you, Felix."

They smiled, laughed and settled back to enjoy themselves. The waiter came with Nora's drink. They chinked glasses. Nora drank, smiling out over the sea.

"You have the most beautiful place in the world."

"Go put on your swimsuit, Nora. I want to have a better look at you. There's a phone in your room. Phone your client and get them to send me a telex. Romano will give you the number. We have a small office in the beach house fully equipped for business. We have something to celebrate. Tonight, alone in this beautiful place, you and I are going to celebrate."

"You don't have a wife?"

"They proved far too expensive. Three of them, Nora. All living the high life off Felix. How it goes, I suppose. How's Ralph?"

"Haven't seen him in years."

"Why didn't you want to marry me, Nora?"

"First, you didn't ask. Second, I was married to Ralph."

"Go put on your swimsuit."

"Back in a minute."

Nora first finished her drink. Felix dived into the pool. Walking away, she looked back. As that friend of Randall's said, the man whose name she could never remember, 'it's not all bad'. The man called Romano was waiting to show her to her room. Nora suspected the room was next to Felix's bedroom. In the luxurious room, her case looking lost by the side of the bed, Nora used the phone and called Henry. Henry picked up immediately.

"Five million and one per cent of the gross. Send a telex. This is the number."

With the phone down, the deal done, Nora changed into her bathing costume and threw a towel over her shoulder.

"Oliver Manningford! That was his name. One of the godfathers of James Oliver. James Tomlin and Oliver Manningford, both of them actors."

When Nora returned to the poolside she was still smiling, an idea growing in her mind. If she could get Oliver and James parts in the movie, Randall would be pleased.

"You're very smiley, Nora."

"We've got something to celebrate."

"Your body is just the same."

"Thank you, kind sir."

Nora put her towel over the chair she had been sitting in and walked to the edge of the pool. Gently, so as not to disturb her hair, she walked down the steps into the water. The water was cool and soothing. The waiter came back with fresh drinks. Out over the ocean a seagull was flying. After her small flat it was paradise on earth.

"I have one personal favour, Felix. The author has two friends who are English actors. I want you to give them parts in the movie."

"Consider it done."

"Just like that?"

"You said the telex is on its way."

It was clear to Nora, everything having gone so easily, that Felix Kranskie had expected to pay a lot more for the rights to make the movie.

Dinner was served by the pool, Romano fussing over every detail. The wine went down making Nora feel mellow. The telex from Henry Stone confirming the deal, along with a copy of Felix Kranskie's reply, sat watching her on the side of the table. Nora's mind, lulled by the most expensive wine she had ever been given, thought through what she was going to do with half a million dollars. Money, despite what Randall had to say about it in *Masters of Vanity*, was nice. In her old age she was not going to run out of money.

"What do you invest your surplus money in, Felix?"

"Stocks and shares. You have to own something tangible. Bonds and cash are too vulnerable to devaluation. Governments print money and lower the value of their currency for when they have to pay it back. Inflation, Nora, you got to stick with good old property and equities. The big trick in life is holding onto your money... You like the taste of the truffles?"

"So that's what it was. It's almost musky. Lobster and truffles!"

"Most expensive food on earth."

"You like being rich?"

"Who doesn't? As people, we are all the same. Only wealth makes us appear different. The American dream."

"The book exposes the vanity of the rich."

"So what? People like movies about the rich. Everyone wants to have more money. The more you have the more you want."

"Randall Holiday, whose real name is Randall Crookshank as you'll see on the final contract, said fishing by the side of the Zambezi River made him the richest man in the world, despite not having a nickel."

"Don't believe what people say, Nora... Are we going to make love?"

"I don't know. Are we?"

"I never got enough of you. Why I want more."

"Life's sad, Felix. All this and you want an old lover."

"We're not so old. I like talking to you. I like you."

"Have another glass of wine."

"I mean what I say."

"Let's go to bed."

"It's a pleasure doing business with you, Nora."

"You too, Felix."

They both laughed. They sat quietly, happy with each other's company. The daylight was going. A ship's lights were moving far out on the ocean. There was not a sign of Romano and the waiter.

"Let's finish this wine, Felix."

"Why not? We have the whole of our lives ahead of us. What a beautiful evening. I just so love the smell of the sea."

The sex, when it came, was remarkably good. Some men preferred older women, Felix Kranskie being one of them. They talked on in the dark, the salt smell of the ocean pervading Felix's bedroom. With a film contract and the sex out of the way they talked of many things. Both were well travelled with many varied experiences. The conversation flowed, neither of them getting bored with the other's company.

"It's so nice to talk to someone who knows what they are talking about. The young ones, most of them, have only their bodies. They think it is enough. Why men get bored with the bimbos so quickly."

"Is this a compliment, Felix?"

"It's the truth. By the end of a couple of years, when the sex had worn off, all three of my wives lost their interest for me. It wasn't so much being bored with each other as having nothing to say. So they went off. They still had my money and I'd had the prime of their youth. A good trade, I suppose. A use for some of my money. But it's sad. Why can't we have both? Good sex and friendship? Never seems to happen."

"You have any kids?"

"I'm infertile. Can't have kids."

"So am I."

"Why are you laughing, Nora?"

"When I didn't get pregnant with you those years ago I went to see the doctor. I thought Ralph was the one with the problem."

"So you had sex with me to get pregnant?"

"I wanted children."

"Would you have told Ralph?"

"Probably not. We're all bad people when we want something."

"You used me!"

"We used each other. A two-way trade. I'm sorry. I thought you didn't care. Just another one-night stand. We didn't know each other. We just got into bed. You knew I was married. In the old days, they called it adultery. Anyway, why didn't you wear a condom? Did you know then you were infertile?"

"I would never have known I had a child." Felix looked away, the sound of his voice trailing off into the night.

"There are many things in life we never find out about. Do you think a lot worse of me for knowing?"

"It was a long time ago. I only found out about the infertility with my third wife. Men always think it's the woman. In the future, will you always be honest with me?"

"I'll try."

"There's so much in life that sucks."

"You want me to go to my bedroom? It's usually best in life not to tell the truth. Most people say what they think the other person wants to hear. It's called being nice. Part of the charm of life."

"Don't go, Nora. You know, with all my money and all the people who work for me, I get so damn lonely. You've been honest. Maybe that's worth being used all those years ago. We've both had our flings and here we are. Makes you think. What happened after Ralph?"

"Nothing. I couldn't have children. The point of marriage is having children and making a family."

"We're lost, Nora. Both of us."

"Probably."

"And even when people have children they still get divorced. What a lovely world... You loved Ralph, didn't you?"

"Yes I did."

"So you weren't being unfaithful to him?"

"He wanted children. So did I."

"What a shame. We're both going to leave this world with nothing to show for it."

"Your movies will last forever."

"You think so?"

"The good ones will. Let's both of us make sure *Masters of Vanity* is a good one."

"Always the girl of business."

"A good movie is more important than business. Do you like Mozart?"

"I love his music. The older I get the more I love his music."

"So do I."

"He was so young when he died."

"But his legacy has lasted for centuries. All that pleasure he has given to so many people."

"You know what? Let's pretend we're young again and go skinny-dipping down at the ocean. It's dark. No moon. The stars will light our way."

"You're an old romantic. Lead on, Macduff... What if we get caught?"

"Who the hell cares? To get down to the beach we'll wear our dressing gowns. Come on, Nora. Let's have some fun."

Wearing dressing gowns and sandals they walked down the path to the beach, Felix leading the way. In the house, Felix had popped the cork of another bottle of his expensive red wine. Nora had no idea what time it was. They drank the wine from the bottle like a couple of hobos, passing the bottle back and forth, both of them giggling like schoolchildren. There was no one down on the beach. Nora took off her sandals, liking the feel of the sand through her toes. Up above, the heavens were endless, both of them stopping to look. The planets twinkled among the millions of stars. Coming up from the ocean was the thinnest of sickle moons. A warm, soft breeze was blowing from the ocean. Felix put the bottle of wine upright on the sand, took off his dressing gown and ran down into the sea. Nora let the silk dressing gown fall to her feet, took a deep breath and ran after him. They splashed and laughed in the starlight. When they came out of the water, refreshed, sober and joyful, Nora's hair soaking wet, Felix couldn't find his bottle of wine. There was still no one to be seen on the beach. For a long minute they searched the beach for their dressing gowns. The starlight caught the silk of Nora's where she had dropped it next to her sandals. Felix quickly found his. There was no sign of the wine bottle Felix had left sticking out of the sand. Hand-in-hand they walked across the beach to the dunes and the path that wound up the cliff to Felix's house. Along the top of the cliff they could see the outside lights that people had left on thinking to protect their houses. The pool lights were still on up at Felix's.

"Thanks for the wine," came a deep voice, the man hidden in the dunes. "Quite a display, Mr Kranskie."

"Have you got a flash camera?"

"Don't worry. The wine's good enough payment to keep my mouth shut. Anyway I don't own a camera. Fact is, I don't own anything. I'm a bum. A happy-go-lucky bum. What a beautiful night."

"How do you know it's me?"

"Watched you come down your path."

"What did you do for a living?" Felix had taken back control, his voice cold.

"I'm an out-of-work actor."

"Come and see me tomorrow."

"Thanks for the wine. I won't mention anything. Swimming naked in the sea. Nothing better. You always have to watch for sharks. In and out of the water. But you know that or you wouldn't be where you are."

"Enjoy the wine."

"I have. Once upon a time I could afford such wine."

"What's your name?"

"Julian. Julian Becker."

"Are you any good as an actor?"

"Some said I was. It's all about luck in the movie business. You should know that. Didn't have the breaks."

"You have to make the breaks in life. Just maybe you've made one."

"That would be nice. Enjoy the rest of your night. You both sounded so happy. I envy you. I want to be happy. I'm sick of living on the beach on my own."

"You want to stand up so I can see you, Julian?"

"Not really. I'm rather comfortable after drinking your wine. I thought you'd abandoned the bottle. It's naughty to litter the beach... Goodnight. With a bit of luck I'll see you tomorrow, Mr Kranskie."

Nora's heart was still thumping, the powerful, deep voice coming out of nowhere having frightened her. Whatever you did in the modern world, there was somebody watching. Felix was standing up ahead. The night's magic had gone. Their moment together had gone, replaced by reality. In the house, Nora said she had better go to her own bedroom.

"Good night, Nora. If that bastard goes to the press we'll be all over the tabloids. Kranskie, skinny-dipping on a public beach!"

"I'm sorry, Felix."

"So am I. Life's never smooth. There's always something waiting."

"What are you going to do?"

"Give him a part. Hope he comes up tomorrow. Keep his mouth shut. It won't do you any good either, Nora."

"I'm not sure. I'm a publicist, don't forget. We could turn this to our advantage. We're both single. Both the right age for each other. What have we got to hide? There's no law about swimming at night in the sea. Clothed or otherwise. 'They closed the biggest contract in movie history and ran naked into the sea.' What a send-off for *Masters of Vanity*."

"You know, you might be right." For the first time since the voice frightened them Felix was smiling.

"I know I am. Now, may I come and sleep in your bed? Henry's going to get here tomorrow with the full contract. Then we'll have to behave. Or maybe not. Give this voice from the dark a part if he's any good. The whole story has a lot of mileage. 'How I got the part. Caught the director skinny-dipping on the beach with a beautiful woman!'... Laugh, Felix. You got to laugh at life and not take it too seriously."

"You think he'll come here tomorrow?"

"Probably. If he's got any sense. Now, can I come to bed? It must be nearly morning."

"What annoys me most is leaving the security gate open at the top of the path. You can't let your guard down for a moment in this lovely world. He ruined our evening."

"Don't be silly. That voice will stay in our minds for the rest of our lives, reminding both of us of our lovely evening. Who cares about a stray man? All the heavens were watching."

"Julian Becker. Somewhere back in my mind I know that name or my mind is playing tricks with me."

"A good sleep and you'll remember everything."

For a long while after Felix fell asleep next to her, Nora lay awake thinking. Through the window she could see the shadow of the sickle moon. A swell had come up in the ocean, the gentle noise of the waves lapping the shore coming into the room. Felix snorted once in his sleep... The next thing Nora knew it was morning, the sun flooding into the room. Felix had gone. Nora got up and looked out of the bedroom window. Felix was walking back through the security gate, accompanied by Romano. Nora heard snippets of their conversation. The hobo, or whatever he was, had gone. Romano was carrying the empty bottle of wine. With Felix's money and fame there was always a risk, the rich always needing security. Randall was right. Life was better on the banks of the African river, anonymous, no money to be stolen, not a care in the world. As Romano turned to lock the security gate in the long fence that went round the property a man came up the path. He was tall, well built, over six feet in height, his body richly tanned by the sun. All he wore was a loincloth. His big feet were bare, his long hair blowing in the wind. The man reminded Nora of a younger version of Randall's grandfather, the actor, Ben Crossley. Felix and the man got into a conversation through the iron mesh of the locked gate, Nora unable to hear what they were saying. Romano, ever the servant, stood back. Felix unlocked the gate. The man strode into the property, smiling all over his handsome face. The three men walked round the pool and across the lawn into the house. She could hear them laughing. Instinctively, Nora knew she was looking at Mark Fletcher, the chief protagonist in Randall's book. Instead of getting dressed and joining the men, Nora got back into bed. She was the publicist, not the film director. She wasn't needed... Nora fell back into sleep. When she woke, the clock by the side of the bed said it was almost noon. She had been dreaming of Randall. She was happy. Dreaming of Randall always made Nora happy. She got up, looked at her tangled hair in the mirror, sighed and started the brushing. A girl her age had a lot of work to do. Nora's day had begun.

Now the publicist, no longer the lover, Nora walked to the room Felix had made into an office. She was still thinking of Randall. She gave the girl at the other end of the line the name and address in Zimbabwe of Jeremy Crookshank and waited. It had not been difficult to remember the name of the farm. Many times during their travels around the bookshops together Randall had talked about World's View, a place he cherished as much as the Zambezi Valley. The girl came back on the line and Nora wrote down the phone number of the Zimbabwe farm.

"Would you like me to dial?"

"Thank you."

Nora waited, expecting the line to be engaged. The farmers in Zimbabwe shared what Randall had called a party line. The phone rang, the sound coming to Nora all the way from Africa. Her hair was a mess. She would have to wait until she found a hairdresser. Skinny-dipping! At her age! It had to have been the wine.

"Bergit. Who's speaking?"

"Nora Stewart from a beach house outside Los Angeles in America. I'm Randall Crookshank's publicist. Are you his stepmother?"

"That I am. What's wrong with Randall?"

"Nothing, I hope. We've lost touch. When I left London he was going to look for a place in the country. I've sold the film rights to his book. Do you have a contact number?"

"When Randall goes off into the bush you have to wait."

"His share is two and a half million US and a share of the gross."

"My goodness. How much is that in Zimbabwean dollars?"

"I have no idea. So you don't have a phone number?"

"No, I don't. When you make contact, give Randall our love and ask him when he's coming home."

"His home is in England."

"When you've lived in Africa for any length of time, your home will always be Africa."

"I met your brother at the British launch of *Masters of Vanity*. Over three million sales so far."

"My goodness."

"How is everything in Zimbabwe politically?"

"So far so good. You can never tell with politicians. When Randall makes contact don't forget to tell him to call the farm. I have to go. We're driving into Harare for a sale tomorrow morning. Tobacco auction. We start the drive after a day's work. We live in the bush, miles from anywhere."

"Have a nice evening."

"We will. Lunch after the sale at Meikles Hotel tomorrow. It's our last sale of the year. Goodbye, Nora."

"Goodbye, Bergit."

Nora stood for a long moment thinking. People's lives could be so different. A tobacco auction in the middle of Africa. It made her smile. Bringing her thoughts back to herself, Nora realised she was hungry. She hoped someone was going to give her lunch. Her hair was a mess. Skinny-dipping at her age! Still smiling, not caring about her hair, Nora walked through the house to the lounge. Felix and the hobo were sitting comfortably talking. Nora raised her eyebrows when she saw the man was wearing nothing under his loincloth. Everything was big about the man including his smile. Having let her have a good look, the man crossed his legs and pulled down the loincloth. Felix had not noticed. They were both drinking beers out of the bottle, the cold beers wet from condensation.

"So, Mr Becker, now we understand each other, my friend here, Nora, and I can relax. Do you have friends in the media?" Felix was being professional, as ice-cold in his demeanour as the beer. All vestige of Felix's hollow laughter, that Nora had heard earlier, had gone.

"Please call me Julian."

"Do you have any clothes?"

"I have a bag hidden in the bushes. Not much but enough."

"You don't wear underpants?"

"Not really. The way I live, there isn't much point. And to answer your question in what I hope is a job interview, I have only enemies in the press. They ruined my career, Mr Kranskie. Which is why you and the lovely Nora can relax." The man had got to his bare feet as Nora approached to where the two of them were sitting.

"Any chance of lunch, Felix? I'm starving. His stepmother has no idea where we can contact Randall. Remarkably, I got through to their farm in Zimbabwe. They were about to drive into Harare for a tobacco auction tomorrow."

"This is Julian Becker."

"Hello, Julian. Don't you ever wear clothes?"

"Not unless I have to." Close up, the man was spectacularly handsome, his blue eyes brimming with confidence.

"So, you say you were an actor, Julian?" said Felix, taking back the conversation. "What is your experience?"

"As a young man soon out of drama school I went to England and joined the Bristol Old Vic. Nothing is better than Shakespeare. They always gave me the parts of bad people. Something to do with my being American, I suppose. Underneath their stiff upper lips the British resent us Americans. Their empire had almost gone and the power of America was rising. But they taught me how to act. Oh yes they did. But please, the lady is hungry." He was looking confidently at Nora as he smiled.

"You could go back to the beach, find some clothes, and join us for lunch. You don't mind my asking Julian to lunch do you, Felix?"

"Oh, no. Feel free... And what happened to Shakespeare?"

"There wasn't any money in it. A great company, the Old Vic, but no money. When I returned to the States, I was offered the juvenile lead in a movie. *Home is the Hunter.*"

"I remember it. It was a big success."

"A huge success. It made the producer a lot of money."

"So, what happened to your career?"

"I was caught in bed with the producer's young wife. A man burst into my trailer with a camera. Did a lot for the movie but not for the producer. Made him look a fool, despite all his money. He swore to me I would never get another part in a movie or a part in a play. And he kept his word."

"Now I remember. It was a brief splash all over the media... So you can act, Julian Becker?"

"I used to think so."

"Excuse me a moment. While I'm gone, I trust you not to make a pass at Nora."

"You have my word."

"How does lunch round the pool sound to both of you? Romano can find you a swimming costume, I think they call it in England. So much of the language is morphing into one. English is so universal. Now I remember why your name sounded familiar. Jensen Sandler. So he really cut you out. Did it teach you to behave yourself?"

"Not really."

Felix went off into the rear of the house. Nora and Julian sat smiling at each other while they waited. They heard Felix call lunch round the pool for three. Inadvertently, Nora licked her lips.

"So you really are hungry?"

"And you really got screwed by the press?"

"Why, despite being invited to lunch, I would never have talked about what I saw last night."

"For a brief moment in time, both of us were happy."

Felix came back into the lounge carrying his copy of *Masters of Vanity*. He was also carrying a bathing costume, a pair of long shorts and a shirt.

"I hope this shirt is big enough. You can change in the study. And, after lunch, take this book back to the beach and read it. I'm going to turn it into a movie. You do read books, Julian?"

"Mostly good ones. A few bad ones I find left behind on the beach. I'm a scavenger. Surprising what you pick up. Thank you for the shirt. You won't mind if I leave the buttons undone?"

The big man got up, took the clothes, and walked across to the small study.

"So what you think, Nora? You're all smiley."

"Mark Fletcher. Down to a T. If he can act. Did you see his movie?"

"I don't think so. Just remember the scandal. Scandals live a lot longer than movies. Or books. Or their authors. It's a good scandal that gets the public's attention."

"And what about Jensen Sandler?"

"I can handle Jensen. A good argument through the press will do wonders for the movie. Let's see what happens. When is Henry coming through?"

"When he's drawn up the contract."

"If he worked at the Old Vic they must have taught him something."

"I hope so," said Julian coming back into the lounge.

"That was quick."

"So, what's the book about?"

"The rich and famous. The high world of finance."

"Sounds like the perfect ingredients for a successful movie if the book has a good story. Got to have a story. Despite the depth of Shakespeare's philosophy he always had a good story."

"Did you play Hamlet?"

"Only once in drama school."

They laughed, Julian eating more than Nora thought was possible, Romano bringing out seconds and thirds.

"In my business you have to stock up while you can. You never know where your next meal is coming from. Thank you for lunch and the conversation, Mr Kranskie. I'll read this book and come back to you. Now, if you'll excuse me I'll change back into my own clothes and go back to the beach. There's a spot under the trees where I like to read and think. Nora, a pleasure to meet you."

They watched him walk back into the house and return dressed in his loincloth.

"I'll close the gate as I go out."

Silently, they watched as the iron gate swung too and automatically locked. They sat silent until Julian was out of earshot.

"What do you think, Felix? Is that your Mark Fletcher?"

"I'm going to watch his movie. Someone in LA will have a copy. Make some enquiries. But yes, I think I can make that man into Mark Fletcher."

"Why did you give him the book?"

"People have to believe in their character to make him real. It'll take him a couple of days to read the book. See what he says. See if the people in the book excite him."

Later, while they were drinking coffee in the shade of the big umbrella, Romano came out of the house and across to where they were sitting.

"Mr Henry Stone is at the airport. He's on his way. I gave the cab driver directions. Will there be anything more, Mr Kranskie?"

"Thank you, Romano. Phone my lawyer and tell Keith to come to the house. He can bring Mellany if he wishes. Is Mr Stone on his own?"

"I think so."

"Make all the arrangements, Romano."

"Where is the nearest hairdresser, Romano?" asked Nora.

"We can have one sent to the house if you wish," said Felix.

Nora smiled. It was good being rich. Everything came to you. She would have to find Randall and bring him back to America for his own good.

"What are you smiling about, Nora?"

"The fortunes of life. How they can turn. Randall broke on the bank of a river. Julian, stony broke on the beach. Makes you think."

"You have to have something to give. Randall Holiday can write. We'll just have to see if Julian Becker can act. He certainly looks as if he can fill a screen. What you want to do, Nora?"

"Go and lie down with a good book. Relax. Be thankful for what I have. Not everyone has been so lucky in life, Felix. Will you sign the contract tonight?"

"Once Keith has agreed to the small print. You go and relax. I'm going to sit here to do my thinking. About the movie. About what I want to do. You have to plan every detail of a movie before you start filming. Hard work. That's what makes a good movie. Hard work and a lot of meticulous planning. I get so excited about my life when I have something to do.

3

*H*enry Stone arrived half an hour after the hairdresser, wearing his trademark spotted bow tie and waving to Nora as he passed the open door of her room. An hour later Nora's hair was finished.

"How much do I owe you, Sandy?" The man was undeniably gay and quite lovely, his hands when not doing her hair flapping at the wrists.

"Don't be silly, Nora. Everything is taken care of by Mr Kranskie. He's such a darling. Now, doesn't that look nice? And no running into the sea, naughty girl. I'll say bye-bye. Romano, sweet boy, will you see me out."

"You've done this before?"

"Those famous actresses are so demanding."

Henry Stone and Felix were sitting round the pool when Nora joined them.

"Keith Fortescue can't join us until tomorrow morning," said Felix.

"It's a standard Villiers film contract. We'll leave the reading to Keith."

The evening passed, the unsigned contract on the table in front of them. Henry had been given a room. Nora let the two men talk and went to bed early, sleeping in her own room. Both she and Felix needed a good night's sleep. Keith Fortescue arrived from Los Angeles at nine o'clock in the morning. They had just finished breakfast, all three of them bright and chirpy. For Nora, there was nothing better than a good night's sleep for improving her concentration. She left the house to go for a long walk on the beach when the three men began talking business. No one seemed to notice her leaving. The May morning was cool, clouds in the sky, a good day for walking. Felix, now they had guests in the house, treated Nora like a business associate, only his eyes telling her otherwise. The lawyer had not brought his wife. Dressed in trousers and wearing a wide-brimmed hat, Nora let herself out of the gate by punching in the security code, making sure the gate was shut behind her. Down the winding path through the dunes Nora looked for Julian, but he was nowhere to be seen. The tide was on its way out, bits of flotsam and jetsam left at the high water mark; bits of broken wood that had floated; a paper cup; an empty packet of cigarettes. Where the small waves were lapping, the sand was clean, a seagull strutting the edge of the water looking for pickings. Seeing Nora, the bird called and flew off out to sea.

The big bird was very beautiful. Happy, content, sexually satisfied by Felix, Nora walked and walked up the beach, her sandals held in her left hand, the wet sand cool on her feet and between her toes. It was so good to be happy, Nora cherishing the moment. By the time the sun was at its zenith, Nora was far from the house, happy to leave the men to their business. Then she saw him far away in the distance, the tall body wearing only a loincloth unmistakable. In one hand, Julian was carrying a fishing rod, the big single-piece rod towering over him. On his shoulder was a fish half the size of Julian. They kept on walking towards each other, Nora smiling. Instead of reading the book the man had gone fishing.

"Good morning, Nora. Or is it good afternoon?" Julian looked up at the sun, the dead fish staring at Nora, the loincloth flapping just hiding Julian's genitals, kept in check by a leather belt. Attached to the belt was a sheath-knife and a small leather bag.

"What is it?"

"A shark. It's a surf fishing rod but I fish from those rocks you can see behind me in the distance."

"Can you eat shark?"

"It's very good. In Australia, they call the meat of the fish, flake. The Aussies like eating flake. You can buy it in any of their fish and chip shops. Your hair looks nice. I'll dry most of the fish and live off it for a week. My lucky day. And now I meet you on the beach. Funny how luck comes in threes. First Felix, then the fish, and now you."

"Isn't that fish heavy? Why don't you put it down?"

"The weight of the fish doesn't bother me."

"I thought you'd be reading the book."

"Finished it last night. I have a battery-operated reading light for emergencies."

"You're more organised than we thought."

"I've been bumming around the world for almost twenty years. You pick up good ideas. So far on this beach I've been lucky. The beach patrol hasn't told me to move on. I used my charm."

"Was it a man or a woman?"

"A woman, of course. Will you walk with me, Nora, back to my camp among the dunes?"

"What did you think of the book?"

"The writer knows people. What's he been through to feel so much?"

"A terrorist war in Rhodesia. They killed his cat. He was nearly killed in the attack. Why he went to England. He made good money in his uncle's London business and lost it."

"What happened?"

"A woman. Inter-company jealousy. There was an associate company in America... That's the biggest fish I ever saw."

"Big teeth. You got to watch the big teeth. There are sharks everywhere."

"So you've been to Australia?"

"Among other places."

"Having read the book, who would you like to play?"

"Mark Fletcher, of course. I've always wanted to play the man who screws everyone and gets away with it. He's a big man. I like big men. Do you think Mr Kranskie is serious?"

"We'll only find out. Felix, his lawyer and the Villiers editor are talking through the contract... You gutted the fish. Some of the entrails are dripping down your shoulder."

"You have to throw back something. Come on, let's walk. It's so peaceful. Just the two of us on this end of the beach. The crowds stay nearer the houses."

"How old are you, Julian?"

"I'm forty-six. I'm forty-six years old. Exactly the same age as Mark Fletcher. Now, isn't that a coincidence? You see those tall trees there? That's where I'm camped."

"You were far from your camp when you frightened the wits out of us."

"I'd gone for a walk and found myself a half-empty bottle of wine someone had left on the beach. Found myself a comfortable spot among the dunes and drank the wine. A gift from heaven. I was lying on my back with all that beautiful wine inside of me looking up at the stars."

"How did you know it was Felix Kranskie?"

"A good guess. It was too dark to see his face. But I knew I was lying close to the path that led up to his house. I'd seen him before. Recognised him from his photograph in the newspapers and magazines. Famous people are easily recognised. I didn't know it was his bottle of wine. That was just my luck. What's he going to do about Jensen Sandler?"

"Tell him to mind his own business. It was a long time ago. Jensen Sandler will have forgotten it. Men like Jensen have a string of wives."

"He hated me."

"Jealousy can be powerful."

"Are you married, Nora?"

"Not for many years."

"You're having an affair with Felix?"

"How do you know?"

"The way he looks at you."

"We have a history."

"Unfulfilled love. It's as powerful as jealousy."

"I was married at the time. I thought my husband was infertile. I was trying to get myself pregnant. Turns out I was infertile."

They walked on in silence.

"Here we are."

"Where do you hide your valuables?"

"Under the sand. My fishing bag. My rod. My knife. My bag of clothes."

"Why's the rod so big?"

"So I can cast out over the surf to where the big fish swim."

Julian walked away from Nora and up to a clump of trees. With the length of rope he had unearthed from the sand, he hauled the big fish by its tail up into a tree, the shark's eyes and teeth still clearly visible. With his food hanging in the tree he walked back towards Nora smiling, the blue eyes penetrating to Nora's vitals. She felt like a girl of sixteen.

"Won't someone steal it?"

"No one likes a shark. People think you can't eat them. My fish will be safe... So, Nora, do you think I can play Mark Fletcher? Good. I can see the answer by your smile. Come and sit on the log. We don't have furniture in the beach home of Julian Becker. But it's comfortable. Full of peace. Will you help me get the part? I have to look to the future. You can bum around until your forty but after that you need money to survive. I need to make some real money. Like Mark Fletcher. Only I'll act a part for it and not steal."

"What do you do when it rains?"

"I have a tarpaulin which I get under."

"And when it's cold?"

"You train the body to ignore discomfort. It's all in the mind. Sorry I can't offer you a soft drink. But please sit down."

"Are you using me, Julian?"

"We all use each other, Nora. Part of the human condition. If I play Mark Fletcher the way I know I can play Mark Fletcher after reading the book, I'll be doing you all a favour. We'll all make money. So, what you think of Julian's lair?"

"I think you're barking mad but who cares? Tell me about your travels."

Nora sat herself down on the fallen branch and stretched out her legs. Julian sat on the sand.

"Where do you want me to start?"

"At the beginning."

"Well, there we were, enjoying a little sexual pleasure, when in bursts this man with a camera, his flash-bulb blinding my eyes."

"What was her name?"

"Do you know, for the life of me I can't remember. Something like Sally or Lily. They all blur into each other after so many years. They say you always remember your first lover. And your last."

"Have you had your last lover, Julian?"

"Don't be silly. Think Mark Fletcher. You want some tea? I can make a small fire from the driftwood and boil the kettle."

"What else have you stashed under the dunes?"

"Everything a man needs to survive."

"I'd love some tea."

"Black tea. I don't have milk or sugar."

"Black tea will be fine."

"What's he like?"

"Who are you talking about?"

"Randall Holiday. The author."

"I just wish I was twenty years younger."

"If I get the part, I want to meet him. He made Mark Fletcher. I want to act Mark Fletcher. He can help me get into the character."

Julian got up, poured water from a Coca-Cola bottle into an old kettle and made a small fire.

"Go on with the story of your life. Poor girl. By now, everyone will have forgotten her."

"But Jensen won't have forgotten his damaged pride. There will be a fight. Vanity is another of man's powerful drivers. Jensen Sandler will do everything he can to prevent me from getting the part. If he doesn't, the press will dig up our history. Every journalist loves a scandal. Scandal sells newspapers... The trick is to get the fire going enough to put the kettle in the flames."

"What happens when you get sick?"

"I don't get sick. I can't afford it."

The kettle boiled quickly. Julian brought out two china mugs, put a teabag in each and poured over the boiling water, stirring the teabags.

"After use, I dry the teabags and use them again. Three mugs of tea from one teabag. The last one is pretty thin. Now, here's the trick. I stole some mint from one of the gardens. The mint was growing through the fence. Never miss an opportunity. I dried the mint and put two leaves of dried mint in my tea. Try it. Mint tea. Better than anything."

"Did you ever get married?"

"No one wants to marry a bum without any money, whatever he looks like. There's been plenty of fun but nothing permanent. Marriage is all about future security. Someone to look after you. Children to support you in your old age. Money comes and goes, Nora, however hard some people try to keep it. Family is meant to be forever. The happy future. And that doesn't happen so much in this day and age... Be careful. The water was boiling. My intention, if Felix gives me the part, is to buy myself a small farm somewhere far away and become self-sufficient."

"One big part will bring others. I could be your publicist."

"Would you do that for me, Nora? I wonder why? Nobody wanted to do anything for me after Jensen Sandler ruined my career. No, that's probably wrong. I ruined my own career by sleeping with another man's wife."

"Nowadays, Felix is much bigger than Jensen. If Felix wants you, nothing will get in his way. Publicity is good. Someone once said bad publicity was better than being ignored."

"Blow on the surface of the tea before you drink it, or you'll burn your tongue."

"My goodness. It's quite delicious."

"You see?"

For an hour, Julian talked about his travels. After drinking his mint-flavoured tea he had stretched out on the sand in the shade of the trees, his big hands behind his head, as he rambled on about the life of a travelling bum. Bits and pieces like the bits and pieces washed up on the beach. The man had a strong charisma, the smallest story made big by Julian, the nomadic life a kind of perfection. Nora wondered if in the pre-history of man, when everyone was a nomadic hunter and gatherer, people weren't happier than living in flashy condos, everything provided with money earned through other people. It made Nora wonder where she was going.

"What's this Randall Holiday like, Nora?"

"A shorter, younger version of you. He called his first book *The Tawny Wilderness*. He loves the bush of Africa more than the suburbs of London... I'd better go. They should have finished their business. A publicist's work is never done."

"You'll let me know?"

"Of course we will. Thanks for the tea. Enjoy your shark."

"Why are you giggling?"

"I've never met anyone like you in my whole damn life."

"Here. Take the book and give it back to Mr Kranskie... Why do we always defer to people we want something from by calling them mister?"

Impulsively, Nora got up from the log, walked across to Julian and kissed him on the forehead. Then she left, not looking back, the shark's dead eyes watching her as she passed. It made Nora shudder. As if someone had walked over her grave.

Further down the beach she found people. Normal people. Nora smiled, found the side path up to the house, opened the security gate by punching in the code and walked past the pool into the house. The men were in the lounge drinking coffee, all three looking relaxed.

"Where've you been, Nora?"

"Walking the beach."

"Meet anyone interesting?"

"Julian. He's read the book. Wants to play Mark Fletcher. Have you all signed the contract?" She put the copy of *Masters of Vanity* down on the coffee table.

"Signed and sealed. You want some coffee?"

"I just had some tea. Mint tea on the beach. It was delicious."

When Nora sat down and tried to listen to what the men were talking about she found herself thinking of Julian. Could a man from the beach, despite his acting history, step into the shoes of Mark Fletcher, the ultimate shark in the world of big business, however many times Julian read the book and however much he talked to Randall? She could only hope for the man that such a thing was possible. To Nora, acting was a whole different world.

"He caught a shark," said Nora into a brief silence. They all looked at her.

"Who did?" said Henry Stone.

"Julian. Julian Becker. The man who would like to play Mark Fletcher."

"Won't we need someone famous? Who's Julian Becker? Never heard of him. Anyway, it's nothing to do with me anymore. I've sold the film rights. Keith here is going to drive me back to the airport. You coming to New York with me, Nora? There's still lots of work to do now we have a film contract. And we want Randall back in America. The moment you stop the promotion is when you start losing momentum . I want a big surge in media interest now the book is to be made into a film."

"You should meet this Julian before you go."

"Of course. If you say so, Felix. Wonderful doing business with you."

"You'll stay to lunch, Henry? There are plenty of flights to New York. Take a little time to relax."

"You think I should?"

"Romano can take you to the airport, Keith. I want to thank you so much for being with us so quickly. Nora, is Julian coming up to the house to talk to me? He read the book faster than I expected."

"He said good books read quickly. He wants to play Mark Fletcher."

"Does he? I have a copy of Julian's one and only film. The office delivered it while we were finalising the contract. The three of us can watch. I enjoy other people's opinions. After lunch we will watch the movie. What would we do without archives? I have a scriptwriter in mind. It's going to be a blockbuster. I'm putting in some of my own money to make the production. I won't have any trouble finding investors. You want to put in some money, Henry?"

"We're book publishers, not film producers."

"Of course you are."

Keith Fortescue packed his briefcase and left. Like most of the lawyers Nora had known, the man was in a hurry. They ate lunch round the pool, the ocean beyond a backdrop to a successful negotiation. They were all happy. They were all going to make money.

After lunch they watched *Home is the Hunter*, Julian dominating the screen. Nora was impressed. Far more than she expected. When the projector stopped running, Felix was silent, a knowing look on his face.

"Oh, he's got it," he said after a long silence. "He's got the power. Fills the whole damn screen. In all my film career it will be the first time I have found my leading man on the beach. You agree with me, Henry?"

"How old is that film?"

"Twenty years... You fancy a walk on the beach? Let's go and find him. Nora can lead the way. No wonder Jensen Sandler was so pissed off with Julian for sleeping with his wife. Jensen was jealous. Of Julian as an actor. The actor's got all the attention. I'm going to phone Jensen and ask him if he wants to invest some money in my new movie. He's been after me a couple of times."

"Will you tell him who is playing Mark Fletcher?" asked Nora.

"No. We'll keep it as a surprise. If Jensen gets mad I'll say I had no idea he had once produced Julian Becker. Oh, what fun. Jensen can be such a pain in the arse. Do you have a swimming costume with you, Henry? You'll have to take off your bow tie. They are banned on the beach. Sorry. Pulling your leg. It's all coming together. Your one per cent of the gross, Henry, is going to add up to a lot of money. So, it's to the beach."

They were still smiling at each other while Henry went off to change.

"You'll stay the night, Nora?"

"Of course I will."

They sat quietly and waited, both of them comfortable with each other's company.

"You want a dip in the pool?"

"Not really."

"I want a swim in the sea. How do I look?" said Henry.

All three burst out laughing. Henry, wearing only a swimsuit with a towel thrown over his left shoulder, had tied his bow tie, spots and all, round his neck.

"Looks good, doesn't it? Oh, well. Rules are rules." Smiling, Henry took off his tie and left it on the wrought-iron table.

"One of my rules in business is to do the deal and get the hell out of the way. Now I've broken my rule, Felix. Another rule is to never outstay one's welcome. I hope I haven't created a problem by breaking two of them."

"You're most welcome. Without you, Henry, the book would never have been published."

DOWN THE PATH, Henry dropped his towel and ran across the beach, splashed out to sea and dived head first into a small wave, Nora and Felix watching. The sun was hot.

"He should have brought a shirt or he's going to burn."

They walked down to the edge of the water, collected Henry and meandered on down to the beach.

"You see that distant clump of trees? That's where we are going."

Nearer, they could see the smoke from Julian's fire. When they reached the trees, Julian was eating a fillet of his fish, the rest of the shark still hanging in the tree. Felix introduced Henry.

"I'd give you some tea but I only have two mugs."

"Henry has to get back to New York. Give us a portrayal of you as Mark Fletcher. There's nobody down this end of the beach. You can call it an audition. I watched your movie. I want to see what that man in the film looks like twenty years later."

"I don't have a script."

"Then use your imagination. Some of the dialogue from the book must still be in your head."

"You're serious?"

"Never more in my life."

"Give me time to think. You can sit on the log."

"Take all the time you need."

Nora, not sure what was coming next, watched the transformation. The long hair, bleached by the sun, was tied back by a rubber band into a ponytail. Julian's look became serious. From his bag in the sand he pulled out an old jacket and draped it over his shoulders. His back straightened, his eyes changing to ruthless. Then Julian opened his mouth, the voice commanded everyone's attention. In a flash, Julian Becker was somebody else.

"I don't give a shit if you go bankrupt, Lucas. You sold me your business. You should have read the details in the contract. You made certain financial statements which are wrong. I have told my people to attach every one of your assets, including your home. I want my money back. You're a fool, Lucas. You left yourself wide open. In business, you can never trust anyone. Now get out of here. This business now belongs to me and you are no longer a part of it. Have a nice life. Nice doing business with you."

Nora, looking back, thought Julian had deliberately played the brief scene in front of the hanging shark, the dead eyes staring from behind Julian, part of the fish's body cut open and eaten. The man had morphed in front of them. When the piece was finished, Julian had thrown the jacket off his shoulders onto the sand in front of the shark and walked away down to the sea, leaving all three of them speechless.

Five minutes later Julian walked back, all full of charm and played out another scene from Randall's book. This time with an imaginary woman. The new Mark Fletcher was charming. A cavalier. Every girl's dream. Julian then walked back down the beach. The third scene, when it came, showed the man of vanity, the rich man who had everything he wanted, a man in love with himself, while hidden behind the spectacle was an element of uncertainty, a man who needed power and money to hide his inferiority.

When the performance was over, Nora and the two men sat tight on the log to absorb what they had seen.

"Where can I get hold of you, Julian?" asked Felix.

"On the beach, Mr Kranskie."

"If you move, please let me know. I'll have the contract drawn up. How was the fish?"

"Perfectly delicious. I always enjoy eating a shark."

This time nobody laughed. Felix got up, stretched himself in a gesture of self-satisfaction, shook Julian's hand, patted him on the shoulder, looked around at the lair raising his eyebrows, and went up to inspect the dead shark hanging in the tree.

"So you think Mark Fletcher is a shark?"

"He's only concerned about himself. Couldn't give a shit about anyone else, man or woman. But he can turn on the charm. Has a sharp brain. Knows what people want and how to manipulate them. The perfect man of business who doesn't care how many people he destroys in his pursuit of personal wealth. What I like about the book is that at the end the author exposes him. Destroys him. Takes away his wealth and all you find is nothing. And, of course, all his friends leave him. Including his money-grabbing wife and their pampered, never-done-a-stroke-of-work children. Randall Holiday strips him naked so you can see the nothing. The end of the book gives me some hope for the human race and makes you wonder about the whole damn capitalist system."

"You want a sad end to a movie?"

"It's not sad. It's exhilarating. The triumph of the film will be in the destruction of Mark Fletcher. A warning to all of us of the consequence of uncontrolled greed."

"Will you be moving your camp? Would you like to use my beach house? Romano will be happy to look after you. You can read the book again. You can get the feel of luxury again and find out why so many people spend their entire lives in pursuit of money. Come up to the house tomorrow morning before lunch. In the afternoon I have to be back in LA. And Nora has to go back to New York with Henry. We all have a lot of work to do. You have made me think, Julian. Producing a movie, you have to be able to bring all the characters and the story together. See the whole picture. Like Randall Holiday who wrote the book. I think I'm going to enjoy working with you."

"And Jensen Sandler?"

"I have a plan. A good one. In the end, money trumps emotions. Look at Mark Fletcher. People like Jensen need money to protect themselves."

"I was a fool to have slept with his wife."

"We're all fools, Julian. The trick is not being caught. If you require some help bringing up your things my staff will help you. There's a lot of luck in life. A whole lot of luck. Lucky I left my wine bottle standing in the sand when we went for a dip in the sea."

They walked back, Nora trailing the men. She was thinking sadly. She had slept with Felix. They would do it again. But Nora doubted if there would be anything permanent. Once Felix had finally satisfied himself sexually he would move on like the rest of them. Life for Nora never seemed to change... In front of her, the sun was still beating down on Henry's bare white shoulders, bringing Nora back to reality.

"You're going to burn, Henry."

"No I'm not. I covered myself in sunscreen before leaving the house. You have to be organised. In New York, living in a flat and working in an office I'm lucky to see the sun through the window let alone feel it. No, I'm well protected. Got to protect yourself. What a day. An audition on the beach. So, Nora, tomorrow we fly home together. Now all we have to do is find Randall Holiday."

"Do you tell your wife when you are coming home? The time of your flight?"

"I like to surprise her, Felix. She's my third wife and a whole lot younger."

"Do you trust her?"

"I've learned never to trust anyone."

"What a world."

"You can say that again."

Nora kept quiet. There were always two sides to a story. From what she had heard, the young wife, in exchange for moving from an ordinary life of having to make her own living, had signed a pre-nuptial contract which left her with little in the event of a divorce. If Henry wanted to have extra-marital affairs she had no power to prevent him from screwing who and when he wanted. Money! It made Nora laugh. She was getting cynical in her old age. The trick was to enjoy life as it came. To worry about tomorrow when tomorrow came. But however many times she told herself to live in the present her mind was always thinking of the future. Of Randall, and what Randall was doing right that moment. She stopped and turned to look out to sea. Looking back down the long beach she could still see Julian's clump of trees. The other way, the two men, deep in conversation, were slowly moving up the shore. She had never asked Henry if he had any children. She would have to ask him. Nora sighed, moved her sandals from her left hand to her right, and began to walk up the beach. The sun was hot on her uncovered forearms. She was going to burn.

THE NEXT DAY, the first flight was full. They had two hours to wait and went to a bar. Romano had dropped them at the airport in the car Felix kept at his beach house. Felix had driven his own car back to LA.

"Do you have any children, Henry? I never asked you."

"One from my first marriage. Why we had to get married. He's married with children. Lives his own life and doesn't think much of a father with a wife younger than his daughter-in-law."

"Grandchildren?"

"Two. A boy and a girl. The seed goes on... You want another drink?"

"Why not?"

"Flying is so boring."

"Don't you think you should phone your wife? Trust her for once."

"You know, I think I will."

"Do you love each other?"

"Very much. That's the irony. If I lost Susan I'd kill myself. I can't imagine why a girl so young and beautiful would want to marry an old man like me."

"You're not old, Henry. Have confidence in yourself. Go and phone her."

"Thank you, Nora. Are you going to be Julian's publicist?"

"I hope so."

"From homeless to living in luxury in the blink of an eye."

"He's going to be good. Very good."

"You like him, don't you?"

"Of course I do. Now, go phone your lovely wife."

THE FLIGHT DRONED ON, both of them keeping their thoughts to themselves. Susan had been at home and happy to hear from her husband. Henry was lucky. He had someone waiting for him at the other end. At the airport they ran towards each other, Henry dropping his luggage to embrace his young wife. To Nora, there was no doubt about it – they loved each other. Nora left them embracing and melted into the crowd. She was jealous, a feeling she hated. Outside the terminal building, she put her luggage inside a waiting taxi and gave the driver the address of her apartment. She was lonely. Was that the end of her second affair with Felix? She didn't know. She didn't really know about anything. She sat staring into nothing all the way home. She had made a lot of money but had she really gained anything? Money was protection to Nora. When she had enough, the rest made no difference.

Her apartment was quiet and empty. She turned on the answering machine, a brief moment of hope flooding her mind. She listened to the messages but none were from Randall. Randall, Felix and Julian, and here she was all on her own. There was no point in moping. She made herself a pot of coffee, took it into the lounge and turned on the television. She was home. This was her life. Everything was back to normal.

PART 4

SEPTEMBER TO OCTOBER 1989 —
"ABSOLUTELY SPIFFING"

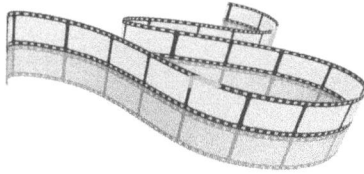

1

$\mathcal{A}$t the end of September, when Felix's film went into production, the leaves were falling in the Welsh valleys, Randall Crookshank totally oblivious to the fact another man had written a film script based on his novel. He had just finished the last sentence in his new book making him sad that all the people who had kept him company in his woodsman's cottage had gone. Finishing a book was like having a door slammed in his face. Outside the room that Randall had turned into his study, his desk pushed up against the window, the autumn sun was shining among the trees. Randall got up from his desk, stretched his arms both ways, holding his hands up towards the wooden ceiling, patted his handwritten manuscript, and looked around the tatty, oh-so-comfortable old room. In the four months he had been writing he had never looked round the room, always going straight to the desk to bury himself in his story. As usual, when he had finished a day's writing, he was hungry and needed a walk. Smiling, Randall went to the small kitchen and made himself sandwiches. With his sandwiches and a flask of tea in his backpack, Randall went for a walk in the woods, the occasional bird calling, the leaves falling, the village, far away in the valley, hidden by the trees. Down the path he had trodden so often as he worked out the plot of his book, he passed the disused mineshaft to the coal mine that had provided work for the villagers, the mine now worked-out, the Welsh miners all out of their jobs. Half the houses in the village were empty. The trees around Randall were tall and beautiful, different to the mopane and msasa trees Randall had grown up among in Rhodesia. Apart from an occasional oak tree, with its bulging roots, he had no idea of the names of the trees, or even the names of the birds and the butterflies, the thought making Randall nostalgic for his native Africa, making him want to go home.

"You cannot escape where you were born, old cock. Where your roots went in... Oh well, that book's finished. Now what the hell do I do with myself? And if I don't get a screw my hormones are going to explode."

The big oak, his favourite spot for sitting under and thinking, had gnarled roots bulging out of the ground, just perfect for sitting on. Randall took the pack off his back, sat down in a comfortable spot on the root of the oak, and pulled out his plastic box with the egg sandwiches he had stuffed with raw onions, sinking his teeth in with relish. When he'd finished his lunch he drank the tea. He was happy with the book. Whether Villiers Publishing would be happy with the book he doubted. There was no strident Mark Fletcher. No sign of the rich and famous. Just an ordinary couple with a young family living happily with a mortgage in a London suburb, a life Randall envied and knew he would never have. *Love Song*, the title he had finally given the book, was a soft book full of happy people in contrast to everything else Randall had experienced in the world. Even the in-love were kind of each other's children. It was Randall's first 'light and fluffy' novel. He hoped the readers would like it. He had certainly enjoyed writing it, tucked away in the hills among the Welsh valleys, the sound of the sea distant but clear. Writing books made Randall feel happy. He was lucky. Putting the lid back on his sandwich box and moving to the soft, leafy ground between the roots of the tree, Randall lay back and looked up into the branches, quickly falling asleep.

When he woke, the tea he had poured into the plastic cup had gone cold. Randall got up. He had made up his mind. He was going down to the village and into the one and only pub. If he got drunk, he would hire the one and only taxi to bring him back to the cottage. Randall shut and locked the door, his only worry losing the manuscript. If the only copy was lost it would be lost for all eternity, not that Randall thought that really much mattered. The birds were singing, the long twilight just beginning, the perfect end to a summer's day. It was time for Randall, after four months of seclusion, to go back into the world. Time to see James Oliver, to be a father and communicate with other people. On the occasional times he had made the hour-long walk down to the village to shop for his food, Randall had passed the Rising Sun but never gone in, the threat of going down the slippery slope into alcoholism always in his mind, the brief pleasure of getting drunk far outweighed by the subsequent pain. But his book was finished. If he ended up with a raging hangover it would not matter. He had eaten his box of sandwiches. His stomach was full.

"The way to go is to never start drinking on an empty stomach."

When Randall walked into the thirteenth-century pub, ducking his head, the date carved into the old oak beam just above the door, the shadows in the sleepy village had lengthened into fading light, the sun now long gone. The height of the entrance made Randall smile, imagining how small people must have been when the first Rising Sun had been built. A middle-aged man wearing an apron was standing behind the bar, the wooden counter black with age.

"When was this actual building erected?"

"Bits of it five hundred years ago, according to local legend."

"We were all a lot shorter back then."

The Welshman looked at Randall and waited.

"I've been living in the hut in the woods. Do you own the pub?"

"We know who you are."

Again the man waited.

"I'll have a pint. You don't do cold draught beer in Wales. In Zimbabwe, where I come from, the beer is always cold."

"We know where you are from, Mr Holiday."

"My name is Crookshank."

"Not according to the cover of your book. You look exactly like the man on the back cover."

After what Randall thought was four months of anonymity his cover was blown.

"Please call me Randall Crookshank."

"If you say so."

The man sang his words, the lilting sound of his Welsh accent pleasant to Randall's ears. The landlord drew the pint and put it in front of Randall.

"That's a quid."

"Thank you, Mr Landlord."

For the first time since Randall bent his head to walk through the door, the man gave Randall a smile.

"So what you doing in the woods all on your own?"

"Writing a book."

"Don't you get lonely?... If you don't mind, I'll have one with you."

"Put it on my tab. When I'm writing I don't want people around me."

"Then why come to my pub?"

"I've finished the book. Now I'm lonely."

The man drew himself a pint, Randall waiting. The man was probably in his fifties, with a good belly on him.

"Cheers, Mr Crookshank."

"Cheers, Mr Landlord."

"What brought you to Wales?"

"The only place I could find far enough away from the noise of people... Do people come into the pub? What day is it?"

"Saturday. You're lucky. Saturday is locals' night. They wait for the sun to go. Kind of a tradition. They like the big log fire in the winter and the company. Why they call it the public house. Anyone can come in if they behave themselves. You have a funny accent, Mr Crookshank. A bit nasal."

Randall smiled, saying nothing. From his wooden stool at the door he looked back into the pub, old oak beams, black with age, holding up the low ceiling, the fireplace, with benches on either side, big enough for people to sit in. Randall had a picture in his mind of Welshmen, their faces still black from a day working the coal faces, bent over the fire holding their pints of beer, happy to be above ground. The door opened as Randall studied the cold fireplace. Two girls came in, both of them young, both of them wearing hiking boots with packs on their backs. They were happily talking. Instead of coming up to the bar they sat at one of the empty tables, put their packs down next to them on the ground and waited. The landlord went to the end of his bar, opened the hatch and went across to his customers. He had left his pint on the bar in front of Randall. One of the girls looked at Randall and smiled, before turning her attention back to the landlord. The girls ordered food and half pints of shandy. The landlord walked back and went into the kitchen to the side of the bar, giving the cook the order. Randall, not to make his lust obvious, turned back to his beer. The landlord came back behind the bar, lowering the hatch.

"Tourists, Mr Crookshank, or whatever you call yourself."

"Randall. Please call me Randall... What's your name?"

"Taffy." The man laughed.

"Are you serious?"

"All Welshmen are called Taffy... Do you want to meet those girls? Months alone in the woods is a long time... Congratulations on the movie."

"What movie?"

"The film the Americans are making of your book. I saw it on the television. The man was interviewing your publisher if my memory is right. We knew by then you were up in the woods."

"Who told you?"

"It's a small village, Randall. Not much to talk about. You rented the cottage from the local council and gave them the name of Crookshank. Fred Winters wanted to know who you were. He made enquiries. Who knows, you might have been a criminal." The man's smile told Randall the criminal part was mostly a joke.

"Oh, so that's it."

"You don't know about the movie?"

"I've been deliberately out of contact. You can't write a book with other things on your mind. Mental interruptions are as bad as people."

"They said it's one of the big Hollywood directors making the film."

"Did they?"

"Aren't you interested?"

"Not really... What's your proper name? Who's in the kitchen?"

"My wife. The kids are long gone. You spend all that time bringing them up and then they go. You wonder why you spent all the energy... Joseph. My name's Joseph, Mr Holiday."

"Why did you call me Holiday?"

The man looked from Randall to the table and the girls. When Randall turned round the girls were listening. Randall turned back to the bar.

"I like writing books but not the aftermath. You lose your anonymity, something I hate. The one thing a man should have is his privacy."

"They know who you are."

"Does it matter?"

"To them, it does."

Randall finished his pint and ordered another. A man had come in and taken the stool next to Randall. The landlord pulled the man a pint and put it down in front of him. The man was obviously a local, neither man having spoken.

"You want food, Randall?"

"I should but want to drink. I used to be an alcoholic. Probably still am."

"We all are," said the man next to him. "Cheers, old china. To happy days."

Randall smiled. He was feeling comfortable. The first pint of beer was having its mellowing effect. For a long while the three men said nothing. The girls were chatting, no longer looking at Randall. Randall broke the silence.

"You're joking about the movie, Joseph?"

"No, I'm not. You didn't know?"

"I'll believe that one when I see it. Give the man next to me another pint. And another one for the both of us. If I fall off the barstool send me back to the hut in a taxi. I'm going to enjoy myself."

"The taxi man is always waiting outside when the bar closes at ten thirty... What you call the new book?"

"*Love Song*"

Randall drank, the beer going down well. By the time he finished his third pint, he didn't care who he was or what they thought of him. The girls had come up to stand behind him, giving their table to a family. The pub had filled up. Half the people up at the bar were standing. His months of peace and tranquillity were over, saturated by people. He was enjoying himself, enjoying the beer, enjoying the company. He bought the girls drinks. A man was always welcome in a bar when he bought the drinks. In his mind, the thought of the film kept coming and going.

"Can I use your phone tomorrow, Joe? Not now, tomorrow when I'm sober. Here's my credit card. Run it through for two hundred quid and tell me when I've drunk it, today or tomorrow. I'll sign for it now."

"You didn't say where you were?"

"Only way I got peace. Only way I could write the book. To the Rising Sun and everyone in it. Cheers, everyone."

Randall knew he was getting drunk. It was how it was. Once he drank he talked a lot of rubbish. The girls, still drinking shandy, had moved away. The man next to him bought him a pint. They were both going to get drunk together. Drinking companions. Drinking companions, hopefully without memories. The book was finished. The rest did not matter. Randall had meant to ask the man his name.

When Joseph rang the bell calling for last rounds, Randall went to look for the taxi. His drinking companion had gone to the toilet and not come back. Joseph said his bar-tab was still in credit. In the back of the taxi, Randall thought of Nora, of how happy she would be with all the publicity generated by a movie. Had he really enjoyed himself? Drinking with strangers was empty. The taxi dropped him back at the cottage, Randall paying the man with cash. Randall went to bed. He was lonely, not properly drunk, and unhappy. It was always the same at the end of a book.

RANDALL SLEPT through into the morning. Surprisingly, he was free of a hangover, lucky Joe closed his bar at half past ten. He made a cup of tea and went into the study, standing with the mug of tea in his hand. He looked at the finished manuscript, touched it with the flat of his hand and smiled.

"Thank you, Felicity and Michael. For being such good company."

Felicity and Michael were the main characters in the book. Randall looked out of the window. He was bored. He had nothing to do. The idea of phoning his publishers or Nora left him flat. They would want to involve him in the making of the movie. Books and films were all about publicity, the media happy to suck him dry. He thought of his two-and-a-half-year-old son but couldn't face talking to Amanda. If there was a film in the works she'd gush all over him. Did he want her back, even if she left Evelina? He wasn't sure. Once bitten twice shy. People rarely changed. Amanda wouldn't want him as much as his fame. Anyway, he had no idea how to entertain a small boy to make his son want to be with him. Life was complicated. Randall finished his tea, gave the finished handwritten manuscript a last glance and left the room. There wasn't much point in staying in Wales but he didn't know where to go. He had no home other than World's View in Zimbabwe. Life was complicated. The one and only good thought in his mind was not having to worry about money.

"Shit, I wonder how much they are going to pay me for the movie?"

It was no good thinking of going to Zimbabwe, even for a holiday. October was suicide month, the stifling hot and sticky build-up to the rains, when everyone was inclined to lose their tempers. And if he went home with nothing to write, what would he do with himself all day? After the months of seclusion, the idea of buying a small farm in the English countryside had lost its attraction. He had nothing to write. It was all about having something to write.

"Nora would know what to do. Such a pity she isn't twenty years younger."

Thinking of Nora made Randall smile.

"I wonder who they've got to play Mark Fletcher?"

Going into the bedroom, Randall put on his walking boots, picked up the stick he had cut from one of the trees, and walked through to the outside door. A good walk in the woods always made him feel better. He would think through the next step in his life and make a decision.

When he opened the door the girl from the pub was standing outside. She looked uncomfortable.

"I was scared to knock."

"Are you alone?"

"Lucy didn't want to come. Thanks for last night's drinks. My name is Meredith. Are you going for a walk? Would you mind if I came with you?"

"How long have you been standing here?"

"Half an hour."

"I'd better make us a flask of tea, Meredith. I'm so pleased to see you. We can walk through the woods down to the sea. Maybe I'd better make us some sandwiches. Do you like hard-boiled egg sandwiches? I boil a dozen at a time and keep them ready for when I get hungry."

"I like anything. Can I help?"

"Of course you can. Come in. My name is Randall. I was a bit drunk last night. You went off with Lucy."

"We thought you wanted to talk to that man. Pubs late at night are so noisy... There's a few clouds about but a lovely day for a walk."

"It's a lovely day."

Happy, excited, Randall led the way back into the small kitchen. Meredith was the pretty one. The one who had first caught his eye. The silent bite. That swift exchange of glances that said more than words. Body language. They knew. Both of them knew. Why both of them were happily smiling as Randall cracked open the eggs.

"Where are you from, Meredith?"

"London. Kensington. Not the posh part. We share a flat with two other girls. When London gets too much for us we go hiking in the country. All year you work hard for two weeks of pleasure. The rest is all pressure. All go."

"When do you have to be back in the office?"

"Another week. How'd you know I work in an office?"

"Not much else to do in London. I used to work for my uncle. Part of his business was developing property. I did the Westcastle development before the property crash."

"Are you married?"

"Not any more. My son turns three in February. My wife went off with a woman... You think that will be enough sandwiches?"

Outside it was beginning to spit rain. Randall looked up at the sky, turned and checked the door was locked, thinking of his manuscript lying on the desk inside the cottage.

"I have a small fold-up umbrella in my backpack, Meredith... I like the name Meredith. I'm always looking for names."

"I carry a plastic raincoat."

Through the woods, rustling the fallen leaves with their boots, they walked up the hill away from the village. The walking helped Randall forget the feeling left by the booze. Drinking to get drunk was so stupid. If nothing else, the evening of drinking had brought him Meredith.

"Joe told you where I was staying?"

Meredith said nothing. They walked on in silence, Randall understanding. It was never right for a woman to be seen chasing after a man. Or was she chasing the writer? Randall never knew anymore. In the old days he could work out when a girl was interested in him and not his money. From the top of the hill they could see the sea. Not the beach.

Behind the tall trees, far away, was the sea. The sun was trying to come out. The sea was flat, the water a dark green, cold and menacing.

"I suppose that's the Irish Sea. Quite a climb. Gets the heart pumping. In Rhodesia, the only sea we had was Lake Kariba, a man-made dam. During the time of the Federation when the two Rhodesias and Nyasaland were all one country. That's all changed. Now, the three are Zimbabwe, Zambia and Malawi. Have you ever been to Africa?"

"I'd like to go."

"They say if you drink the water of the Zambezi you will always want to go back to Africa. It's an addiction, they say."

"Are you addicted to Africa, Randall?"

"Very much so. I was born in the back of a truck between two African rivers. The rivers had flash flooded. My father delivered me. He couldn't get my mother to Salisbury and the hospital."

"That would make a good story."

"Please, no more stories about me."

"Do you like writing books?"

"More than anything. It's being part of the selling I hate. You become meat. Edible meat, everyone having a bite."

"Joe said you just finished another book."

"Come on. Let's run the last bit through the trees."

Still not sure what Meredith was after, Randall led the way down the hill, coming out onto a cliff. The coastline was wild, a small fishing village over to the left. A fishing boat was coming into shore, headed for a small pier in front of the village. There was no wind. The rain had stopped spitting. Next to him, the city girl was breathing heavily, her hands on her hips.

"What a beautiful view. Why don't we sit and eat our sandwiches? Do you like sugar in your tea? I twisted some sugar into wax paper if you want to make it sweet... Is it me or my book, Meredith?"

"You, Randall. When we first looked at each other I didn't connect you with a book. Why should I? Only when Joe talked loudly about you did Lucy twig you were that famous writer."

Randall hunched down, bending his left knee, and picked at the grass with his fingers.

"What do you do?"

"A legal secretary at a law firm in the Inner Temple."

"They're making a film."

"So I heard."

"Fame and money. Too much money turns to poison. It can destroy a person."

"Why you've been hiding in the woods, I suppose... I don't take sugar in my tea."

"Neither do I. Have a sandwich. The bread's a bit stale. I tried to go into the village as seldom as possible."

The girl took a sandwich from the plastic container Randall had taken from his backpack, along with the flask of tea.

"They're delicious."

"Of course they are. I made them."

They laughed. They were comfortable with each other watching the fishing boat closing with the jetty, the grass too wet for them to sit on.

"We could buy some fish and have fish for supper."

"Are you inviting me to stay?"

"We could have a whole week of peace. Lucy can come and stay. Save you both money."

"Mackerel. There's nothing better than fresh mackerel... Who was that man you were talking to in the bar last night?"

"I have no idea. We were drinking companions. When you drink like that it's better not to remember. We all talk so much rubbish when we drink."

"Why we left."

"I thought so. There's no alcohol in the cottage, I'm afraid."

"That's wonderful. We can both talk sense... Can I read the book?"

"The new one? It's in hand script."

"Even better. More personal. Like reading a letter from a friend... I wish I could write. I hate working in an office. But you have to make a living. Tell me more about Africa."

"First, tell me about Meredith."

"Is it the writer looking for a story, or a man looking for a friend?"

"A man looking for a friend."

"Did you love her?"

"I thought so."

"I thought I loved my partner. We never married. Lived together.

People are rarely what you think they are. It's all surface. All appearances. All trying to get something out of each other. I hate it."

"So do I... Have another sandwich."

"Lucy has to go back to London this afternoon. She's a lawyer working for a different practice now. How we became friends. She had a phone call. There's a problem. There's always a problem."

"Did you tell her where you were going?"

"It was her idea. She knows I want to write."

"Ah, then it's the book, not me."

"Not the book you wrote or the famous author. I wanted to talk to a person that writes. No, that's an excuse. I don't know. Can we play it by ear? Typing briefs is so boring. There has to be more to life than a nine-to-five job just to get a salary."

"Work is the curse of the drinking classes."

They both laughed, the awkward moment still lingering. Life, thought Randall. It never changed. But he wanted her. That much was certain.

"Does she expect you back before she leaves?"

"Probably not. In the flat, we come and go as we please. No one has to explain themselves. It's a free world."

"Yes, I suppose it is... What was he like?"

"We screwed each other's brains out. Come on. Let's go down. They're unloading the fish. You think they'll sell us fish off the boat?"

"I don't see why not."

They walked slowly along the clifftop looking for a path down to the beach. Most of the fishermen were sitting on the side of the boat, their feet dangling. They were waiting for the catch to be offloaded, their work done.

"Nobody's come for the fish. We might be lucky... There's the path."

Randall led the way. Down on the beach, more shingle than sand, the pebbles crunched under their feet. The pebbles were polished, washed by the sea. Randall wanted to hold her hand.

"Look. There's a piece of amber. When I was a kid we went to Aldeburgh for our summer holidays. We kids spent hours looking for amber on the beach. Dad grew up in Liverpool. Aldeburgh reminded him of when he was a boy. They use amber in jewellery. We'd better hurry. A refrigerated truck is pulling onto the jetty. Let's run."

In her hurry, Meredith slipped and stumbled, Randall steadying her before she fell over. It was the first time they had touched.

"Thanks, Randall. Hiking boots and pebbles on the beach don't go well together. You want to go for a swim later?"

"You got to be kidding. I only swim in warm water."

"Were there wild animals in your Africa?"

"My mother was killed by lions."

"Oh, God. I'm so sorry."

"We'd better try running or we won't get any fish. Zambezi bream. That's my speciality. You can put a line in the water without bait and pull out a fish quicker than it takes to say your name."

"You're kidding."

"Not much. We used to get the pan hot before going down to catch the fish. The Zambezi Valley is wild... Hey, guys. Can you sell us a fish? Mackerel. You got any mackerel?"

The men kicking their heels over the side of the boat said nothing, all of them looking at Meredith. The backdoor of the truck was open. Two men were loading boxes of fish into the truck. No one took any notice of them. Another man, considerably older than the rest, appeared from inside the boat, leaning on the rail, looking down at them. Meredith smiled up at him enticingly.

"You got any mackerel, captain?"

"All we got, lady."

"Can we have two?"

"Help yourself."

Randall moved forward and handed up two ten pound notes.

"Is that enough?"

"Take what you can carry... Boys, we got beer money."

The old man disappeared and came back again, handing down an old newspaper to Randall.

"For wrapping the fish. Gut them when you get home. You live in the woods? Saw you walking down the hill. Enjoy the fish. You got a funny accent. Where you from?"

"Zimbabwe. That's in southern Africa."

"Is it now?"

"Enjoy the beer."

"Enjoy the fish."

With Randall's backpack stuffed with fish, the weight of the fish pulling on the straps over his shoulders, they walked back up the pebbled beach.

"You gave him far too much money. The fishmonger makes most of the money. Do you ever wonder if any of those men have read your book? There isn't much to do on a fishing trawler until they run into the fish. No television... Is it heavy?"

"We'll be eating fish all week if you stay."

"Oh, I'm going to stay now we have all that nice fish."

They laughed, Meredith doing a skip as she turned and looked back at him, their eyes meeting. They heard the refrigerated truck start up and drive away. When Randall looked back the fishing boat was all on its own. They walked on slowly, neither of them in a hurry. The sun had come out from behind the clouds.

"What did your father do in Liverpool?"

"He is the manager of an insurance company. Forty years with the same company. By the time he retires, he'll have paid off the mortgage on the house. The days of loyalty to a company are over, he says. Now the staff change jobs every time they get a better offer."

"If everything is about money we're all in for a sad awakening. Why I love Africa. On the farm, it's all about the tobacco crop, the sheep, the cows and the people. The kids take the tractor and trailer to go play football. The farm school team is the best in the district. When they come back having won you can hear them singing. They're happy."

"You have a school on the farm?"

"Not just for World's View. The kids walk miles to the school from the neighbouring farms."

"Do they learn anything?"

"You'd be surprised how much they learn. The president, Robert Mugabe, was a schoolteacher before he started his liberation movement. There's a snag though. When they learn to read and write they don't want to be labourers on a farm. Some of them get pretty frustrated. Africa's transition into the modern world is going to get ugly unless the newly educated find employment. It never stops. You solve one problem and create another."

"How are we going to cook the fish tonight?"

"I'm going to make a fire and cook them over the coals. We're going to have a fish party. Just the two of us. You really going to stay, Meredith?"

"Of course I am. We'll sit round the fire and talk. Just the two of us."

Back at the cottage, both of them pleasantly tired from their walk, Randall found a knife and went outside to gut the fish. Meredith stayed inside. Randall thought she had gone to the toilet. With all the fish cleaned, the guts buried in the small vegetable garden, Randall made ready with the fire. Whistling to himself, wondering what was taking Meredith so long, Randall pulled up a big lettuce, cut a cucumber and picked a handful of tomatoes, just enough for a nice big salad. All the time he was thinking of Meredith. As his guest, a girl alone, any sexual approach would have to come from her.

"What's taking you so long?" he called into the house.

"I'm reading your book."

"Which one?"

"The one on your desk... Do you have a title?"

"*Love Song.*"

"The chapters have headings but not the book."

"I like to think a lot about the title. I want Nora to give it a read."

"Who's Nora?"

"My publicist. She's American."

"Is she pretty?"

"She's in her middle fifties."

"I didn't ask how old she was. Is she pretty?"

"Yes, she is. Very pretty."

"You like her a lot?"

"She's a lovely person... The fish are done. I've put the biggest two on one side. A green salad, and baked potatoes in the ashes of the fire. I pile old ashes on the spuds wrapped in tinfoil and then make the fire."

"I'd better stop reading."

Feeling pensive, Randall waited for the girl to come out. It was always the same with his books. At the end, when he had finished them, he had no idea if they were any good. During the writing it was different. Whatever Meredith said about the book it would be difficult for him to believe, especially if she said she liked what she had read.

Meredith walked out of the cottage, smiling at Randall, a knowing look on her happy face.

"I can see them so clearly."

"Who you talking about?"

"The people in your book. Felicity and Michael."

"They're just ordinary people."

"That's what makes them interesting. I can relate. How on earth did you learn to write?"

"Book by book. It gets easier the more you write. Have you ever tried?"

"Only in my head."

"Try putting it down on paper. There's plenty of paper in the cottage."

"I don't have my typewriter."

"Then use a pen. You can borrow mine. I'm finished with writing for a while."

"Would you go for Nora if she were a lot younger?"

"Like a bullet... You want to walk to the village to get your things before I start the fire?"

"I'm tired of walking. We can go tomorrow."

"Have lunch at the Rising Sun. We can go out on a date."

Meredith walked to the weather-beaten old table where Randall had left the fish.

"*Love Song*. It's a beautiful title. You haven't asked me what I think of it."

"I never do that... What are those birds?"

"Blackbirds. The most common bird in Britain. That and the sparrow... Will you read it if I write something?"

"I'll be your mentor."

Without warning, Meredith came straight at him, took his face in both her hands and planted a kiss right on his lips.

"You're a darling, Randall. An absolute darling. Give me those. I'll wash them and make a salad dressing. Do you have any garlic?"

"Lots of garlic. When the rest of the fish has dripped out we'll put them in the store cupboard. We don't have a fridge. If they start getting ripe we'll make them into a nice big fish stew."

"You didn't kiss me back."

"You're my guest. While you are a guest in my house I am your only protection... Why are you giggling?"

"Are all you colonials so old-fashioned? This is England at the end of the twentieth century."

"It's not. It's Wales."

"And if I write a lot of rubbish, are you going to tell me?"

"Probably not."

With his hormones screaming, Randall followed Meredith into the kitchen. The back of her trousers were tight, riveting Randall's attention.

"This is fun, Randall. All the way from Africa just for Meredith... If we had booze this whole thing would happen a lot quicker."

Randall dropped the salad in the sink. They were just touching each other. Meredith turned on the tap and washed the lettuce. Trying hard to control himself, Randall walked into the small store-cupboard, found four large potatoes and a roll of tinfoil and went out to start the fire. At the outside tap, Randall washed the potatoes. When everything was ready, the fire crackling, he walked back into the house. Meredith had made the salad dressing and was sitting at his desk, reading his manuscript. Between making the fire and seeing her reading his book, his hormones had come under control. The girl said nothing, her back to Randall. Randall went back out into the garden. The sun had gone down behind the trees. The birds were singing to each other. Randall stood and listened. Behind the woods, he could hear the sea. A wind had come up making his fire burn quickly. Randall put on more wood. She was right. A drink would make it a whole lot easier, reducing both their inhibitions. Having been sober and celibate for so long, Randall wanted more. Much more. He wanted a lifetime companion. All the money in the world would not help a man on his own. Standing alone, listening to the birds singing, he waited for the fire to cook the top of the potatoes. There was no sound from inside the house. His book had got between him and Meredith. After ten minutes, Randall had a look at the potatoes, sticking in a fork. Making sure the underside was nearest the heat of the fire, he put them back into the ashes and made up the fire. Cooking over a fire was Randall's speciality. The trick was to cook the spuds without burning them black. The tinfoil helped... A movie. They were making a movie of *Masters of Vanity*, an idea so big it was difficult for him to comprehend. Maybe Nora wasn't what you would call pretty but she still had that something, that same sexual pull that was drawing him to Meredith. He would have to give Nora a ring. Give his agent a ring. Speak to Henry Stone. Find out what was going on. It was time to get out of his foxhole and face the world. His mind drifting, Randall forgot the fire and walked off into the woods, closer to the birds. The birds did not stop singing. There were lots of them all making a chorus. She was nice. He would have to be careful not to ruin anything. Sitting down under an oak tree, Randall could still smell the smoke from the fire. Everything in Wales was so much gentler than Africa. There was no fear of predators. No need to carry a gun.

"Where are you, Randall?"

"Listening to the birds, the most beautiful sound on earth. You know, birds never sing out of tune. Always pitch-perfect. That's a fact."

"Your fire's going out."

"I'm coming. You must be hungry. All we've had are sandwiches. It's good to eat when you are really hungry. The food tastes so much better."

"There you are."

"Hello, Meredith. It's quite dry under the tree. You want to sit down next to me?"

"You write so beautifully. It's all so alive. I can see the pictures as clear as seeing them on television... Move over. Where am I sleeping tonight?"

"There's one bed and the couch in the lounge. You can take your pick."

"How big is the bed?"

"Very small. It's a one-man cottage just right for reclusive writers."

"The leaves are so soft... You can't eat acorns."

"I know. I tried."

"Are there any cats around?"

"Why?"

"They'll eat our fish."

"No cats. Just you and me. I love the gloaming in England. The twilight."

"We're in Wales."

"Of course we are."

Lying back, looking up at the branches, Randall was acutely aware of Meredith lying next to him, her hand an inch from his. Neither of them moved. It was a perfect moment. One inch.

"You can now hear the sea."

"The wind's come up. The potatoes will still be cooking. Won't take long to grill the fish... Are you happy, Meredith?"

"At this moment, I've never been happier."

"Neither have I."

They lay still, more conscious of their almost-touching-hands than their empty stomachs. They were being watched from up in the tree. The small animal was still, its big tail curled up behind its furry body. Meredith pointed up at the squirrel.

"That's a grey squirrel looking down at us. They eat the acorns. They're not indigenous to the island. Dad said in his youth they paid a shilling for the tails. He shot the squirrels with his airgun. The squirrels were considered vermin. I hate the idea of killing anything. There are still a few red squirrels left nearer to Scotland."

"Where did the grey squirrels come from?"

"I have no idea."

"In Africa, they imported wattle trees from Australia. It had something to do with the tanning industry. Leather. That sort of thing. Now the wattle is a menace to Africa's indigenous trees but you can't get rid of them."

"A bit like you lot invading Africa."

"Something like that. The idea is good to start with but you have to see what happens. That squirrel looks so cute. I think he's laughing at us."

"Now, why would he laugh at us?" After pointing out the squirrel, she had brought her hand back down still an inch from Randall's.

"They know a lot more about us than we think... Do you think squirrels love each other?"

"I'm sure they do. Hemingway in *Islands in the Stream* says cats can love humans and humans love cats. I mean, really love each other."

"That's such a nice thought. I love cats. Hemingway. Now there was a man who could write books."

"We'd better go cook us some food."

Meredith moved her hand away, breaking the tension. When Randall looked up in the tree the squirrel had gone, hidden by the leaves. He got up, put out his hand and helped Meredith to her feet. As they walked away from the tree she kept on holding his hand. The fire was almost out. With a pile of dry leaves Randall brought back the flames, putting on more small pieces of dry wood.

"How much money did your father make? A shilling was probably a lot more money to a boy in those days."

"I never asked him. Are the spuds cooked?"

With a stick, Randall pulled one out of the fire. Meredith handed him the fork.

"Still a bit hard in the middle but not burnt on the top. When the fish are done, they will be perfect."

"We need a bottle of wine."

"Probably."

The light was going gently. A perfect early autumn's night. The wind had dropped. They could still hear the sea. He wanted to give her a kiss. Instead, he walked to the weather-beaten old table and put the two largest fish into the griller. The griller was old and rusty.

"In Africa we call it a *braai*. If you burn the griller in the fire regularly the rust doesn't stick to the meat. Here it's a barbecue, same as Australia. *Braai* is Afrikaans. The language of the Boers. A kind of bastard Dutch that's grown up over three hundred years in Africa."

The wood had blazed and settled down. Randall built up bricks on either side of the hot fire and placed the griller with the fish over the fire just high enough from the flames to do the cooking and not burn the fish... Randall stood back to admire his handiwork.

"Where are we eating?"

"Inside. I don't have a folding table."

"You've done this before, Randall."

"Ever since I can remember we cooked over an open fire. Part of our African culture."

"How long will it take?"

"A couple of minutes on each side of the fish. Never overcook fish. The Japanese eat it raw. They call it sushi."

Without warning, Meredith put her arm around his waist and gave him a hug. Randall let go the griller having turned over the fish. They kissed. A soft kiss full of meaning, a kiss that spoke more than just animal lust. Randall let it pass, not wanting to take the embrace through to its conclusion, the build-up more important than the climax. There was going to be a climax. For both of them.

"I'll go make up the salad... She'll be almost home by now. Back in the flat. I'm so lucky to have a good friend. Don't you miss your friends?"

"I miss my family. I miss not knowing my son."

"And you miss Nora."

"And I miss Nora."

"How much will you both make out of the movie?"

"A whole big bunch of money if I know my Nora. The inside of Nora is soft as butter. The outside as hard as nails. Especially when it comes to making her clients money. It's a tough world out there in the marketplace. My agent drafts the contracts. Nora does most of the work... There. How does that look? That side is almost cooked."

Randall twisted the griller and put it back on the bricks, poking the fire underneath. They both stood back, their hands touching, just the backs, Randall not sure if he should take her hand or not. It was all in the timing. Acutely conscious of the sexual undertone, Randall poked the spuds out from the fire with his stick, picking them up and dropping them quickly into an old wooden bowl.

"Will you carry the potatoes? You can take off the tinfoil and have a look. When they cool a bit we can press them so they burst open in the middle, and stuff them with butter. Real butter, not margarine. Add a little salt... There you are, Meredith. The fish is cooked. Supper is about to be served."

"Are you going to leave the rest of the fish out all night?"

"I'll do that after we've eaten... I'm so glad you decided to pay me a visit. When a book is finished I get lonely."

They ate inside without turning on the lights, just able to see what they were eating, the last of the daylight washing Meredith's face. Her skin was perfect. Not a blemish. Not a sign of make-up. Their feet touched under the table, again sparking the sexual pull. When they had eaten, Randall went outside and brought in the rest of the fish. Far away, an owl was calling, answered by its mate. Inside the cottage it was almost dark. Meredith had undone the top of her blouse. She was not wearing a bra. The playtime was over. With one hand on her breast, Randall pulled down the zip of her trousers. She was clutching the front of his pants.

"Fuck me, Randall. Please fuck me."

Her voice was deep and husky. He could still hear the owls calling, then nothing. They were deep inside of each other, no thought in the world.

When Randall woke in his bed in the dark of the night, she was sleeping next to him, their bodies entwined. Outside in the woods, everything was quiet. Randall smiled, stroking her naked body, the body as smooth as silk. Meredith began to wake. This time they made love slowly, like a love song. Exhausted they lay awake side by side, holding each other's hands.

"I'm definitely going to call it *Love Song*."

"I think I'm going to love you, Randall."

Randall said nothing. Love came slowly. Lust came quickly. Time would tell them where they were going. Real love. Not spoken love. That was what Randall wanted. A love that would last forever. For the rest of his life. For all eternity. Then he drifted back into sleep and his dreams. When he woke the light was pouring in through the open window. By the window, Meredith was standing naked, looking out into the woods.

"Aren't you cold?"

"It's so beautiful. So quiet. Earlier, the birds were singing. You were sound asleep. You look so vulnerable when you are asleep. Do we have to go into the village?"

"We don't have to do anything. We have a whole week to ourselves. But what about your clothes?"

"I'd forgotten about my clothes."

"Come back to bed."

Back in the bed Randall pulled her in close. Her skin was cold. Within a minute they were both sound asleep.

By lunchtime, everything was back to normal. They had walked slowly into the village, holding each other's hands. It made Randall feel like a child. A naughty child. He thought of making phone calls and changed his mind. Making contact with the real world would have broken the spell. The magic. The magic of two lovers in the woods. They had lunch at the Rising Sun, neither of them wanting to drink alcohol. Mrs Joe's food was good. Joe left them alone. He understood. Meredith's bag was next to the table, ready for Randall to carry back into the woods. Instead of making chit-chat they ate quietly, chewing their food as they looked into each other's eyes. Both of them were smiling. Soft, knowing smiles that said everything. They were going to have a week together in paradise, all on their own.

"You can keep the rest of the money, Joe," Randall said up at the bar. Meredith had gone to the door. "Thank you, Joe. I owe you one."

"My pleasure."

The man had a distant look on his face, as if he had lost something. Randall understood. Love, like life, was transient. One minute you had it and then you didn't. Joe's wife had come out of the kitchen, neither of them seeming to notice each other. Picking up the bag, Randall walked to the door.

"Don't you want to get the taxi?" The soft, replete look of satisfaction was still on her face.

"I want us to be alone."

"Isn't it heavy?"

"Life's heavy, Meredith."

"It may rain."

"And again it may not. I don't want to lose our moment."

"You're a romantic."

"Probably."

"Do you have to be a romantic to write books?"

"You have to be a lot of things to write books."

They walked back. Randall moved the bag from hand to hand as it grew heavy. The weight of the bag didn't bother him. He could still hear her husky voice in his mind: the 'please fuck me, Randall'. Her words had surprised him. They were all animals when it came down to it, himself included. The driving force of life was procreation, the romance made up by man.

"What's for supper, Randall?"

"Fish."

"I'd forgotten the fish. What are you going to do at the end of the week?"

"I don't know. I don't want to know."

Randall put the bag down. Meredith sat on it. They had not used a condom which was probably wrong. There was always reality. After a while they walked on. There was no more talk of writing or talk of his books.

2

----

*A*t the end of the week, when Meredith had to go back to London and her job in the Inner Temple, they were both satiated.

"What are you going to do, Randall?"

"Remember our time alone in the woods for the rest of my life."

"I hate my job but I have to do it. Make a living. You're lucky."

"Maybe. I was lucky on the banks of the Zambezi River. I was lucky in the woods. Hopefully, I will always be lucky when I am at my desk writing my books. The rest can be a nightmare. So, what did you think of it?"

"Your book or our love affair?"

She was smiling, the smile waning, a passing smile. He shouldn't have asked her about his book, the thought of love more important to Meredith than his damn book.

"What do you think of my writing, Randall?"

"You can make pictures out of words. That's what counts. The rest will come. That's just practice. Your English isn't bad. Better than mine when I started. You have to live to find good stories. Got to have a good story. All the fancy writing in the world won't make up for a good story."

"What do I write about? All I can do are three-page short stories... Are we going to see each other again?"

"Of course we are."

"They'll want you to go to America. Where they are making the film."

"Probably. You can come over."

"I can't leave my job. The job, Lucy and the girls in the flat are my only security. My only permanence. What are you going to do about your son?"

"I don't know. I can't bring him up on my own. Maybe he's better off with his mother and Evelina. With his mother he has stability. With me he'd be all over the place. Can a single man bring up an almost three-year-old boy? You have to be practical in life."

"You can ring me when you come back from America. Whenever that is. And you're right. I'll never forget this week in the woods. And don't worry. I'm far too street-wise to get myself pregnant. It's likely we'll just go our own separate ways, taking with us this memory. Every time in the future, however old I get, when I eat mackerel I'll think of Randall Holiday."

"Not Randall Crookshank."

"You're going to be so rich and famous you'll have forgotten all about Crookshank."

"But not Meredith."

"No, not Meredith. This was a once in a lifetime memory... I think I hear our taxi coming through the woods. It's all over."

"Don't cry, Meredith."

"What else can I do? Life is so cruel. It gives, only to take away... I must try and stop being silly. Life is made up of bits and pieces. Good bits and bad. That's what you called it, Randall, in *Love Song*. Life's mosaic. You see, that's one thing I will always have of you, Randall. I will always have your books. No one can take them away. No one can destroy them."

"You liked *Love Song*?"

"Of course I did, you idiot... We'd better go. The driver is hooting his horn."

Outside the cottage Randall put the key in the door and locked it for the last time. He was sad. He had lost something, not just the week but all the months he had spent in the woods. They were going together, no point in Randall staying in the woods any longer. He put the key in the small flower pot next to the door, picked up their bags and walked down the garden path towards the waiting taxi. They had ordered the taxi two days before when they had walked to the village to shop for food. They got in and sat in the back, holding each other's hands. The taxi driver had put the bags in the boot of the car. The man dropped them at the small railway station and left. Alone, the only travellers, they sat on the wooden bench and waited for their train. Another part of Randall's life was over. They changed trains twice on the way back to London, the world of suburban and urban England sucking them back. All the rows and rows of semi-detached houses. All the people. Instead of saying what they were thinking, they spoke small talk to pass the time away. It was late afternoon when they arrived at Paddington Station to catch the Tube, the railway station quiet on the first Sunday afternoon in October, Meredith due to start work at nine o'clock in the morning. They both found themselves trolleys and stood looking at each other, neither knowing what to say.

"Do you know, a week ago you and I didn't know each other. It seems so ridiculous. We part here, Randall. This is it. Where are you going to stay?"

"With my grandmother and uncle if they'll have me."

"Won't it be a surprise?"

"Life is full of surprises, Meredith." He was smiling at her, both understanding each other's thoughts.

"You can say that again. Who would have thought this would happen to me? Well, goodbye, Randall. Best of luck with the new book."

"I'll give you a ring in the office tomorrow."

"You do that."

"Say hello to Lucy. And thank her. What would we do without friends?"

"I can't even imagine."

Meredith put out her hand. Randall took the hand and held it. They were both crying. Meredith broke away, gripped the metal rail of the trolley hard and pushed it down the platform, her back to Randall as she walked away.

"Phone you tomorrow, Meredith."

She didn't turn round. He watched her show her ticket to the ticket collector and disappear through the gate. Was it over or was there a more normal life beginning? Randall wasn't sure. Trying to remember which Tube line to take to get to Hyde Park and the townhouse of his uncle,

Randall began pushing his trolley down the platform. Outside the gate, he left his trolley in the line with the rest of them, picked up his suitcase and walked towards the emblazoned entrance to the London Underground. Halfway there he changed his mind.

"What are you doing, Randall?" he muttered. "You're not broke."

In the train, he had suggested a taxi to Meredith.

"I'm not after your money, Randall. Or your fame."

In the back of the taxi outside the station Randall again changed his mind.

"The Savoy Hotel," he told the driver.

He'd make his phone calls from the hotel and decide what the hell he was going to do with the rest of his life. Then he'd surprise his grandmother. Later he'd visit Amanda and Evelina and surprise his son. The new book was safe inside his suitcase next to his knee. He was still thinking of Meredith on her way home to her normal life. By tomorrow lunchtime she'd be back in the routine. By the end of a week the cottage in the woods would be fading from her mind, her ordinary day-to-day life taking precedence. She was right. He would probably have to go back to America. Back to his own life. Back to all the rubbish of money and fame with all its clamouring, everyone making money. He was part of them. They had got him. They owned him. There was no turning back. All that hope of fame and fortune he had had when he first started writing turning to nothing compared to a week alone in the woods of Wales with a happy girl. He would phone her in the morning and see what happened.

"Life's full of shit."

"Sorry, cock. What you say?"

"Nothing."

"You staying at the Savoy?"

"I hope so."

"Blimey. You must be rich. Why you put your case next to you?"

"It's got something in it I don't want to lose."

"Oh, it's got money."

"It's a book."

"Who cares about a book?"

In his room in the Savoy Hotel, Randall put through a phone call to America.

"Hello, Nora. It's Randall."

"Where the hell have you been?"

"What's the matter, Nora?"

"Get yourself on the next plane to New York. They're making a film."

"I heard about it. How are you, Nora?"

"Better, now I have you on the phone. Do you know how much of an idiot a publicist looks when she doesn't know where to find her client? Nice to hear your voice. Did you finish it?"

"Every word."

"What's it called?"

"*Love Song.*"

"I like it already. Next plane, Randall. No shilly-shallying. We've got a lot of work to do. Do you know what time it is?"

"I have no idea. Probably Sunday afternoon."

"I was having a nap."

"Go back to sleep. I'm staying at the Savoy in London."

With the phone down, sitting on the bed, Randall wasn't sure what to think. Part of him was excited by the thought of the movie, part of him wanted to run back to the woods and hide away from all the predators.

"Maybe, when I get back from America, Meredith. If everything hasn't changed by then."

Randall lay back on the bed. He was thinking of Nora. It was nice to hear her voice. At that moment, lying on his back on a strange bed in a strange hotel room, Randall wondered what was the point in his life. What it was all about. What it was like to stay happy. What it was they all wanted. Where he could stop and be content. He didn't understand it. And likely never would... Only later, when he got hungry, did he leave the room and go downstairs to the dining room. He was back among people. The noise and all the nonsense. Sitting down at a table in the big dining room, surrounded by important-looking people, Randall had never felt more alone. The women at the tables were all rich, dripping in diamonds, all making polite conversation.

"What can I get you, sir?"

"A life in an African forest."

"I don't understand, sir."

"Neither do I."

The key to his room was on the table in front of him, making the man obsequious. He smiled up at the man and ordered his supper.

"You haven't ordered the fish starter."

"I've had enough fish."

"Very well, sir."

The man was positively cringing, making Randall want to be sick, the power of money reducing the poor man to nothing. Or was it the tip, the man trying to make himself some money? Two tables away it seemed as if he had been recognised. They were all looking at him. Randall smiled uncomfortably and got up from the table. He was going to have a drink in the bar.

"Forget my order."

"As you wish, sir."

Apart from the bar and alcohol, there was nowhere to run. He had it all and yet he had nothing. Alone in the woods they were fine. It wouldn't be fair to a nice girl like Meredith to throw her into the world where it didn't matter who you were, provided you had a pile of money.

Randall found the bar and walked inside.

"Double Haig whisky, Mr Barman."

"Coming up."

Down the bar a girl was smiling at him. She had seen him put his hotel keys on the bar. It was starting all over again. The whisky came and tasted good, sliding down his throat like silk.

Three hours later, still alone, Randall left the bar to go up to his room. He was drunk. He had left the barman the kind of tip they expected at the Savoy. The girl had gone off with an old man. In the room, Randall drank down two pints of water to minimise his hangover and got into the strange bed. In the morning he was going to America.

When Randall woke, his mouth dry, it was ten o'clock in the morning. From the phone beside his bed Randall dialled Meredith's office.

"Meredith who, sir?"

"She's just come back from leave."

"There are many people who work here. I don't know a Meredith. Do you know her surname?"

In the whole week in the woods they had spent together she had never told him her surname.

"No, I don't"

"Well then I can't help you. Sorry."

"Please, you must…"

"Good day to you, sir."

Before Randall could say any more the phone went down at the other end. They had had a week. A week for both of them to remember. Randall had gone from everything to nothing in the blink of an eye.

"And that's life, you idiot. That's life."

Not wanting to look sorry for himself in front of his grandmother or Amanda, his young son probably not even knowing who he was, Randall booked his flight to America and ordered a taxi to Heathrow Airport, the bill for one night in a swank hotel so big it caught his breath.

"What a mind-bending waste of money, Randall Crookshank."

He had been drunk, slept badly and not had his breakfast. Or his supper. Just the peanuts and crisps up at the bar, and the best part of a bottle of whisky.

"Rich people must be out of their minds."

The receptionist, a woman of middle age dressed immaculately in a severely cut uniform, just looked at him, saying nothing. He had paid his bill and that to her was all that mattered. He had paid the bill and ordered the taxi in the name of Holiday, even his credit card part of his fiction.

At the airport, he was fawned over once more in the first-class lounge, free everything while he waited for the plane. Travelling first class removed a lot of the hassle, the price making Randall feel sick. He was going to sit his arse on a seat. The rest of it was all show off, what his publisher, readers and fans expected from a bestselling author whose book was being made into a Hollywood film. Meredith and the woods seemed a million miles away. The flight was called and Randall went on board. On the plane, Randall found his seat and sat down. The man he had pushed past was wearing glasses on the end of his nose, immersed in paperwork. The man looked important, ignoring Randall. Feeling guilty at not having seen his grandmother Crookshank or his son, Randall stared at the back of the seat in front of him, happy the man with the snooty look wasn't talkative. *Love Song* was in a small bag on his knees, his suitcase in the body of the Boeing aeroplane. The book was all he had left of the woods. She would read it again, that much he was certain. Poor Meredith, stuck in a lawyer's office. Poor Randall stuck in an aeroplane. The plane took off, Randall looking out of the small window next to him. Once the plane took off the old man went to the toilet. Probably why he had taken the seat by the aisle. Back in the seat, the man replaced his spectacles and went back to work.

"Don't I know you?"

"I hope not... Sorry, that didn't come out the right way."

"You're that author. I read your book. Don't often read novels. Friend of mine lent me a copy. I'm in corporate business. You look too young to have been in the executive suite. How did you learn enough to make up such a story? Aren't they making a film?"

"I believe so."

"You don't know?"

"Why I'm going back to America."

"What's that accent?"

"Rhodesian. Oh, now it's called Zimbabwean."

"And you knew the inside of corporate America?"

"It's a long story."

"It certainly was. What's your name again?"

"Randall Holiday."

"I remember your face from the back of the book. Saw you on television. Have a good flight, Mr Holiday... Good luck with the film. What is the world coming to?"

Not wanting to argue, Randall turned away to look out of the window. The man was English. One of those frightfully-frightfully, the accent almost nauseating. Probably had a title.

"Prostate problems. Why I take the aisle seat. If I had your seat by the window I'd be pushing past you every hour."

"I'm sorry."

"Getting old. We all get old in the end. The body starts breaking down. I work to keep my mind off my problems. What did you do in Rhodesia?"

"We're tobacco farmers. Dad came out after the war. He had a Rhodesian friend. Or rather, his father had a Rhodesian friend. My grandfather was killed at Dunkirk. The Germans sank the *Seagull*."

"I'm sorry to hear that."

"Why everything changed."

"Yes, I suppose it did."

The man wasn't so bad after all. Meredith flashed back into Randall's mind, his mind soon back on the beach talking to the skipper of the mackerel boat. The airhostess moved by, smiling at the passengers, just touching the top of the seats on both sides of the aisle.

"Could you bring me a sandwich, miss? I haven't eaten since yesterday's breakfast." The girl smiled. She was pretty. The plane flew on, further and further away from Meredith. Randall wondered if anyone was going to meet him at the other end. He had left a message with Henry Stone's office, giving them the number of his flight. Henry was away. Everything in Randall's future was uncertain. He had no home. No permanence. His family and friends were scattered all over the world... When his food came, the tray passed over the man with the prostate problem, the crust had been cut off the sandwiches. It was all so ridiculous. What was a loaf of bread without its crust? Randall devoured the sandwiches and asked for another plate.

"You are hungry." The pretty girl this time was smiling right at him.

"The aftermath of too much booze."

Randall ate the second plate of sandwiches, no idea what was inside of them. The old man had got up again and gone to the toilet. The plane flew on, chasing the sinking sun, no clouds outside the window, just the eternal empty wilderness of a universe, the earth so small and insignificant, none of them really knowing where the world was from or where it was going, a brief moment of life without a purpose. Randall dozed off, the half sleep producing only a shadow of a dream. The girl woke Randall, the food trolley in front of her.

"Sorry. Not hungry after all those sandwiches."

It was all so weird being up in the sky, the only reality the inside of the aeroplane. Randall dozed off again into a deeper sleep. In the sleep he found Meredith. They were laughing. They were happy... The loudspeaker, warning them of the descent into Kennedy, woke Randall from his dream. The old man was putting his papers back into his briefcase.

"I wish I could sleep like that on an aeroplane. Just one more visit to the toilet and we'll be on the ground. You got someone meeting you?"

"I have no idea where I'm going."

The old man gave him a queer look, put his briefcase on the floor in front of him, and got up to go to the toilet.

So that's it, thought Randall. You put it in and piss it out again.

"You all right, Mr Holiday?"

"My ears won't pop... There you go... Wow, that was painful."

Like so many times in Randall's travels he had met a man he would never meet again. The Boeing came in to land, touched, and retouched the tarmac. When the plane taxied in and stopped, the seatbelt lights went off. People got up. The aircraft doors opened. People moved off the plane. In first class, the transit from the aircraft to gate twelve at the terminal was pleasantly quick, Randall looked around holding his suitcase and the bag that contained his book. Then he smiled. A young, familiar face was smiling at him. The old man from the plane had gone.

"Thanks for meeting me, Johnny. I haven't booked anywhere to stay."

Johnny Stiglitz, Henry Stone's junior assistant, shook his hand.

"You're in the company's apartment. We have three of them. Have to look after our authors. That all you've got? How you doing, Randall? Henry's in LA with Felix Kranskie, the producer and director of your film. Congratulations. Your book's come a long way since I met you here the first time. You'd been hiding somewhere in the African bush. What you been up to, Randall? The whole world's been looking for you."

"Writing a book. Meeting a girl."

"Ah. There's always a woman. Let me carry that case."

"Where are they filming?"

"Mostly in Kranskie's studio. One office looks much the same as the rest of them. They'll do shots of New York to give it authenticity. The book sales are still good. They'll want you for more publicity. Got to keep your name in the eye of the public. Nora's got a pitch about your months of hiding in the woods. She's good at picking up soundbites that catch the ear and imagination of the public. 'Reclusive writer comes out of the woods with a *Love Song*.' That is the title of your new book? It's all go in New York. All go in America. Did you get any sleep on the plane?... Taxi!... Here we go, Randall. Nice to see you again. MaryJane's excited you're back. She wants to type *Love Song*. You liked what she did on your last book."

"Have you finalised the title? MaryJane didn't like 'The Woman Who Stole My Wife'. Too many words."

"Not yet. Publication is on hold. No problems with the book. We're still concentrating on pumping every yard of mileage out of *Masters of Vanity*."

"Who's playing Mark Fletcher?"

"Julian Becker. They met him on the beach! Can you believe it? The rumour is Nora and Felix are old lovers. How she sold him your book. Good old Nora. She got five million and one per cent of the gross. Henry wants to know where to send you your half after expenses. He's got it in a trust account earning you interest. Julian Becker wants to meet you."

"Are they still into each other?"

"I think so. Why do you ask?"

"Nothing, really. How old is Kranskie?"

"Nora's age."

"Seems both of us have been having fun. So, where's this apartment?"

"Manhattan. Close to the office. Good to see you, Randall."

"So, it's still no title for my book."

"Still no title... The film's going to be big. Very big. There's a whole argument about Julian Becker and another producer. All over the tabloids. Years ago, Julian screwed the producer's wife. The public are loving it. Nothing like a scandal. The media feed on scandal."

"Why's he want to meet me?"

"To get to know more about Mark Fletcher. They had an audition on the beach. Can you believe it? It's all over the papers. Sent the book sales through the roof for a couple of weeks. Nora's good. Really good."

"Is she going to marry Kranskie?"

"I have no idea. I don't think so. You going to give me dinner for meeting you at the airport? MaryJane's at the apartment making sure everything is ready for you. Just kidding. She's waiting for you. The famous writer. We can all go out together."

"You've got it all planned."

"Of course I have. MaryJane's got a friend. The four of us."

"You really look after me."

"Of course we do. You're famous. You make us money. What it's all about. All your books are going to sell millions of copies if we have anything to do with it. Books are all in the marketing."

"Not in the books?"

"That helps. Just kidding. Without a good book it wouldn't work. I've booked you to fly to LA tomorrow. Oh, and I told your grandfather you're coming. They're giving Ben Crossley a part in the film. He wants you to phone him."

"How's his health?"

"The cancer is still in remission. Nora's making a story about you and your famous grandfather. It never stops. This one never stops getting better. You got to feed the media, Randall. Got to keep feeding them... Why you looking so glum?"

"I'm thinking of Nora."

"Nothing to be glum about. She's the best publicist a man can get. You owe a lot to Nora Stewart. Though she did all right out of your film rights. Like keeping it all in the family... We on for dinner?"

"Of course we are, Johnny. Dinner for four. You're all going to be my guests."

MaryJane opened the door of the apartment and flew into Randall's arms. The flat was swank, everything shouting money.

"What's in the small bag, Randall? You won't let it go."

"My new book."

"*Love Song*. Love the title. Can I type it for you? Here, give me the bag. With me it will be as safe as houses. Oh, Randall, it's so good to see you again. A film! Can you believe it? We're working on that title. *Nothing Lasts Forever* was good but not good enough. Not for a writer with a Kranskie film behind him. Kranskie is just about the most famous director/producer in Hollywood. How Nora Stewart does it at her age I have no idea. Rumour is she and Kranskie are as thick as thieves. An old love that has burst back into flames."

"She's not that old."

"Well, past menopause... What's the matter, Randall? Have I said something?... Are we all going out to dinner? Polly can't wait."

"Whose Polly?"

"My friend. She wants so much to meet a famous author."

"But not me."

"What are you talking about? You're the famous author whose book is being made into a film. Just the four of us. I booked us a table."

Randall gave MaryJane the bag with his book. Johnny had taken his suitcase through to the main bedroom. Randall was tired. Very tired. People were exhausting.

"You want to change, Randall, before we go out?"

"No. We're only going to eat. Maybe a drink or two will wake me up. Where's this Polly?"

"She's waiting for us at the restaurant. I'm hungry. You like this place, Randall?"

"Absolutely spiffing."

"What's that mean?"

"Totally unbelievable, MaryJane. An old expression I learnt in Rhodesia from an ex-Indian army colonel who had gone into tobacco farming when the British left India in 1947. He had a million good stories to tell. Now it looks like he might lose his tobacco farm. But he'll always have his memories. Absolutely spiffing."

Everyone but Randall was full of energy. MaryJane took him by the hand and led him to the door. Johnny had gone ahead and found them a taxi that was waiting in front of the building. They all piled in. MaryJane was a good typist but sexually not his type. Neither was Polly. Randall was thinking of Meredith. What she was doing... After the meal and two glasses of wine Randall had had enough. He was mentally and physically exhausted.

"Sorry, folks. I'm lousy company tonight. You mind if I go get myself some sleep?"

"But Randall, the night hasn't yet begun."

"That's the trouble, MaryJane. It has begun. I'm five hours ahead of you. There will always be another day."

"Oh, poor darling. You're dog-tired and we're being selfish."

"Let me pay the bill. You three stay and enjoy yourselves. See you in the morning, Johnny."

"Are you sure, Randall? The night won't be the same without you."

"There's a man dying to meet you up at the bar, MaryJane."

"Which one?"

When MaryJane turned round the man smiled at her. Randall got up from the table and put a hand on Johnny's shoulder. At the desk, Randall paid the bill. When he looked round, the man at the bar had joined the table. They were all talking animatedly. Outside in the street it was beginning to rain. Randall flagged down a taxi. He had written the apartment's address on a piece of paper.

"Got to be organised, Randall Crookshank, or whatever you want to call yourself."

"You talking to me?"

"Can you find that address?"

"Sure I can."

"Then home, James, and don't spare the horses."

"My name isn't James."

"Most probably not."

Back in the flat, alone, Randall gave a deep sigh of relief. He ran himself a bath, got undressed, climbed into the tub and lay back in the warm water. When he woke, the water had gone cold. He felt better... He dried himself and went to his bed. He was soon asleep, back in his dreams, back on the banks of the Zambezi River. Without a toss or a turn, exhausted, Randall slept right through the night. When he woke, the doorbell was ringing, making Randall look at his watch.

"Did I or didn't I change the time?... Coming."

Johnny Stiglitz was smiling.

"Did you sleep?"

"Like a baby."

"We got to go to the airport."

"How was the evening?"

"We all went on to a nightclub. It's all go, Randall. New York rocks. Are you packed? I'll take your new book and give it to MaryJane."

"You will be careful with it?... Never unpacked."

"Come on. The cab's waiting."

"It's all go in America."

"You can say that again."

"Have you ever caught a vundu? It's a fish. I caught one last night. Weighed all of fifty pounds."

"What are you talking about, Randall?"

"My dreams. I caught a fish in my dreams."

PART 5

OCTOBER 1989 TO MAY 1990 — "ON THE
SPUR OF THE MOMENT"

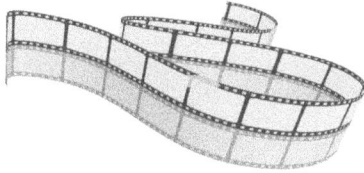

1

"You're on, Mr Becker."

"Can't a man have a shit in peace, Mickey?"

"They're waiting for you. Are you dressed?"

"Of course I'm not. My trousers are round my ankles."

"Mr Kranskie will be getting impatient. He hates being kept waiting."

"Do I have time to wipe my arse?... Are you still there, Mickey?"

"Of course I am. Mr Kranskie told me to go get you. They can't start the next scene without you."

"I need five minutes to get into character. You can't just turn it on and off."

"Of course you can't. Five minutes. I'll tell him. You know which scene it is?"

"Of course I do. I spent three hours memorising what Mark Fletcher has to say. And how he says it."

"I understand, Mr Becker."

"I don't think you do. I don't think any of you do."

Ten minutes later, his hands washed, impeccably dressed, Mark Fletcher walked out of the toilet and strode down the corridor, bursting onto the set, an arrogant man impatient of people. The smile of total confidence was on his face. His back was straight. His mind firing on all cylinders. In the moment that he walked into the story, Julian Becker didn't exist, left behind in the toilet, the words, the voice, the commanding appearance the master of the masters of vanity. He was rich, getting richer with no concern for other people, the world made just for him. Totally unaware of the real world, Mark Fletcher strode across the stage, the dialogue flying. Without interruption they played out his scene. At the end, when it stopped, Mark Fletcher stood still, the film crew looking at him. The silence was pregnant. Slowly, the man changed. The body relaxed. The old, whimsical smile of Julian Becker was back again.

"Good morning, Mr Kranskie. Sorry I was late. How are you all? Did it go all right?... And who, may I ask, are you, young man?"

"Randall Holiday. I wrote the book."

Julian gave the man, who looked in his twenties, a knowing smile. After reading the man's book so many times he knew all about Randall Holiday as well as Mark Fletcher. Authors put themselves into their books.

"Did I get him?"

"I'm not sure. I can see inside my characters as I write them, but I never know exactly what they look like. Filming is all new to me. The only side of a film I ever saw before was in a cinema. It'll take a little time to get used to you being the man who lived in my head. It's a bit as though you've stolen him from me."

"Do you want us to do it again, Mr Kranskie?"

The cameraman looked around at everybody and then back at Felix Kranskie.

"Not for the moment. First, I want to see how it looks on the screen... Right. The next scene is between Deena and her mother... Wanda, are you ready?"

"Yes, Mr Kranskie."

"Can I go, Mr Kranskie?"

"Of course you can, Julian. Why don't you take Randall down to the beach house for the weekend? If we have time, Nora and I will join you."

"Did you like that scene?"

"You'd have heard all about it if I hadn't."

Never quite sure what the director was thinking, Julian took Randall to one side where they waited, watching the new scene unfold. Deena, played by Wanda Worthington, was the sexual interest for Mark Fletcher at the start of the film. She was now talking to her onscreen mother about the man and his money she was hoping to marry. The woman playing the girl's mother came out of context and Felix stopped the filming. The woman tried again. And again. Julian could see she wasn't concentrating.

"You got to stay in the part, Anthea," whispered Julian too far away for the woman to hear him. He was tense, feeling for the woman. Acting was so simple when it went right. Impossible when it went wrong.

Taking the author of the book by the elbow, Julian walked him off the set. It was Friday afternoon, filming almost over for the week, the actor's union laying down the rules. The biggest surprise meeting Randall Holiday was the age of the man. The man was a boy.

"How old are you, Randall? I was expecting to meet a much older man."

"I'll be thirty-two in December."

"How do you know so much about the internal workings of the world's financial system?"

"Observation. Watching people. Reading the magazines and papers from all around the world. I worked in the City of London. Built a fancy apartment building on the Thames, turning a worthless, obsolete industrial site into a place of incredible value. Creating wealth out of nothing. Making so much money out of nothing intrigued me. It's the foundation of capitalism, making the public believe a house or a share is worth vastly more than you paid for it. You create a public competition and appeal to people's inherent greed. The snag comes when the bubble bursts. It happened to me. One minute I was living in a swank apartment bonded to the bank, having invested twenty per cent of my own hard-earned money, the next I was underwater and broke. Not a penny. Before that, my uncle's company had had an associate company in New York. I went over on a visit after winding up the project and stayed longer than I should. Her name was Hayley Oosthuizen but you don't need the details. She wanted me to stay in America. My wife, who had gone off to live with a lesbian, came out to America and surprised me. She supposedly wanted to make a go of our marriage again. Hayley's father had offered me a job with the American company which pissed off my uncle. When I went back to my wife Hayley made sure the American offer was withdrawn, and back in

England my uncle didn't want me working for him anymore. Said I'd been disloyal. Taken a better offer from Tinus Oosthuizen. I was wrong. Uncle Paul was right. I learned a lot about big business in that time in America. Sometimes, you grow up quickly. If you are lucky you don't grow up at all."

"Where are you staying?"

"At the Fairmont Century."

"I've been living in Felix's beach house down the coast since he gave me the part. I have a small, cheap hotel room during the week. I'm saving my money. I've been playing the part of a housekeeper while I read your book over and over, waiting for the scriptwriters to finish the script. When I've finished filming I'm going to get the hell out of the way again. You either lead them, or follow them, or get the hell out of the way. I prefer the simple life I've led for twenty years, bumming my way round the world. But at forty-six I need to make some capital so I can benefit from those masters of vanity who maintain the wealth of your capitalist system. I'm going to retire to the country... Why are you smiling like that, Randall?"

"You and I have a lot more in common than *Masters of Vanity*."

"Let's get the hell out of here and go walk a beach. How long are you staying in America?"

"I have no idea. My publishers own me. I do what I'm told when I'm not hiding away in the country. They tell me I have to be nice to everyone who have made my book so successful. Gratitude. Makes sense. Trouble is, you lose your independence. You belong to your public. And the public can be fickle if you don't behave yourself."

"Do you drink?"

"I do, but I shouldn't. There's an alcoholic in all of us... Will Nora and Felix really come down for the weekend?"

"Probably not."

"I like Nora."

"Ah. I've got it. Our Nora has more sexual pull than is good for her at her age."

"Is she going to marry Felix?"

"Probably not."

"How do we get to the beach house?"

"Don't be silly. This is Hollywood. I'm a big-name actor. Or about to be. You're a big-shot author. We have a car and a chauffeur. Compliments of Felix."

"Sounds perfect."

"Nothing is ever perfect. We learn that as we get older. You wrote one hell of a good book, Randall Holiday. One hell of a book. And we're going to make ourselves one hell of a movie. Trust me. If you are going to do anything in life do it properly. We can talk in the back of the limo. Tell me more about yourself and how you visualise Mark Fletcher. The world's full of shit. Full of predators who take what they want. Too many people with political and financial power like your character in the book. They all lie. They all cheat. They all steal. But people want to be them. Want the lifestyle of the powerful and rich. Chances are, all those smart-arses who run the world will take us all down. They'll either bankrupt us or blow us up. And they lead us around by the nose, poor, simple, ordinary people doing what we are told, hoping to make a living. Sitting alone in my hideaways I've had too much time to think. I wish I could write but I can't. But act I can. I played Hamlet at drama school. Even joined the Bristol Old Vic in England soon after leaving drama school in the States. Another time. Another place. Another life. But it's all in my memory. The plays. The people. Even a girl I once loved when I was young and innocent. When I thought people loved each other for themselves and not for their money. She was an actress. Her name was Holly. She too was on a scholarship to the New York drama school... There's Trent, the chauffeur. Hi, Trent. This is Randall Holiday who wrote the book. Felix has let us go. When can you drive us to the beach house? Good. Then we'll go... In the end Holly went for an older man with a lot of money. She wanted to make her future while she was still good-looking. She dumped me. As soon as I finished drama school I went to England and after that back to America to make my one and only movie. Which I screwed up by screwing the producer's wife. I'm sure you've heard about my fight with Jensen Sandler. He's calmed down a bit since Felix let him buy a ten per cent stake in *Masters of Vanity*... So, Randall. What's life all about?"

"You tell me."

"You have a woman?"

"Her name is Meredith."

"I thought it might be Nora."

"An affair with Nora with the difference in our age would have to come to an end. I respect and like Nora Stewart too much to create a problem in her life. You have to be realistic... What's this beach house like?"

"A small piece of paradise. Not so much the house. The surrounds. How I met Felix. I was living on the beach. I'll show you my lair. I rather think you'll like it, Randall Holiday... Am I going to be all right as Mark Fletcher?"

"I think so. But underneath he's not the shit you think he is. He too was caught up in the system. We all are."

"Unless you get the hell out of the way."

During the drive out of the city both of them were quiet, looking out of their respective windows from the back of Felix Kranskie's limousine. They had driven to the Fairmont and picked up Randall's things. The traffic was bad, people going out of town for the weekend, their hard work at last having a purpose. Julian felt sorry for them. All those hours in an office, followed by a struggle to get out of the city for two days of relaxation, their minds still full of their work and all its problems.

"Poor bastards. What a life. All in pursuit of money." Looking across, Randall seemed not to have heard him.

Once out of the built-up area the car picked up speed. Julian began to relax. The ocean, when it came, was beautiful, the houses along the cliff a soft yellow, washed in the evening sun. To have a man in the car he had only just met, but knew so much about from reading his book, was a strange experience. Trent parked the car, took Randall's luggage into the house and began the drive back to LA. Julian introduced Randall to Romano. Julian went into his bedroom and changed while Romano showed Randall his room. In his shorts and open shirt, Julian was ready for a walk down the beach. When they walked past the swimming pool to the security gate they were both wearing shorts over their swimming costumes, both carrying beach towels and wearing sandals. Julian punched in the security code and led the way out down the path to the beach. The beach was almost empty of people, the sea gently lapping the shore. Out to sea was an ocean-going cruise liner, far enough away for Julian not to be able to see the people on board the ship. A band was playing, the sound of the music drifting to them across the water, the sound irritating Julian.

"I should have invited a couple of girls, Randall."

"Maybe not. Women require all one's attention. I'm not quite ready for people."

"You see those trees in the distance? That was where I lived. A beach bum. To be ignored. Now I'm making a film."

They walked on, both of them feeling uncomfortable, neither of them knowing what to expect from the other. Strangers, with only the book and the movie in common. Julian racked his brain for something to say that would break the tension.

"What made your family leave England and go out to Africa?"

"How did you know?"

"You're in the public domain. People know you come from Zimbabwe. It's all in the papers if you bother to read them."

"It's a long story."

"I like long stories. Why I liked your book."

"Why did your ancestors come to America? For an adventure? To escape poverty? In the hope of finding a future? When we are young we all think the grass is greener on the other side of the fence. My father says that after the war England was grim, everything rationed and jobs difficult to find. There wasn't any money in England anymore. No one then realised the British Empire had come to an end. India got its independence two years later in 1947, which my father said should have warned him. Before the war, my grandfather had met a farmer from Rhodesia who had been a pilot in the Royal Flying Corps during the First World War. Grandfather lived on the Isle of Wight and was chief engineer for Short Brothers who made the Solent Short flying boat. The Rhodesian was the test pilot on a long flight to a lake in Switzerland. Grandfather flew with him and they became firm friends. When Grandfather went down in his sailing boat at Dunkirk, Harry Brigandshaw helped my family. Harry was rich from the family company he inherited in England. I'm not quite sure why he had come to England between the two world wars but he still owned Elephant Walk, his farm in Rhodesia. I think there was a management problem making Harry leave his farm and come back to live in England. The company is the same company now run by my uncle Paul, who is married to Beth, Harry Brigandshaw's daughter. It's the same company I worked for on the Westcastle project next to the River Thames. Instead of joining Harry's

English company my father went out to Rhodesia and met my mother. He had heard so many stories about Africa from Harry. If he hadn't gone to Africa I wouldn't have come into this world. The chance of life is pretty slim. Only after my father had been farming for some years did Rhodesia, a self-governing British colony, declare itself unilaterally independent from Britain. By then Ceylon, Burma, Malaya and most of Britain's African colonies had been given their independence. In a matter of twenty years Britain had become a country of little consequence in the world. It was all Soviet Russia and the capitalist United States. I was seven years old when UDI was declared. My father had married again after my mother was killed by a pride of lions soon after I was born. In 1980, along came Robert Mugabe after a seven-year bush war, and Rhodesia became Zimbabwe. No one in Zimbabwe quite knows the future but they all hope. I gave up hope after our farm was attacked by terrorists at the end of the war. Life has strange twists and turns for all of us. No one really knows what's going to happen to them. Most of it's chance. Like you meeting Nora and Felix on this beach."

"They were skinny-dipping,"

"I don't believe it... Why are we stopping?"

"This was my lair under the trees, where I was living... Are you going back to Zimbabwe to live now you've made so much money out of your writing?"

"My heart wants to. My brain warns me against it. At the end of his life, when he knew he was dying, Harry Brigandshaw went back to Elephant Walk. Africa has a strong pull on all of us who have been part of it. It becomes more than just our home. Yes, one day, when Africa stabilises, I'd like to go home. It's a wonderful place to have a family. Towns are too full of people, always on top of you. In London or New York you can't get away from people. I prefer the peace of the bush on the banks of an African river... You mind if I take a swim?"

"You go ahead, Randall Holiday."

"My real name is Randall Crookshank. Holiday was my publisher's idea."

"For a man your age you've had quite a run."

"I just hope there are more places to run to. More things to do. One day soon I'm going to run out of writing material... I like your spot. The kind of place a man can think."

"Where do you think the world is going?"

"That's something nobody in history has ever been able to predict. You just go through it as best you can... You coming for a swim?"

"Why not?"

"Glad we came down to the beach house. Gives me time to reorientate myself to life in America. It's different to England. And very different to Africa. You know, I still miss my cat. That night of the terrorist attack they killed my cat. Just missed me. Not only would they have killed me, Julian, but you'd still be living under those trees."

"It's not all bad."

"What my friend Oliver Manningford always says. He's also an actor. As well as Nora, I asked Mr Kranskie to give him a part in the movie. And a part for my friend James Tomlin. My son's name is James Oliver. My two friends are his godparents. You ever been dumped twice for a woman, Julian?"

"Not even once."

"He's a toddler. Makes you think."

"We should open a bottle of whisky when we get back to the house. It'll stop all this serious thinking."

"Now you're talking. But before we start drinking I want to phone my grandfather. He's also got a part in the movie. You see, that bullet that killed my cat could have changed so much for so many people if they'd hit me instead of my pussy cat. You ever loved an animal, Julian? And had the animal love you back? All part of living on a farm in Africa. Everything is natural. In a city, everything you do is artificial. You even walk on pavement and never touch the soil. Horrible. Not the life that was intended for us. You got to see the trees. Smell the ocean. Hear the birds. Without Mother Nature what would we be? Sometimes I think the modern world so many people crave is turning us all into robots. Or money-grabbers where materialism is the only path we go, chasing more and more of this money we try to store away, something we probably can't do. How do you store forever an entry on a bank account statement? Or store value in a share certificate that says you own a piece of a company you have never seen? Everything in the modern world is done on trust. Can you really trust other people? I don't think so when it comes to money. Does a diamond really have value? Or a bar of gold? They're only worth what another man will pay for them. You can't eat them or love them. They are made of material. Money only has value when we turn it into food, into warm clothing, into a comfortable home. And does it matter how big and impressive the home is, once you are comfortable? Were you not comfortable under the trees? You're an educated man, Julian. You could have made yourself a fancy career. But you chose to live under a tree because it was comfortable. I envy your life as a bum far more than your life as a big-shot Hollywood actor. I hate being a successful writer. I love writing my books but I hate the consequences. I was once a bum waiting tables, happily living with Amanda in a bedsitter. The best time of our lives together."

"But you got to have money for your old age, Randall. I don't want the money as much as its protection. Money gives you protection from the problems of life."

"Why are we never satisfied?"

"You tell me."

To Julian, the man was becoming an enigma, the look in Randall's face so far away. For a man who looked so young, being so sad was wrong. Instead of running down to the water's edge and jumping into the sea with joy, the author walked slowly across the sand and into the water. Deciding he didn't want a swim after all, Julian sat down on the sand. The sun was colouring red as it left their world. The breeze had come up. Julian shivered, a premonition, as if someone had walked over his grave. The young man down in the water was in pain. With all that was happening to him he should have been happy, enjoying the pleasures of life. Julian watched Randall swim slowly out into the ocean before swimming back and walking up the beach, picking up his towel, drying his hair and shaking the water out of his ears. On the man's face was the same, faraway look of sadness. Of loss. Of finding no hope in what he was doing.

"You all right, Randall?"

"Never been better. Why didn't you come in?" The eyes looking at Julian said something different.

"The wind came up."

Slowly, side by side, Randall still in his bathing costume carrying his shorts and his sandals, the towels over their shoulders, they walked back up the beach to Felix Kranskie's beach house. Julian punched in the security code at the gate. The sun was down, the sky slashed in red, red clouds pointing like daggers across the pale-blue sky. At Julian's request, Romano had put a bottle of whisky and two glasses with a bucket of ice out on the table next to the pool.

"How you like your whisky, Randall?" Julian unscrewed the cap on the bottle and threw the metal cap over his shoulder, causing the author to frown, not at the open bottle of whisky but the piece of rubbish on the ground.

"I've drunk it neat. I've drunk it with soda. I've drunk it with lots of ice and water. It's what the damn stuff does to me that's the worry."

The wind was going down with the sun, the air was warm and only the music coming from the house next door was an irritant. Julian got up, picked the cap off the ground and put it in his pocket, making Randall smile. Julian looked across at the neighbour's house.

"Why do people have to play their music so damn loud?"

"They want attention, mostly."

"Pour your own, Randall."

"Thanks, Julian... There, now that looks good. To your health, to hell with your wealth. Glad to meet you. And yes, you're going to make one hell of a Mark Fletcher. They'll be all over you like a rash, offering you new parts in a dozen movies... So, here's to the famous actor. May you always prosper. Down the hatch, Julian. It's time to do some drinking and forget our trials and tribulations. Let's have some fun."

"Welcome to America."

Bit by bit, they were getting to know each other. People, thought Julian, were not that different. The man was right. A litter bug was a litter bug whether or not he had a servant to pick up the rubbish or not. In his not-so-distant past, when someone left an empty bottle on the beach he had picked it up and put it in the bin.

Romano, always looking after the guests, brought out a tray of snacks and put them on the white wrought-iron table. They both smiled their thanks at Romano.

"You want a meal later, Julian?"

"Probably not, Romano."

The drinking began.

"Tell me all about Holly. The first love is usually the one we remember... These snacks are good. Mr Kranskie is lucky to have him."

"Would you have liked to be a servant?"

"We're all servants, Julian. I write for my readers, the same way Romano made those snacks for us. We're all working for someone."

"Beach bums don't work for anyone."

Forgetting the drinks, the snacks and Randall Holiday, Julian went back into his memory. They had been young. Both of them innocent. Holly was eighteen when he first met her in drama school in New York. They were both exactly the same age, sharing the same birthday, the quirk that had brought them together. Still not old enough to legally go out to drink in the clubs, Julian's friends had thrown him a party.

"Is it really your birthday? It's my birthday too. How old are you?" She had a smile that lit up the room for Julian.

"Eighteen."

"Now that is a coincidence. You and I are born on exactly the same day."

He could still see her face. Exactly as it was on the day of the party. They were both shy, the coincidence breaking their shyness, drawing them together, making the first, stumbling conversation that much easier. Outwardly, they appeared confident. Inwardly they couldn't think of anything to say that wouldn't sound silly among their friends, where the best party conversation was always the most trivial. Unlike some of her friends, Holly had one drink the entire party, Julian getting drunk, egged on by his friends. Only afterwards, away from other people, did the two of them talk, two youngsters in a strange city far from home. She was beautiful, no doubt about it, but underneath there was something for Julian that was far more important: they were going to be friends. A month later, when they found each other's bodies, they found another similarity: they were both virgins. In the months to come, Holly convinced herself she was never going to make a career out of acting. Her teacher, when asked directly, had admitted that only six per cent of drama school students were still in the theatre five years after leaving the college. Despite Julian saying the woman had to be wrong, it had taken the passion away from Holly, making her look at her life and her future and where she was going, the money word creeping into her conversation. From then on she drifted away from him. By the time she went off with the older man who had made a pile of money in New York City before he was thirty, Julian had joined the ranks of the cynical. From then on, women had been physical for Julian. Sexual partners. Never more than convenient superficial friends. When he made a success out of his first movie and screwed the producer's young wife, he had lost all hope of finding more in a woman than sexual satisfaction. When Jensen Sandler chased him out of the acting business in a rage of jealousy and humiliation, Julian had gone on the road, exploiting his charm and attraction for women, never once getting emotionally involved with anyone.

"You ever had a flash, Randall, of something better in this life? That was me and Holly. That one, brief flash of hope that I still so clearly remember and never stumbled over again. Looking back I now know it was love. I was lucky. Most of us never love anyone in our lives. We tell them we love them when we want something out of them... How's your drink going down?"

"Far too well."

"When we get into the real world we find there isn't any lasting emotional softness, that a material reason is somewhere lurking in the background."

"What happened to Holly?"

"She married her rich man."

"Did she stay with him?"

"Don't be silly. He was screwing around like the rest of us. She waited her time, collected her evidence and took him to the cleaners in the divorce court. It was all over the papers, in America as well as England. By then he'd really made himself rich."

"Did you ever see her again?"

"I thought we might get back together again. Find our old magic. When she saw I was broke without an acting future my Holly wasn't interested. All that money had made her as hard as nails."

"Was she happy?"

"Only the good Lord knows."

"You'd better watch it, Julian. Once I became a successful writer, Amanda came back to me bringing my son, smiles all over her face."

"Did you want her back?"

"Yes. But not for her reason. You be careful with Holly. *Masters of Vanity*, the film, can well make you screaming famous... Do you think one bottle is going to be enough? The thought of having to do all those publicity performances is making me sick. All that self-adulation. I hate being interviewed for television. Appearing ever so humble and having the interviewer gush all over you. Enough to make a man puke. But it's all about being a successful writer. The book is only a minor part of the equation. The reality is exposure to as many people as possible. Nora understands. Why I love our Nora. She tells me it's all an act and to forget about making people think I'm wonderful so they'll read my book. I call it arse-creeping. My publishers call it business."

"So you think Holly might try to get back in my life?"

"If she isn't married, she will."

"She'll be forty-six. We share the same day and year of birth."

"Have another drink, Julian. This whisky is tasting so good and we don't have far to stumble to get to our beds. At this stage in the drinking I don't give a care about my tomorrow's monstrous hangover. I'm getting drunk, Julian."

"So am I."

"Here's to Holly."

"Here's to Amanda."

"Do you think we'll ever be happy again?"

"Most probably not. To women, Randall. You can't live with them and you can't live without them. Life and lust are pretty much fundamental. Without the lust of a man for a woman, and the lust of a woman for a man, mankind would not even exist. It's the fundamental building block of life. Something so obvious but somehow dirty that they tell us to sweep it under the carpet and look at life through the noble eyes of righteousness. They give us rules to abide by to protect the moral righteousness of mankind. Build it into our minds from an early age. They put the fear of God into us to make us behave ourselves. To give us self-control. Or end up in the burning fire of hell for all eternity. One way or another we are all being manipulated but don't let that interrupt our drinking."

With the second bottle of whisky, Romano brought them a tray of small sausages, with a stick stuck in the middle of each. Julian smiled. They both ate the sausages in between swigs of whisky. The sun had long gone down. The music from next door had stopped. Both of them were drunk, talking a whole lot of rubbish and enjoying themselves, their lives in the present, the past and future of no importance. Luckily for both of them they got up to go to their beds before opening the second bottle of whisky.

"It was the sausages, Randall. You got to eat when you're drinking."

"Drink two pints of water before you go to sleep. Helps the hangover."

"Did we solve any of life's problems?"

"I don't think so... To bed, to sleep, perchance to dream?"

"What would we ever have done without William Shakespeare?"

Julian helped Randall stumble away from his chair. Together, arm in arm, more for support than companionship, they made their way into the house and parted, heading for their respective bedrooms. From Randall's room came a bang and a slap and the one word 'bugger'. Julian smiled, drank some of the water Romano had left by the side of his bed and took off his clothes. He was well and truly drunk. On his back under the covers Julian thought of Holly. He was still thinking of Holly when he drifted off into sleep.

2

The next Julian knew, it was morning. He was woken by Romano with a hot cup of coffee.

"Mr Kranskie and Miss Stewart have arrived. They are asking after you."

"How is the guest?"

"He broke a chair on his way into bed. How are you, Julian?"

"Still drunk. Why do we drink, Romano?"

"A foolish habit. Did you escape from yourselves last night round the pool?"

"All the way. By the end of the bottle I had no recollection of myself whatsoever."

"Then the evening was a success."

"Where are they?"

"Having a swim."

Romano left to organise the breakfast, a superior look on his face. Mouth parched, Julian drank his coffee, got out of bed and dressed himself. The day had begun. The game was on again. The game of films, money and people.

"You're right, Randall. We were happier as bums."

Outside in the corridor Julian found a dishevelled Randall blinking his eyes.

"Do I look as bad as I feel?"

"Nora's here with Felix. We're both back on duty."

"I feel like a piece of shit."

"Better go back and tidy yourself. It's all about appearances."

"There's always a price to pay for everything. I enjoyed last night. Don't remember the end of it. There's a broken chair in my room. Probably me. Sorry. They say the biggest problem for an alcoholic is not having hangovers. So I'll survive. Are they on their own?"

"Probably not. When making a film, I'm told, Felix likes to travel with an entourage. Keeps him focused."

"See you later. Make excuses for me. I'm going to stick a finger down my throat and try and be sick. Oh, for the peace of Africa. I hate having to be polite with a hangover."

By the time Julian walked out into the garden and across the lawn to the swimming pool, his back was straight, his look confident, a man in control. Once again he was Mark Fletcher for all the people gathered round the sparkling pool, the ocean beyond, the sun warm, a few light, fluffy clouds up in the sky. He was back playing his part. An old man was watching his approach, a look of understanding in a wise old pair of eyes. The man's white hair was long, down to his shoulders. A white beard covered most of his face. His clothes were different to the rest of the party, reminding Julian of the way people dressed in the eighteenth century. The man cut away and met Julian before Julian reached the pool. The man's right hand was outstretched. He smiled, their eyes meeting as Julian shook the outstretched hand.

"You must be Julian Becker. Where's that reprobate grandson of mine? My name is Ben Crossley. More out of politeness than anything, they've given me a small part in your movie."

"It's not my movie."

"But it will be. Felix showed me yesterday's shoot. For some reason he wanted my opinion. Nice of him to ask me to the lunch party. Everyone's here. My goodness, you remind me of myself when I was young. So, where is he?"

"An hour or so ago, he was in his room throwing up. Don't tell Nora. It's all my fault. I got him drunk."

"He's not meant to drink alcohol."

"So he said. We wanted to get to know each other. I wanted to find out more about Mark Fletcher. How are you, Mr Crossley? Or do we call you Ben?"

"My cancer is still in remission. Surprisingly for me, life goes on. Poor Randall. His wife went off with a woman and stole his son. What a sad life we all have. At my age, I look back and wonder what it was all about."

"So do I, Ben. So do I."

"Then we're going to be friends. Let's go across and talk to Nora. Without Nora none of this would have happened. Does he know how much he has made from the film rights?"

"I don't think so... Hello, Nora. Randall's on his way. You look absolutely fabulous."

"You old flatterer. Felix liked yesterday's filming. Looks good, Mark Fletcher. So, here we are again. Back where it all started. Come and mingle. The party is just getting started."

When Julian looked round for Ben the old man was walking across the lawn with his back to the party. Julian watched him go into the house to look for his grandson. It gave Julian a spasm of jealousy. He had no family himself. For a long moment, Julian stood wondering what had happened to his grandparents and all those other people in his biological history that had boiled down to him. Randall was lucky. He had a grandfather concerned about him. And, like so many other things that had gone wrong in Julian's life, it was all his own fault.

"What's the matter, Julian?"

"Life's very lonely on your own... Come on. Let's join the party. I need a drink... Have you been to see a plastic surgeon, or is that the wrong question, Nora?"

"Of course I have. With all the money I made from the film I had to do something with it. What's the use of money sitting in the bank? He's a friend of Felix's. Many film stars wouldn't get parts without all the nips and tucks. All my facial wrinkles have gone... Where's Randall? He should be mingling... So, what you think? Do I look like a woman of forty?"

"Not a day over thirty-five."

"Good. Then money has a purpose. We only have one life. Might as well make the best of it. Randall told me on the phone he's finished another book. This is going to be some party. Everyone from the movie is here. Scriptwriters to meet Randall. All the actors. The media are over on the other side of the pool. Felix invited them. You look good. A man of substance. Get ready for the cameras. What did you two do last night? Here they come. Why is it you rarely see one person with a camera? There's always a phalanx competing with each other. Get ready to play Mark Fletcher, the star of your movie. Don't forget, Julian, I'm your publicist."

"Didn't you invite the media?"

"I gave Felix a list of people to phone. He likes to be in control. They all want to interview Randall. The way he disappeared fascinated the press. They think he's hiding a good story."

"Poor Randall."

"What's the matter?"

"I got him drunk. It's all my fault. Do you know, Randall hates people. Especially people he doesn't know."

"Does he know how much money he's made?"

"He didn't mention it. I don't think money interests Randall. He likes the peace and quiet of solitude so he can think and write. We have a lot in common. His grandfather has gone to talk to him. When he hears the vultures are waiting, our author is going to want to make a run for it. Multiple questions don't go down too well on a hangover."

"I've got people asking about you, Julian. All the backchat with Jensen Sandler has made you interesting. There's a lot more to come for Julian Becker. But first we finish *Masters of Vanity*... Here he comes. Oh, dear. He looks awful."

"He broke a chair stumbling into bed. You'd better go and help him. Did you know he has a thing for you, Nora? Oh, that look speaks louder than words. You like our Randall. Naughty girl. Now, off you go. And remember, you're only as old as you feel... Gentlemen and ladies. How are we today? My name is Julian Becker, masquerading as Mark Fletcher. Now, please. One question at a time."

It was all one big game and none of it very interesting. The chit-chat began. A waiter with a tray of drinks offered Julian a drink. The beer was cold and still in the bottle. It tasted good. The trick was to drink just enough to conquer the hangover. Wanda Worthington gave him a wave. The press were moving past him, making Julian look round. Randall looked positively awful. His grandfather had a hand on his shoulder. Nora broke from the party and walked towards Randall. Randall saw the approaching media and looked over his shoulder. Nora gave him a light kiss on his lips and took him by the arm. Randall was trapped. Julian felt sorry for him. The young man was a writer, not a means to further the film's publicity. Julian caught Randall's eye and gave him a smile of encouragement. Randall looked desperate. The vultures had landed. They had got him. The same waiter offered Randall a drink. Randall took the nearest glass and drank it down. His grandfather frowned. Nora, talking ten-to-the-dozen to the press, hadn't noticed. Wearily, Randall took another drink off the tray, took a sip, smiled around and looked up at the sky before walking forward to answer all the questions. Julian had forgotten the man had once been in commerce, had a degree in economics. Randall was back in business, doing what he should for the common good. He looked at his grandfather and again at Nora, smiling at both of them, the look telling them both he knew his duty. Wanda had taken Julian's arm, coming up on him from behind.

"When are we really getting together, Julian?"

The girl had snuggled up into his arm. Together, the two of them joined the party round the pool, leaving Randall and Nora to the media.

"Who's the man surrounded by the press?"

"The writer. The poor bastard who wrote the book."

"Oh, good. Can I meet him?"

"Get in the queue, Wanda."

"Felix said we looked so good together, Julian. I'm going to be a star. Isn't it wonderful? Don't look so sad."

Half an hour later, when Randall had had his third drink, everyone was happy, the news cameras flashing, the reporters scribbling away, Nora's new face smiling, everything going as planned. Even Felix Kranskie looked pleased with the party, free publicity being every film director's dream. What it did to the life of the young man from Africa, no one really cared. They all had what they wanted. The money machine was back in play.

FELIX KRANSKIE WRAPPED up the film in the spring, a third of his budget spent on publicity, the advertising making Julian famous, a name on everyone's lips. Nora's finale was the première, every vulture in the media industry coming in for the kill to interview and photograph the stars, all the usual suspects walking up the red carpet to promote themselves as much as the film. Jensen Sandler, no longer Julian's antagonist, was happy with his ten per cent investment, shaking Julian's hand in front of the cameras. It was all one big publicity stunt after another, one big competition, everyone desperate for attention, big smiles and self-deprecation, everyone feeding off each other's celebrity. Happy with the money now safely in his bank account, Julian joined in the game. All through the evening, he hoped to see Randall Holiday, but there was no sign or talk of the author, neither Nora nor Felix mentioning him. Felix, radiant with Wanda Worthington on his arm, was the centre of attention. Nora looked sad, Julian suspecting her affair with Felix, like the film, was over. When the lights came up, Nora sitting next to him, Julian was ready to go.

"Let's get out of here, Nora. It's finished. Over. Our work is done. Is he, to put it politely, dating Wanda? She's young enough to be his granddaughter."

"But she wants to be a movie star. She wants to be famous."

"Are you upset?"

"I've learnt to take life as it comes. We had some fun. Made some memories. What more can a girl expect?"

"Why didn't Randall come to the première? His grandfather is here. How is the old man? He looks tired. Old age gets to people. You want to make a bolt to a nice, small restaurant I know that's cheap, pleasantly insignificant, the food the best of Italian, and no one will find us?"

"Are you asking me out?"

"Friends, Nora. You're my publicist. Let's have some fun. Celebrate now I have enough money to buy a place for myself away from the crowd."

"But you're going to do more movies? The press reviews are going to praise you to the sky. The important columnists had a preview so I know what they are going to say in tomorrow's newspapers."

"Maybe. Maybe not."

"He went back to Zimbabwe. He's living in a cottage on his father's farm without a phone. Oliver Manningford and James Tomlin were there tonight, but not Randall. They say they haven't heard from him. The man's become a recluse."

"Is he writing?"

"Probably."

"Are they publishing more of his books?"

"The one about his lesbian wife is due out before Christmas. They're calling it *Nothing Lasts Forever*. Henry Stone hasn't put the same amount of advertising money behind it as he did for *Masters of Vanity*. With the author out of the way, and not prepared to make a book tour, the publishers are inclined to lose interest. Randall says he's got enough money to last him two lifetimes. He's not interested in what goes on with the publishing. His first love is Africa. Good luck to him. Right now, like you, I've had enough of this... You'll have to wave at everyone and make a grand exit into the limo. Round the corner we'll jump out of the car and catch a cab. Freedom, Julian. Did you like the standing ovation at the end of the movie? Nothing more I can do for them now. My work is done. So is yours. Let's get the hell out of everyone's way. Are you still in those cheap digs I've so carefully kept from the press? I miss Randall. He was the one real person among this whole charade, some of it my own work... Why don't we go back to my flat and I'll cook you a late supper? Home-cooked food. When did you last have home-cooked food, Julian? Now smile. They are pointing the cameras at you. They want that big one for their papers tomorrow. Felix thinks we are going to gross ten million dollars this weekend. Why Jensen Sandler was so happy to shake your hand."

"What's it going to be?"

"Bacon and eggs. And an evening of peace."

"Was it all worth it, Nora?"

"I don't know. You tell me. Are you talking about the movie or are you talking about life? For a brief moment I thought Felix and I would have something permanent. Be able to grow old together when the rest of the game was over. Now I'm empty. All that new money in the bank but Nora Stewart is empty. Nothing. Nothing now or in the future. All the plastic surgeons in the world can't alter your real age... Do you ever get lonely in a crowd, Julian? That's how I feel tonight. In all this lavish world we see around us tonight, there's nothing of real value. None of it ever lasts."

Nora, instead of crying, was trying to smile. Putting on a face. Taking her hand, Julian walked her out of the theatre and into the limousine hired for the occasion.

"Round the block, Trent, find us a cab and the rest of the night is yours."

"As you say, Julian. How did it go?"

"They all loved it. America's going to love it. So is the world. People like a movie about successful people and they like it better when a thief gets his comeuppance. Exit Mark Fletcher. Welcome the old Julian Becker from down on the beach."

"It all looked good from where I was sitting in the limo."

"You're a good driver. A good friend."

"Just doing my job. Earning a salary. There's a cab over there. Have a good evening. You're a star, Julian. Something, however hard you try, they'll never let you forget. There's a price to pay for everything. You two go and enjoy yourselves in private. You deserve it. You've both made a lot of people a lot of money. Look after yourselves. If you don't work with Mr Kranskie on another film, this is probably the last time Trent will drive you."

"Enjoy the rest of your life, Trent."

"I'll try."

IN THE BACK of the car, while Trent was talking, Julian had been holding Nora's hand, trying to give her comfort. He helped Nora out onto the pavement. The cab driver was waiting, the backdoor to his cab open. Julian put his hand through the open window of the limousine and gave Trent's shoulder a squeeze. He too had his problems. His wife, sick of his inability to move up in the world, had left him. Trent, unlike Randall, didn't have any children. In that he was lucky... Nora gave the cab driver the address of her apartment. Looking back, there was no sign of the limousine. Trent was back in the heavy traffic among the crowds of people, the only thing left of their friendship the memory of their deep conversations alone at the Kranskie beach house. Life was sad. So transient. So temporary.

When they arrived at the apartment block, towering skyscrapers all round them, Nora, on the side nearest the sidewalk, got out first. This time there was no doubt: Nora was crying. When he came round and joined her on the pavement, he again took her hand, gently wiping the tears from the top of her new cheeks.

"What's the whole damn point in living, Julian?"

"Let's go upstairs and find out. One door closes, Nora, and another opens."

"Are you coming on to me?"

"I thought you'd never notice. From that time in my lair on the beach when you enjoyed my mint tea, there was something between us. Whatever it was, let's go upstairs and enjoy it. For one night we don't have to worry about other people. What they are doing or what they are thinking."

"There's one thing about it. With all that money in your bank account you've so carefully saved, you won't have to dry your teabags and make them stretch to three cups of tea."

"You remembered."

"I couldn't believe it. This is America."

"You never know. In an unstable world, however much the politicians try to tell us different, who knows if one day I'll be back drying my tea bags? And you know, that third cup of tea was always the best when it was the last of the tea."

"Which life is better? Now or then?"

"Then, definitely. Ask Randall. I'll bet he's sitting in that cottage under the African sun right now, writing away, happy with his life and himself... That's better, Nora. You're smiling. Your tears have gone."

"Who was that woman who came up to you when you first got out of Trent's limo? She seemed to know you well."

"Her name was Holly. We used to be more than friends. Like you and Felix."

"Are you going to see her again?"

"I don't think so. What she wanted from me was my fame. She didn't want me. Randall warned me. When he made all that money, Amanda wanted him back. Why are people so materialistic?"

"Part of human nature."

"Isn't bacon and eggs a bit too British?"

"That was Randall. He liked it with pork sausages and tomatoes."

"Do you have sausages?"

"Come and find out. Welcome to my home, Julian Becker."

"Thank you for the privilege."

At the open door, Julian bowed, Nora curtsied, and both of them laughed. Inside, the door shut and locked, they were safe from the world. Nora put on some classical music, the music both gentle and beautiful. The curtains were drawn, the one standard lamp the only light in the room. Julian, watching Nora pour them a drink, was thinking of Holly. That first re-encounter was horrible, probably for both of them. Julian had thought her a fan. The woman was old, despite all the glitter she was wearing.

"You don't recognise me, do you, Julian?"

"Now I do. It's the voice. Your voice hasn't changed. It's Holly. How are you, Holly?"

"But everything else has changed?"

"I'm sorry, Holly. You caught me unawares. This is my opening night."

"Of course it is. I'm so proud of you. One of the six per cent. Top of the class. You made it, Julian. Don't you want to take me with you into the cinema? You don't have a wife and you're not with a woman. I'm sure for the big star of the night they'll find me a seat next to you right up at the front. You remember how we talked about being stars in drama school?"

"I can't, Holly. Everything tonight is planned."

"You could if you wanted to."

"You left me for a man with lots of money."

"I'm sorry."

"Have you come to see me or the man in the headlines?"

"Oh, Julian. I'd so love to be with you."

"They're calling me. Got to go."

"Are we ever going to see each other again?"

"I don't think that thought has entered your head for years."

"Why are you being so horrible?"

"You've got plenty of money. You don't need me."

"Do I look that different?"

"We were young. Two Americans wrapped up in Shakespearean theatre. It's over. Has been ever since you dumped me, Holly."

In a hurry, with the news cameras trained on him, Julian walked away, leaving the only love of his entire life standing alone, no one taking any notice of her. When Julian looked back she looked at him hatefully. In that look, the myth of Holly exploded. He was free of her. The girl that had stayed in his mind for so many years had gone, replaced by a tarted-up, middle-aged woman with hatred written deep in her eyes, for once not getting what she wanted.

When Nora put the glass of whisky in his hand, with the right amount of ice and water just as he liked it, he was unable to speak. A part of him, a treasured part that had lifted up his spirits in the darker moments of his life while bumming around the world alone, had gone. Torn to pieces. Shattering the best of his dreams. He sipped the drink, shook his head, the long hair moving across his shoulders, and put down the drink on the small side-table next to where he was sitting.

"Now you're the one looking sad, Julian. What's the matter?"

"Holly. We were so young. I've never since loved another person. Maybe I was lucky. The beautiful girl of eighteen has turned into a bitch. She knew all about me. My not being married, not having a girlfriend. That once, so long ago, beautiful young woman, has turned into a scheming bitch... Come and sit next to me. Who's the composer?"

"Haydn. When I get the blues I close the door and put on a Haydn symphony. Within a few minutes I feel better. Music like this is so uplifting... Do you think she'll try and find you again?"

"I hope not."

"They call them stalkers when they check up on you like that."

"The price of fame. No wonder Randall made a run for it into the middle of nowhere. He showed me the area where his father farms on the map. It's up on the Zambezi escarpment. You can't run further than that."

"Cheers, Julian. To a wonderful success. May you have lots more of them."

"Thank you for everything, Nora. With my new money I can buy my freedom, be at peace. You know the most important thing in this life, Nora Stewart? It's being at peace with yourself. I had it once while living in my lairs. And I'm going to have it again."

"Can I come with you?"

"Only if you find peace. Something you won't find in your business."

"So I've got to give it all up? No, I couldn't do that. My work is who I am. You and Randall are artists. I'm just a businesswoman in the business of making everyone who hires me lots and lots of money. Money that makes the world go round. However much you try, you can't live without money in this lovely world of ours."

"So you won't run away with me?"

"Maybe tonight."

"Are you really going to cook bacon and eggs?"

"Only if you are hungry for food."

"You're flirting with me, Nora."

"Of course I am."

She sat down next to him, both of them comfortable with each other's company, both of them with a drink in their hands, listening to the music. Julian took Nora's free hand, gently fingering the palm. From outside they could just hear the New York traffic, a raw hum beneath the tranquillity of the orchestra. Despite trying not to, Julian was back thinking of Holly. Once, sometime after they had started going out together, they had travelled up to London and had gone to the first Night of the Proms at the Royal Albert Hall, the centre of London's music. They had stood in the standing-room-only part of the auditorium with all the young, impoverished and happy Londoners. By then they had been lovers for months. Inwardly, Julian sighed. Nora was feeling the inside of his hand, both of them miles away in their memories. The second drink came with the end of the Haydn symphony. The third, a good slosh of whisky poured by Julian, with the end of a song by Frank Sinatra. In the silence between the different pieces of music the traffic sounded louder. By the end of the fourth drink neither of them were interested in food. By the end of the fifth stiff whisky they were falling all over each other, both of them in the present, the dreams forgotten, the physical need imperative. They got up from the couch and, holding hands, walked into Nora's bedroom. Nora had turned out the light. The curtain was drawn, the apartment in darkness, only a faint light from outside penetrating the chinks in the curtain. They both took off their clothes and got into bed. Slowly, gently they aroused each other, building into a frenzy, a final rush that ended in a climax for both of them. They lay back, side by side, Julian never more sexually satisfied. Holding hands, neither spoke a word, no reason for words from either of them. For that moment, both of them were at peace, with each other, and the world. All the dark side of life had gone for Julian, Holly's look of hatred no longer worrying him. The whisky made Julian want to sleep, the soft happiness with Nora next to him wanting him to stay awake as long as possible. When Julian woke in the night, he was still lying on his back. They were still holding hands.

"Are you awake, Nora?"

"Did you drift off?"

"That was the best sex of my life."

"Wasn't too bad for me."

"Now we really are friends."

"You can say that again. You know, they say you should never mix business with pleasure. We've broken the golden rule, Julian."

"I don't care."

"Neither do I. Are you hungry?"

"I could eat some bacon and eggs. Just no more whisky. I hate hangovers. You're incredible, Nora. Just plain incredible."

"Maybe a little soft music?"

"I'd love some music."

In the dark, they both pulled on their clothes. They were happy. Both of them were happy. The traffic had gone down, the hum not so intrusive. Nora put on another piece of her classical music, turning down the volume. They went into the kitchen.

"You've got to think of the neighbours. The thing I hate most living in an apartment is the sound of my neighbours, their music or their arguments. Why do people only think of themselves?"

The food was ready quicker than Julian had expected, Nora as efficient with her cooking as she was with her business. They sat at the small kitchen table, eating in silence, both of them hungry, concentrating on the food. When they had cleaned their plates of food they went back to bed. They were soon sound asleep, Julian sleeping dreamlessly through the rest of the night.

In the morning, when Nora checked her messages, the other world thrust back into their lives, shattering their moment of peace.

"Got to go, Julian. A publicist's work is never finished. Can you find your way back to your digs?"

"I hope so." Julian was smiling. Nora had showered and dressed, her make-up reapplied and was ready for business, a brief thought of Randall on his African farm making Julian envious.

"Are you going to take the part Jensen Sandler offered you?"

"I don't think so. Once bitten, twice shy."

"What about the others?"

"Let me think."

"Don't leave it too long. Another cliché – strike while the iron is hot. People have short memories. What's on your agenda for today?"

"Absolutely nothing, I'm pleased to say. You want to go to lunch?"

"Not today. You want to look at my work schedule?"

"Not particularly."

"It just never stops. Success, however much some people think otherwise, only comes with hard work and attention to every detail. What are you going to do today?"

"Think of you. Our night together. Is there more to us, Nora?"

"Only time will tell."

"Let's go down in the lift together. That was a night to remember."

When they parted outside the building, Nora getting into a cab with her briefcase, Julian stood on the pavement and watched the taxi move out into the traffic, Nora quickly lost in the rush and bustle of the day. It made Julian feel sad. No one in the modern world had time to savour anything. The sun was shining high above the tall buildings, the air dulled by the traffic's pollution. Looking up it was difficult to see the real blue of the morning sky. Julian began to walk down the pavement, avoiding the oncoming people bent on the start of another day's work. He walked aimlessly for half an hour thinking of Nora, thinking of Holly, thinking of what he wanted to do with the rest of his life. Did Nora want a future with an actor, a one-time itinerant bum? He doubted it, every time he asked himself the same question. They had both used each other, however successfully. A one-night stand. The travel agency was one block from Julian's apartment. With his mind made up, Julian quickened his pace. The digs were on a monthly rental, easy to give up. His passport was valid. He had money in his bank account that was earning interest. When he went through the door of the agency only one of the girls was talking to a client, the other girls' chairs vacant. Julian sat down in one and smiled. The girl was young and pretty.

"How do we fly from New York to Zimbabwe?"

"Where in Zimbabwe? There are two main international airports – Bulawayo and Harare... Don't I know you?"

"I live round the corner."

"Of course. You're Julian Becker. I read your interview in a magazine about the film you're in."

"Was it worth reading?" Julian was smiling, with a quizzical look on his face.

"Of course it was."

"Harare. The farm is a hundred and twenty miles from Harare. How long will it take to get a visa?"

"First class, of course?"

"I'd prefer economy. I'm saving my money."

"When do you want to go?"

"As soon as you get me my visa."

"You're not really Julian Becker?"

"I'll be back in half an hour with my passport. Please work out my itinerary. I presume I'll have to change planes, unless there is a direct flight from New York to Harare?"

"You'll fly via London."

"What's your name?"

"Henrietta."

"It's a lovely name."

"I'll need yours to book the flights."

"Julian Alan Becker. With one C and a K. Book my flight in the name of JA Becker. Thank you, Henrietta. I'll pay you once the flight is booked. You see, the author of the book that the film was made into, is a Zimbabwean. He's back on his father's farm, having a rest. I need a rest, so I thought I'd go join him."

"Does he know you're coming?"

"I'll tell him when I get there... Can you manage that for me? Don't look so surprised. Life is full of surprises."

Outside, next to the travel agency, was a florist. Julian went inside and chose two dozen red roses, writing out a note thanking Nora for a lovely evening.

"The man downstairs on the door will give them to Miss Stewart. His name is Josh. When will they be delivered?"

"As soon as possible. They are lovely."

"Yes, they are. Thank you. Have a nice day."

Feeling happy, even a little excited, Julian walked the last block to his digs. Once again, he was going to get the hell out of the way.

3
_____

Julian arrived at Harare Airport on the last Thursday in May, no one knowing he was coming, no one knowing where he had gone. It was always better to disappear than to start an argument with a publicist or an agent, especially when the publicist had been his lover. They had not made love again, Nora saying she did not want to get hurt, the failed affair with Felix Kranskie still rankling her. He had still not accepted another part in a movie, despite the offers. *Masters of Vanity* was proving a runaway success at the box office, boosting Julian's career to the height of stardom. As he had hoped, flying economy, they had left him alone. Through customs and immigration without any problems, Julian found the Hertz kiosk in the main concourse and rented himself a small car, showing the girl the international driving licence Henrietta had so carefully organised when she booked him a car.

"What's the road like to Centenary West? Do you have a map you can give me?"

"Tarred all the way to the small village of Centenary. They tarred all the roads during the war to make it more difficult for the terrorists, or freedom fighters as we call them now, to lay land mines."

"Will someone be able to direct me to a farm called World's View?"

"Ask at the police station. Everyone knows everyone in the farming areas."

"How do I get onto the right road?"

"From here you drive into Harare and find Second Street. You drive up Second Street Extension and turn into the Lomagundi Road. After that you look for the sign to Centenary just after the hotel you'll see on the left of the road. I'll write it all down for you and mark the map. Give my best to the Crookshanks. Did you know Randall is back again? He's a famous writer."

"As a matter of fact I do. How do you know the Centenary so well?"

"I'm Randall's sister, Myra. I got sick of working at the bank and got a job at Hertz. I was going to join Randall in England but he kept disappearing. There's not much future for a white girl in Zimbabwe. How do you know Randall, if I may ask?"

"Hasn't Randall mentioned me?"

"He cut himself off in the cottage... Oh, now I've got it. You played in the film version of the book with our grandfather. The booking was in the name of JA Becker. I didn't put two and two together. The film hasn't come out here yet. Probably take months, if not years. America isn't much interested in Zimbabwe. Are you going straight up to the farm or having a look around Harare? It's very pretty. Lots of jacaranda trees. I'm off duty tomorrow for three days. We could go up together. What a strange coincidence. Does anyone know you're coming, Julian? That's your first name isn't it? Randall talks about Julian and Nora."

"I came on the spur of the moment."

"I can book you into Meikles Hotel for the night and come to the hotel tomorrow morning. Or you could buy me dinner. You'd almost think someone had planned this. I'm Randall's half-sister. There's me and Craig from Dad's second wife. Randall's mother was killed by lions a long time ago."

The young girl was smiling at him. Another customer was standing behind Julian. Myra gave him the keys to the car, not bothering with the map or the directions.

"You want to leave about eight o'clock in the morning, Julian?"

"That sounds about right."

"Never met a film star before. I'd phone Randall and tell him you're at the airport but he won't put a damn phone in the cottage and Mum and Dad won't run his errands. Anyway, Randall hates being disturbed when he's writing. Do you live in America?"

"Most of the time."

"Takes us about two hours to get to the farm."

"It really is a strange coincidence."

"Not really. There aren't many of us whites left in Zimbabwe. I'd love to come to America. Now that would be really exciting. Nice to meet you, Julian. You'll find the car in the Hertz parking lot just outside the building."

"You say your name is Myra?"

"That's right. Myra Crookshank. Anyone will tell you how to get to Meikles Hotel once you drive into the centre of town. Now, don't forget to drive on the left side of the road."

The girl's eyes were twinkling at him. She was flirting. He would have to be careful. There were always problems. Even on a safari.

"Thank you, Myra. You've been most helpful."

"You're welcome. All part of the service."

They were both laughing out loud as Julian walked away from the kiosk. Outside, he easily found his rental. With his small suitcase on the seat next to him, Julian started the car, put it into gear and began slowly to move out of the parking lot, careful to keep on the left side of the road. Out on the road, Julian gained his confidence. She was far too pretty. She was going to be trouble. Nice trouble, but trouble.

"Men and women! When do we ever stop?" Julian was whistling. The sun was shining. The air so clear he could see forever over the bush on both sides of the road. He was in Africa. Expecting to see a lion or an elephant at any moment, he drove on towards the capital, its tall buildings away in the distance. A car passed him on his right side coming the other way. He would get used to it with a little concentration. Tomorrow he'd let the girl drive. Life really was full of strange and pleasant coincidences. He should have asked her if the cottage had a spare bedroom. Not that it mattered. From all his years bumming around he was comfortable sleeping on the floor.

Once in the centre of the city, Julian stopped the car and asked for directions. The man pointed up the road to a tall building with the name Meikles up on the top. Opposite the hotel was a public garden. Julian parked the car and walked across the road into the hotel. They were waiting for him, big smiles on the girls' faces at reception.

"You can take your car round into the hotel parking at the back of the hotel. Enjoy your evening. Myra said you should expect her at seven o'clock. You'd better reset your watch."

"Do I have time to change?"

"You have three hours, Mr Becker. Would you like me to book a table for you in the restaurant for eight o'clock?"

"That would be kind of you."

"Table for two in the main dining room at eight."

The young girl was grinning all over her face.

"You know Myra Crookshank?"

"We went to school together. Have a pleasant stay with us, Mr Becker."

"This isn't a date, you understand. Her brother is a friend of mine."

"I know all about it."

"I mean, I'm far too old for a girl as young as Myra."

"You're never too old, Julian. You don't mind my calling you Julian? I've never met a Hollywood film star before. I'm looking forward to seeing your movie."

"That's very nice of you."

Julian put the rental in the parking lot and walked into the public garden, time on his hands. If she was going to drive him up to the farm, he probably owed the girl dinner. Up in his room, Julian took his clothes off and lay down on the bed. He was tired. Travelling halfway round the world was tiring. Within minutes, Julian was fast asleep, deep in his dreams. When the phone rang beside the bed it was dark outside. For a moment, Julian had no idea where he was. Trying to focus, Julian picked up the receiver.

"What time is it?"

"Seven o'clock, Julian. I'm downstairs. Look, I'll see you tomorrow morning. You sound half asleep."

"It was a long flight, Myra. I'm sorry."

"I thought you might need company in a strange city. Get some sleep. Do you want me to phone my mother and tell her you are coming?"

"If you think you should. Give me half an hour to shower and dress."

At least, for Randall's sake, he had done his best. When he went down, Myra was waiting for him in the bar. From the Hertz uniform, she had changed into a dress, the top nicely cut and showing part of her breasts. Whether he liked it or not, the game had begun.

Mentally wiping his brow, Julian took the seat next to Myra up at the bar.

"So, what are we having, Myra?"

"I hope I wasn't forward arriving for dinner."

"Whatever are you talking about? The thought of driving alone on the wrong side of the road into the heart of Africa was not the part of my journey I relished. The least I can do is buy you dinner. Now, tell me all about your family. Your brother wrote a book that is going to live for a very long time."

"Has he made any money? He won't even tell Dad. It's probably a few thousand dollars. Why he had to come home."

"More like five million of our United States dollars after tax. Just don't tell him I told you."

"So what is he doing living in the cottage?"

"Doing what he likes best. Writing a book."

"I don't understand men."

"Having fame and fortune can bring with it problems. Why I am here without telling anyone other than Nora. I thought on the farm with Randall I'd get some peace."

"I'm sorry, Julian. I didn't understand."

"It all looks glamorous. Money and fame don't make you happy. Mostly, they give you problems, as half the world wants a piece of you. I'm running away. World's View was the furthest place I could think of. Randall understands. Now, what would you like to drink? I'm having a cold beer. I'm thirsty. That nice sleep upstairs has made me feel a whole lot better. My time clock was all wrong."

"A gin and tonic would be perfect. It's so exciting to meet an American. I wish I could go and live in America but they won't give us Zimbabweans a work visa, or whatever you call it in the States. Dad says Mr Mugabe wants us out of his country, the last ten years of his government have given them time to put their own people in charge. Especially the army and the police. The more Mr Mugabe gains in confidence, the more pressure he's going to bring on us whites to leave the country. They are talking about designating the white farms for expropriation now the ten year period of transition written into the Lancaster House Agreement that gave Zimbabwe independence from Britain has come to an end. I can live in Britain because my mother and father were born in England but what would I do? I have no tertiary education… Cheers. That does taste good. Working in that kiosk can get hectic. You got to get it all right. Check their driving licences. Make sure of the payment and the deposit. A girl has to keep her wits about her. Now, with all this farm designation, Dad thinks they'll come after World's View. Who's going to run the farm after Dad goes is another story. But don't let me bore you with our politics. But it is worrying. You never know where you stand, what's going to happen to you in the future if you stay. Five million dollars. So Randall will be okay. So will Dad and Mum. It's just Phillip, me and Craig. There was a girl in Dad's life before he married Randall's mother. She didn't want to live in Rhodesia. Wise girl, looking back. She's a famous artist. Before they split up and Dad married Carmen, Dad and Livy Johnston, the name she paints under, bought a block of flats in Chelsea not far from the Thames. Dad used the profit he made from a particularly good tobacco crop. In those days, you could get your money out of the country. Now the flats are worth a fortune. But it doesn't help me. Sorry, Julian, I'm rabbiting on about myself."

"How is Randall? The divorce from his wife and the loss of his son was devastating. And now he's rich and famous she wants to come back to him… Thank you, Mr Barman. Give me another of those cold beers. That first one hit the spot."

Not knowing what to advise Myra about her future in Zimbabwe, he had tried to change the subject. The barman, a black Zimbabwean, had been listening to their conversation, seemingly wiping glasses with his cloth. Wherever you went in the world there were problems. The moment you had anything of monetary value in life, there were always people trying to get it away from you. Nothing ever changed. In America, they called it politics. In the new Africa, from what he had heard, they called it the struggle for freedom. Who was more right or wrong depended on which side of the fence they were from: the man behind the bar over-polishing the glasses, or Myra sitting next to him? The girl was agitated. Probably why she had latched onto him. Instinctively, like his family when they had arrived as immigrants to America, she was looking for a way out of her problem. With luck, the girl's intention wasn't to seduce him but to find a friend. A friend that could help her out of a dilemma. Julian felt sorry for her. Having to contemplate leaving the country of your birth was horrible.

"Haven't you talked about this to Randall?"

"He's too wrapped up in his books. Anyway, I don't want to worry my brother with my problems. But time goes by so quickly. I've got to do something."

"Let's take the drinks into dinner."

"Or we can finish them. I'm sorry, Julian. Some call it panic. Right now in Zimbabwe there are a lot of us whites in a panic."

Julian looked at the barman and back at Myra, picked up his glass of beer and drank it down. Myra finished her gin. They got off the barstools and walked towards the dining room, Myra showing him the way. When the girl had got off her barstool she had brushed her hand along the side of his leg. He would have to be careful. He was arriving at the parents' farm to see the brother, not to seduce or be seduced by their daughter. However nice she looked. However much he enjoyed her company. The girl was obviously intelligent. If there was one thing Julian didn't much like in life it was frivolous people. Idle chatter that had no meaning. To make it worse, as Julian followed her into the main restaurant, the girl had the cutest bottom, a tight little bum that was wiggling enticingly right in front of him. At the door to the restaurant, Myra looked over her shoulder and smiled at him, trying to put in the hook. Julian swallowed. Confident, Myra marched on into the dining room. A man came across and showed them to their table, giving Julian undue deference. The girl at reception must have told him. They sat down at a table near the window, the fawning man handing them each a menu. The man bowed and left them to read their menus.

"So, Julian, how does it feel to be famous?"

"I'm not sure. Depends on how people look at me."

"Is my brother famous?"

"He would be if he let them do what they want. They love him on television. That's how you become a celebrity. As a film actor you're exposed all the time. Nothing's perfect, Myra. Maybe you should enjoy Africa for as long as you can. There are always problems wherever you go. You solve one problem and create another... What's good to eat?"

"All of it. In Zimbabwe, we have the best beef in the world. And the Kariba bream is as good as it gets... You're right. I shouldn't complain."

"You think we should drink a bottle of wine?"

"Why not? We don't have to drive until tomorrow. I'll catch a taxi up to my flat. It's only just up the road. I used to share the flat with Craig until he finished his degree in the social sciences. Now he works for the government and has his own apartment. He lives with a girl. She's a local Zimbabwean. They were at university together. She's nice. You'll like her. They are very happy together. Jojo has solved Craig's problem. Maybe I should find myself a nice man and settle down. Craig and Jojo share a passion for wanting to help people. The less fortunate. Those without a farm or a block of flats in England. Or five million dollars from writing a book. Not everyone is lucky in life, according to Craig and Jojo."

"Are they going to get married?"

"Jojo is trying to get pregnant. Only then do they want to get married. For the sake of the kid. My brother is full of all this new liberalism. You want some fish? Or let's go for the steak. A nice juicy steak and a bottle of red wine. Can't get better than that."

"When you say Jojo is Zimbabwean, what is she?"

"Oh, you mean is she black? Jojo is Shona. Like the man behind the bar who was listening so intently to our conversation. You're not from the South, Julian?"

"I'm from all over really. Certainly hung my hat in a lot of places. Steak and red wine. Sounds good to me."

"How long have you been an actor?"

"I made my first film some twenty years ago and seduced the producer's wife. The husband had me ostracised from the business. From then until *Masters of Vanity* I was a beach bum living on my wits, moving from place to place."

"So, you're a naughty boy." The girl was smiling right into his eyes.

"I was young and foolish."

"Aren't we all?... Thank you, Barry. We're going to have the steak."

"A rare steak for Myra." The man took her menu and looked at Julian. "How do they like their steaks in America?"

"Medium rare for me. And a bottle of your best red."

"A South African Nederburg Cabernet should do the trick."

The man left with the menus, a knowing smirk on his face.

"You've been here before, Myra?"

"Dad's favourite restaurant when he comes into town."

"Do you have a boyfriend?"

"Not at the moment. Men with potential are difficult to find in Zimbabwe. In the old days, the daughter of a tobacco grower would have a line of suitors. Now, with the family farm probably worth nothing, it doesn't really help. Anyone with brains and ambition has already left the country. We whites call it the brain drain. Mr Mugabe calls it good riddance. He doesn't consider us whites to be Zimbabwean. He thinks we stole the land. Colonialism isn't exactly popular anywhere in the world right now. It makes some of us smile when the world looks down their noses at us. Whatever would the world have looked like without colonialism? There wouldn't even be the mighty America. When Dad first moved onto World's View it was bush. Never been farmed. The land had never been used. He turned it into a productive farm employing hundreds of people. We even have our own school on World's View so the kids can start an education. The people have lifetime security. Some people might call it feudal, but it works."

"You don't have to defend yourself."

"Probably guilt. You'll see tomorrow how we live. The big house. The swimming pool. The English garden. Servants all over the place. Craig says the comparison of how we live and they live is downright disgusting. The ultimate disparity in wealth. The very rich living side by side with the very poor. When you look at it that way it's no wonder they hate us and want us gone, whatever the consequences to themselves and the country's economy. Craig says you should never look rich in a poor man's country. He's probably right. All rather sad... Oh, good, here comes Barry with our wine. Let's live for today. So nice of you to invite me to dinner. Or did I invite myself, Julian?"

"We invited each other... Racism has been a problem in America for centuries. Probably still our biggest problem. People like the familiar. Their own kith and kin. People with similar backgrounds. Similar cultures. It's always been difficult to mix people of different cultures and backgrounds... Thank you, Barry. The wine tastes good. Pour away."

"Enjoy your evening."

"I'm sure we will." The man left and came back with the steaks, putting the plates down in front of them.

"When do you go back to America?"

"That all depends on Randall. Did you tell them we are coming?"

"I spoke to my mother. She's looking forward to meeting you. Nothing of much excitement happens on the farm. Not since the end of the bush war. And that kind of excitement wasn't very pleasant... You're going to be a sensation."

Myra took up her glass and put her elbows on the table, holding the full glass of wine with both hands, looking over the top of the glass at Julian. Then she drank. A long drink that took half of the wine. She looked at him again, the look reaching right into Julian's genitals. He sipped at his wine trying to regain his control. The girl was even better than Wanda Worthington, his co-star who had seduced Felix Kranskie away from Nora. Julian picked up his knife and fork, looked down at his plate and began to eat. Myra was right. The steak was as good a piece of meat as Julian had ever eaten. For a long while they both ate in companionable silence. Julian, just in case, had tucked his feet back under his chair. They ate and drank, smiling at each other, neither of them taking any notice of anyone else in the room. They finished the steak and the bottle of wine, Julian ordering them another one. The candle on the centre of the table was dripping wax slowly down its diminishing stem, the small bowl of flowers in front of it washed in the soft light of the single candle. She had her hand out on the middle of the table, next to the bowl of flowers. Knowing he was doing the wrong thing, Julian touched the girl's hand. Slowly, Myra stroked the top of his hand. They were in their own world. Just the two of them.

Halfway through the second bottle of wine, a three-piece ensemble playing in the background, Myra again stroking the back of his hand as she smiled at him, a look of certainty came into her eyes. She leaned halfway across the table. "I never make love on the first date, Julian... Can we just pretend this is the second?"

Not sure whether to laugh or take her seriously, Julian did nothing, his mind swinging from what he wanted to the consequences. If only the girl wasn't Randall's sister. There were always problems. Always decisions.

"I'm not sure if you're being serious, Myra."

"Neither am I. It's one of Randall's stories. Of an Australian girl he met in London in his heyday as an executive at BLG, when he was developing a block of flats. By then Amanda had left him for Evelina."

"And what happened?"

"They made love of course. What else would Randall want to do?"

"You're naughty, Myra."

"But nice. You fancy a brandy with a cup of coffee?"

"We'll get ourselves tipsy."

"Drunk more likely. It's been wonderful meeting you, Julian."

"Brandy it is."

Julian lifted his arm to Barry who was standing thirty feet away from them watching his customers. The man reacted instantly. Fame, sometimes, wasn't so bad.

"We'd better not mention this evening to Randall or my parents."

"I was thinking the same."

"Who knows where tonight will take us? Who knows? That's the best part of life. You never know what's going to happen. This morning, whoever would have thought that Myra Crookshank from Zimbabwe would be dining with Julian Becker from Hollywood?"

"The ex-beach bum."

"The man who for years didn't even have a home. I like your stories, Julian. I want to hear more of them."

With the second bottle of wine gone, and the brandy and coffee on the table, Julian threw caution out of the window. It was as much in the girl's interest to keep their evening a secret from her parents as it was in his. Parents of young, pretty girls never liked to be told of their daughter's sexual affairs. Neither did brothers... They were holding hands across the table, Myra's foot rubbing the back of his leg.

"You mind if I stay the night? It's a bit late to find a cab. And you mustn't drive one of our rentals after drinking a bottle of wine. We can sleep nicely and go to the farm in the morning."

"Are we going to behave ourselves?"

"Probably not. I'm on the pill if that's what you're worried about. And no, Julian. I don't sleep around. This for me is a very rare occasion. Instant chemistry. It's like that sometimes. You know, right from the beginning. You've got the keys. We don't need to go to reception. Anyway, it's none of their business."

Julian signed the bill. The dining room was now half empty. He had added fifteen per cent to the bill for Barry. Upstairs, the lights still on, they fell onto the bed, both of them clinging to each other. Slowly, carefully, using all his experience, Julian made love to Myra. A while later, he turned off the light, both of them content. Through the open window an owl was calling from the garden outside. The air was cool through the mosquito screen that covered the window. Myra had gone to sleep, sleeping on her side. Julian sighed contentedly and turned on his side. As Oliver Manningford had told him many times while they were making *Masters of Vanity* into a movie, 'it's not all bad, Julian. It's not all bad.' Within a minute, Julian was fast asleep.

SURPRISINGLY, the next morning when a young black woman brought them their tea, neither of them had a hangover. They decided to skip breakfast and drive straight up to the family farm.

"I expect you'll want to visit America?"

"Don't let's jump the gun. One step at a time. Was last night as good for you as it was for me? You're grinning like a Cheshire cat so I'll take that as an affirmative. You mind if we call at my flat so I can pack a few things? If you don't want to drive in on Monday, someone in the block will be coming into town and can give me a lift. On the farm, I'll try not to look at you and tip off Randall."

"You want to bath first?"

"Why not? We can bath together. You ever want to burst into song? It's how I feel now."

Julian watched the naked girl get up and walk to the window, where she stood with her back to him looking down into the public garden across the road. He was right. She had the cutest bottom. Life was going on, what they had done just part of it. Did it matter taking advantage of Randall's sister? He hoped not. And, anyway, who knew what was going to happen? With Myra. Or in general. Life went on. It was how it was. Piece by piece. Or as Shakespeare had said, each 'petty pace, from day to day, to the last syllable of recorded time'. And in that flash of his time at drama school in New York, Julian thought of Holly. She was still in his mind. The young Holly. When they were both young. Before both of them became cynical. Before Shakespeare's 'petty pace from day to day' had sucked the goodness out of both of them.

"I'm sorry, Myra, for taking advantage of you after last night's wine."

"It takes two to tango... Just listen to the sound of that dove singing. He's so beautiful." She turned from the window showing her full frontal before searching the room for her clothes and putting them on a chair.

"I'll run the bath. Drink your tea, Julian. Tea first thing in the morning is an English tradition. Don't look so worried. They're not going to find out as neither of us are going to tell them. Can you sing?"

"Not really. I'm an actor."

"Have you been in love?"

"Just once. A long time ago. A whole life away."

"I've never been in love. I'm still hoping. You got to keep hoping, Julian. It's what keeps us going."

Dressed, they went downstairs, Myra leaving Julian to book out of the hotel. She had taken the keys to the car and gone to look for the rental. When she came back, parking outside the entrance to the hotel, Julian was waiting on the pavement with his small suitcase.

"You don't mind driving?"

"What it was all about. Jump in and relax. I know the road like the back of my hand. You sure you don't mind missing breakfast?"

After stopping at her flat, they drove out of town, quickly reaching the rural area, farmland on both sides of the speeding car. She was a good driver, totally in control.

"You mind if we don't talk when I'm driving? I like to concentrate. Despite the farm fences animals can stray onto the road."

On both sides of the road the farmland was lush, the fields ploughed in between the lines of the trees. They passed through some hills and came out between groves of orange trees. They had passed the lone hotel on the left. Julian relaxed, enjoying the scenery, happy to be driven on what to him was the wrong side of the road. He was wondering what Randall would think of him pitching up out of the blue. If the man was too wrapped up in his new book he would go on safari. Their brother Phillip, according to Randall, was in the safari business. Whichever way it went, he had got the hell out of the way. The money was good from being the star of a film, but the constant attention was sickening. No one back in America would leave him alone. Which made him think of Nora, the best publicist in America, who never missed an opportunity to publicise her clients, to thrust them into the headlights of the media. It was tiring and somehow demeaning, a false frenzy to get the public's attention, a constant promotion to sell tickets for the movie and promote his new career. Poor Nora. She had had a hard time mixing business with pleasure, first with Felix and now with him.

"Aren't those purple hills on the horizon just beautiful? You live in a beautiful country, Myra."

The girl didn't reply, the car driving on further and further from civilisation. Julian was feeling hungry. He should have eaten breakfast. Occasionally, he saw small signs pointing up dirt roads, with the farmer's name on the signs. All the names seemed to be English surnames, only one a Dutch name. Just over an hour after leaving the suburbs Julian saw the Crookshank sign, Myra slowing before the turning left down the dirt road, the car shaking from the bumps in the road.

"It's the corrugations," Myra said. "They grade the roads every now and again. Ten minutes and I'm home. As we drive, the land on both sides belongs to my father. We're just not sure for how long. Sorry about the silence. I don't like accidents... That dam over there was built by Dad."

"It's enormous."

"Dad says the one thing you need to farm successfully is water. Lots and lots of water. The rains are spasmodic in Zimbabwe and only last for a few months. You have to store the rain so you can irrigate the crops in the dry season. Dad says growing a good crop is the most difficult thing in the world. You have to watch every detail and know what you are doing. There she is up on the hill. The house looks out onto the whole countryside from all sides. Why Dad called the farm World's View. From that ridge you can see forever. Welcome to World's View. My home. The best place in the whole wide world."

Nearer to the long bungalow up on its ridge they drove through a line of gum trees, the trees towering high above the car. They came out next to a lush English garden, the sprinklers lazily swishing the water between the trees, each tree ringed by a bed of flowers.

"What kind of trees are they, Myra?"

"Msasa trees. All the trees, other than the Australian gum, are indigenous. That's Mum and Dad coming out of the house. They must have heard the car. The cottage you can see at the end of the ridge is Randall's. Come and meet my parents. You'll love them."

"Everything is so beautiful."

"You can say that again. After we've had a late breakfast down at the pool we can go for a swim... Hello, Mum and Dad. This is Julian Becker. He's come to see Randall. What we call the Hertz extended service."

Making himself concentrate on playing the part of a friend of Randall's, Julian stepped out of the car. The man in his sixties had his hand held out. They shook hands.

"I hope Randall won't mind my coming unannounced."

"You're lucky. He just finished the new book. Right now it's just the editing. All a bit much for me. I find it hard enough to write a letter. He's talked a lot about you, Julian. Welcome to World's View. Stay as long as you like. Don't meet too many Americans in Zimbabwe. The odd tourist but that's Phillip's business. It's a lovely surprise to have our daughter back on the farm. Three boys and a girl. Myra gets spoiled. This is her mother Bergit. She's not German. Just named for a German. It's a long story. It all goes back to a man called Harry Brigandshaw. Did you get breakfast? I don't think I've seen a man quite so tall since I was in the Royal Navy. That was just after the war. We all had to do our National Service... Here he comes... Randall, your friend has arrived."

"Julian, you old bugger. Lovely to see you. So you escaped the predators."

"You don't mind?"

"Don't be stupid. Anyway, I just finished the new book. Now I want to relax. Lucky you bumped into Myra."

"I was hiring a car."

"Of course you were. There's a spare room in the cottage. You can stay as long as you like. How did the film go down?"

"Better than even Nora expected."

"Ah. Nora. How is she?"

"She sends her love."

"If she was twenty years younger or I was twenty years older, I'd have wanted to marry Nora. Come on in. How are you, sis? Thanks for driving my friend up to the farm. Getting to the Centenary is a lot easier when you know the way. You're looking radiant, Myra. Have you found yourself a new boyfriend? I've been telling you to find yourself a nice young man. Just make sure he doesn't go queer on you. Just a joke. That kind of lightning doesn't strike more than once in the same family. What's Julian been telling you about me?"

"That you're rich. Sorry, Julian, I couldn't resist. Mother, dear, my esteemed brother is now worth five million dollars, the movie has been such a success. US dollars. Not our worthless Zimbabwean dollars. Can you believe it? All for doing what he enjoys most. There aren't many jobs that make you happy and pay so well. Mum, you mind if Silas makes us some breakfast? Silas, Julian, has been on the farm as long as Dad. A friend to us kids far more than a servant. But oh can he cook up a breakfast."

Julian took his suitcase out of the car, the family all talking at the same time, giving Julian a pang of nostalgic jealousy at their closeness to each other, something he had lost after losing his own family when they didn't want to know him after the scandal with Jensen Sandler's wife. There was nothing happier than a happy family. A black man had come out from inside the house and was standing on the veranda, his white teeth ablaze as he grinned down at Myra. Randall picked up his suitcase. The woman called Bergit ordered them breakfast, the black man going back into the house. Far away, Julian could hear the sound of a tractor. They all trooped into the house. Randall's father smiled at Julian.

"Not much goes on at this time of the year on the farm. The rains won't come again until the end of October. We can have some tea on the veranda. When we heard your car we told Silas to bring the tea. All very British. But that's what we are. At the height of the British Empire there were Englishmen all over the world. Growing tea in Ceylon or tobacco in Rhodesia. The Portuguese did the coffee in Brazil. When I was born in England before the war, the Union Jack flew over a quarter of the world's surface. One in five people were subjects of the king of England. Or that's what they told us at school. All a bit bizarre when you look at today's world. Britain's only importance now is as part of the European Union... How long will it be before the United States loses its world hegemony, Julian? Empires come and go. We can only hope the British Empire did more good than harm. Only history will tell us... A film actor. Don't think I ever met one before."

"Have you read *Masters of Vanity*, Mr Crookshank?"

They walked through the lounge onto the veranda where they all sat down.

"Please call me Jeremy. Not yet, to answer your question. It's difficult to read a book written by a son. Far too personal. Bergit has read the book. Says it was very interesting. Out here on the farm we don't understand much of the machinations that go on in America. We only get local television. Most of that is Mugabe's propaganda. Sometimes it's better not to know what's going on. Some call it living in a fool's paradise."

Julian looked out to the distant purple mountains, the vastness of Africa spread out before him. In all that great distance he could see no sign of man.

"To live among this for so many years could never be called foolish... I believe that picture on the wall in the lounge is a portrait of Randall's mother. Randall spoke of it many times. Your home is very beautiful, Mrs Crookshank."

"We think so. But please, call me Bergit. In this day and age you must appreciate what you've got when you've got it. When will your film be coming to Zimbabwe?"

"I'll ask them when I get home. Make a point of it. You know what they say. As long as you see the film you don't have to read the book. But millions have, Jeremy. You should read your son's book. Understand him better. By the time I met Randall I already knew all about him from reading his book. Getting to know his characters was part of my job. And a writer's characters, according to Randall and many other writers, are a composite of the author's experience. Why the book and film have proved to be so good. Your son has done a lot of living. You should read it, Jeremy. You really should."

The trick, for Julian and Myra, was not to look at each other. And it was working, the only flutter, Randall's comment about his sister looking radiant. It was difficult for Julian not to look at her. They drank the tea that Bergit had poured out into delicate teacups sitting on the silver tray, the teapot silver, the sugar bowl silver, all of it reminding Julian of a bygone age. Sitting there in the farmer's house, sipping tea, talking small talk, trying not to look at the man's daughter, was like something from a nineteenth-century period movie, except it was happening at the end of the twentieth. He was glad he had come. He was glad he had made love to Myra. They would have to wait and see what happened. Another servant, dressed in long, coarse white shorts and a long white shirt that hung to his knees, was carrying a tray of food down the lawn towards the table next to the swimming pool, the smell of the cooked bacon making Julian's mouth water. He wanted to look at Myra and smile at her. Instead he concentrated on listening to Randall talking about his new book.

"Can I read it, Randall?"

"I'd like you to. Get a fresh pair of eyes. I'd like your opinion. An artist's opinion. Come on, let's all go down to the pool before your breakfast gets cold. After your breakfast, I'll show you round the farm. Can you ride a motorcycle? It's the best way to get around. Good to see you, Julian."

Conscious of being in a world that soon would not exist, Julian, again forcing himself not to look at Myra, followed Randall down to the pool. The parents had gone about their own business. The sprinklers had been turned off and the grass was wet under Julian's feet.

"Are you two having an affair?"

"What do you mean, Randall? My word, am I hungry."

"You two have been too careful not to look at each other. Look, it's nothing to do with me. Dad hasn't noticed. He's far too naïve. In his day a young girl of good breeding stayed a virgin until she was married. Or that's what they liked to believe. Anything untoward was not a subject for discussion. All us men are pretty much the same, Myra. It's the nature of the beast."

"You're far too observant."

"I'm your brother. I know you far too well. How does that look, Julian? You two tuck into the food. I'm going to jump in the pool."

"What are we going to do now you've finished the book?"

"I've no idea, Julian. I hate finishing a book. Everyone goes. All the people who have kept you company over the months, have been your friends, just vanish from your head. You must know the feeling from acting. From being Mark Fletcher for all those months."

"You don't mind, Randall?"

"It's none of my business what Myra does with her life. Just don't hurt her."

"Of course I won't."

"Good. Enjoy your breakfasts."

They ate in silence while Randall swam up and down the pool.

Under his shorts, he had been wearing his bathing costume. Julian felt uncomfortable.

"You can always go back with me on Monday. This time you can drive."

"Maybe I should."

"During the weekend you and Randall will talk each other to a standstill. I'll leave you both alone. Mum and I like to talk. By then, you'll have seen everything on the farm. Stay at Meikles. You've got plenty of money. I'll get hold of Phillip. He can take you on a safari. If Randall wants a change he can come with you. What do you think, Randall? The Crookshank brothers again on safari. You'll need something to do. Maybe you'll want to go back to America with Julian. You can't hide in the bush for the rest of your life. None of us can. With all your new money you can invite your sister to come on a holiday. I'd love to see America. My job at Hertz isn't the most stimulating job in the world... How's your breakfast, Julian?"

She was grinning at him, rubbing the back of his leg with her foot under the table. Julian smiled back. There were worse things in life than a safari with the brothers, and taking the sister back to America. Randall got out of the pool, dried himself with his shirt and sat down at the table."

"What's the point in having money if you don't use it, Julian?"

"Exactly what I was thinking."

"Good. That's settled. Come and read my book while Myra talks to Mum... It's such a beautiful day."

PART 6

AUGUST TO OCTOBER 1991 — "THEY ALL
HAVE THEIR AGENDA"

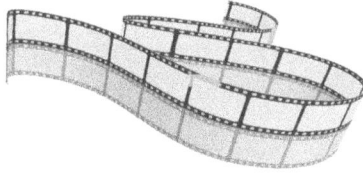

A year after Randall Crookshank went back to America with Julian and Myra, World's View was designated for expropriation by the Zimbabwean government, the final push to remove the British colonials from the country building up its pace. Randall was in New York when he heard the news from Myra. She and Julian were living together in a house down the beach not far from the lair Julian had shown to Nora. Julian was keeping his feet in both camps. A new movie with Julian in the lead, produced by Jensen Sandler, was coming up. Money, as usual, had won the day.

"Dad's devastated. His whole life is in disarray. Not only is he going to lose the farm he has built and worked so long, they are going to kick him out of his home. All that familiarity. The comfort of home. They are saying in the block that there won't be any compensation. Not that it matters. Anything they get will be in worthless Zimbabwean dollars, because you can't take your money out of the country. What's going to happen to Silas and the labour force is worrying Dad as much as anything. Some of them have lived on the farm for several generations. Now it's going to go to one of Mugabe's cronies as compensation for supporting him. Dad says they know absolutely nothing about farming. They'll bring in their political followers and turn the highly productive land of World's View into subsistence farming. In a few years the whole place will revert to bush."

"When are they going to throw him off the farm?"

"Dad doesn't know. He doesn't know whether to plant a new crop or not. He thinks they want him to grow a new crop so they can confiscate the farm when Dad's reaped and cured the tobacco. Why they are not telling him to get off the farm right now. Then the new owner will make some cash money by selling Dad's crop on the tobacco auction floors."

"Is he all right?"

"He's terrible. So is Mum. The thought of living back in suburban England, surrounded by noise and people, is not exactly appealing. All their friends are in Zimbabwe. They don't know anyone in England other than Grandmother and Uncle Paul. And over the last forty years he hasn't seen a lot of his brother. They were young men when they last knew each other and now they are old men. It's devastating. One of the other farmers who was designated has shot himself. Committed suicide. Put a nine millimetre pistol to his head and blew his brains out."

"Do you think we should go over and help them?"

"What good would it do? They've got to leave. There's no alternative. And if they have to leave World's View they might as well leave the country. Our family are lucky, still having British passports and that block of flats in Chelsea. The chap who shot himself was a fourth generation Zimbabwean. His great-grandfather had come up on the pioneer column with Selous."

"Do we know him?"

"Of course we do. You don't want to know his name. Make you even more miserable. How are you, Randall?"

"A lot better before this phone call. So what's he going to do?"

"They're all running around the Centenary like chickens with their heads chopped off, not knowing who's going to be next."

"Is it legal?"

"Don't be bloody stupid. What's legal in Zimbabwe is what suits Robert Mugabe. He's clever. He's been biding his time. Now he's fully in control he's going to force us all out of the country."

"What's the world going to say?"

"He couldn't give a damn. He knows he's got to stay popular with his own people to stay in power. He's throwing our farms to his cronies to keep them happy. Did you ever read George Orwell's *Animal Farm*? Mugabe's keeping his pigs happy or they'll turn on him."

"It had to happen."

"Of course it did. Colonialism is an anachronism. And with Mandela out of jail, and talk of a one-man-one-vote election in South Africa, it's going to happen to them as well. They'll be going down the same path of land restoration, the cornerstone of the black freedom charter. Just a matter of time. You lose political power, you lose everything. Always has been. The world's changing and it's changing rapidly."

"How's Julian?"

"Learning his lines under the trees on the beach. Oh. And there's another bit of news. I'm pregnant."

"Was it planned?"

"By whom? I need to get myself married. Time's passing me by."

"Does Julian want to get married?"

"He's excited about being a father."

"And poor Jojo still can't get herself pregnant."

"Kind of ironic don't you think? How's James Oliver?"

"I saw him in the spring when I went to England."

"Life's a bugger."

"You can say that again."

"We're coming to New York for the launch of your new book."

"That's something. I'll phone them on the farm when you stop talking. What do you want? A boy or a girl?"

"Doesn't matter. Now I'm pregnant I want a whole brood of them."

"Look after yourself, sis."

Randall had been writing an article for *Newsweek* when the phone had rung. Now everything he had been going to say had flown out of his head. All he could think of was his father. A lifetime of work that now had no value, monetary or emotional, nothing left for an old man to look back on with satisfaction. A life unfulfilled. Worthless. And everywhere in the world, other than the Centenary Block, they would think Mugabe was right. If Randall were to write an article defending his father he would be laughed at. The wrongdoers were the greedy colonials, not the black majority. Colonialism in Africa had been wrong. The tables had now turned. How it was. Nothing he could do about it. If the Zimbabwe economy collapsed without the support of the white farmers, the problem would be Mugabe's and all the poor sods left to starve. The price of freedom and democracy. Randall got up and went to look out of the window.

"If I was a black man in Zimbabwe I'd hate the whites with the rest of them. Kick them right up the arse. My poor, bloody father. It'll kill him. With or without a gun. A whole life tossed down the drain."

To add to Randall's feeling of doom and gloom, outside it began to rain, people in the street down below scurrying for cover. Like Randall, the room had gone cold. All he had was four walls, however much those walls cost him to rent. All that wonderful space in Africa was just a memory. Trying to control the bitter feeling in his mind, he went to the phone and dialled the number of the farm. The phone rang and rang. Randall waited until his stepmother picked up the phone.

"You must be devastated. Myra just phoned me."

"Hello, Randall. Your father's in a bit of a state but he'll get over it."

"Is he going to plant another crop?"

"I don't think so. I'm packing right now. There are lots of little things I want to take to England. The one in a real state is Silas. You know what he just said to me? 'What happens to the sheep?' We can leave him money but he says they want to kick him and his family out of their house in the compound. He wants to know where he must go."

"But why kick out the labour force?"

"Who knows? They have their own people they want to bring onto the farms. Their own supporters. I don't understand politics."

"So what are you going to do?"

"Go back to England. Live in one of those Chelsea flats when one of them falls vacant. Take walks up and down the Thames. Go to the theatre. I haven't been to the theatre in years. Someone said that when you're bored with London you are bored with life. It'll be a whole new chapter in our lives. I'm sick of all this politics. I hated the bush war. It's time to leave Africa and go home."

"Do you consider England home?"

"I don't know what to think."

"And Phillip and Craig?"

"Phillip's safari business will go on. Craig is happy with Jojo. He's the one who has assimilated. We'll be all right in London, thanks to Livy Johnston persuading your father to invest in the Chelsea flats. You know she wanted to marry him if he'd gone back to England. And if he'd gone we wouldn't have got married and there'd be no Craig and Myra."

"You know she's pregnant?"

"What! The little witch. She didn't tell me. Does Julian know?"

"He does now."

"Did she get herself pregnant without telling him?"

"I think so."

"That kind of subterfuge doesn't usually work out. Have either of you got a green card, or whatever they call it, to live permanently in America?"

"Not yet."

"Is he going to marry her?"

"Only time will tell. The latest craze is being a single mother."

"At least the kid will be an American and have a future. I'm going to be a grandmother. I can't believe it."

"Would you like me to fly out and give Dad some moral support?"

"What's the point? We've got to go. No point in prolonging the agony. We'll soon get used to living in England. You can fly across the pond and pay us a visit in Chelsea. All go and see a play. Have you ever thought of writing a play, Randall? That would be exciting. We could all go to the first night of a Randall Crookshank play in the West End."

"You're wonderful, Bergit. I truly don't know what we would have done without you. Look after him."

"I always do... And write us a play."

"I'll think about it. Poor Silas. It's always the poor people who suffer the most. All the politicians ever care about is themselves. Whether in Harare, London or Washington. None of them really give a damn about the Silases of this world. They only care about themselves."

"How's New York?"

"It's raining... Why, when something is so devastating, do we all end up talking about the weather? Who shot himself?"

"You don't want to know."

"Poor bastard."

"He's the lucky one. He's out of it."

As Bergit put the phone down in the lounge of World's View, Randall could hear her crying. Getting up from the chair next to the phone, Randall went back to the window. He stared out of the window seeing nothing. Inside he was crying. For his father, for Silas, and all the other poor sods about to lose their jobs and their homes… It was six o'clock in the evening. Time to drown his sorrows. The one advantage of being a practising alcoholic was being able to drown his sorrows. Now, despite all his money, he had lost the one place in the world where he could go to for sanctuary. To make sure he didn't get drunk and fall over in public, Randall made himself a sandwich. The food tasted good. Food that everyone who had money took for granted. With food in his stomach to absorb some of the alcohol, Randall left his flat, going down in the lift, and walked out into the rain. Putting his face to the sky, he let the rain wash his face. Aimlessly, his raincoat closed up to his chin, he walked on down the pavement, not sure where to go. There were so many bars and nightclubs in Manhattan. Without realising his purpose, Randall arrived outside Nora Stewart's block of flats. Josh was standing at the door. With Randall beside him, back in the lobby, Josh rang up to Nora's apartment.

"You want to speak to her?"

"Ask her if I can come up."

Josh smiled and pointed to the lift.

Upstairs, Nora was waiting outside the door of her flat.

"What's the matter, Randall?"

"My dad's been kicked off his farm. I need some comfort or I'll end up in some bar falling off the barstool. How's the launch of *Nothing Lasts Forever* coming along? Can I come in?"

"Of course you can."

"Can I have a drink? I ate some food."

"You poor thing. A few glasses of wine can't do too much harm."

"Oh, and Myra's pregnant."

"Is she now?… Is he going to marry her?"

"Who knows in this wonderful world? At the moment, my life is going round and round in circles and getting nowhere. Even if the new one tops the bestseller list, which I doubt, gays aren't some people's favourite subject, I won't feel a thing. I've already done what I wanted. My stepmother wants me to write a play."

"You're soaking wet."

"It's raining outside. I've been wandering around the streets and found myself outside your block of flats. Am I being a nuisance?"

"No client of mine is ever a nuisance."

"Tonight, I need a friend."

Inside the flat, Randall took off his raincoat and gave it to Nora. He shouldn't have mentioned Myra being pregnant. Nora and Julian had been lovers just before Julian had flown out to see him in Africa and taken a three-week safari with himself, Myra and Phillip. The trip through the African bush that had convinced Julian he wanted to see more of Myra and take her back with him to America. One girl's gain. Another girl's loss.

"How are you, Nora?"

"The same as usual. Working. Making everyone money. The pre-sales of *Nothing Lasts Forever* are good but not that good. The sales will grow over the years as more and more people admit they are gay. At the moment, no one wants to make a movie about your book. But that may change."

"Have I interrupted anything?"

"Nothing that can't wait. Sit yourself down. I'll open a bottle of wine. Which would you prefer, red or white?"

They were smiling at each other.

"Red would do just fine."

Sitting on the couch in Nora's lounge, Randall felt a whole lot better. Nora always made him feel better. She came back from the kitchen with the open bottle of wine and two tall glasses, put them on the coffee table and sat down next to Randall, gently taking his hand.

"Is that better?"

"A whole lot better. I'm lonely, Nora."

"So am I. I don't have anyone. You at least have James Oliver."

"He barely knows me from a bar of soap."

"But he's still your son. They can never take that away from you. Do you want to pour the wine? What's your father going to do?"

"Go back to England. He's lost everything. His whole life."

"Nothing seems to work in life. So, now she's pregnant."

"Nora, you're crying."

"Sorry. I'm being silly. Is Julian coming to the launch?"

"He says so."

"Pour the wine, Randall."

"Did you have a good day?"

"You know he sent me two dozen red roses before he took the plane to go out and see you. He was telling me something I didn't want to know."

"Cheers, Nora. Our little world of peace on a couch, a bottle of red wine on the table, a little classical music maybe. Without Nora, where would I be?"

"Probably not in New York. Do you want to stay in America?"

"Let's first drink our wine. To a better life, Nora. Where people don't hurt each other. Where some good things do last forever."

"To your new book."

"To your health. To hell with wealth... It's delicious. Perfectly delicious."

"Do you have a steady girlfriend?"

"Not really. When you're rich and famous you're not sure what they are after. Young girls, like my sister, do what suits them. They talk about love but don't mean it. They usually want something. Myra wants to permanently escape Africa and not have to find a job."

"You shouldn't talk that way about your sister."

"The truth never hurts. At least she was honest. We use each other, Nora. All of us. Whether we admit it to ourselves or not. We're a selfish bunch, us humans. Ask any politician. Have you ever once heard of a politician doing something that isn't in his own interest? They talk a lot of twaddle about doing it for the good of the people. Like we tell a girl we love her when all we want is her body. Or all the girl wants is our money. We live in a world that lies through its teeth."

"I wish I'd had kids."

"I wish I hadn't married a lesbian. But they look after him. I can't complain. I couldn't bring up James Oliver on my own even if I tried. If I got custody, chances are I'd marry the first girl who came along to have someone to look after him. And what would that do for anyone? He's probably better off with two mothers and no father. My book should give Amanda something to think about. At least that's something. You know, of course, that we humans are all screwed in the head. But that's what we are. A conniving species. Nothing we can do about it."

At the end of Randall's moralising diatribe he felt better. Nora had let go of his hand. The wine was tasting good, sending a warm glow through Randall's whole body. They would be all right in England. Life went on until you were dead. For better or worse. Nothing in life was ever perfect.

When he looked round at Nora she looked straight into his eyes. She too was hurting. She must have thought she loved Julian. A one-night stand that hadn't worked out. Satisfaction, like life, didn't last forever. It made Randall smile cynically as he watched Nora fill up his glass without adding to her own. She was probably trying to get him drunk. The game went on. What the hell. More than once he had fantasised about himself and Nora. What it would be like sleeping with a much older woman. He would have to watch the wine not to make another mess in his life. Like Julian, one-night stands were often too convenient at the time but hurt the other person. They were business associates. Maybe friends.

"What's going through that writer's mind of yours?"

"Moral integrity. Words most of us have forgotten."

"What's moral, Randall?"

"Doing that which is right, opposed to that which is wrong."

"Do you know the difference between right and wrong?"

"I hope so. Do you, Nora?"

"I'm not sure. Maybe right is giving us pleasure. Being nice to people. Helping people. I want to help you, Randall. Drink your wine. You'll feel better."

Not sure where the conversation was leading, Randall sipped his wine. Nora's knee was now touching his.

"I'd better go, Nora. Can't unload my problems on my publicist. I've just made up my mind. I'm going out to Africa."

"You'll be back for the launch of your book?"

"Maybe. Maybe not. Does a book launch have to have the author? They're buying my book. Not buying me."

"That would be highly irresponsible."

"Isn't being responsible being with my family in the time of their need?"

"Are you going to do another of your disappearing acts?"

"Probably. Sorry. Have to go. Thanks for the wine and the company. You've helped me make up my mind. We can't break the rules, Nora. You know that. For so many reasons, it wouldn't be right."

"When are you leaving?"

"Now. As soon as I've booked my flight. I'm going home. For the last time. To say goodbye to World's View before it no longer belongs to my family. I've got nothing here for me in America any more than I have in

England. One last trip. One last wallow in the past. I can write wherever I go. The one big advantage of being a writer."

"Finish the bottle of wine."

"I don't think so, Nora."

"I'm so damn lonely."

"I know you are. But we still have to behave ourselves. I do silly things when I'm drunk."

"That's what I was hoping."

"A brief respite and then the regrets."

"Haven't you thought of it?"

"Many times. But it still doesn't make it right. Relationships have to have a future. Ask Julian."

"Is he going to marry her? I doubt it. Men are all the same. Felix or Julian. I'm going to end my life all on my own."

"We'll always be friends."

"I want more. Why do we always damn well want more?"

"I could have been your son."

"I wish you were. No, I don't mean that. At least finish what is in your glass. Do you want to use my phone to call the airline? Go on. Before I make a bloody fool of myself. Your sister is going to end up with everything I wanted. A good man, a good home and children. I've got all this money, famous friends and famous clients, and I've got nothing. Absolutely nothing."

Randall got up and went to the phone. The number of South African Airways was in the phone book. When Randall turned back, Nora was looking at him, tears in her eyes.

"Four hours' time. I can catch a cab to my flat, pack and go to the airport. With luck, this time tomorrow, I'll be home on the farm."

"You're leaving me. Why is it everyone leaves me?"

For the second time in a day Randall left someone crying. A hug, the hug he had wanted to give her, would have ended in disaster. Nora was desperate. First Felix going off with Wanda Worthington and now Julian with a pregnant Myra. Josh found him a taxi. Back at his rented apartment, Randall packed his bags. The ticket was waiting for him at the airport. All he had to do was sign his credit card receipt and get on the plane. At Harare Airport he would hire himself a car and drive up to the farm. He had written a letter to the landlords giving them notice. Randall felt empty. Like Nora, he had all that money and nothing to do with it. Catching the SAA stop-over flight so quickly was an omen. He was, for once in his life, doing the right thing. He had booked first class, the only seats left on the plane. The last journey had begun. On the aircraft, to make his flight easy to London, Randall took a sleeping pill, curled up in the large reclining seat and went to sleep. His long dream, the perfect dream, was full of wild animals, all of the animals smiling at Randall. In his dream he was gloriously happy.

"Mr Crookshank! Are you awake? We are starting our descent into Harare Airport. Did you sleep well? I can't remember seeing a passenger sleep for so long without waking."

"I took another sleeping tablet after take-off at Heathrow. Thank you for waking me. Do you know my sister used to work the Hertz car rental at the airport? It's so good to be home."

"You'd better buckle your seatbelt."

With the belt buckled, Randall sat staring out of the window. He was content looking at the African bush in all its sunshine, the great open space unbroken by humanity. He was back in his dream, only this time he was wide awake. The air hostess had gone about her business, checking her passengers for their seatbelts. She sat down across from him against the galley and smiled at Randall. The girl, like so many girls in Randall's life, was pretty. She had spoken with a South African accent similar to his own. Despite his years living in England and his time in America, he still spoke in what he liked to think of as a Rhodesian accent. Happy, smiling to himself, he felt the aircraft touch the runway, bounce and settle down. He was home, back on the soil of Africa, whatever the meanness of the politics that was awaiting him. Politicians, with all their greed irrespective of the colour of their skin, came and went. Africa, the land of Africa, would always stay the same. The bush, the sunshine, the wild animals and the smiling people. Randall wanted to sing he was so happy. Despite his new British passport he was a Zimbabwean.

EVENTUALLY HE PASSED through the airport and the open road was soon in front of Randall, the road to the farm with all its memories waiting.

The first person he saw on World's View as he drove up to the house on its hill was his father. Randall got out of the car.

"Randall! What on earth are you doing here? Bergit only spoke to you the other day in New York... It's so good to see you!"

"How are you, Dad? I was at a loose end and was lucky to catch flights so easily. I've got an idea. Instead of going to live in England you could buy a house in Harare and you wouldn't have to leave Africa. You'd still have your friends. Or with Phillip's safari business based in the Victoria Falls, you could buy a house at the Falls. Help him with his safari business. That will never stop. Mugabe needs the tourists and their foreign exchange. Craig isn't going to leave Africa. I might even buy myself a place at the Falls. A good place to write. So, what you think?"

"Are you out of your mind?"

"Probably. Mugabe's government won't last forever. When they find they don't have any food to feed the people they may give you back the farm."

"You always were an optimist."

"Got to look on the bright side of life. England's cold and wet and swarming with people, everyone living on top of each other. You'd go mad having to permanently be polite to people. Four walls, Dad. However expensive, you'd still be spending most of your time locked up between four walls. Don't you remember?"

"There are compensations."

"There'd be compensations living at the Falls. Most of all, you'd have something to do that you like most. You wouldn't have to leave the bush. Everything would still be familiar. You can take the cats and dogs. Give Silas and his family a job. You see, now you're smiling."

"Kids. What would we do without our kids? Come and give your old man a hug. Don't usually hug my children. But this is an exception."

"Old school, Dad. You got to break out."

The hug made both of them emotional. Neither of them spoke as they walked up onto the veranda of the house. The rented car's door was still open, his luggage in the boot. Randall stood looking out over the bush to the far distant purple hills, the view even more beautiful than usual. There was no smog, no haze, nothing to lessen the perfect view. World's View. All the way to heaven through a clear blue sky, a white cloud motionless above the bush. Far away, just visible, a pair of birds were circling lazily high in the sky, the cry of the birds both evocative and emotional for Randall.

"At least we had it, Dad. Most people don't have anything like this in their whole damn lives. All the politicians in the world will never be able to expunge from your memory the sheer beauty of this view. World's View. Your home. We were all so privileged. Not by money or the house. Not by servants. But by the glory of the place where we lived."

"I'm still going to live in England. The fight to stay is finally over. You're still young. I'm old. And yes, I'll sit in a chair with half a view of the Thames River and think of my life in Africa, lucky my life was fulfilled. Building this farm out of nothing was an adventure. The great adventure that became my life. I won't have to worry anymore in England. Whatever happens to money they take care of people. It's called the Welfare State."

"If it doesn't go bankrupt fulfilling all its commitments. Politicians love to promise what they themselves won't have to fulfil. Mugabe and Mandela promised their people the return of their land and everything in it. But land and mines only have value when they are skilfully worked and managed. They have to be productive or they are no damn use to anyone."

"That's Mugabe's problem, not mine. Never stay in a man's house when you are not welcome. They don't want us, despite producing for Zimbabwe the best agricultural economy in Africa. They call Zimbabwe the breadbasket of Africa. But not for long. The farm has stopped working, Randall. I'm still paying the labour force but when I have to go they will be on their own. Yes, I could give Silas a job if I moved to a town. But for how long? I'd just be extending his family's agony. They are going to have to adapt and make the best of being governed by their own people. This farm will belong to the people. He can stake a claim to a piece of the land and grow some maize, run a couple of cows, grow some fruit and vegetables. If the rains are good it will be enough for his family."

"And if the new owner doesn't want him, what then?"

"He'll starve. Along with the rest of them. But what can I do? How can I still remain responsible? World's View is no longer my farm. Mugabe has kicked me out. And there's another reason I don't want to stay. I don't want to watch their misery. Since I arrived in Africa, the population has multiplied by seven. The country was thriving, enabling the population to grow. But without modern farming methods and highly organised bank financing, backed by the value of a privately owned farm, the land won't be able to sustain so many people. It's a modern world. You can't go back to subsistence farming or they'll have another revolution. And if they don't revolt they'll just starve or depend on the charity of foreign NGOs. Charity should begin at home. You can't rely on foreigners to forever feed the people while blaming the people's poverty on colonialism. No, they want us out. I've got the message, loud and clear. I'm going. Go and see your stepmother. She's in the kitchen helping to prepare the supper. You're just in time... You want a drink?"

"I wouldn't mind one."

"And that was another one. We all drink too much. It started during the bush war. Good to see you, Randall. It makes my heart sing to know that someone cares a damn."

"You're very brave, Dad."

"What else can we do? Stiff upper lip, old boy. You probably don't remember all that crap. It was during the time the British had an empire. But life in Britain will go on. It always has. People adapt. I'll adapt. I'll get up to something in England... Is that enough ice in your whisky?"

"Just perfect."

"Cheers, Randall... You know, it really is the perfect view. When I first stood on this hill the name just came to me. There wasn't a house or a barn or ploughed land. But I had the vision of what I wanted to create from nothing. World's View. Let's drink to the wonderful life we have had in Africa. How's the writing going? How's your son? And how's my pregnant daughter? Will he marry her?"

"Probably not."

"The world really has changed in my lifetime. But he will look after her?"

"Of that I'm certain."

"How long are you staying on the farm?"

"As long as you."

"Don't you have a book launch?"

"They don't need me as a writer, they only need me to promote the sales of my books. The part of writing I hate. Telling people how bloody clever I am. Which I am not, as you, Dad, would be first to point out."

Randall finished his drink, both of them standing in silence looking out over the view. Shaking his head, Randall put the empty glass down on the low wall of the veranda. With a smile of sympathy at his father, Randall walked into the lounge on his way through to the kitchen. Bergit's face lit up with a smile.

"That was quick, Randall."

"No point in sitting around. What's for supper?"

"Roast guinea fowl."

"My favourite."

"I must have known you were coming. How was the flight?"

They both laughed. Randall walked forward quickly and hugged his stepmother. When they stood back to look at each other, both of them were smiling. Life went on. One door shut. Another door opened.

"What are you going to do in England?"

"Catch up with old friends. Make a new life. We're not dead, Randall. We just lost our farm and our home. A whole new challenge. Nothing wrong with that. And if the place blows up Craig and Phillip will have someone to run to. They can take away your home, your business, everything material that you possess. But they can't take away yourself. You remember, they tried that during the war. You were lucky they only shot your cat."

"I still love that pussy cat."

"Everything is now ready in the oven. I'll join you both on the veranda."

"You sound a whole lot better than you did on the phone."

"I had a good night's sleep. Thanks for coming all this way, Randall. It means a whole lot to your father. Go back and talk to him."

WITHIN THREE WEEKS, Randall was back on the aeroplane, this time seated between his father and his stepmother. The removers had filled three shipping containers with everything in the house. All the moveable farm equipment had been sold. The farm bank account had been closed after the labourers were given a year's wages in lieu of notice. Not all in the labour force were unhappy to see the back of the white farm owner. The afternoon they drove off the farm, no one in the car looking back, the drums were playing in the compound, the celebration expected to go on all night. Not everyone liked a boss. They drove, mostly in silence to Harare Airport. Craig and Phillip were there to see them off and for Craig to take possession of the car. Only when they reached cruising height did Randall's father speak.

"I think the unkindest cut of all was hearing those drums. So much for trying to look after people. Sometimes you don't see the picture from the other side. They're glad to see the back of me. A year's salary. Plenty of beer. Oh, well. When I think of those drums again I don't feel I've let anyone down by not fighting the government to stay longer. Good luck to them. In twenty years' time they'll all look back and say we were good riddance. They'll end up working the farms properly. We taught them how to grow tobacco. I've never travelled first class before. Always watching my pennies. Thanks for buying us the tickets, Randall. I hope you can afford it. So, here we go. Back to old Blighty. When I came out after the war I travelled by boat. In some ways I feel a load has lifted from my shoulders. Building the farm was a fight. Holding onto it a bigger one. September shouldn't be too bad in England. And my mother's excited. Paul's meeting us at Heathrow. I have an idea to take a holiday on the Isle of Wight before the winter sets in. Relax a bit. The tension's really gone. Like a balloon that's been pricked. All those childhood memories of the Isle of Wight are coming back to me. I can see the *Seagull*, Dad's boat that he used at Dunkirk to get those soldiers off the beach. I'm sure he died happy. Doing what was right. Trying to save their lives. He did many trips from the beaches to the waiting ships before the dive bomber blew the *Seagull* to pieces."

"You're not feeling bitter?"

"Why should I be feeling bitter? I had one of the best lives in Africa a man could possibly experience. What they do with the farm is now up to them. Good luck to them. And you, Randall. What are you going to be doing in England? Or are you going back to America?"

"First the launch of *Nothing Lasts Forever*. And then we'll see. I might find a quiet spot and write a novel based on your lives in Rhodesia. Probably no one will give a damn about a colonial farmer. But I'll enjoy writing it. Give me something to do. The one thing I'm lucky about is not having to make any more money. To me, just spending money for the sake of spending it is pointless. It's showing off. As kids, you both told us kids not to show off."

"We're both looking forward to seeing James Oliver."

"So am I."

"How is Amanda?"

"Still with Evelina."

"Are they happy?"

"I hope so. Probably not quite so happy when they read *Nothing Lasts Forever*. Unlike you, I was bitter when I wrote the book. It got the bitterness out of me. I don't care anymore. So long as the boy is happy. I'm sure Amanda has been a good mother. She's a good person. Just a lesbian. In the book they live happily ever after. Let's hope they do. Who am I to judge?"

Both families were at Heathrow Airport when they landed. The Crookshanks and the Wakefields. The reception committee for the last of the colonials returning to Shakespeare's 'precious stone set in the silver sea'. Everyone hugged as was the custom when no one wanted to discuss a problem. Randall smiled somewhat cynically. His Uncle Paul, who had fired him from BLG for being disloyal, talked about everything other than the business where Randall, with his hard-earned degree in economics from night school, had made the company so much money by developing Westcastle.

"How's the property market, Uncle Paul?"

"Recovered very nicely. You should have held onto your flat at Westcastle. Anyway, you obviously don't need money these days. First class. Jeremy says you paid for the tickets. One of these days I'm going to read your book."

"You don't have to be embarrassed about it."

"Of course I don't. Never been a big reader. Beth saw the film with some of her friends. Why did they call it *Masters of Vanity*? Huge success at the box office so they tell me. You must have made a fortune. Beth said it was all about rich people. People like to watch movies about rich people. You're staying with us, of course. Still in the same townhouse in Hyde Park. Your grandmother is waiting for you at the house. She's getting old. How long will you be staying with us, Randall?"

"Tonight. Tomorrow I fly on to America. Villiers are launching my new book."

"Who are they?"

"My publishers."

"You young people move around so quickly. Will you have time to see your son?"

"Probably not."

The uncomfortable moment over, they all walked out of the terminal to the parking lot, Randall getting into the back of his uncle's car. He was being ungrateful. Without his uncle's help he would never have been able to get his degree in economics. Flying to America so quickly had come on the spur of the moment, as much to get away from the memory of his debacle at BLG as to please Nora.

In the Hyde Park house, Randall dialled Amanda's home number and got the answering machine. He put the phone down without leaving a message. Only then did he phone the airline and book his flight.

'You're going round in circles,' he told himself when he put down the phone. When he walked out of his uncle's study and into the lounge they were all talking animatedly to each other. At the moment, for all of them, World's View was a million miles away, in the past with the rest of the British Empire where history would say it belonged. Life went on, irrespective of losing a farm or being fired from a job. With a drink in his hand, Randall sat down, made himself comfortable and listened to the babble of conversation. His grandmother was smiling from one to the other, happy to have her son back in England. Her family. Her legacy. What her life had all been about. Harry Wakefield, Bergit's brother, was talking about his work. Feeling detached, on his own, Randall thought of Meredith and what had become of her. After two years, Randall still had no idea how to get hold of Meredith.

"You want another drink, Randall? You look far away."

"I was. In another world. Writer's drift off, I'm afraid. How are you feeling, Dad?"

"Just fine. Glad to be with my family. My mother is so excited to see us. Paul says you are going tomorrow. Thought you would stay a few more days. How are you getting back to the airport?"

"I'll catch a cab. You don't have to worry about me."

"There isn't any animosity between you and my brother?"

"Of course there isn't. Working for BLG seems so long ago I barely remember it. Thanks, Dad. I'd love another whisky."

Supper was served, the Wakefields left, his grandmother, tired by all the excitement, was helped up from her chair and went to bed. Randall, tired like the rest of them, was shown to his room by Beth, the daughter of the late Harry Brigandshaw and a prime architect of everything in their lives. Randall, thinking of the story of the man whose father had been the first in the family to go to Rhodesia, toyed with the idea of writing a series of fictional books based on the Brigandshaw family. The trouble was, he didn't know enough about the Brigandshaws, only snippets as they had affected his family. In the small room, the door closed, the house quiet, Randall took off his clothes and got into bed. With his hands behind his head, looking up at the ceiling, the bedside lamp still on, he contemplated the rat race he was going back to in America, everyone chasing sales, the mantra of sell, sell, sell propelling everything. Soon he was thinking of his son, wondering if it was not better to leave the boy alone, parents squabbling doing more harm than good to their children.

"Maybe one day, when you're grown up and the world has settled down, we can go on safari and I'll show you the beauty of Africa."

The words came out in a whisper. A whispered dream, a hope for the future. Leaning up, his elbow in the pillow, Randall turned off the light. Tomorrow he was going to America. Quietly, half content, Randall went to sleep.

2
_____

The book launch for the media took place at the Plaza Hotel, three days after *Nothing Lasts Forever* hit the American bookshops. When Randall arrived the gay rights pickets were already in the street outside the entrance to the hotel, gay men and women screaming at the guests as they arrived. For Randall, the verbal abuse reached the brink of being physical the moment he was recognised as the author of the book.

"I was the victim, not you," shouted Randall, losing his temper. "I'm not allowed to see my son. We called it fiction but it wasn't. You lose your son to a calculated plan by two women and see how you feel. Don't give me shit."

"We have as much right to bring up children as you do."

"But not my son. I made him. You didn't. Now bugger off before I give you a clout."

"You wrote the book to make money."

"I wrote the book to show people what happened to my son, lady. I have no argument with girls being lesbians. I do have an argument with a woman who deliberately got me to make her pregnant with the full intention of going back to her girlfriend."

"How can you be sure it was intentional?" A man, tall and aggressive, had stepped in front of the woman.

"She got herself pregnant, didn't she?"

"There's always two sides to a story. We gays have a right to live as we like and not be belittled by writers like you."

"Have you read my book?"

"Of course I haven't."

"Then read it before you make a fool of yourself. In a book character, I told my wife's side of the story. Good writers always tell both sides of a story. The main male character in the book's gripe is losing his son to a premeditated plan by two women."

"Are you sure it was premeditated?"

"Why don't you go and ask them? Now, please get out of my way."

"We know your history. You're a colonial. A racist. As well as a gay basher."

"My father has just had his farm confiscated in Zimbabwe, so don't give me that shit."

"You whites stole their land. What do you expect? Come on. Punch me."

"You'd like that wouldn't you?"

"Oh, you have no idea how much I'd like my picture in every newspaper in America."

Controlling his temper, Randall walked through the picket line and into the lobby of the hotel. Nora, who had been looking through the glass door, was waiting for him.

"What was all that about, Randall?"

"A publicity stunt. And like a fool I almost fell for it. Wow, those gays really hate me."

"The book isn't anti-gay. If it was it would not have been published."

"How are you, Nora? Is Henry Stone here?"

"Everyone has arrived except the press. They're all outside looking at the protest. Did you say anything?"

"Probably too much. One of them was trying to get under my skin. And he succeeded. They always say any publicity is good publicity."

"We'll see. Have you prepared your speech?"

"I had. Now I'll have to change it. Tonight's going to be fun. Why is it always my fault?"

Instead of making the serious speech about the process of writing a book, Randall made an apology to all the gays and lesbians outside the hotel. In particular he mentioned his happy early life with his ex-wife Amanda. At the end of the short address he suggested everyone from the picket should come inside and join the reception. For the first time since he had arrived outside the Plaza Hotel the press were smiling. Knowing the heated verbal exchange had been caught on camera, Randall made a point of going up to the tall man and offering his hand. The man looked around at the expectant reporters, saw how the argument had changed and shook Randall's outstretched hand. Nora, now smiling, put a drink in the man's hand as the television cameras filmed the exchange. The launch was all about getting good publicity and selling books.

"Do you have anything to say, Randall?" asked the CNN reporter.

"Yes, I do. We may all be different, some more different than others, of different sexual orientation or different skin colour, but basically we are all much the same. There is lots of food on the table. Lots to drink. Turn up the music. Let's have a party. We've all only got one life to live. Let's enjoy ourselves. And please, those of you who have just come in from the picket, there's a free copy of my book for each of you. I'll be happy to sign each one of them. Read my book. You'll understand more about me. And, hopefully, more about yourself. And if you find I keep you company on a lonely night, even better. To living together in harmony. That's the biggest wish I try to write into my books. I hope you enjoy the reading."

Like everything else in life, Randall found experience made his job easier, especially the bullshit that was required of him in front of the media.

Across the room, Julian Becker was smiling at him, a knowing look on his face. Next to him was Myra, basking in the limelight of a famous lover and a famous brother. She was holding Julian by the hand and looking up at him adoringly. Randall walked across to them, the two young men from CNN following. Nora had taken the tall man by the elbow and was showing him the table spread with food. She looked over her shoulder, caught Randall's eye and winked. The seven-piece band up on the stand at the back of the reception room was wooing the crowd with a Madonna song, the female singer getting into her stride. The big, overhead chandeliers sparkled with light. The drink, as it usually did, was making people talkative. Randall, with a soft drink in his hand, his wits about him, looked around. A pretty girl smiled at him as he passed, the girl sending Randall a clear message of invitation. The idea appealed. Not for the first time in his life after a long break, Randall was horny.

"How's Mum and Dad?" Myra was snuggling up to Julian.

"How are you, sis? That dress is quite something."

"Are they happy in England?"

"Julian, thanks for coming. Are you staying in the movies or going back into seclusion?"

"Oh, we're staying in the movies, aren't we, Julian?" Myra, looking radiant, was smiling into the CNN camera, the man with the microphone catching the conversation.

"I thought you were the one looking for a hideaway. How are you, Randall? Like me, once you are in, it's difficult to go back to old habits. You must come visit us in my fancy beach house. We can take a walk alone down the beach and talk. Now we are both on camera. So smile. What was it your friend Oliver Manningford used to say?"

"It's not all bad."

"What are you drinking?"

"Lemonade. Nora's instructions."

"How long should we stay?"

"An hour. You both want to come back to my apartment? I gave the landlord notice when I went to Africa. I don't have to leave for a month."

"Where are you going to live?"

"Probably England. I can come and go to America but I don't have permanent residence. Now we've lost the farm I don't want to go and write in Zimbabwe."

"What happened to the book you wrote in the farm cottage?"

"It didn't work. When I read it back after I returned to America, I found it didn't work. It happens. Haven't written a word since."

"That's not good."

"It's bloody terrible. A writer has to write or he's miserable. Life is funny. When you finally get what you wanted so badly it isn't what you expect. There's so much going round in my head these days there isn't enough room for a book. We'll see. Hope springs eternal. Good to see you looking so happy together."

The silence that followed was louder than words. Randall, getting the message, stopped himself from asking about the baby. While Julian answered questions from the press, Myra stood back, instinctively touching her stomach. She looked at Randall, the movement of the side of her face suggesting a shrug. There were going to be problems. Right there Randall knew there were going to be problems. It was usually best for a woman to explain before she got herself pregnant, instead of laying a trap. The last thing Randall needed in his life was finding himself in the middle. He gave his sister a smile of understanding. The press walked away. There were many celebrities at the launch, people in show business using every opportunity to put themselves in the way of the press. The two men, instead of looking for another subject, went to the table that was serving the drinks, their work over for the evening. The tall gay tried to start a conversation with one of the men and was ignored. Myra was looking at him as Nora, holding the hand of a young man a good twenty years her junior, joined them in the corner by the pillar where they were standing.

"It's sad your grandfather wasn't here tonight. Do you miss him?"

"I didn't really know Ben Crossley, sis. He came into my life. But yes, I do. Apart from Phillip he was my last blood connection to my mother. He fought that cancer for years. We had some truly good moments together. Made our memories. One generation dies and another is born."

"Why don't you write a biography of your grandfather?"

"I could but I don't know enough about him. Anyway, I'm a fiction writer. A story teller. I'll let a professional Hollywood non-fiction writer do a book on Ben Crossley. You know he left me and Phillip a fortune? Ridiculous how one minute you're on the bones of your arse and the next you've got more money than you could spend in five lifetimes. Money has never been my motivating force. But it's good for Phillip. If Mugabe throws all the whites out of his country at least Phillip will have money. You don't need vast fortunes in life but you have to have enough to live on. Ask Julian. In the end you can't survive without money... So, Nora, have you met my sister? We were thinking of going back to my apartment for a quiet evening."

"Don't be ridiculous. I'm taking my two favourite clients out to dinner. Everyone meet Timothy Wendel. Tim's an aspiring actor, aren't you, Tim? Tim, please meet Randall Holiday and Julian Becker. And Myra, Randall's sister from Zimbabwe. I've heard a lot about you, Myra, from Randall. Once the rest of the press have gone we can go to dinner. I booked a table. Do you have a lady in mind who would like to join us, Randall? I'm sure there are lots of girls who would like to spend an evening with a famous author. Glad you made it, Julian. I've got a whole lot of new publicity ideas to talk to you about."

Trying not to shake his head with amusement, Randall looked over Nora's head to find the girl who had smiled at him on his way to talk to Julian. The young aspiring actor reminded Randall of a puppy dog. Julian was also trying not to smile.

"Excuse me. There's a girl over there I think I know."

"Invite her to dinner."

"That's exactly what I'm about to do."

The young man said nothing as he clung to Nora, a confident smirk on his face. Randall hoped for Nora's sake they were friends and not a male escort hired for the evening to cock a snook at Julian and his new young girlfriend who had conveniently got herself pregnant. Women scorned, in Randall's experience, had the habit of being catty, of wanting to get their own back on a lover that had rejected them. Life, Randall thought, as he walked across the crowded room, could be sad. Nora was lonely. He felt sorry for her. At the least the man called Tim, probably in his late twenties, was using Nora. Using his male body to get himself a film career. People used each other. It was the way of life. Denied by everyone... The girl he was about to use was smiling at him as he approached. Like Randall, she had an agenda. Being a famous author put him on many people's agenda.

"Hello, I'm Randall."

"I know who you are. I love your books."

"Are you enjoying the evening?"

"Enjoying it much more now the author has come to join me. You handled them so well. Standing outside so long, they were hungry. Just look at them over there at the food table. My name is Kaitlyn."

"Do you have a last name?"

"Why do you ask?"

"Oh, it happened in the hills of Wales while I was writing one of my books. She never told me her surname. Now I can't find her."

"Did you love her?"

"Probably. I'm not sure. After my wife Amanda I'm not sure what love is all about."

"Love is what life is all about. If we don't have love we don't have anything. Kaitlyn Harvey. I'm a junior reporter for the *New York Times*. Like all journalists, what I really want to write is a bestselling novel. The trouble is, I can't write fiction. I can't invent a story. How do you do it, Randall?"

"At the moment I'm not sure."

"Writer's block?"

"You want to join us after the reception? My publicist is taking us all out to dinner."

"Who is all of us?"

"Julian Becker and my sister. Nora and her new boyfriend. There will be six of us."

"Sounds nice and intimate. Despite writing about a lesbian you like women, Randall. That's nice. Could you get me another drink?"

The chat-up had begun. Nothing had changed. Smiling to himself, he went to get the girl a drink. He was thinking of Meredith. So often, since their week in paradise in the woodman's cottage, when Randall met a girl that he liked, his thoughts went back to Meredith and what had happened to her. Across the room Nora caught his eye and he nodded. He had forgotten to ask the girl what she was drinking. A waiter passed with a tray of drinks, Randall taking one of them.

"I've no idea what it is, Kaitlyn. You didn't say what you are drinking."

"Does it matter so long as it's alcohol? Why do we all drink so much? Wherever you go they offer you a drink."

"Don't tell me. Why I'm drinking lemonade. I'm an alcoholic most probably. Once I've had a couple I go down the slippery slope. Cheers. What is it?"

"Don't we all?... I've no idea. Probably vodka. Are you taking me with you to dinner?"

"On one condition. The evening has nothing to do with the newspapers."

"You've got a deal. Are you going to drink alcohol at the restaurant?"

"Oh, yes. Once business is out of the way it doesn't matter if I make a fool out of myself. Anyway, there's nothing more boring than being the only sober person at a party. You have to join in or it isn't fun. If my friends are all talking crap why shouldn't I join them?"

"I don't talk crap as you call it. Drunk or sober."

"That's quite something, Kaitlyn. Mostly, all of us talk crap at one point or the other. Why we drink together hoping none of us remember what we said."

"*Masters of Vanity* was serious."

"You read that one too?"

"If I hadn't, I wouldn't be here."

The girl was watching his eyes closely, Randall not sure if she was putting on a show to impress him. Behind the seriousness he could feel the sexual pull. As the waiter passed again, Randall put his empty lemonade glass on the tray and took a glass of red wine. The girl was smiling at him seductively, the game now on.

"That's better, Randall. You have my word of honour I will not report anything you say in the newspaper. Maybe if we hit it off tonight you can give me an exclusive."

"Oh, we will."

"I think so too. How's the red wine?"

"Delicious."

They talked small talk and began to enjoy themselves. By the second glass of wine the girl was twice as attractive. The reception was thinning out. All through their conversation Randall had to turn away and sign copies of his book. Most of the people were from the picket line, all of them smiling.

"I never thought of the actual author keeping me company."

"But that's how it is when you read a book. Have a good read, Naomi."

"If I wasn't a lesbian I'd go for you."

"I've been down that route. Have a good life."

"You two have a good evening."

The press had mainly gone. A few hands enjoying the free booze were keeping to themselves next to the drinks table. Nora came across. She was still holding Tim's hand, making Randall wonder if there wasn't more to their relationship.

"Time to go, Randall. Hello. My name is Nora Stewart."

"Kaitlyn Harvey from the *New York Times*. Randall has invited me to join you for dinner."

"Julian's outside getting two cabs. I hope you'll give our book a good review, Kaitlyn."

"You can bet I will."

The girl was smiling. As so often in Randall's life he was going out to dinner with a girl he had known for less than an hour. Tim was looking at Nora with a look of awe. As if he couldn't believe he was holding her hand. The look, behind the aura of awe, was sexual, the puppy dog look having gone. When Nora caught her lover's eye she was smiling. They understood each other. If Nora had been twenty years younger she would have been Randall's date. At that moment Randall envied Tim. When they collected their coats, Tim and Nora were still holding hands. For both of them, Randall hoped they were making more than just a memory.

Julian and Myra were waiting outside with the taxis. Nora told the drivers where to go. To Randall's surprise and pleasure the taxi drove all the way to Brooklyn and stopped outside a small restaurant. When people wanted to impress they spent their money in a swank restaurant. The restaurant was Italian with the name of Guido's. For Nora, she was among friends. Randall took a silent bet with himself the food would be good.

"You've been here before, Nora?"

"Oh, yes. When Guido first started his restaurant. We were both starting our careers. A long time ago, but you never forget the food in a good restaurant."

Inside, the restaurant was packed. The owner greeted Nora like a long-lost friend. A woman at a table close to where Julian was standing froze as she ate her food, the spaghetti dribbling off her fork. They were shown to their table. The table was set for six, a bottle of Italian wine already on the table. A waiter popped the cork, Guido having taken their coats. Everything was ready for them as Nora had ordered. The large, bulbous bottle sat in a straw base, woven with a flat base to support the bottle. After the moment of interest in Julian Becker the restaurant settled down, the people getting on with their evening. The food began to arrive at their table, each small plate put in front of them. For Randall, eating out was about the taste of the food, not the surrounding décor. The food was delicious, each course as good as the last. Julian poured out the wine, not wanting their chit-chat to be interrupted by the presence of a hovering waiter. They were all enjoying themselves. When the first bottle of wine was finished another was put on the table, no one having had to ask. Kaitlyn, with a good start on the vodka at the reception, soon lost her inhibitions. Tim just listened to the conversation. Once, Randall caught Nora looking at Julian. With the wine floating his mind up to the ceiling he found his thoughts looking down at the table. Life was full of complications. A pregnant girl without a job, a husband, or a country to live in. A young man adoringly looking at a woman who in more normal circumstances would have been his mother. A vivacious young girl trying to make a career for herself out of journalism, grasping with both hands a surprise opportunity. The only person Randall's mind, high up on the ceiling, couldn't see was himself.

"Randall! Randall, are you all right?"

"Sorry, Nora. I was off on one of my imaginary trips. It's one of a fiction writer's problems. You can float your mind out of your own body, seeing things as clearly as if they were in front of you. The only thing you can't do is touch."

"What were you seeing?"

"All of us. And our lives. I'm sorry. I was being rude. What were you saying, Nora?"

"When are you going to write another book?"

"When I find another story."

The food kept coming, Randall stopping himself from floating back up to the ceiling by slowly sipping his wine. Kaitlyn was doing her best to chat him up. For some reason, Randall was not in the mood, the thought of his sister's uncertainty and Nora's clutching at straws with Tim making him sad. It was all too often in life that people did not get what they wanted, the day to day mundaneness overwhelming all the hopes. When the coffee came Randall had fought and won his battle and not gone down the slippery slope to drunkenness. He was happily tight but not drunk, not dancing with a chair when he got up to go to the toilet. The only one stone-cold sober was Myra, thinking of her baby, a baby whose future Randall had contemplated when his mind was up on the ceiling; when he had looked down at Nora and wondered where she was going, making a lover out of the son she had never had; and Julian, now the famous Hollywood actor, who had been much happier as a penniless bum living under a tree on an empty beach by the sea. Life in all its complications. If only he could look down at himself and know where he was going.

When the evening was over the three parties ordered separate taxis,

Nora and Tim walking outside to their cab holding hands, Myra and Julian quiet, Kaitlyn with a look of expectation. They all got into their taxis.

"Where do you want to go, Kaitlyn?"

"Wherever you're going, Randall. That was such a lovely evening."

"Yes, it was."

"Is he going to marry her?"

"You saw she was pregnant?"

"She kept holding her stomach."

"My poor sister. A girl from the African bush. Totally out of her depth."

"What does Julian want?"

"I don't think he knows. Not long ago our famous Julian Becker was a beachcomber. It happened to me. In the British property bust I lost all my money having lost my job from my own stupidity. Life can change so quickly. Myra will have to find out. But life, and new life, will go on. It always does."

"You're sad, Randall. Why don't we go back to my place and I'll cheer you up. It's just around the corner. I'm not rich like you and Julian. I live in Brooklyn in a one-room apartment. But I love it. There are good people living close to me. We help each other. You want to come and see? Tomorrow's a holiday. We have the whole weekend ahead of us. I even have a nice bottle of wine we can drink together. How does that sound? Let's relax. See how it goes. Get to know each other better. I want to hear all about your life in Africa. Why wouldn't you answer your sister's question about her parents?"

"She wanted to know how they are. Frankly, I don't know. You'd better tell the driver where we're going. Life is so complicated."

"Not always."

The bottle of wine tipped them both down the slippery slope and into bed, the copy of *Nothing Lasts Forever* Kaitlyn had been given at the launch by the side of the bed. As a junior reporter at the *Times* Kaitlyn had many jobs to do. They had discussed it before they undressed and got into her bed, the big double bed the dominant furniture in the one small room.

"Have you reviewed a book before, Kaitlyn?"

"Not really. I was asked to stand in for my boss. At the moment I don't care about anything but sex. Why do we all get so sexual when we drink?"

"Removes the inhibitions. The caution. Blurs our judgement."

"Is our judgement blurred?"

"Only if you get pregnant. These days men and women who only have one sexual partner in life are something you only find in ancient fiction. Maybe it was always fiction."

"Then why do we do it? Want it so much?"

"To enjoy ourselves. To make ourselves happy."

"Have you had many girls in your life?"

"Far too many. Why, in all probability, I'll end up a happy but lonely old man. In the end, after so many affairs, you find one is much the same as the next. That the idea of finding that one soul mate that will satisfy all aspects in our life just doesn't happen. I don't think I've ever seen a couple without problems. Marriage, and all its legal and religious rigmarole, is to protect our children. To give them a safe home and a secure upbringing. Are Julian and Myra going to be happy living together for the rest of their lives? Now, they think they should for the sake of a baby. The way our parents looked after us. My mother was a drunk. How she got herself killed. And I miss her every day of my life. Why, like her, I drink too much."

"You're being far too philosophical. Let's go to bed. Let's pretend the next half hour is our lives. The now and present. A time to enjoy. To forget old lovers and enjoy the moment. Sex is physical, Randall. What satisfaction is romance unless it ends up in a comfortable bed? Come here, tiger. I'm drunk. But who cares? When we fall in love we'll count it a bonus."

"Are we going to fall in love?"

"Stranger things have happened."

An hour later, their carnal lust finally satisfied, they fell asleep into happy dreams. In the dark of the night Randall woke into panic, not knowing where he was. His heart was pumping, his head pounding. Randall knew he was still half drunk. Trying not to remember what he had done, he went back to sleep. In his dream, a woman's voice was shouting 'where are you, Randall' from the pitch dark outside his bedroom window. The girl's scream in his dream woke him, his whole body sweating.

"What's the matter?"

"I had a nightmare. I should never drink booze."

"Go back to sleep. You'll feel better in the morning. Do you want me to turn on the light?"

"Did we make love?"

"Of course we did."

"Did we take precautions?"

"I'm not an idiot, Randall. Go back to sleep. I was having such a lovely dream. In case you've forgotten, my name is Kaitlyn."

"Where am I?"

"In my flat in Brooklyn. You're safe, Randall. Give me a cuddle."

"I feel sick as a dog."

"Are you going to be sick?"

"It's not that bad. If I don't want to ruin my life I must stop drinking."

"Writers and journalists. It goes with the territory. Hemingway drank too much."

"And Hemingway shot himself. Put the barrel of a twelve-bore shotgun in his mouth and pulled both triggers."

"Now you're making me nervous."

"I'm sorry. It's true."

"Then find a nice girl. Settle down. Have a family. And stop drinking... I'm only kidding. Go back to sleep. And if you want to be sick, the door to the bathroom is on your side of the bed. The one next door to it is my little kitchen."

"What an evening."

"You can say that again."

"How's your hangover?"

"I don't have hangovers."

"My mother didn't have hangovers. They say that is even more dangerous. That if you really suffer the next day you don't drink so much."

"Life's to be lived, Randall. Not to be worried about."

"You're right. I'll be better in the morning. Good night."

After a few minutes of lying quietly on his back the room stopped going round. The first, faint light of dawn was seeping round the side of the curtain. Then he was back in his sleep, the voice of Meredith no longer calling through the window.

. . .

IN THE MORNING, embarrassed by his behaviour and knowing he had made himself a two-day hangover, Randall made an excuse about having to see his publisher, put on his clothes and left. There was nothing worse than getting drunk and making a fool of himself. Back in his own flat Randall tipped what was left in the bottle of Eno into a glass of water and drank it down while it was still fizzing. He had ruined his weekend by poisoning himself with alcohol. He tried reading. He tried thinking. He tried sleeping when he got into bed. Nothing worked. His whole body had rejected him. The pleasure from a few hours of partying just wasn't worth it. Had the sex been any good? He had no idea, far too drunk to remember. His life was a mess. He had made a fortune, made himself famous, and his life was one big mess. Where was his spot on the banks of the Zambezi River? Where was the cottage in Wales? Where was Meredith?... The phone rang making him curse. There was always someone after him. The dreadful noise was splitting open the inside of his head. He picked up the handset and put it down, stopping the ringing. Within a minute the phone rang again. Randall, leaning out of bed, unplugged the phone. He was wide awake, the whole long day ahead of him. So much for launching a book. The whole point of his life had come to nothing. Later, feeling hungry, he made himself breakfast. The food helped, calming his stomach. The two pain killers he had taken began to diminish the pain in his pounding head.

"Now what the hell do I do with the rest of my life?"

Feeling jaded, bored, the pain still in the back of his head, Randall went back to bed. Making his mind go blank, he drifted off into a troubled sleep.

When he woke, feeling worse than when he had gone to sleep, he lay on his back trying not to think of alcohol, the only sure way out of a hangover. Stumbling into the bathroom Randall turned on the taps. His mouth was dry and felt like the bottom of a birdcage. Carefully, Randall lowered himself into the water, the taps still filling up the bath. Water from the cold tap in his mouth made little difference. He lay back, his whole body prisoner to the hangover, his stomach, his limbs, his head, even his toes aching. Through the pain he thought of his father and his life in Rhodesia. Like his father, his own life had come to an end. He had nothing left in him to write. The only way to stop the pain in his body was to go to his local bar and have himself a drink. Drown all his sorrows.

Dressed, Randall plugged in the phone and ordered a cab. He went downstairs. The taxi was waiting outside the swivel door to his block of flats. He had nothing now or in the future of importance to do. After running through the rain, he got into the cab. At three o'clock in the afternoon the small bar was almost empty. Randall ordered himself a beer. The first beer tasted terrible. The second not so bad. The third beer Randall enjoyed. He sat staring into his empty glass, the barman waiting for him to order.

"I either have another, get drunk and fall off this barstool, or I go home."

"Go home. You look positively dreadful."

"Great! Thanks. But I'll take your advice. If it's stopped raining I'll try and walk home. You got enough money?"

"More than enough. Look after yourself."

All the way down the street he was trying to remember the girl's name. Three beers had made him drunk again. Without having to think he found his way home down the old well-trodden path from the bar. When he opened the door to his apartment the phone was ringing. Randall pulled out the plug. He was well and truly finished. In the small cabinet above the washbasin in the bathroom, Randall found his bottle of sleeping pills. He took two of them and got into bed, the combination of the pills and the alcohol knocking him out. When Randall woke twelve hours later he was feeling almost normal.

Soon after Randall plugged in the phone it rang. He picked up the handset.

"Randall Holiday. Randall Crookshank. Take your pick."

"It's me. How are you, Randall? Wonderful news. When I phoned my boss and told him you were my boyfriend he said I could write the review. He wants me to not only review your book but write a piece on the author. You must have been so busy. Every time I phoned it rang and rang. Being a famous author must be so tiring... Are you still there, Randall? It's me. Kaitlyn. When can we have a really good sit down so I can find out all about Randall Holiday the person? If you give me lots of story I can stretch the piece into more than one article. I'm so excited. It's such a big break for a young journalist. What are you doing now? I don't mind working on a Sunday. I'd love to see your apartment. For a man like you who is so well known and rich it must be quite something. I always wanted to know a famous person... Are you there, Randall? Afterwards, we can go out to dinner. I'm going to be a book critic. Isn't that exciting?"

"Have you read the book?"

"Not yet."

"Shouldn't you read the book before the interview?"

"You're what's important, Randall. People want to know all about a famous author. The celebrity."

"I thought it was all about my book."

"Don't be silly. It's about the author. The celebrity. The public want to know about you, the famous author. Wow, you really can make love. It's all so exciting."

"Am I your boyfriend, Kaitlyn?"

"Of course you are. We slept together. Sex that good doesn't stop. I'm feeling randy. I can find a cab and come round now. It's all so exciting. You do want the right story in the press?"

"What do you mean? Are you threatening me?"

"Don't be silly. Of course I'm not. I want the real inside story of Randall so I can write the best article of my life. I would never threaten anyone, Randall. What we did together is our business. So, can I come round? I really, really enjoyed our evening. There are going to be lots more of them."

"I'm not in the best of moods right now."

"Even more reason for me to come round, you poor darling. Let Kaitlyn look after you. You are alone? You said so much to me the night before last."

"I was drunk."

"We were both a bit tipsy... Are you lonely, Randall? They say famous people get lonely in the midst of all that attention. Let me help you. We can have so much fun together. Or have you started a new book? We could talk about it. I know your address. Just say yes and we'll have so much fun together. So, what you say?"

"I'd love to see you Kaitlyn."

"I'm on my way. I'm so excited you just have no idea."

Still not sure if the girl was using their one-night stand as leverage,

Randall sat down plonk on his sofa. Why was it in his new life people always wanted something? No one ever phoned to give, they phoned to take. Even Nora Stewart and Henry Stone had an agenda whenever they phoned. Thinking of Nora he wondered if he should first clear the proposed article with his publicist and decided against it, not wanting to tell Nora he had slept with Kaitlyn. Randall sat back in the sofa and let his mind go blank.

WHEN RANDALL OPENED the door to his apartment the girl had a smile all over her face. She was even prettier than he had remembered. Both arms open, she flew at him and gave him a kiss, rubbing her crotch hard into his. She pushed him backwards into the flat, slamming the door shut with the back of her foot. Within a minute, both of them were naked, the love making short, sharp, and mutually satisfying.

"Wow. How does that feel, lover? Do you not feel a whole lot better?"

Both of them were smiling, naked on the couch.

"The interview was just an excuse. Today is Sunday. The day of rest and love for each other. Why don't we leave business until tomorrow? How was your meeting with your publisher?"

"I didn't have one. I was drunk when we went to bed. I thought I'd made a fool of myself. Taken advantage of you. Used my celebrity to get you into bed."

"Are you happy now?"

"Much better, thank you."

"What do you want to do? There's a symphony concert at the Met this afternoon. Do you like classical music?"

"It's one of my passions. Along with traditional jazz. Music, painting, fiction writing. It's all the same. Just different forms of creative art."

"Then we've got a whole lot more in common than a good roll in the hay."

"How did you know where I live?"

"There's nothing secret from the *Times*."

Wondering how people knew so much about him, Randall put the kettle on to make a cup of tea. He was feeling better, a smile back on his face, hopeful the girl was after his company and not the article she was going to write for the *Times*. From a background on an African farm where the animals and bush were more likely company than people, he knew he was naïve.

"Do you mind if I ask you some questions? I mean, time is short. If we want to listen to music we don't have to see the orchestra. Turn on the music channel. You do have cable? Of course you do... What are you doing in the kitchen?"

"Making a cup of tea. It's a British tradition they brought with them to Rhodesia. When guests arrive you always make them a cup of tea. Not that we had many guests on the farm. We were miles from the nearest farm. The only social life was the Centenary club. Cricket, tennis, squash and a whole lot of drinking. We all drank too much. Where my problem started."

"All this furniture must have cost you a fortune."

"I rent the flat furnished. I have a multiple entry visa into America. Nothing permanent. Why I've never brought property or furniture. Buying, and having to sell when you leave, doesn't make any sense... How does that look? You can put in your own sugar. You do drink tea?"

"Sometimes... But you could buy this apartment and everything in it?"

"Probably."

"I'd love to be rich. Famous journalists make big money."

"Being rich isn't all it's made out to be. It makes you a target."

"I think it would set me free. Money gives you freedom. And you don't have to worry about every damn thing you buy. I'm always up to the limit on my credit cards. A girl has to look good. Clothes cost a fortune... If you married an American you wouldn't have any problems staying in the States. If you don't own all this, what do you do with all the money you earned in royalties? I'm sure Nora and your agent got you a good deal. It's in their best interest."

"It's in the bank."

"You should invest in property. A swell car. Show off a bit, Randall. Nothing wrong with showing off when you are rich. What's the point in having money if you don't show it to people?"

"What are you doing there?"

"Turning on my recorder. You don't mind? I'll only say nice things about you, Randall. A lot of people would give their eye teeth to get a piece about themselves in the *New York Times*. We can help each other.

It's the little snippets in an article that make it worth reading. People want to relate to a celebrity… So you don't mind?"

"Do what you have to do."

"Don't you think you should put on your trousers?" Kaitlyn was giggling, the small machine on the coffee table in front of the sofa where they had made love recording everything. "I like tea with two spoons of sugar. Come and sit next to me. The lovely thing about modern life is you don't have to go out. You can get all the entertainment you need from the television. I love living in New York. All I need is lots more money and life will be perfect. I'm suddenly so lucky having you as a boyfriend. You don't have to put on your trousers unless you want to, Randall. So, are we staying in for a nice lazy Sunday on our own or are we dressing up and going out? I don't mind. I love dressing up. Let's turn on some classical music. Or you can find the traditional jazz channel you say you like so much. I'm just so excited. My boss says if my articles on Randall Holiday appeal to the public he'll give me a raise. Let's just say we're helping each other. And when we get hungry you can send out for some food and not have to worry about cooking. Have you thought about getting married, Randall?"

"Not recently. My problems with a lesbian wife have left me wondering about marriage. But read my book. It's all in *Nothing Lasts Forever*."

"Now. Let's start at the beginning. Where were you born?"

"In the back of a truck that was stuck between two swollen African rivers. My father delivered me. He was on the way into Salisbury to get my mother to the hospital but I couldn't wait. It was raining cats and dogs. A dark and stormy night in Africa. How's that for the start to your article?… It was a dark and stormy night…"

"You've got to be kidding."

"Of course I am. I'm pulling your leg."

"So where were you born?"

"In the back of a truck… Drink your tea before it gets cold."

On the table, silently, the small tape recorder was slowly going round and round.

When the doorbell rang, Randall was still sitting on the sofa in his underpants telling Kaitlyn his life story, the girl skilfully pulling more and more out of him. She was going to be a good journalist.

"Who the hell's that?"

"You'd better answer the door. And you'd better put on your trousers." Kaitlyn gave up being the competent journalist and began to laugh, stroking his naked leg.

Randall got up. The doorbell rang again, a long ring that wouldn't stop.

"I'm coming! Hold your hat on... Why are people so impatient?"

Stumbling around in his haste, Randall tugged on his trousers and pulled up the zip. The bell was still buzzing. "Hold on!"

When he opened the door, Myra was smiling at him, the tall Julian Becker a pace behind her. They were both smiling. Big, broad smiles all over their faces. Julian's long hair was tied in a ponytail at the back of his head, both of them dressed casually.

"You wouldn't answer your bloody phone, so we decided to come around. We have some wonderful news. Are you going to invite your sister in?... Hello, Kaitlyn. This is a nice surprise. Did we interrupt something? Naughty boy, Randall. You can make us some tea. What was wrong with your telephone?"

"I pulled out the plug. Good to see you, Julian. Why are you both looking so damn happy? Are you two getting married or something?"

"Exactly. Julian's going to make an honest girl out of me or they were going to throw me out of the country. My visa has expired. We're getting married at the beach house at the end of the month. Everyone is invited. Felix Kranskie and Jensen Sandler and all Julian's friends."

"Have you told your mother?"

"Of course I have. They're coming over. Isn't it wonderful? Kaitlyn, do you want to come to my wedding or is your visit with my brother business?"

"Both. Randall and I are lovers."

"You naughty boy. But who am I to preach?"

"Dad's coming to America?"

"Of course he is. His daughter is getting married. He's going to give me away. Mother is over the moon."

"Have they decided where to stay?"

"Not yet. Still with Gran and Uncle Paul. They're liking London. Seeing their families. Going to the theatre... Aren't you going to give me a hug?... There we are. And tuck your shirt in."

Randall shook Julian's hand. "Welcome to the family, Mr Becker. I hope you and my sister have a wonderful life together. Are you having a honeymoon?"

"We're going out to Africa, big brother... I'm going to be an American. A citizen of a real country and not one that's going to become a banana republic if President Mugabe continues to destroy his country's economy. Phillip and Craig can't come over. So we're going to them. Julian wants a honeymoon on the banks of the Zambezi River... Let's go and make us all some tea. From being bored to tears in good old Harare my life is now so exciting I could burst. And Julian's making another film. Right after we come back from our honeymoon."

"It's all a bit sudden."

"Life's full of surprises. What makes life worth living. I'm going to be a wife and a mother. Can you believe it?"

"Are you really making another film, Julian? I thought you had now made enough money to get the hell out of the way."

"Probably. I'm just not much good at organising my finances. I leave that to my accountant. He pays the bills and signs all the cheques. I know how to live frugally but don't understand the modern financial world."

"I imagined you on an island, walking the beach, far away from other people's shit."

"Have you started another book?"

"Not yet. That's the problem. I can't get the hell out of people's way."

"Life changes. You have to go with the flow. Being a father brings new responsibilities. Sometimes we have to do what is right for other people and not be selfish... Isn't that a tape recorder on the table?"

"Kaitlyn was doing an interview. She's been asked to write the review for my new book. And an article on me."

"Can you turn it off? I hate those things. They have a habit of coming back to bite you. How Jensen Sandler found out I was having an affair with his wife and got me slung out of the theatre. He set a trap and recorded his wife telling her friend she was having an affair. Sent a news photographer to follow her and catch us in bed."

"You said he did you a favour."

"Maybe he did. Who knows in this crazy world?"

Later, when they had finished their tea, and Kaitlyn and Myra were talking the hind leg off a donkey, Randall looked across at Julian sitting silently in his chair. The man had the look of a deer caught in the headlights of a car, the look of fear deep in his eyes. Randall felt sorry for him. The man was trapped. By his celebrity, and now by Myra and the prospect of having a kid. Like so many others Randall had met through his turbulent life, Julian Becker was going to have to conform. And by the look on his staring face, he didn't like it. When Julian's eyes moved towards the conversation on the sofa, Randall looked away so as not to embarrass his friend, the thoughts in both of their minds better not said. But at least the women were happy. And that was something.

"Sorry, Myra. What did you say? I wasn't listening."

"What are you going to do about James Oliver?"

"At the moment, I have absolutely no idea. You'd better ask his mother, or his mother's lover. So far they haven't asked for money but that time will come."

Again Randall didn't look at Julian. Soon after, the girls went home to get dressed to go out to dinner, Julian and Randall doing what they were told. Kaitlyn had picked up the tape recorder and put it in her pocket. For the moment the celebrity interview was over. At the door, as the girls were leaving with Julian, Julian had agreed, at Myra's suggestion, to give Kaitlyn an interview for her newspaper, the first exclusive Julian had given to anyone. That time they had both looked at each other, their eyes meeting, the mental shrug understood by both of them. They were all going out to dinner, the two men having to behave themselves, a whiff of Randall's last months with Amanda coming back to him, Randall wondering how long his sister's marriage to Julian would last. Like Amanda, Myra wasn't an artist, someone who would be content on her own and not require constant attention. Remembering his week of peace and joy in the Welsh valley with Meredith, Randall stood silently in front of his closed front door.

"If only I had found out her surname."

Going into the bedroom, Randall found a fancy set of clothes and laid them out on the bed. He had given Kaitlyn the price of the taxi fare back to her flat so she could bath and change. They were all to meet at the restaurant in the swank Plaza Hotel. Like he did so often with his own son, Randall was thinking about Myra's unborn child. What kind of life the child was going to have. How many people would be involved in the kid's upbringing. The only thing certain, apart from a life, was the child was going to be an American.

As Randall put on his fancy clothes and looked at himself in the mirror, he made up his mind. After the wedding, conveniently timed at the end of the lease on his flat, he was going back to England to look for a place in the countryside. He wanted to write, the only thing that gave him satisfaction.

PART 7

OCTOBER 1991 TO AUGUST 1992 — "ON THE
ROAD AGAIN"

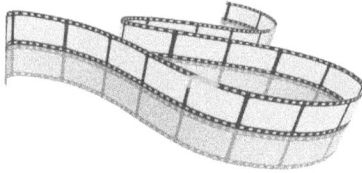

1

---

*J*ulian Becker had to laugh. It was all about publicity, not a wedding, Nora Stewart having done her job wringing the last drop out of promoting Julian to his public. Even Myra had gone through the mill, the farm girl from the heart of Africa with a beautiful tan was skilfully plastered with make-up, her hair done just right. Her family, when they flew into LA for the wedding, had the surprise of their lives, Julian not sure if the old man approved of him or the new look of his daughter. Randall, when he arrived at the beach house, was remote, far away. For Julian, marrying a girl half his age also had its problems judging by the expression on the mother's face. The woman had just celebrated her fifty-fourth birthday, making Julian six years younger than his future mother-in-law. As for the father, the old British colonial, the world he now found was indeed strange. Julian had tried to get to know the old man, the British reserve with its upper-class accent difficult to penetrate. The smiles, when they came, only showed on half the old man's face. From being the guest on the farm who had come to visit his son, the father having no idea Julian was having an affair with his daughter, everything had now changed. Even doing the right thing by marrying the daughter was having its problems. The old man had a habit of walking the beach alone, Julian not sure if the loss of his farm had anything to do with it. With so much going on in his life, his house flooded with people, Julian did not have time to think of other people's problems.

The caterers arrived with two trucks the day before the wedding, setting up chairs and tables and all the rest of a wedding's paraphernalia in the garden. What with Jensen Sandler and the new movie, Nora's publicity stunts and the wedding, Julian had lost control of his life, the flow of people through his house overwhelming. Would he have married the girl if she wasn't pregnant, Julian asked himself? He doubted it. Ever since Holly had left him for a man with money, he had never trusted women's motives. Affairs which came without responsibility were preferable – being a bum had had its advantages. When he had no money none of his girlfriends had any interest in marrying him. He was a vehicle for fun, not a prospect for the future. Would any of the people now in his life have anything to do with a man in a loincloth combing the beach for a living? Even the idea was a joke. Maybe Randall would have understood. Nora and Felix Kranskie, always with the prospect of more money in the forefront of their minds, had turned the beachcomber into Mark Fletcher and swallowed him whole... As the hour drew closer for the minister to marry them in front of all those rich people, Julian wanted to run. He wanted to be that man in a loincloth with all that freedom back in his life and not a responsible husband and father. As the traditional wedding with its traditional music being played by a small orchestra next to the pool built to its climax, it felt like he was facing a firing squad, if not a jail sentence. Myra looked radiant. As the old man, a full smile on his face, walked his daughter between the rows of chairs and the standing guests, Julian, looking over his shoulder, was in panic. For a brief, overpowering moment, Julian wanted to make a bolt. If only he hadn't caught Felix and Nora skinny-dipping on the beach, none of what they were doing to him now would have happened. But he stayed, and through all the fog of misunderstanding, Julian found himself married. He was Mr Becker of Mr and Mrs Becker, with a father-in-law, a mother-in-law, a brother-in-law, and a son on the way.

"Happy wedding day, Myra."

"I'll make it up to you, Julian, I promise."

Not sure what she meant, Julian walked his new wife away from the minister's dais and up the aisle between the rows of chairs, the orchestra playing Mendelssohn. The caterers had laid out the food and drink on beautifully decorated tables around the pool. Far away over the heads of the nine-piece orchestra, a cargo ship, loaded with containers, was making its way out to sea. A team of waiters and waitresses stood waiting to serve the guests. At the end of the aisle, Julian broke from Myra, put his long arms in the air and turned his eyes up to heaven. The guests broke away from where they had sat during the brief ceremony, Felix Kranskie the first to shake Julian's hand. Nora, with her toy boy Tim a pace behind, was kissing Myra on both cheeks. As the media took photographs, Jensen Sandler gave Julian a hug, talking into his ear, not one of the words encouraging. Wanda Worthington, who had played opposite Julian in *Masters of Vanity*, told him how lucky he was to be married, her brief affair with Felix Kranskie long in the past. Kaitlyn, the girl who had tried to corner Randall, was working the crowd looking for new celebrity material. With Randall now shortly on his way back to England, the articles on himself and Randall had given her status. By the time Julian was handed his first drink the caterers' staff were working hard, the guests swarming the tables. The orchestra stopped playing as the waitress, prettier than paint, offered Myra and Julian their drinks for the toast. A seagull was crying up high in the sky as it flew out to sea. For Julian, the sound made him long for a walk alone on the beach. The bride's parents, looking aloof, even a little bewildered, were standing away from the people milling round the tables, no one taking any notice of them. With Julian and Myra flying to Africa the next day, the two were returning to England and the uncertainty of their new lives. Julian watched as Randall walked across to them with three drinks clutched in his hands. Like his parents, Randall looked lost.

"Why don't you go over and talk to your parents, Myra? I'll deal with the media. Kaitlyn seems to be enjoying herself."

"Isn't she? Nora looks so happy with Tim."

"She's got him a part in the Sandler movie. Be fun if he turns out any good. Quite a day."

"You can say that again. Are you all right? At one point I thought you were going to make a run for it... My parents look lost."

"What's wrong with Randall?"

"Says he can't write. Driving him nuts. His latest idea is to look for a small farm on the Isle of Man."

"Where is the Isle of Man?"

"I have no idea. I'm so glad we posed for the wedding photographs before the ceremony."

"Go talk to Jeremy and Bergit. They look so out of it."

"Wherever they go, the old Rhodesians look out of it. You felt a bit out of it when you visited World's View. Now Dad has nothing. He says without the farm his life has no purpose."

"What's he going to do?"

"Sit around and wait to die. Says his life is finished. You go and talk to the press."

"What are you going to make up to me?"

"Having made you marry me because I got pregnant. Were you going to make a run for it?"

"I didn't. That's all that matters. I can't wait for tomorrow when we get on that plane."

"Neither can I. Do you love me, Julian?"

"Of course I do. Now go talk to your parents. Must be awful to lose your country. Never thought of it. No one is ever going to lose America."

"Except the people who owned it before Columbus. Mugabe just made sure he didn't make the same mistake. My poor parents. When Dad was born, the British had an empire. Now they have nothing. Just a small island attached to the European Union."

Myra leaned up and kissed him, tears running down her small cheeks.

"What's the matter?"

"I just hope we're going to be happy. The three of us."

"We will. Off you go."

Julian, playing his part, moved from guest to guest as he walked towards the media, doing his best to remember everyone's names.

A while later, when Myra went into the house to change out of her wedding dress, Julian followed her.

"Let's get out of here. I've booked us a suite in the Royal Hotel. They're all getting drunk. Most of them won't even notice we've gone. It's a long flight tomorrow. I'm sick of people. Is there something wrong with me?"

Julian sat down in a small armchair and looked at his wife. She was naked, sitting in front of her dressing table mirror. The bulge in her belly was pronounced as she leaned forward. Her breasts were firm, the nipples protruding. Julian tried to smile, his long arms hanging over the arms of the chair, his long legs out in front of him. Neither of them spoke. Their bedroom was on the other side of the house from the pool, the noise from the party outside on the lawn a mixture of music, voices and laughter. Julian hoped his friends were enjoying themselves. When Myra finished touching up her make-up she turned to him.

"Do you mind if I lie on the bed for a while? The baby makes me tired. Sounds as though they're all enjoying themselves."

Julian smiled. Myra got up and went to lie on the big bed. Julian closed his eyes, his body relaxing, his mind drifting away into the past, the long ago past when he had first gone to New York as an eighteen-year-old on a scholarship to drama school, his whole exciting life at last in front of him. When he opened his eyes and looked at Myra she was sound asleep, breathing softly. Julian got up and gently pulled the sheet over his wife's naked body, the round, pregnant belly well pronounced.

"Whoever you are in there, you're going to have a better childhood than mine, sonny boy. No foster parents for you. No father in jail. No mother killing herself. I'm going to look after both of you. And if you are a girl you are going to be my princess."

Happy with his thoughts, Julian went back to his chair and made himself comfortable. In her dreams, Myra looked happy with a faint smile on her sleeping face. He closed his eyes, returning to the drama school and a young boy full of exciting dreams. Like now, with a wife asleep on her wedding day, life then was just as strange. Julian, instead of joining his guests, put his head back and looked at the ceiling and let himself think of his past.

When Julian was six years old his father had got drunk in a bar and had an argument with a man who had beaten him up. Instead of leaving the argument alone, Miles Becker had gone home to their house at the end of the street in Kansas City where he kept his gun. Armed, in a raging, cold temper, Miles Becker had gone back to the bar to confront the antagonist. The man had attacked him again, Miles had shot the man dead, and the police arrested him soon after. Sober, Miles confessed. He was sentenced to death, and Julian's mother committed suicide the day after. Julian was taken away by an old woman who worked for the government. For months, Julian waited for a relative to claim him but none of them came. When Julian's father was executed they put him in a foster home where he stayed for a year, the couple losing interest in a seven-year-old boy with a mind in turmoil. Eventually, three foster homes later, two old spinster sisters, both of them in the theatre, took him in and gave him a life, a life the boy Julian, both his parents dead, was unable to come to terms with until the old ladies found a place for him in New York with a chance to make a life for himself. By then, one of the old ladies had died. In Julian's second year, after his affair with Holly had ended, the second old lady had died. Between the two women they had left Julian enough money to see him through drama school. After his short time at the Old Vic in England, he returned to Kansas City landing the part in the Jensen Sandler movie and ruined every one of his chances by having an affair with the producer's wife. Afterwards when people asked him about his family he said they avoided him because of the scandal, a story that was now part of his life. Maybe one day, long into the future, he would tell Myra the true story of his mother and father.

When Julian pulled himself out of his thoughts and looked at the bed, Myra was still sleeping.

"Maybe not. Bad things are better forgotten."

Closing his eyes, comfortable in the chair, the party noise nothing to do with him, Julian went into a dreamless sleep.

When he woke, stiff from lying in the small armchair, it was almost dark. He could hear the sound of the sea, everything quiet. Julian got up and looked at Myra sleeping peacefully on the bed. Outside when he walked through the house there was no sign of anyone. The tables and chairs had gone. Someone had left the light on at the pool. Leaving his clothes by the side of the pool, Julian dove into the water. The water was cold. He swam up and down the pool in a crawl, the exercise pleasing.

"You'd better put on some clothes, Julian. Dad and Bergit are walking up the hill from the beach."

"How was the reception?"

"Not bad. The food was excellent. The best part of your wedding was the lack of speeches. What happened?"

"Myra went to sleep. The baby makes her tired. What's your agenda?"

"Like you and Dad I'm off tomorrow. If I don't start another book soon I'm going to get more and more depressed. Nora said to wish you a pleasant trip. The rest just ate, drank and went home. People. It's how it works."

"And Kaitlyn?"

"Oh, I'm no good to her anymore. She went off with a group of journalists. There's another party in town. She got what she wanted. So did I. Nothing wrong."

"There's a towel in the room just behind you."

"I'll get it for you. Jensen Sandler said you're not to be late for the start of your new movie... Is Myra all right? When's the baby due?"

"After Christmas... Where's the Isle of Man?"

"Between England and Ireland. Dad was seconded from the navy to an RAF base when he was doing his national service after the war. Spent a week on a radar course. Says the island is quiet and very beautiful. It's also a tax haven like the Channel Islands. The British Isles are a bit complicated. I'm going to bury myself in the country."

"What about women?"

Coming out of the pool naked, Julian took the towel from Randall, dried himself and wrapped it around his middle. Far away over the sea the final red of the sunset was beautiful, the patches of clear blue between the red clouds fading as Julian watched. He could hear voices from the pathway. Randall handed him his shirt.

"I'll get a dog or a cat. I love cats. Maybe fifty acres. They call them smallholdings. Women? I'm not very lucky with women... Are you going to be happy with my sister?"

"I hope so. I'm going to make it work."

"I'm happy for you. You can always visit me on my little farm if you get sick of being chased by the media."

"Goes with the territory."

"Of course it does. We're lucky. Our flights tomorrow are only an hour apart. We can all go to the airport together."

"Is anyone meeting you in London?"

"I don't think so. Maybe Uncle Paul. He's usually pretty busy on a Monday. Phillip will be at Harare Airport to meet you and Myra. Give my love to the big river. Don't forget."

"I won't. How does it feel to have a brother-in-law?"

Julian's mother and father-in-law walked through the gate at the top of the path from the beach.

"I like it... Bergit, Myra's still sleeping. What a sister. Sleeps right through her wedding reception... Well I'll be blowed. Look who's here. Hello, Myra. You're up."

"I'm hungry. Starving. Having a baby makes me tired and hungry."

"We're all going to the airport tomorrow together."

"Why don't we have supper round the pool? I'll make something. We don't have servants. Julian doesn't like people under his feet. How was your walk, Dad?"

"What a beautiful sunset. Reminded me of World's View."

"Do you still miss the farm?"

"Every waking moment of my day. When you've lived in Africa it's difficult to settle down anywhere else. Am I not right, Randall?"

"Spot on. Maybe one day, when Mugabe's gone, we can all go home again. You three stay round the pool. I'll go and help Mrs Becker in the kitchen. Mrs Becker. Has a nice ring to it."

As Julian watched them go off to the kitchen he was thinking of Sally and Joan, the two spinster sisters who had given him back his life. They would be happy for him. In the small room where Randall had found the towel, he got dressed. The warmth of mentally thanking Sally and Joan was tangible. He could feel their presence.

2

a wall of heat hit Julian as he walked out of the terminal building at Harare Airport carrying both of their travelling bags. The heat was overpowering. Myra was hugging Phillip having run into his arms. It was good to see a brother and sister who loved each other. The safari fifteen-seater bus he had travelled in on his previous visit was waiting for them in the parking lot. They climbed in the bus which was stifling hot from having sat in the sun. The journey had been long, Julian not sure if taking a woman seven months pregnant all the way to Africa was such a good idea.

"Why is it so hot, Phillip?"

"October, Julian. Suicide month. When the rains break next month it will cool down."

"We can't go down into the Zambezi Valley in this kind of heat."

"Of course we can't. We're going to the Nyanga and the Chimanimani mountains, seven thousand feet above sea level. Nice and cool and very beautiful. You'll like it. Why Zimbabwe is the perfect country to run a tourist business. Whatever time of the year there's somewhere to go. When's the baby due?"

"In December. Do you have good doctors in Zimbabwe?"

"Not really. The good ones left the country when Mugabe started his black economic empowerment policies. A white man working for the government didn't have any future."

"Are the hospitals working?"

"Sort of."

"Are there any private hospitals?"

"There are but the only hospital I know is the Harare General. You're not sick are you?"

"I worry about Myra and the baby. This heat is terrible."

"Be better when we get going with the air conditioning. How do you feel, Myra?"

"I've got a tummy ache. I hate flying. It's so boring. You just sit for hour after hour. Probably the airline food. How's Craig and Jojo?"

"She's still not pregnant."

"I'm so lucky to be pregnant. I can't wait to be a mother. Have you got a girlfriend, Phillip?"

"There aren't any eligible girls left in Zimbabwe. Craig and Jojo love each other but people on both sides of the racial divide look at them with suspicion. I wonder how their kids will fit into society? The world's so bigoted. No, I don't think I'll ever get myself married if I stay in Zimbabwe."

"You could always go to England and look for a wife. What they did in the old days."

"No English girl in her right mind would want to marry a Zimbabwean and live in Africa."

"Bad as that?"

"Not good. Now the farms are being taken over the economy is going down the drain. Tourism is still okay. Mugabe still has a good reputation overseas. A hero of the new Africa. Equal rights for everyone. You got to have good, well-trained people to run a business. Not some political appointee. We'll see. I always try and stay positive. Can you feel the air conditioning?"

"Has anyone been up to the farm since Dad left?"

"Don't be silly. We're not welcome. The new owner is one of Mugabe's cronies. He's kicked everyone off the farm and brought in his own people."

"What's happened to Silas?"

"I don't know. I just don't know. In the new Zimbabwe it's better not to ask political questions."

"So everyone on the farm lost their jobs?"

"That's about it. When they've gone through the year's wages Dad gave them they are going to be in trouble."

"But where are they living?"

"As I said. Don't ask questions. You're lucky, Myra. You got out of it thanks to Julian... How's Randall?"

"Terrible. He can't write. Gone to England to find himself a smallholding on the Isle of Man wherever that is. With people on top of him all the time in New York he couldn't get a book started. I worry about Randall. All that nonsense with Amanda has soured our brother. Made him cynical."

"He'll get over it. He's Randall... Once the air conditioning washes over you it's pleasant isn't it? Very pleasant. Let's hope the rains break soon. So, Myra, tell me everything. How was the wedding?"

"I slept through the reception. The baby makes me tired. My stomach ache is making me uncomfortable. Having a baby is uncomfortable. All part of motherhood. So, what have you been up to, Phillip?"

"Not much. Working. Making a living. What life is all about."

"Just look at it. Even at the end of the dry season the countryside looks so beautiful. It's wonderful to be home. Even for a short visit."

"America is now your home."

"Of course it is, silly. I was just being nostalgic."

"How's Dad taking it?"

"Not very well. He hates not working. Having nothing to do."

Julian was only half listening to what they were saying, the rhythm of the tyres on the road making him daydream. Up front, over the empty seats, he could see the back of the head of the African driver. They were all sitting at the back of the bus, a Bedford truck that had been converted by Jacques, Phillip's business partner, into the perfect safari vehicle, everything self-contained, tents, cooking equipment all on top of the vehicle covered with a tarpaulin. Julian looked out of the window. Everything looked peaceful. All he could see was bush. After an hour they passed through a village, the driver stopping for petrol. Phillip got out of the bus to pay the attendant. Myra, her head against the side of the window, was asleep, both her hands clasped over her pregnant stomach. She looked peaceful. Phillip and the driver got back into the bus. The journey went on. Myra woke, looked around, smiled and closed her eyes. Phillip, sitting between them on the long backseat, was quiet, thinking. Julian, back into the rhythm of the tyres, let himself think of the film. Jensen Sandler had bought the rights to a novel set in a German prisoner-of-war camp two months after the D-Day landing in Normandy in the penultimate year of the Second World War. Julian was to play the senior American officer. A good scriptwriter had written the movie, making Julian confident. The crux of the story was the relationship of the German camp commander and the senior American officer. At the start of the film, the German has just lost his wife and three young children in an Allied bombing raid over Cologne. During the day the Americans had pattern-bombed the town, leaving it to the British to do the same at night, reducing the buildings to rubble. Julian's character sympathises with the German commander. They both hate war. What was the point of war, they ask each other? Everyone lost. At the end of the film, just as the Allied forces arrive at the camp to liberate the prisoners, the German commander commits suicide.

"You look sad, Julian. Something the matter?"

"Just getting ready for my new movie. You have to work your way into a part. Become the person you are playing. Have his feelings. You have to play your character from the inside... How long did the war last in Rhodesia?"

"Fifteen years."

"Did anyone win?"

"Robert Mugabe thinks so."

"Fifteen years is longer than the Second World War, Korea and Vietnam put together, and you wonder if it will ever stop."

"There are always wars. Always fighting. Part of human nature. Survival of the fittest. Call it what you like."

"Where do we camp tonight?"

"Next to a lake. We've plenty of fresh food I bought in Harare before your plane landed. We'll do some fishing in the lake. Funny going on my sister's honeymoon."

"Who better to look after us?"

"She's always sleeping."

"I don't know much about giving birth. Everything was fine when we left America. She looks so peaceful."

"Yes she does. Thank you for marrying her, Julian. Many men would have run away, or made her have an abortion... Why do people want to kill their own children before they are born? All we leave behind are our children. A generation or two down the line no one even remembers us. The only part of us that goes on is our seed. I'm so envious. I've never met the woman I want to have my baby. In not so long I'll be forty. Then fifty. An old bachelor with nothing in life to show for it."

"He's a good driver."

"Been with us a couple of years. Jobs are not easy to find in Zimbabwe. Someone has to create the employment by making a successful business. I don't think Mugabe understands how it all works. He and his cronies are only interested in themselves. In power. In holding onto power for fear of a backlash. He's turning into a dictator like so many others in Africa who fought their wars of liberation from colonial rule. I sometimes wonder where it will all end... You feel like a beer? They'll be cold by now. We have a connection from the bus to the coolbox and its electric motor."

"Sounds good."

"Shall I wake Myra?"

"She doesn't drink with the baby."

"Of course she doesn't... What's it like to be a film star?"

"Only other people see you differently. I'm still the same inside. Only the outside looks different. Once the baby is born and the film finished I'm out of it. People suffocate me. Fame and fortune isn't all it's cracked up to be. Why everyone chases after it is beyond my comprehension."

"Where will you live?"

"Somewhere quiet. Where a child can grow up in peace and be normal. I hate all the intrusion. All the attention. You're the one who's got the perfect job."

"If it wasn't for the politics. There's always something. I'll get us a beer."

"Thanks for being there for us."

"It's my pleasure."

More than halfway through his life Julian still didn't understand what it was all about. There had to be a purpose, a reason for existence. There were so many religions telling different stories. No one Julian knew had come back from the dead to prove them right or wrong. He wanted to believe in religion to make sense of his life but he couldn't. Maybe one day when it was too late he would find out and find himself in hell. The only future Julian could logically see was through his children. Through the child clasped by Myra in her belly. Julian got up and gave her a kiss.

"What was that for?"

"You're awake."

"I like to daydream with my eyes shut. I'm going to call him Jay."

"Thank you, Myra."

"What for?"

"For getting pregnant."

Julian sat back, comfortable with his feelings. Phillip handed him a cold bottle of beer, the moisture dripping down its sides. Outside, Julian could see a herd of cows in a farmer's field. They were still passing through farmland that had been developed by the white man: strong fences, dams and ploughed fields ready for the new rains and the planting season. Julian drank his beer from the bottle. It was just perfect. He was on his way to the mountains.

"You want another beer?"

"Why not? The family on safari. What could be better? Why do you call farmland the bush?"

"We call everything the bush. You have to leave cultivated farmland for a few years before replanting or the soil deteriorates. My father was a good farmer. All that knowledge wasted. Politics. It's all politics. One minute the solution is communism and now look what's happening in Russia. Do you think Anglo-Saxon capitalism will go the same way?"

"Almost certainly. When a system becomes established it becomes corrupt. Hereditary monarchies have had their day. Man's infused with greed. If he can't make it he steals or starts a revolution. There are always poor people with nothing, ready to listen to a revolutionary. Democracy is becoming corrupt with too many people in politics for their own selfish reasons. Politics has become a career. All this 'doing it for the good of the people' is their way of getting elected. A manifesto for change. Take from the rich and give to the poor. In America big money and big corporations control politics and the politicians. They call them lobbyists. Paid for by business to make sure the best interests of big business are looked after. Man is inherently corrupt, despite what comes out of his mouth."

"I'll get us another beer."

"You do that."

"Were you happier living as a beachcomber?"

"Much happier. No money. No worries. And no responsibilities. Worked well for a while. But you have to have the backing of your own money to get through the later years in life."

"How do you hold onto your money when you've made it? Look at Dad."

"That's a whole other question. Nothing is certain in life."

Further down the road vendors were selling vegetables, black people sitting on the side of the road trying to make a living. Phillip stopped the bus. With the driver he walked back to the vendors, filling a large wicker basket with fruit and vegetables. The journey went on, the farmland no longer on either side of the road. All Julian could see was uncultivated bush and the occasional wild animal.

"What's that one, Phillip?"

"A grey crowned crane. The male is slightly taller than the female. Behind is a wildebeest that some call a gnu."

"They're beautiful."

The light was beginning to fade when they reached their destination. The driver climbed up on top of the bus and undid the tarpaulin. The sun was setting across the lake, the water so still. A rowing boat with two old men was in the middle of the lake. The two old men were fishing from the bow and stern, their backs to each other, the glow of the setting sun highlighting them. Like the surface of the water they were both still, their rods motionless at a forty-five degree angle. Julian doubted either of them had caught a fish. The driver handed down a folded tent to Phillip, Myra watching. She seemed better, no longer clutching her stomach. A bundle of wooden tent poles was handed down next, Julian's offer to help rejected. The driver's name was Sedgewick. Julian wondered why the man did not have an African name. So many of the African leaders had English first names: Robert Mugabe, Nelson Mandela. Why was Mandela, the man about to liberate South Africa from the vile grip of apartheid, named after a British admiral? Or was he? It made Julian curious. A second tent and set of poles were handed down, along with the rest of the camping equipment. They were going to camp close to the water's edge.

The sun slipped down behind the range of distant mountains, the perfect backdrop to the lake. The old men pulled in their lines and stashed their rods, each picking up an oar. They sat on the bench in the middle of the boat and began to row to the shore. Myra was standing with her shoeless feet in the water watching them. They were all going to go for a swim. The evening air was warm but no longer suffocating. Birds were calling, the only sound other than the creaking rowlocks. Julian, standing alone, happy in his soul, watched the two old men run the boat into shore, struggling to climb out of the boat. They were both very old. When they spoke, they both had English accents, the same as Jeremy, Julian's new father-in-law. The twilight end to the day for two old friends in their twilight years. Julian wondered how long they had known each other. He didn't think they were brothers. All those years on the beach had taught him to read people accurately. Sometimes he was wrong. The old men walked slowly to their campsite, one of them carrying two large fish. He was wrong about the fish. The men, a hundred yards from where Phillip was putting up the tents, lit a fire, the flames dancing in the fading light of the day. They were going to cook their catch over the fire. The two old men looked so content with the fish and each other it made Julian envious. Old friends. There was nothing better in life than old friends.

By the time the light went completely they were sitting round the fire, Sedgewick still doing the chores. The beers in the coolbox were still cold. They were camped among a clump of trees, the firelight dancing up into the overhanging boughs throwing shadows. Apart from themselves, the only other reality was the old men's fire, the flames still dancing. They had forgotten to go for their swim despite Phillip assuring Julian there were no crocodiles in the lake. For the first time since leaving his lair on the beach close to Felix Kranskie's beach house, Julian felt he had escaped from the burden of the human race, America a million miles away with all its noise and bustle, the long, tedious flight now worth the effort. He was content. For the first time in a long while, Julian was content. There was peace on earth and goodwill to all men. He was happy. No one spoke. No one said anything. All of them were happy on the side of their African lake.

When Sedgewick put the meat on the fire to cook, Julian's mouth watered. Like the rest of them he was hungry. They were sitting waiting, watching the meat cook over the campfire.

"Tell us a story, Julian."

"What kind of a story, Myra?"

"A good one. You tell the most beautiful stories about your time roaming the world. I love to hear them. A good story around a campfire. What could be better?"

"Well, let me think. There was a time in Australia. We were in the Orbost Forest. That's in the State of Victoria, a three-hour drive from Melbourne. I was camped on my own. All I had in the world was the pack on my back and my sleeping bag. Much like this I was under some trees. It was summer, the grass soft and dry. I made a fire and sat, happy, wondering what it would be like to have a son. To take a son of mine camping in the forest. Take him fishing. Catch two fish and put them on the fire."

"You're making it up as you go along."

"Of course I am. That is the art of storytelling. And the story is coming true. But let me tell you what happened that night in the Orbost Forest..."

His voice low, so as not to disturb the two old men, Julian told them a story. Sedgwick, having left the meat to cook, had sat down next to him. An owl was calling from across the lake. Julian went on and on. Doing what he did best. Entertaining. Entertaining other people... When he finished telling his mostly fictional story they all sat still, no one talking. During the telling, Phillip had turned over the meat. Later he got up and made the salad in a big wooden bowl, the salad dressing he poured over the lettuce already made and kept in a jar. Mixed in with the lettuce were tomatoes and cucumber. Fresh salad from the hawker on the side of the road. At the other camp, one of the old men was playing a guitar and singing. The man could really sing, making Julian prick up his ears. The second old man joined in, his voice croaking. Chances were they were drinking. They sounded so happy, content with each other's company. Both fires had gone down leaving a red glow, the fat from the meat spurting the occasional flame as Phillip tended the meat. Sedgwick had gone to the bus, coming back with four glasses, a corkscrew and two bottles of red wine. All part of the safari service. Phillip popped one of the corks and poured out three glasses of wine, the wine warm from the day's heat but still delicious. Myra had told him not to pour her a glass of wine. Julian thought of Randall and hoped he had conquered his alcohol addiction. In life there was always a problem. From the dark they could hear the two old men laughing. An owl began hooting, a distant call from the other side of the lake. When Julian looked across the water he could see the stars reflected in the surface of the lake. It was very beautiful. Looking up he could see three layers of stars going all the way up to heaven, the one a long splash of light as if the gods had thrown it out over the heavens.

"Tell me about the stars, Phillip."

"That one is the Southern Cross." said Phillip, pointing. "You can find south by drawing a line through the stars. Above is the Milky Way."

"And the owl? What kind of owl?"

"A spotted eagle owl. They are very common. They are calling to each other, the male and the female. Chances are they have a nest with chicks. They sit all day in the trees guarding the nest, the male usually fifty yards or so away. They are my favourite owls. Such a beautiful call... How's the wine going down?"

"Any chance of some of that meat? If I had to bet I'd say the guitar player was a professional. One old singer in America, whose name I can't remember, went on singing in clubs into his nineties. He had to change the way he covered the strings, his fingers were so arthritic. But he played and sang. People flocked to hear him. By then he was rich. Did it for the pleasure of entertaining other people. Making them happy."

"You want to eat now? The potatoes Sedgewick wrapped with tin foil and put under the fire before it was started will be ready. Baked spuds dripping in butter. My favourite. Why are you so quiet, Myra?"

"I'm enjoying myself. You don't have to talk when you are enjoying yourself. You think our baby can hear that music, Julian?"

"Of course he can. I've heard most mothers sing to their babies in the womb. Makes them appreciate music later on."

"I can't sing... Are you being serious?"

Like the wine, the food was delicious, Julian eating more than his fill, his old instinct from his days as a bum making him finish whatever he could find.

"Why don't you get fat, darling? That's your fourth helping. If I ate that much I'd end up fat as a pig."

"You're smaller than me."

"Can I just have a sip of your wine? A sip won't hurt the baby. You're all getting tipsy... Thank you, husband... Now I'm going to the tent. The old men have gone quiet... Just look at that moon."

"You want me to come with you?"

"Don't be silly. You're on safari. Do they have lions in the Nyanga, Phillip?"

"Lots of them. But they won't worry you." Phillip was smiling.

"Are you being serious?"

She kissed Phillip, then Julian and smiled at Sedgewick, took the torch and went off to her bed. Julian sat back in his canvas chair, his long legs stretched out to the fire, the glass of wine held in both of his hands on his lap. Later, Sedgwick took himself off to his tent. Together, Julian and his new brother-in-law finished the second bottle of wine. When he walked to the tent and went inside the mosquito net was hanging from the centre pole over his wife, protecting her and the baby. The small torch showed him she was asleep. Julian took off his clothes and got under the net. Gently, without waking her, he took his wife into his arms. Outside, intermittently, the owls were still hooting to each other, the one calling, the other one answering. A soft, cool wind was brushing the side of the tent. Without realising what had happened Julian went to sleep. When he woke in the dark of the night he was still holding Myra. His one arm had gone to sleep making Julian turn over. More comfortable, with their naked bottoms touching each other, Julian went back to sleep. In his dream he was out on a rowing boat fishing with his son. The boy was ten years old. The boy caught a fish, crying out with excitement. When Julian woke the morning sun was peeking into the tent. Myra had gone. He could smell the woodsmoke from the morning fire. Julian lay awake enjoying the sound of their voices. Sedgwick brought him a mug of tea. When he got up, having pulled on his trousers, he went outside and stretched. He was getting used to drinking tea in the morning. The two old men had gone. So had their boat. Across at the morning fire, Phillip was frying bacon, the smell making Julian hungry.

"Good morning, everyone. What a beautiful day to be alive."

Julian walked down to the water's edge. He was thinking of the days when he had no money, drying tea bags to make them stretch to three cups of tea, fresh mint instead of milk, the flavour of mint tea coming back to him. Like now, those were happy days. In those days, unlike in the tent with its thin mattress, he had slept on the ground. When he walked back Sedgewick was serving breakfast. Soon after they broke camp. The journey went on. Higher and higher towards the distant range of mountains. Each night they stopped by a river or a lake. They were in the Nyanga National Park, a legacy of Cecil John Rhodes, the founder of Rhodesia. There were no signs of lions, only the spoor of nocturnal leopards. On the tenth day of their safari Phillip spotted a leopard stretched out on the bough of a tree. The animal, its yellow eyes narrowed, just looked at them. They all backed away. When Julian looked back the animal was still watching him from the tree. The leopard looked so comfortable. That afternoon, camped by a small stream, Myra complained of pains in her stomach. By the time the sun went down Julian knew they had a problem. By the estimate of Myra's gynaecologist back in America the baby was not due for another eight weeks. In the middle of the night Julian woke in the tent to find his wife writhing. Julian went into panic. They were in the middle of nowhere.

"Phillip! Myra needs help. Wake up. For God's sake wake up. We've got to get her to a hospital. Where's the nearest hospital?"

"Mutare. Nearly two hundred kilometres. Take us a couple of hours. We'll break camp."

"Leave the bloody tents. I'll pay for them."

"What's wrong?"

"I don't know. She's writhing."

"Has her water broken?"

"Can't see anything in the dark."

"Let's go. Sedgwick, bring what you can. We can drive back again."

Phillip drove the bus. The road wound down from the Nyanga mountains, Phillip driving as fast as possible. Myra lay out on the backseat groaning with the pain. The journey was endless. In the small town as dawn was breaking they stopped at the first petrol station to ask directions. The lone petrol attendant was half asleep. He didn't know anything about a hospital. They knocked next door at a house. No one answered the door. Phillip drove to the central police station. The woman at the desk told them where to go. In the panic, Phillip missed the turn. At the government hospital there were no doctors on duty. Julian's worst nightmare had begun. No one, so far as he could see, knew anything. They all tried and passed the buck, suggesting someone else could help. No one seemed very interested. The woman was having a baby. The father was in panic. Everything to them seemed normal. Half an hour later when the gynaecologist arrived at the hospital from his house in the suburbs he said Myra needed a caesarean. He was going to cut the baby out of her womb.

"Will the baby be all right?"

"I don't know, Mr Becker. Not until I get inside your wife and find the problem. I'll do my best. What were you doing on holiday with a seven-month pregnant woman?"

"It's our honeymoon."

The man was old. Past retirement. A white man with a look of sadness. There had been no thought of a problem when they left America. Everything had checked out normal.

When the man cut the baby from Myra's womb, Julian was watching. The baby, a boy, did not cry. Myra's eyes had gone up into their sockets. The baby was dead, the old surgeon shaking his head. When Myra opened her eyes she asked for her baby. When told her boy had died she shut her eyes.

"I want to die."

"You're not going to die, Mrs Becker. The cord in your stomach had twisted and strangled your baby. I've never seen it before in all my years. I'm so sorry for both of you. The good news is you are young. No reason why you can't have another baby."

"It's all my fault. I got myself pregnant. It wasn't an accident, Julian."

"It doesn't matter."

"You're right. It doesn't matter. Nothing matters now. You can't blame anyone but me. When you do something wrong in life, God punishes you. What are we going to do?"

"Catch the first plane back to America."

"Can I see my dead baby?"

"Not today, Mrs Becker. There will have to be a funeral. You can see him then. It's best to see your baby and to come to terms with your tragedy. I'm so sorry. There was nothing anyone could have done. I'm going to give you another sedative. After a good sleep you'll feel better."

"I'll never feel better. Leave me alone."

THE FUNERAL TOOK place two days later in the church. Before the funeral, on a slab in the mortuary, they had been shown the baby. He was lying on his back naked. There was nothing covering him. They turned and clung to each other, Julian only thinking of himself. Of what Myra had said. That she had planned her pregnancy to get married and stay in America. Was there anyone in the whole wide world he could trust? Who was she anyway? A woman he had bumped into at an airport, and had a one-night stand. The thought of the baby had brought them together. The mutual excitement of becoming parents. Of having a purpose in life. Leaving a mark. Leaving behind something more important than their own trivial lives. Who was an actor? Did it matter? Did all the money in the world really matter? There had to be a purpose in life and for both of them that had been children. Now they had nothing. Nothing to bind them. Nothing to make them whole. At the end of the long, sobbing hug they had not even looked at each other, neither wanting the other to see what they were thinking.

At the church funeral Phillip did his best. After the short ceremony, the small body was taken to the funeral director's furnace and cremated. They were given the remains in a fancy jar the man called an urn. Julian paid the bill. Not knowing anything about the procedures of the Church of England, he had given the priest two one hundred dollar bills. They got in the bus for the drive to Harare and the international airport. Phillip had booked them the flight. In the bus, nobody spoke. Phillip sat in the middle of the bus to leave them alone. Sedgwick was driving. Sedated, Myra went to sleep, Julian not sure if their marriage wasn't over. They had a long journey to take. They would have to see. Trust, the most important relationship of two people, had been broken. If you couldn't trust a person how could you live with them for the rest of your life? The thought of finding some other woman with whom to have his children was equally appalling. And he was old. He was going to go to his grave without any purpose from his life. Was everyone, including himself, so damn selfish? Did people only think of themselves? Of what they wanted, to hell with the real feelings of other people? The thought made him sick. He could see at the end of the seat the small jar of cremated remains. His future. Everything that he had longed for all his life. As Julian sat staring blindly out of the window, the rhythm of the tyres on the road mocking him, all he had ever wanted was a family. The two feet that separated him from Myra could have been a million miles. Not even hope came into his mind. What had started had now been finished. Despite his new fame and fortune as a Hollywood actor he was completely on his own. She had used him. Simple as that. And like so many other times in his life he was only thinking of himself instead of the young girl who had just lost her baby. It made him realise how horrible he was. A despicable person. But that was how it was. A member of the human race, a race they all tried to say was so wonderful. So caring. So concerned with other people. All of it bullshit.

3

They reached the airport just in time, an hour before take-off.

"Sorry about the tents."

"Look after her, Julian."

"I'll try. I'm not at my best right now."

"None of us are."

"Good luck with your business."

"Good luck with your new film."

The small talk over, they walked through into the transit lounge leaving Phillip standing, a sad look on his face. The plane was called and they walked out onto the tarmac. The first leg of their flight was to Johannesburg in South Africa where they would change planes.

"Do you hate me, Julian?"

"I feel sorry for you, Myra. I feel sorry for both of us. We wished for a dream. We all hope our dreams come true. Most of them don't."

"What are we going to do?"

"I don't know. Why didn't you tell me you had intentionally got yourself pregnant before we got married?"

"I was scared you wouldn't marry me. Make me have an abortion. I didn't have a country. I was desperate. People do desperate things in desperate situations. There was no future for a white girl in Zimbabwe."

"You used me."

"We all use each other, Julian. It's part of human nature. Don't worry. We can get a divorce. I won't want anything... Will I be able to stay in America?"

"Probably."

"Why did you leave the urn on the bus?"

"So it wouldn't remind me for the rest of my life that I don't have a family. Never have since a boy of six."

"What are you talking about?"

"We all hide things, Myra. My father shot and killed a man in a bar. My mother committed suicide. They executed my father. I grew up in foster homes until two old spinsters looked after me. They were in theatre and paid for me to go to drama school."

"You poor darling. And I thought we had problems in Zimbabwe."

"I wanted a family."

"Why didn't you tell me?"

"Would you have wanted your son's grandfather to have been a murderer?"

"Probably not."

On the plane, Myra took his hand. The long flight home had begun.

"What were their names? I'd like to meet them."

"Sally and Joan. Both of them are dead."

Only then did Julian look at Myra. She was crying. He had made her cry.

"I'm so sorry, Myra."

"What do you have to be sorry about?"

"Give me back your hand."

"Why?"

"We have to support each other. There's nobody left."

"Will I be able to have more children?"

"We can find out."

"I couldn't go through that again."

"Neither could I. How long's the flight to Johannesburg?"

"A couple of hours... Why does everything always go wrong in my life?"

"Join the club."

She was smiling, wiping away the tears. After everything, she was smiling. The aircraft had reached cruising height. A stewardess offered them coffee and cake. Life around Julian was normal, the real world going about its business. They said time healed everything. He had to believe it. Hope, Sally and Joan had told him, springs eternal. He would have to hope.

AT JAN SMUTS AIRPORT JULIAN phoned Nora Stewart to tell his publicist they were coming home and give her news of the baby. He wanted to tell somebody. Nora cried.

"Don't cry for me, Nora. It's over. We have to get on with our lives."

"I had three miscarriages."

"You never told me."

"Why should I? Jensen Sandler will be happy to hear you're coming back. He doesn't trust you. I'll meet you at the airport. The press will have to be told."

"Why?"

"They're expecting your wife to have a baby. It's news. We can't hide it. They know Myra was pregnant. She couldn't hide her belly. Got to go. I'm late for an appointment. Thank you for phoning."

The long, tedious journey continued until they landed in Los Angeles. Myra had spent most of the journey sedated. Despite Julian's revelation of his parents' deaths they had found little to talk about. Nora, who had been in Los Angeles visiting clients, was waiting with the media.

"Did she go to Africa to have an abortion, Julian?"

"Of course not."

"Isn't no longer being pregnant too much of a coincidence, Mrs Becker? Why did you have an abortion? Was your marriage a sham to stay in America? Aren't you Zimbabwean? Didn't your father just lose his farm?"

"Shut up, you bastard. Leave my wife alone. She's just lost her baby. Don't you have any feelings?"

"Are you going to stay married?"

Before Julian could hit the journalist, Nora stepped between them, shaking her head.

"Leave him alone, Julian. He's just doing his job."

"How low do you have to sink to get a story?"

Walking through the concourse the barrage of questions went on, Julian sick of the whole business. They wouldn't leave him alone. They thought they owned him. Myra, walking next to him, was white as a sheet. Nora, letting them go ahead, engaged the reporters. Julian could hear her say there would be a press statement giving them the details of Myra's illness. By the time they reached Nora's car in the parking lot, Julian had made up his mind. He had had enough of being famous. Had enough of people.

At the car Myra told him to sit in the front. Nora was driving them back to the beach house. She had that look on her face. That know-all look of 'that's what happens when you break the rules and marry a girl half your age'. The slight smile said she was almost pleased Myra had lost the baby. She had not forgotten or forgiven their brief affair. It was human nature to take satisfaction from other people's problems. Instead of thinking of himself or Myra, Julian thought of Nora, an old woman with plastic surgery on her face in a desperate attempt to make her look younger. A woman whose chances had passed her by. Three miscarriages. It was hard for Julian to imagine Nora's pain, the pain growing as she grew older, alone, only her business to keep her going, to give her an interest. When she looked at him again Julian put his hand on Nora's knee. From the backseat Myra could not see what he was doing. Nora resented the hand and pulled her knee away, Julian's gesture missing its point of sympathy. Throughout his life Julian had found women difficult to understand.

At the beach house Nora said she had to go back to Los Angeles. She was due to fly back to New York in the afternoon.

"You be ready for filming, Julian. I gave Jensen my word you wouldn't muck him around. You try anything silly and you'll be out of the film business for the rest of your life. Look after yourself, Myra. We'll be in touch."

Julian could feel Nora's stress. Everything was back to business. He watched the car drive away. When he turned back to the house Myra was looking at him, fire in her eyes.

"You had an affair with that woman. You know something? She was glad I lost the baby. She's a bitch."

"During her marriage she had three miscarriages. Don't be too quick to judge people. I'm going for a walk. You want to come?"

"No I don't."

Inside, the house was emotionally cold. He walked through, across the lawn, let himself out of the security gate and walked down to the beach. For the first time in a long time Julian had no idea what he was going to do. Women! You couldn't live with them and you couldn't live without them. The best thing to do was leave everything alone. Pretend their lives were normal and see what happened. Poor Myra. Poor Nora... Down the beach he found a flat pebble and threw it at the sea, the stone skipping over the water. An old trick he had learnt as a boy. He looked up at the sky. The sky was still blue. He looked around. There was nobody on the beach. Stripping down to his underpants Julian ran into the water. He swam and swam, beating the mental pain out of his body. When he got out of the water a couple were standing next to his clothes.

"Are these yours?"

"They were."

"Shouldn't you be wearing a bathing suit?"

Shaking his head, still wet from head to toe, Julian pulled on his clothes. It never stopped. People. It truly was a wonderful world.

Back at the house, Myra was lying on a chaise longue next to the pool. She was wearing a bathing costume, her stomach no longer protruding, the wound from the operation still livid.

"How was the beach?"

"Lovely. I took a swim in the sea."

"I made some lunch if you're hungry."

"I could eat a horse."

THE WEEK he had saved from being back early, Julian used to take himself into character, to make his mind think like a B-17 bomber pilot in the midst of a war, a man who had thrown bombs out of an aircraft to kill women and children convincing himself he was right, blaming the Nazis and Hitler. By the time the cameras rolled on the lot he was Colonel Josh Landau of the United States Air Force, a Jew fighting a righteous war of revenge. For all the weeks of filming Julian was moody, the character's life no longer knowing right from wrong staying with him. For most of the time he stayed in a room near the set, going back to the beach house as little as possible. Myra did not seem to mind. Never once did she visit the studio to see the process of filming, to watch him dressed up in a World War Two uniform. It was better for both of them. They both needed space. Being largely set in the German prison camp, the story was more important than the scenery. After three months the job was done, Julian and most of the actors mentally and physically exhausted. Without Myra knowing, Julian put the beach house on the market, packed up his things in his temporary room and went home. Once again Julian had been frugal not to waste his money. He told no one what he was doing, not even Nora Stewart. Jensen Sandler shook his hand and they parted.

"You'll be ready to help with the publicity, Julian?"

"Of course I will," Julian lied.

"I'm spending a third of the budget on marketing the film."

"Of course you are, Jensen. You're one of Hollywood's best producers. It's all in the marketing."

"You've got to sell the movie if you want it to succeed. They say the turnover at the box office is in direct proportion to the amount you spend on advertising. Why films without money behind them don't succeed."

"I'll leave that all to you, Jensen. I know nothing about business. Thanks for the ride."

"You're a good actor."

"I hope so."

"When we top the ratings I'll be looking for you again. You don't spend all that advertising money on an actor and not use him again."

"I'll keep my fingers crossed. Give my love to your new wife."

With twisted smiles and a final handshake his film career was over. In the camper he had just bought for his next journey, Julian drove home to the beach house.

"There have been realtors all over the place. What's going on, Julian?... Who owns that vehicle?"

"The film's finished. We're going on a journey."

"Where to?"

"I have no idea. We'll find out when we get there."

"Are we selling the house?"

"I hope so. I'm putting all our money into six what the man called 'global equity funds'. Sixty per cent in stocks and forty per cent in cash and bonds. Whatever all that means. I had some help from Felix Kranskie. He's good at investing his money for the future. We'll never have to worry about money. After a year or two on the road, Mrs Becker, we'll truly get to know each other. Then we can both make up our minds."

"You've got to be kidding."

"Matter of fact, I'm not. If you don't want to come I won't force you. It's up to you to make up your mind."

"What about your film career?"

"That's history."

"Does anyone know?"

"Only you. Why work when you don't need money? You can only eat one meal at a time. The rest is showing off. I'm sick of showing off. I'm sick of everyone trying to use me. They all want a piece of you when you are famous. And according to Jensen Sandler, fame is all in the advertising, not the ability of the artist."

"Can I sleep on it?"

"I want the right price for the house. You'll have plenty of time to think."

"Let me have a look inside."

"It's got everything. A shower. Cooker. Television. Plenty of room. They call it a mobile home. What more could two people want? Get in, Myra. Take a look. Be my guest. To quote your brother Randall, 'I'm getting the hell out of the way'."

"You're quite mad, Julian."

"I know I am. But it's fun."

When Myra climbed out of the camper, a vehicle almost the size of a bus, she was shaking her head. There was no look of excitement. No look of adventure.

"Shouldn't we rather sell the house after we've gone a month or two and found out if we like what we are doing? What are we going to do with ourselves? You can't spend the whole day staring out at the passing scenery. Do you have wild animals in America? What are we going to be looking at? And when we stop, all we'll meet are strangers. Won't it be dangerous? In the house when we go to bed we turn on the security system. It makes me feel safe. In this we'll be exposed to criminals. To anyone who feels like robbing us. Out there they rape young women. You read all about it in the papers and see it on television. The news is full of problems. I mean, if after a month we find we want to go home it won't be any good if we've sold our home. When you were a bum you didn't have anything worth stealing. Now you are famous. People will recognise you. You can't just run away and expect people not to remember. You've got a whole new film coming out. You'll be all over the news, in every cinema across the country. However much you want to escape, they won't let you. You are who you are, a famous actor. That will never change. The newspapers will catch up with you and say it's one big publicity stunt. You told me Ernest Hemingway disappeared into the heart of Africa for several months and the papers said it was one big publicity stunt."

"And look what happened to Hemingway. He shot himself."

"You can't have life both ways. You can't be rich and famous and retain your privacy. Not as an actor. You have to take both the good and the bad. I know the bad. I lost my baby. But I still have you, Julian. Please don't ruin your life. You can't change what's done. You're famous. A brilliant screen actor. You like acting. Enjoy what you've got. We can go on holidays. We can go on a holiday in the camper. But we still have to have a home to come back to. Nothing in life is perfect. Ask my poor father. But Dad still has money. He's one of the lucky ones. So are you. Invest your money in whatever those things are called so when they won't give you parts we'll still have money. And that will happen, Julian. As sure as night follows day. It's how life works. But if you've got money you can always get by. Maybe one day soon we'll be making love again. You won't be put off by my scar and our terrible memory. Maybe I'll have another baby. Who knows? And then what will happen if we don't have a home? I like this place. So do you. It's familiar. Please don't sell it, Julian. It's our home."

"So you'll come with me on the road?"

"Of course I will. Provided we have something to come back to."

"I just want to get the hell out of the way."

"I know you do. But you've got to be practical."

"If I don't disappear Jensen and Nora will have me on every chat show in America promoting the film."

"It's part of the job. What they pay you for. It's going to be months before they finish editing the film. We'll go on a journey. Take a holiday. Take a break. Learn to physically love each other again. We'll go 'walkabout' as they say in Australia. But we'll have to come back again. It's how it works. How life works. You can't change anything however much you might want to try. Got to go with the flow, Julian. Got to go with the flow."

"Do you like our camper?"

"Of course I do. Now come inside the house. I'm hungry. I made a curry. A 'damn fine curry' as one of Dad's old friends in Rhodesia used to call it. He lived in India before the British Raj came to an end. Always said there was nothing better than a 'damn fine curry'... After we've eaten I'll do some packing for the road."

"You know something? I wish I'd stayed down on the beach."

"No you don't. Give me your arm... Why are we never satisfied? Seems so silly. We get what we want only sometimes and when we do it isn't enough. Most people would give their eye teeth to be in your position. Most of us go through life without achieving anything. We watch films and read books to take us into a fantasy world to get away from our mundane lives. You're part of their fantasy. Part of their escape. Be grateful you're doing something for other people. Most of us don't have the chance."

Julian let her lead him into the house. She was right, of course. But it didn't help, the thought of having to promote his new movie making him sick in the stomach. Inside, the house looked familiar. That was something. It made him smile. Why were women so often right? Julian picked up the phone and began phoning the agents, telling them he was no longer selling the house. Their attitudes immediately changed, the charm that went with selling thrown out the window. One of them was actually rude, telling Julian in future not to waste her time. Julian tried to apologise. The woman put down the phone. People only loved you when you were making them money.

"You'd better phone Nora and tell her we are going on holiday. Tomorrow I'll finalise all our outstanding accounts. The ones that send us monthly accounts I'll pay in advance. That accountant you had to do your bookkeeping would have been a problem. You need looking after, Julian. Why you have a wife. Where shall we eat? I'll make sure Jensen Sandler's accountant pays what they owe you direct into our savings account. When we return from our travels you can decide on a longer-term investment."

"You've learned a lot. What would I do without you, Myra?"

"Is that sarcasm?"

"Of course it's not."

AFTER A MONTH ON THE ROAD, travelling down the coast, Myra was proved right. It just wasn't the same as the good old days. Far too often Julian was recognised. When they tried to make friends in the bars and restaurants they expected him to pick up the tab. Or they went awestruck and gushed all over him. On the road, however hard he tried to be a 'normal bloke', as Randall had called it, he was still a celebrity. Nothing could ever be normal. Instead of being new and stimulating the journey was boring. At forty-eight Julian had run out of new things to do. When they found out who he was they looked at him differently, never as a potential friend. Never as a couple to have fun with.

"We'd better turn back."

"I was thinking the same. It doesn't really matter. We have some friends at home. Even if they can only talk about money or how well they are doing. You want me to drive?"

That night, in an outside bar at the beach, Julian got himself drunk. They had parked the camper nearby in the campsite. Everyone was dressed in their swimming costumes, running down to the water to cool themselves from the heat. Surprisingly Myra drank drink for drink with him. When they left the bamboo bar and their bamboo stools they had to support each other. They were drunk. Both of them had the giggles.

"Did we pay the bill?"

"I think so. Haven't been this drunk since I left Africa. No one recognised you. We got some privacy."

Back in the camper, having fumbled the key in the door, Julian opened a bottle of wine. Getting the cork out was difficult. They sat across from each other at the small table, the doors and windows open. A slight breeze had come up from the ocean. They talked of silly things that made them giggle, their only world each other across the table, the bottle of wine and their half-full glasses. Before they went out, Myra had made up the double bed. When the wine was finished, the lights out, the door and windows still open, they fell into the bed. The small light in the camper was out. Julian could hear the voices of people down on the beach and people laughing in the distance. They had both taken off their costumes to get into bed, their old lust transcending everything. For the first time since the caesarean, they made love. And again. And again. Exhausted, drunk, happy, holding each other's sweaty bodies, they fell into a drunken sleep. Julian woke once in the night. He was smiling. It wasn't all bad, he told himself remembering the words of Oliver Manningford.

"I wonder what happened to him?"

"Go back to sleep."

"Are you awake?"

"I wasn't."

"We made love. Are you still on the pill?"

"No I'm not. Now go back to sleep. Haven't you got a hangover?"

"Not yet."

When Julian woke in the morning everything looked different. The trees, the beach through the trees, the ocean, the sun shining on everything. The door to the camper was still open. The people in the tent next to them were up making a fire and boiling a kettle. Julian could smell the woodsmoke. He pulled on his bathers while lying on his back on the bed. Myra was looking at him and smiling.

"You going for a swim? Can I come with you? I don't believe it but I don't have a hangover."

"Neither do I. Come on. Race you to the water."

"Hang on. I've got to put on a bathing costume."

"Well hurry up."

"Why do I smell smoke?"

"They're boiling a kettle."

"That's so Africa... Come on. Last in the water is a sissy."

THE TRICK HAD BEEN to grow his hair well below his shoulders and leave it dangling. To wear his loincloth with nothing underneath, his long legs and big feet prominent. He had grown a beard. The tan on his body was rich. For the first time since *Masters of Vanity* he had got away from them, people treating him like any other camper. The weeks turned into months. With the money he had put away they could go on forever. They made love, morning and night. At the end of July, with Julian conscious of his new film about to go into the cinemas, Myra told him she was pregnant. At first he was frightened for Myra. Then the elation lifted him off his feet. It was like walking on air.

"We'd better go home, Julian. I want to see the doctor. If I have to spend the next six months in bed to prevent any problems I'll do it. This time I am not going to lose my baby. You'll be just in time to promote the film. What a wonderful holiday. You'll have to shave off the beard and cut your hair. Why don't you give Nora a ring? We can find a telephone."

"Do we have to go back?"

"For the sake of the baby."

"Of course. It makes everything so different. I'm going to be a father."

"You don't have to start a new film immediately."

"No one has offered me a part."

"But they will."

"Another month or two on the road?"

"The doctor, Julian. We made a mistake last time by going to Africa. We're not making the same mistake again."

"She'll wonder why I didn't phone her."

"Tell her you were doing a Hemingway. When you burst back on the scene you'll have those journalists drooling. Come on."

"We don't have to go right now."

"Yes we do. Never run away from a problem. Give her a ring. Tell Nora some bullshit story. And tell her I'm pregnant. That's it. Tell her it was all about getting your wife pregnant. The press will love it."

"Isn't that tempting fate?"

"There was nothing wrong with me. Somehow the baby turned in my stomach and strangled itself. Or that's the story the old man told us in Mutare. We'll get the best doctors in LA. The best that money can buy. I'm young, I'm healthy, and I want to have our baby. Let's go home, Julian. We've had some fun. Overcome our problem. The world is our oyster again. Be happy."

"Can I have one last swim?"

"You're a bloody idiot. Come on. Race you down to the water."

In the water, Julian floated on his back looking up at the few clouds in the sky. He was sad and happy, mixed up in his feelings. Paddling with his hands extended, he kept himself afloat. His new life as a bum was over. He was back in the system.

. . .

FOR THE NEXT month they made him criss-cross America. One chat show after another on radio and television. They made him open a rock concert in Miami, introducing the famous band whose lead singer, a man with shaded glasses, only went by one name. In Phoenix, Arizona, they made him open the local dog show. They put his name up to the United Nations offering 'do-gooder' services as a roving ambassador. Every which way they used every opportunity to make him visible to the public and promote *Prisoners of War*. By the time they had finished with him everyone with access to the media in America had heard of the film. The only thing the publicity machine of Jensen Sandler didn't do to him was drop his trousers and stick him up the bum. Not surprisingly with the flood of expensive advertising the movie opened well, the reviews positively influenced by all the publicity. If you told people enough times something was worth watching they were inclined to believe you, even if only out of curiosity. Whether the public thought his new movie was any good, Julian had no idea. But that, he was told, didn't matter. All that mattered was Jensen Sandler was going to make himself a good return on his investment... His privacy shattered, Julian went home feeling as if he had been put through a wringer. They had smoked him dry. The only good news was Myra. She was still pregnant and healthy.

"Your agent has a raft of new movies for you to choose from, darling. You can ask your own price. They are all competing with each other to get on your band wagon."

"It's just not worth it."

"Of course it is. You've got to do something. We can't have you moping about the house with nothing to do, now can we? How are you, darling?"

"Tired out of my mind."

"You poor thing. Travelling so much can be exhausting. Every second time I turned on the television, there you were. Right in the living room. You're so clever, darling. You do it all so well. Nora is tickled pink with you. Says you're one of her best clients. I'm so proud of you, Julian. Come and have a drink. I can't drink but I'll keep you company. Oh, and I sold the camper. It was cluttering up the driveway. With a baby, we can't go on the road again. Once the baby is born I'll want to stay at home and look after him. I know some rich people have live-in nannies. We won't have that though, will we, darling? My mother is so happy for me. They're getting used to London. They haven't heard from Randall for months. He's disappeared. Gone on his travels. He's silly. Should be out promoting his books like you promote your films. Give me a big hug. You can feel my belly. Nothing's moving, of course. Too soon. The doctors are very pleased... What's the matter, Julian?"

"You wouldn't understand."

"Probably not. And the Carmichaels are coming to dinner tomorrow night. You won't believe how many invitations we've had. Everybody loves you, Julian. I'm so proud. The Kricklers insist we go to dinner with them as soon as you got home. Oh, they're all such fun. Our lives are so interesting. They all want to talk about my baby... Julian... Julian... Where are you going?"

"For a walk on the beach."

"Oh, darling, you were going to have a little drinkie. Oh, and Nora wants you to phone her the moment you get in."

Even at the security gate he could still hear her talking. But it wasn't all bad. His wife was going to have a baby. He was going to be a father.

PART 8

SEPTEMBER 1992 TO APRIL 1993 —
"SEEKING MEREDITH"

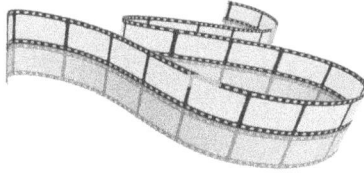

1

The big reunion took place in London at the end of September, the leaves still on the maple trees. It was Oliver Manningford's thirty-ninth birthday. Randall Crookshank, using his real name in England, leaving his pseudonym of Randall Holiday back in America, was the first to arrive. The room in Mrs Salter's house in Notting Hill Gate looked much the same. Mrs Salter had died in the spring when the maple trees in the road outside her Victorian semi-detached home came into bud. The property, along with the rest of the row of three-storey houses, had been sold to developers, the same old game that Randall remembered from his days working for his Uncle Paul that produced Westcastle on the banks of the River Thames. London was all about making money, no one concerned with an out-of-work actor about to lose his home. Oliver had lived in the room for fifteen years, never moving, even when he had briefly touched the face of fame. James Tomlin, their old friend and muse, had given up acting, no longer able to find work. He was living in Cornwall with a girl he had met in the theatre helping her run the family bed and breakfast. Her father had died leaving Ivey the house with its six bedrooms close to the sea in Penzance. Her mother was in a nursing home suffering from dementia. James was due up from Cornwall on the five o'clock train. Ivey had needed someone to help her run the business: fix the drains, keep the guttering in place, a hundred and one odd jobs about the big house. The arrangement suited both of them. Two people who had had their day in the London theatre, approaching middle age with no means of finding an income. They were lovers, lovers of convenience. Ivey was not due on the train. Randall had organised and paid for the party, sending out invitations to everyone he could think of who knew Oliver before he went down to Cornwall to visit James. Like James before he tied up with Ivey Conway, Oliver had no idea what he was going to do for money. Since the developers bought the townhouse the rent on the room had quadrupled. Mrs Salter had valued Oliver's company more than his money. Randall, knowing what it was like to run out of money, was worried for his friend. Randall had offered him money.

"I need something to do more than the rent. When you get to my age they say your looks are going. Or you're too old. There's always an excuse."

"You're not even forty. How many are coming tonight?"

"We'll have to wait and see. They're only interested in you when they think you are famous. Except you and James. Thanks, old friend. You know there's one thing you can never do in life however hard you try? You can't make new old friends. New friends if you're lucky. But never old friends. Good to see you again, Randall."

"You want to come downstairs and help me bring up the booze?"

"Have we got any food? I'm always hungry."

"Big, lanky men are always hungry. The caterers arrive at eight o'clock with hot food."

"Caterers. I'm impressed."

"If you're going to do a job do it properly. Seriously, what are you going to do at the end of next month when they're knocking down this building?"

"Get a job as a barman. I know a lot of bars. I still have a faint glimmer of fame. I'll get by. Maybe later, like your grandfather Ben Crossley, I'll become a famous character actor... Are you ever going back to America? What you going to do with yourself?"

"Travel. Go round and round looking for something to write about. Now I'm in England I'm going to mount a search for Meredith. She has to be somewhere. Next week I'm going to her old place of employment.

They won't help on the phone. I'll make a nuisance of myself until they show me their employment records."

"She's probably married."

"Probably. But I want to know... The beers are cold from the bottle store. I pulled them out of the fridge. Ice for the whisky. All the trimmings. We're going to have a birthday party."

"And if you don't find Meredith?"

"My lovely life will continue."

"Have you seen James Oliver, my godson?"

"Not yet. Amanda's still with Evelina. The publication of *Nothing Lasts Forever* didn't help. Nothing's changed."

"Everything changes and everything stays the same. It's the same old story. Let's go down to your car."

"I bought it to travel around Europe. It's odd driving on the wrong side of the road. I never got used to it in America."

"What does James's Ivey look like?"

"An ordinary girl. A nice ordinary girl. I liked her B and B. It was well organised."

"So you're not going to buy a place in Cornwall and write?"

"I've still got my hopes on the Isle of Man. We'll see... Quite like old times, Oliver. Humping crates of beer up the stairs to Mrs Salter's top floor."

"Don't get all nostalgic. You'll have me getting sentimental."

"What happened to your last girlfriend?"

"Hasn't been one of those since I've been out of work. No woman in her right senses is interested in an out-of-work actor pushing forty. They want a future. They all do."

"Where are you going to live?"

"There's a nice spot under a tree in Holland Park... You ever hear from Julian Becker? He used to live under a tree."

"He's married to my sister. They're expecting a baby."

"Now, he's famous. Really famous. And he's good. Really good... I'll miss these stairs. You and I crawled up them a few times. Pissed in the Leg of Mutton and Cauliflower."

"I met Amanda in the Leg of Mutton."

"I know you did. We've been friends a long time... Is she going to marry him?"

"Who?"

"Ivey."

"Who knows, Oliver? Who knows?"

"Why didn't James drive back with you?"

"Couldn't. I was taking a slow drive back. He had a business to run. People paying money for a room expect everything to be right. James says sometimes they can be a right royal pain in the arse."

"How old are you now, Randall?"

"I'll be thirty-five in December. Four months' time."

"Are you picking up James at the railway station? The three musketeers. We were all so excited those years ago. Young and full of dreams. You were twenty I seem to remember. Ah, memories. What would we do without our memories?"

"He said he'd catch the Tube... They were good times, Oliver. We were all so excited about life. The world was our oyster. It's not the same anymore."

"You're lucky. You've got plenty of money."

"Doesn't make you happy. I want a new challenge. I've done it. Got to the end. Succeeded beyond my wildest expectations. But it's hollow. I loved writing the books. But then people sucked it out of me. They didn't care if the book was any good. They were only interested in making money out of it. You're a performing artist. I like to think of myself as a creative artist. You must know what I'm talking about. To write another book is to just make them money. I've got enough money to last five lifetimes. It's taken the challenge away. I'm bored. Why I've dried up, I suppose. What do you do when you've done it, Oliver? I sometimes think of giving away all my money to some worthy cause. But which one? Most worthy causes are just another form of business for the organisers. They say it's non-profit but they still pay themselves out of donations and drive fancy cars. To give away money is a job in itself, and then what do I do?"

"And all I wanted was fame and fortune... What's in that box?"

"Potato chips and peanuts. Lots of them. I was kidding about the caterers. You live in a bedsitter. Those smart arses don't cater to bedsitters. If we get hungry I'll phone for the pizza man."

"We've got enough booze by the look of it."

"That's the whole idea. When people get drunk they don't think of food."

"Let's get drunk before the guests arrive."

"What I was thinking. To hell with my drinking problem. Your friend only turns thirty-nine once in his life. I'll sleep on the floor. Can't drive drunk. The three musketeers. You want to take that crate of beer? First, everything upstairs. Then we'll open the bar."

"Whatever happens in our lives, the three of us will always be friends. We're lucky."

"I know we are."

"It's not all bad."

"You're right, Oliver. It's not all bad."

James, full of smiles, was the first to arrive. Randall and Oliver had been drinking slowly so as not to ruin the party. They all hugged, everyone feeling sentimental. It was six o'clock in the evening. Through the window Randall could see the sun still on the maple trees. With James's first beer they drank a silent toast to Mrs Salter. They all missed her. She had been so much a part of their lives, their common bond the theatre.

"I would love to have seen her in her heyday," said James. "When she was young. We only remember an old landlady. Looking at some of her old photographs she was a knockout in her youth... Pass the peanuts... I used to have tea with her down in that basement flat. The photographs were on the mantelpiece."

"How's Ivey?"

"Working hard. It's the end of summer. Plenty of people still on holiday. I promised to go back tomorrow. I hate travelling on a hangover. But what can you do? She looks after me. Without Ivey I'd have nothing. I'm lucky. How many people are we expecting?"

"We'll have to see. In the old days people replied to invitations. Not anymore."

"Do we have to run up and down the stairs to let them in?"

"When they start to arrive we'll leave the front door on the latch. There's no one else left in the house. It's the end of an era."

They drank, talked about old times and enjoyed themselves. People started to arrive. By eight o'clock the guests were spilling out into the corridor. Sitting on the stairs. The music was loud. Most of the guests had brought a bottle. They were never going to run out of booze. At nine, Randall phoned the Pizza Hut and ordered twenty boxes of pizza, telling them to pre-cut the food into pieces. The man was told to ring the bell downstairs three times, and if that didn't work to come up to the party. When the pizza man arrived half an hour later he had to fight his way up the stairs. It took the man four trips. Randall paid him in cash and gave him a good tip. The man was smiling. By midnight, most of them were drunk. The party went on until three o'clock in the morning. They had stopped playing music at midnight, so as not to annoy the neighbours. When Randall had to sleep he lay down on the carpet, not a care in the world. Next to him on the floor James was watching his old friends. Oliver, on the only bed, was snoring. It was one hell of a party.

"Goodnight, old boy."

"Goodnight, James. Happy dreams."

Within minutes Randall was fast asleep and in his dreams. The next thing he knew it was morning, the smell of all the leftover booze was nauseating. He was stiff, tired and hungover, all of it worth it. As Oliver had said, however hard you tried, you could never make new old friends.

Later in the day, after a good breakfast cooked by a remarkably cheerful Oliver, Randall drove James to Paddington Station before driving to his father's flat in Chelsea, to the same block of flats his father had bought all those years ago with the artist Livy Johnston, the painter of the portrait of Randall's mother that had hung for so many years in the living room at World's View.

"You look terrible, son."

"Not as bad as I feel. You know what they say. 'There's no pleasure without pain.'"

"How are your two friends?"

"Surviving. Where's Bergit?"

"Gone to buy a ticket to America. She wants to make sure herself that Myra is all right. Talk to the doctors. That sort of thing. Mothers! Rather wonderful, don't you think? Coffee or a drink?"

"Coffee. I'm never touching another drink in my life."

"Glad to hear it."

"What's on your agenda, Dad?"

"Nothing as usual."

"You used to be so busy on the farm."

"Don't remind me... We could go for a walk next to the river. It's stopped raining. It always seems to be raining. I'd forgotten. We were so lucky on World's View."

"Are you going with Bergit?"

"It's a woman's job. Best to let her go alone. I don't want to intrude on Myra and Julian's lives just because I'm bored... You want to go for a walk? Where are you off to next?"

"Tomorrow, when my head feels better, I'm going to the Inner Temple. I want to find Meredith."

"You want to tell me about Meredith? No, it's none of my business. I shouldn't have asked. Life is one long search, Randall."

"Do we ever find what we want?"

"Sometimes. I found your mother and Bergit. I've been lucky."

As Randall walked out of the flat with his father, both of them carrying umbrellas, he looked at the portrait of his mother hanging on the wall. She was smiling at him. It made Randall feel happy. Outside, a bounce in his step, they began to walk briskly down the path next to the Thames. The best cure for a hangover was always exercise. Couples were sitting on the benches. People walking both ways up and down the path. On the road, traffic was passing, leaving behind the smell of petrol fumes.

"It's not quite like a walk down the side of the Zambezi."

"You take what you can get, Randall."

"I'll always miss Africa."

"So will I. You think there will ever be a chance of getting back World's View?"

"You never know. Probably not. What's done is done."

"We can still hope."

"We can always hope. You always have to hope."

"The river's so small."

"But it's safe. The sun is shining. And my son is walking next to me. We have a lot to be thankful for."

2

Randall found the offices of Price, Fulham and Simpson on the fourth enquiry, people pointing a direction but not really caring. They were lawyers with more important things to do than help a stranger. Some of them were wearing wigs and little black bibs. The Inner Temple was reputed to have some of the best lawyers in Britain. The woman at reception was middle-aged, subservient to anyone wearing a wig. Not knowing how to start his quest for Meredith, Randall stood fidgeting. He could still feel the effects of the booze from three days ago. A three-day hangover. It was a record. His stepmother had flown to America that morning, Randall driving her to the airport.

"Can I help you?" The woman's voice had a whine in it. She seemed bored looking at Randall.

"Three years ago you had a young lady working here by the name of Meredith. I'm trying to find her. It's very important."

"Are you a client of ours?"

"No I'm not. I was her boyfriend."

"What's her surname?" The woman was looking away, no longer interested in the conversation.

"I don't know."

"You were her boyfriend and you don't know her surname?" The woman let out a huff.

"It's a long story. We met by chance while Meredith was on holiday in Wales."

"What do you expect me to do?"

"Ask someone. People in the office must remember Meredith. She was very nice."

"I'm sure she was. The secretarial staff change. I wasn't here three years ago."

"You could ask one of the partners if they remember a girl by the name of Meredith."

"You've got to be joking. The partners in this firm have far better things to do than be worried about some girl with the name of Meredith."

"There must be a list of employees from three years ago. We could see their initials, if not their Christian names."

"I'm far too busy. Can't you see? There's a call on the switchboard."

Randall stood his ground while the woman answered the phone. She was very polite on the phone. Randall tried to smile at her but the woman wouldn't look at him. She had stopped looking at him the moment she realised he wasn't a client. There were no rings on the third finger of the woman's left hand. The words 'dried-up spinster' sprang to Randall's mind. He was getting nowhere. When the woman finished her phone conversation by connecting the caller to one of the partners she got up from her desk and turned to a filing cabinet, her back to Randall. Randall waited patiently. The woman fiddled around in an open drawer of the cabinet. When she turned and saw Randall still standing there she became impatient.

"I'm sorry, I can't help you." The woman gave him a fixed stare. They stared at each other, neither prepared to give in. A puzzled look came into the woman's eyes.

"Don't I know you?"

"I hope not. Have a nice day."

"You're that author. I'm reading your book. There's a photograph of you on the back cover."

"You must be mistaken. Can you help me find Meredith? May I see one of the partners?"

"They are far too busy."

The brief pleasure of recognition had gone. The woman looked sour. When Randall reached the door he turned back again.

"Which one are you reading? *Masters of Vanity* or *Nothing Lasts Forever*?"

Randall smiled sweetly and walked out of the office. The woman's jaw had dropped. She was dumbstruck.

Outside in the street, Randall shook his head. Some people could be absolutely charming. The woman was a bitch. Walking fast, he made for the Tube station. He would have to use money. Money usually worked.

Back at his father's Chelsea flat Randall had a look at the London telephone book. He was going to use a detective agency to trace Meredith. There was always a way.

WHEN RANDALL FOUND the office of Ernest Bligh it was not what he hoped. The place was poky to say the least of it. There was no reception. No girl at a desk. Just the one man sitting behind the one desk. There wasn't even a carpet on the floor. Ernest Bligh was in his fifties, a man who had seen better days. He was wearing a suit and a tie, the top of the tie loose, the top button of the shirt undone. He looked tired, even exhausted. A single light hung from the ceiling, the shade at a crooked angle.

"My name is Randall Crookshank."

"I know who you are, Mr Crookshank. You made an appointment." The man did not get up.

"I want you to find Meredith."

"Do you now? And who might be Meredith?"

"My old girlfriend. The trouble is, I don't know her surname."

The man's eyebrows went up, a twinkle coming into his eyes.

"And how long did you go out with Miss Meredith?"

"A week."

"She must have been good."

"She was. I was writing a book in a cottage in Wales. I'm a writer. She walked up from the village and found me. The cottage was quiet. Just right for writing. She had seen me in the local pub. She wants to be a writer. Why she came I suppose. We became lovers."

"I'm sure you did." The man chuckled. He was enjoying himself.

"She had a friend called Lucy who was a lawyer."

"Do you know her surname?"

"No I don't. Meredith's father worked for an insurance company in Liverpool. He was the manager."

"Of the company or a department?"

"She didn't say. She just said he was the manager. We didn't talk much about our families. We were only interested in each other."

"I'll bet you were."

"And books."

"What kind of books?"

"Novels. I write novels. Have you heard of Randall Holiday?"

"No I haven't. I don't read books. Who's Randall Holiday?"

"Me. It's my pseudonym. Writers have pseudonyms."

"Do they now? And why is that?"

"My publishers in America didn't like the name Crookshank. The word crook has a bad connotation."

"Don't tell me."

"How much do you charge?"

"Ten pounds an hour plus expenses."

"How do I know when you are working for me?"

"You don't."

"And you'll charge me even if you don't find Meredith?"

"Of course. It's like looking for criminals. They don't all get caught. I used to work at Scotland Yard. The good old days, Mr Crookshank. Now let me see. We've got a girl called Meredith with a friend called Lucy and a father who works for an insurance company."

"And she used to work as a legal secretary at the Inner Temple. For Price, Fulham and Simpson."

"Then why don't you ask them for her surname? They must have a forwarding address."

"I did. On the phone. And at their offices. They wouldn't help."

"I suppose that's a start. Them lawyers can be a pain in the arse. They never give information unless there's a good reason. I suppose I could phone them."

"You don't know anyone at the firm?"

"Why should I, Mr Crookshank?"

"Will you help me?"

"I have to say it doesn't look promising. A girl called Meredith with a friend called Lucy. Have you any idea how many Merediths and Lucys there are in this world?"

"What about the insurance company?"

"That's possible."

"There we go."

"But unlikely. You want me to phone every insurance company in Liverpool and ask them if any of their managers have a daughter by the name of Meredith?"

"That's exactly what I would like you to do."

"They'd laugh at me."

"But you're a private detective. Can you help me, Mr Bligh?"

"I can try."

"Tell you what. Instead of paying you ten pounds an hour, I'll give you ten thousand pounds if you find my Meredith. Whatever happens I'll pay your expenses."

The man sat bolt upright in his chair before standing up and walking round the desk.

"You've got a deal. You must sell a lot of books."

"Fortunately, I do. I'll put the ten thousand in an escrow account so you know you'll be paid."

"That's very kind of you."

"Difficult to trust strangers in this lovely world of ours."

"That it is, Mr Crookshank. Or do you call yourself Mr Holiday?"

Randall smiled, told the man the name of his uncle Paul's lawyer where he would post the ten thousand pounds, gave him a hundred pounds in cash for expenses, and again shook the man's hand. The man had changed. He was fully alert, his eyes focused.

Outside in the street Randall smiled to himself. It was all about money. The power of money. Or so he hoped. He had given the man his father's number in Chelsea. He would have to sit around and wait.

For a week, Randall kicked his heels. Nothing happened. He phoned Ernest Bligh and got the answering machine. For three days Randall spoke to the answering machine until his frustration exploded. By a miracle, the weather was good for the second week in October. The sun was shining. Shining for days. The British called it an Indian Summer. Randall walked to the Tube station, getting off at Knightsbridge, the good address in the phone book having caught his attention, Randall having imagined a smart and bustling detective agency, not one room with a desk and an answering machine. Mr Bligh was in his office.

"I'm lucky to have caught you, Mr Bligh. When I phone you are out and I get the answering machine. Have you found anything about my Meredith?"

"You owe me another three hundred and four pounds and fifty-four pence for expenses." The man had pulled out a sheaf of expense chits.

"Did you find out anything?"

"Not a thing. I went to Liverpool after getting nowhere on the telephone. Went to one insurance company after another. Manager after manager. All a blank, I'm afraid. I have the receipts for every one of my expenses."

"I'm sure you have."

"Mr Simpson was rather rude to me when I called. Nasty little man. Wanted to know why he should give a detective agency information about one of his ex-employees. When I told him I was working for one of her ex-boyfriends he threw me out of his office. He obviously thought I was lying. That I had a far more sinister motive. I hate lawyers. Period. And your fame hasn't helped. The one lead I found to a Meredith was a joke. The tea lady at Simpson's office thought she remembered a Meredith Shoreditch. When I found Meredith Shoreditch she was my age, Mr Crookshank. Not worth ten thousand pounds, I shouldn't think. But she said she knew you, Mr Holiday. Got all coy with me. When I asked where she met you, she said it was in London. Never been to Wales."

"You used my pseudonym?"

"I thought it might help. We'll have to go back to basics. Where you two met. Apart from Lucy without a surname was there anyone else those three years ago who saw you and Meredith together?"

"The owner of the bar where we met told Meredith where to find my cottage in the woods. The pub was in the valley."

"Can you remember the name of the pub?"

"I only went there when I went into the village to stock up with food. I don't drink when I'm writing."

"Wise of you... Can you remember his name?"

"I think it was Joe. I've talked to so many barmen in my time."

"I bet you have. Some people's best friends are barmen. No offence, Mr Crookshank."

"You're laughing at me."

"Not really. I've met a lot of barmen in my time."

"The pub was called the Rising Sun. That's it. There was a metal image of a rising sun behind the roof of the old building. The man I think was called Joe said his pub was fourteenth century. Might have been fifteenth."

"It wasn't a rising moon?"

"No, definitely a sun. There were metal rays sticking out of the orb. When I'm writing a book I get so absorbed in my characters I don't remember much about what is going on around me. Sort of a world of my own."

"But you remember Meredith."

"She brought back reality."

"You must have details of the cottage you rented. Where you paid the rent. Give me everything you've got. Good detective work is in the detail. How you find criminals."

"She's not a criminal. When I get home I'll check the stubs of my old cheque books. I keep all my records for tax purposes. A kind of habit."

"A good habit, speaking as an ex-Scotland Yard policeman. You can never be too careful when it comes to the taxman. Was the rent deductible?"

"It was. Part of the expense of writing a book. You have to get away to somewhere quiet. I've always tried to be careful with my money. My father says easy come, easy go. I try to hold onto what I make now. Lost it all, once. Dad lost his farm in Zimbabwe."

"That won't help us find Meredith. And your landlord was in Wales?"

"In the same village as the Rising Sun."

"Now we are getting somewhere. Phone me the man's name who rented you the cottage."

"But he didn't know anything about Meredith."

"Leave it to me. Now, may I have what you owe me so far?"

"Of course. Will you take a cheque?"

"From a famous author? Of course I will. Make it out to cash. But you'd better go and cash it for me. Would you care for a cup of tea, Mr Crookshank? Or a cup of coffee? The office next door let me use their kitchen. Like you, Mr Crookshank, I tend to be frugal. The best crooks – sorry, no offence to your name – I have met during my long career as a detective always had flashy offices."

"Then why are you in Knightsbridge, one of London's most expensive places?"

"The bait that catches the fish. Looks good in the phone book, an address in Knightsbridge. Now, tea or coffee?"

"I want to get you that address as soon as possible. Maybe a cup of tea when I've cashed the cheque."

"As you wish."

"The ten thousand is in the lawyer's bank account."

"I know it is."

"Are you going to find her?"

"For ten thousand of your good pounds I'd lift heaven and earth. My wife has expensive tastes. Which bank are you with?"

"Lloyds."

"When you go out turn left, then right and you'll find the high street. There's a Lloyds bank on the corner. All this modern computer technology makes banking so much easier. Any branch can check your balance."

Outside Randall turned left, walked, turned right and reached the high street. There was a restaurant on the corner with an unusual name: 'Camilla's Corner'. It was lunchtime. Idly, Randall looked in through the window. The shock of what Randall saw made him stop in his tracks. Looking at him from the table on the other side of the window was Amanda. Next to Amanda, James Oliver. An older woman Randall recognised as Evelina from their brief introduction at the British launch of *Masters of Vanity* at the Savoy Hotel was on the left. The boy did not recognise his father. He had looked at his mother who was staring fixedly through the window. Randall waved, hoping his son would see him. Amanda put her napkin on the table and got up. The boy turned to talk to Evelina. When the door to the restaurant opened Amanda walked out into the street.

"I thought you were in America. How are you, Randall?"

"He didn't recognise me."

"It's been a while. Better for James Oliver. We don't want him torn between you and me and Evelina."

"He's my son. What about me tearing apart?"

"Why are people always so selfish? They only think about themselves."

"I want to see him whenever I'm in London."

"You can't. It'll upset the boy. As he is, he's happy. Look at him laughing. It's Evelina's birthday. Why we came out to lunch. She prefers going out to lunch. Evenings we prefer at home with James Oliver."

"I'm going to get a lawyer. I want my rights. I've got money."

"You won't do him any good. Anyway, how often are you in London? You could never be a proper father to him. Maybe when he's grown up he'll want to find you. He doesn't know you and that's best for James Oliver. You saw him briefly at the launch of your book, and again two-and-a-half years later on your visit to England. Don't try and disrupt his life."

"Did you trick me to get yourself pregnant? Did you and Evelina plan your pregnancy? Don't look dumb, Amanda. I'm not a fool. It was all too convenient."

"That's a question to which you would neither like me to answer yes or no. What I can say is, the boy is happy. A happy childhood is a gift we all crave. Leave him alone. Lawyers only want to make money. I'm going back inside. Nice to see you again."

"I doubt it."

Randall watched the restaurant door open and close and blew his fuse. He wrenched open the heavy door and stormed inside. A woman looked up from the counter where a man was paying his bill.

"James Oliver, don't you recognise me? I'm your father."

"Mummy told me not to come outside." The boy looked frightened.

"Which mummy?"

"Mummy Evelina."

"She had no right."

"Oh yes I do. Amanda and I are the boy's legal guardians."

"Doesn't change the fact he's my son."

"Go away, Randall. You're making a fool of yourself." Amanda's face was as white as a sheet.

"Is there a problem?" The woman from the desk was now standing behind Randall. She was looking for a fight. "Will you please leave my restaurant or I will call security."

"Oh, so you're in it with them."

"As a matter of fact I am. Please leave. You've made the poor boy cry."

Amanda was now looking at him with a smirk on her face, no resemblance to the woman he had met and lived with in the room at Mrs Salter's next to James Tomlin and Oliver Manningford when the four of them had been so close. And the woman was probably right: he was making a perfect fool of himself in front of the one person in the world he wanted to impress. There was nothing more to be said. Randall, controlling his temper, and stopping the urge for a parting shot, turned on his heel and left Camilla's restaurant. Outside in the street, when he looked back, he could see James Oliver had buried his face in Amanda's lap, Amanda giving him that 'now look what you have done' look. Amanda then smiled across at Evelina who smiled back again. Randall's surge of anger reached breaking point where he wanted to smash in the window. Forcing himself to be calm, he controlled himself.

"You've been a bloody fool, Crookshank. Now you've really blown your chances."

A woman, passing in the street, gave him a queer look for talking to himself. The final look through into the restaurant showed all three women laughing, Camilla now sitting at the table. They were enjoying themselves. At his expense. Remembering the bank was due to close shortly, Randall walked on down the street and into the bank where he cashed a five hundred pound cheque, making sure they gave him change. He counted the exact amount of Ernest Bligh's expenses into an envelope given him by the teller, and walked back to give the money to the private detective. To prevent any further altercation he walked on the other side of the road, ignoring the restaurant where his son was still having his lunch. Even his wish to find Meredith had abated.

At Ernest Bligh's office the door was locked. Taped to the door was an envelope addressed to Randall Crookshank/Holiday. Inside was a note that read 'please slip the money under the door'. Not sure if he wasn't decanting money down a rathole, Randall slipped his own envelope under the door. At that moment in his life he was not sure if anything mattered.

Back at his father's Chelsea flat he found himself alone. His father had gone out... The picture of his mother on the wall in the lounge was no longer smiling at him. The portrait had a whimsical look of sympathy.

When he looked at the artist's portrayal of his mother from different angles the expression changed.

"What's life all about?" he said to the mother he had never known. First he found the stubs of his old cheque books, found what he was looking for, and phoned Ernest Bligh. As expected, he got the answering machine. Without much hope, Randall read out the name and address of the owner of the woodsman's cottage. He felt lonely, desperately lonely. There was a bar down the road not far from the block of flats. He was going to break the rules. He was going to get himself drunk. To hell with his drinking problem.

That night instead of going back to his father's apartment and making a fool of himself for the second time in one day, he asked the barman to order him a taxi and book him a room in the Savoy Hotel. They knew him at the Savoy. They would look after him. His money would look after him. When the cab driver came up to the bar, Randall gave the barman a twenty pound tip, concentrated hard, and pulled himself off the barstool. He was drunk. Very drunk. The cab driver, having seen the size of the barman's tip, gave him an arm and helped him to the cab, and drove him to the Savoy Hotel.

"You going to be all right, china?" The man was a Cockney. Randall, pulling himself out of the cab, paid the man and gave him a ten pound tip.

"With some luck I won't make a fool of myself. Thanks for the offer. I know the way. You've been very helpful." Every one of the words felt thick in Randall's mouth. He was slurring his words. Unsteadily, he walked inside the hotel.

"Mr Holiday! How wonderful to see you again."

"I don't have any luggage."

"We quite understand. You're an old and trusted customer."

The man gave him the key to a room and walked with him to the elevator.

"Will that be all, Mr Holiday?"

"I hope so. I really hope so."

Randall got into the lift, the man leaning in to press the third-floor button. The doors closed and the lift went up. After some fumbling with the key in the door, standing out in the corridor, Randall got the door to his room open. Inside, he walked to the big bed. The cover had been pulled back. Randall, fully clothed, fell head first into bed. He was quickly asleep.

WHEN RANDALL RETURNED to his father's apartment late the following afternoon, his father was not amused. When a guest in a house, even a parent's house, it was polite to tell them what you were doing. Randall made an excuse, avoiding telling his father about James Oliver and about the drink. For three days Randall felt the debilitating effect of the alcohol, the brief three-hour escape from reality not worth his depression. Ten days went by. He was going to try one more time. If that didn't work he was going alone to the Isle of Man to find himself a place in the wilderness as far as possible from a bar. He had to do something or his life was pointless, a day-to-day process achieving nothing. If there was one thing in life Randall had understood, there had to be a purpose in a person's life or all the days of trivia, the getting up, eating breakfast, talking about the weather, making small talk, having lunch, taking a nap, watching television, all of it was pointless. A man had to have a job. A man had to have something to do. If he didn't get back into writing a book his life was no good. First he went to his bank, sure there would be more expenses. Resigned to an empty office, Randall drove his car through to Knightsbridge and called at the office of Ernest Bligh, private detective. Surprisingly, when Randall opened the door, the man was sitting behind his desk.

"Ah, Mr Holiday. Now that is a strange coincidence. I was about to phone you. Do you believe in telepathy? I think there is something in it."

"Have you found Meredith?" A surge of hope went through his mind, changing his mood of doom and gloom to one of elation.

"Her surname is Harding. Meredith Harding. Unfortunately she has moved from her last place of residence and not left a forwarding address. It's a bit like eating soup with a fork. By the time you get the fork to your mouth there's nothing on it. But don't despair. I spoke to Lucy a week ago. Lucy Haynes is doing her best to contact Meredith. When I mentioned your name she was very excited. Apparently, your Meredith still talks about you, Mr Holiday. It could of course be your fame. When you get to my age you are inclined to be cynical. That old 'soup and fork' syndrome."

"You have some more expenses?" The brief moment of euphoria over, Randall felt flat.

"I'm afraid I do."

"If you know her name, can't you find her father? Her family must know where she is."

"Oh, I spoke to him all right. He said if I find out where his daughter is to let him know. Children! Don't tell me. Got three grown-up kids of my own. I never know what they are up to. Every now and again they condescend to remember their parents and tell us what they are doing. In this global age people move around a lot, Mr Holiday. Indeed they do. The world is a global village. Got that from the Russian president! Global village. I like it. If your Meredith should contact you please tell me so I can claim my ten thousand pounds from your escrow account. Now, let me see. The latest expenses amount to ninety-seven pounds exactly. If you have one hundred pounds I can give you change."

Smiling wryly, Randall gave the detective a hundred pounds, convinced he was being milked of his money.

"Would you care for a receipt?"

"I don't think that will be necessary."

When Randall drove to his father's home, first parking his car in the basement, Meredith was sitting on the couch talking to his father. When she smiled a whole new world opened in front of him.

"Lucy says you've been looking for me, Randall. Employed a private detective. What's up?"

"Would you like to come with me to the Isle of Man? I want to find another woodsman's cottage and write a book."

"I'd love to. I left my last job and my flat three months ago. I've been travelling around Europe and got back two days ago."

"You look good."

"So do you."

Smiling, his father got up from the couch.

"I'll leave you two long-lost lovers on your own. She's nice, Randall. We've been having a long chat. Meredith tells me she's finished her first children's book. I'm going out. You two have lots to talk about. Nice to meet you, Meredith. Look after my son. He's important to me. You'll like the Isle of Man. Just the place to write books."

"You don't have to leave, Dad."

"Oh, but I do."

When the door to the flat closed they sat looking at each other. Neither of them spoke. Both of them were smiling. Then they burst out laughing.

"Meredith Harding. If only I'd known your surname."

"We were too busy making love to worry about a name."

"So, you've written a book. Can I read it?"

"First things first. I need a kiss. You have no idea how much I've missed you, Randall. Our week together was full of magic. Just the two of us alone in the woods. I want more."

"So do I. The idea is to buy a small farm. A farm that if the whole rotten world collapses we'll be self-sufficient. Go back into the past of our ancestors. When people and families were happy. Only farmland gives permanent security. Unless your farm is in Zimbabwe."

"Your poor father. He talked of Zimbabwe with such longing. He's a beautiful man."

"Have you shown your book to a publisher?"

"Not yet. I'm too frightened of rejection... You've done so well, Randall. To be close to you I reread your books. I've seen *Masters of Vanity* three times. You're so lucky."

"It's all hollow without another person in my life."

"Women must throw themselves at you. A famous author."

"Can I read your book? What's it about?"

"A fantasy world where the children can talk to the birds and the animals. Only the children. The parents don't understand what's going on right in front of them."

"Where's it set?"

"In a woodsman's hut in Wales. In a Welsh valley. Lots of log fires in winter. Running down to the beach in summer talking with the seagulls. Writing makes me happy."

"Once I've read your book I'll send it to Henry Stone at Villiers Publishing in America. It's better to publish in America. They are better at the publicity."

"Will you, Randall? But only if you like my little book. Just please don't think I'm using you. Who you are as a writer has nothing to do with how I feel for you. Where are we going to on the Isle of Man? I've never been to the Isle of Man. I once met a Manxman. That's what they call people from the Isle of Man."

"I have no idea where we'll be going. We'll drive to Liverpool and put the car on the ferry to Douglas. You can see your parents. Your father told Ernest Bligh to tell you to phone him when he found out where you were."

"I should have told them I was spending the summer travelling around Europe. I was being selfish."

"It's inherent in all of us. They'll love to see you."

"Don't tell them about my book. They'll only be interested once it's published."

"I suppose they will... Want to go for a walk?"

"When are we driving to Liverpool?"

"I thought tomorrow morning. There's no time like the present. Where are you staying?"

"With Lucy... It's all so wonderful to see you again."

"Do you have another book to write?"

"Lots of them. We can write together. You do have another novel in your head?"

"I rather think one is coming to me." The block that stopped a new book coming into his mind was crumbling. He could see to the other side.

"Let's go for a walk. As much as I want to, making love on your father's couch wouldn't somehow be right. And what if he came in? But a kiss won't be wrong."

"If we touch each other we'll end up making love. Better go for a walk. We have so much to talk about."

Meredith smiled, blew him a kiss across the three feet that separated them, picked up his hand and led him to the door. They were smiling. Down by the river they stood under a tree on the grass and kissed each other. They were lovers in their minds. The physical would come later.

The next morning, before Randall and Meredith packed their suitcases in the car to begin the journey to Liverpool and the Isle of Man, Randall phoned the lawyer and told him to pay out the ten thousand pounds, the best money he had ever invested.

"What was that about, Randall?"

"A debt I had to pay... Goodbye, Dad. I'll keep in touch."

"Have a safe journey, both of you. I won't come down to the car."

"When's Bergit due home?"

"Next week. Everything's fine with Myra."

"Give her my love."

Smiling at the portrait of his mother on the wall, Randall shook his father's hand in the traditional English way. His mother was smiling at them.

"Take care, Dad."

"I will."

RANDALL'S first job when they reached Liverpool was to find the ferry and book them through on the first boat to Douglas. The ferry was leaving in four hours, enough time for Meredith to visit her parents.

"That works, Randall. Or we'll be bogged down. My parents will want us to stay... If we don't find a room to ourselves I'm going to explode. Have you ever made love in the back of a car?"

"Not recently... Too many people."

"I think there are. Come on. I'm taking you home. But brace yourself, Randall. Fathers don't seem to mind so much what their sons get up to. It's considered normal for men to sow their wild oats. Fathers think daughters should only have sex when they are safely married. You can't believe how many single mums there are these days. Why it's a girl's job to look after herself. Once we get to Douglas we'll find a nice little hotel and fuck the brains out of each other. Then we'll go travelling round the island. It gets cold on the Isle of Man in winter. I remember that from growing up in Liverpool. We're just in time to find ourselves a place and get tucked in for winter. Are you ready, Randall? Good. Let's go see the Hardings. You never know. My brother or sister may be visiting."

"Is your father retired?"

"Not yet. He's spent forty years paying off the mortgage on the house and still hasn't finished. Had to borrow money against the house to put my brother through university. When he's finished paying it off he's going to retire to the country. What a life. All those years of drudgery sitting at a desk in an insurance company working off debt and waiting for a pension. Doesn't seem worth it. Now I'm going to blow in and blow out again."

"We could spend a few days with them."

"Are you mad? My hormones would explode."

Randall held back at the house, calling Meredith's father 'sir'. It was Saturday afternoon, the old man watching football on the television. There was no sign of the brother or sister. The father was more interested in the game. The mother cried when she hugged her daughter. The home was comfortable. Well lived in. A typical suburban home.

"What do you do for a living, Randall?"

"I'm a writer. Novels. That sort of thing."

"Haven't read a novel since I was at school. Had to read them for my 'O' levels... Just look at that. Liverpool have scored."

They drank tea while the father carried on watching the game, Randall sitting on a chair in silence. Meredith and her mother had gone into the kitchen. He could hear them talking ten to the dozen. The women were happy. The old man was happy watching the football, not touching the cup of tea his wife had put on the side table next to him. With not the slightest interest in English football, Randall sat back comfortably in his chair and let his mind wander. The only time Randall got interested in sport was when Zimbabwe were playing cricket or rugby, the two sports he had enjoyed at school. To be polite, he drank his tea. When the game was finished, Meredith and the mother came back from the kitchen. The father was switching channels, looking for another sport to watch.

"I've told Mum we're booked on the afternoon ferry. We'd better get going, Randall."

"Goodbye, Mr Harding. Very nice to have met you."

"Watching golf after football is so boring."

"Yes, I suppose it is."

The old man stayed sitting when Randall put out his hand. They shook hands, the old man still looking at the television. Mrs Harding smiled at him.

"Look after her, Randall. I think of her every day."

"That I promise you."

"I'm going to read your books."

"You don't have to."

"We'll look for the film when it comes on television. We don't go out much."

The old woman saw them to the car. At the car she kissed Randall's cheek. She was crying, a tear touching the side of Randall's face.

"It's all about our children. I miss them so much. But they have their own lives."

"Once we are settled in we can drive over for a visit."

"That would be nice. Very nice. I'm going inside before I start howling."

Mother and daughter hugged for a long moment. Randall opened the door to the car for Meredith to get inside. They were on their way. Randall knew he was lucky in more than one way. He wouldn't need forty years to pay off his mortgage. Through the front window, Randall could still see the father sitting in front of the television.

Soon after they went on board the wind came up. The car, along with four others, was securely tied down on deck. They stood by the side of the ferry for a long while watching the city of Liverpool recede. There was a bar on board that had caught his attention. Douglas, according to the man who had checked over their ticket before boarding, was a hundred miles to the northwest. The sea became rough, the ship rolling. Some of the passengers left the deck to find the restrooms. Randall and Meredith, arm-in-arm, stood happily, their faces to the wind. The journey was expected to last past sunset, the ferry docking in twilight. Clouds scurried across the heavens, the sun, low on the sea, going in and out, shining directly into their eyes. They both had winter coats on, buttoned up to their throats. Randall smiled. Africa, the warmth of Africa, was a long way away, the thought making him nostalgic, the longing to go back home overwhelming. But he was going to an island between England and Ireland. Where it was cold. Where he knew no one other than Meredith. The idea of what he was going to write became clear to him. If it was not possible to physically live in Africa, he would go back in his mind and live in a book. A series of books that would keep him happy as long as possible. He was going back in time to the first Brigandshaw arriving in Africa at the end of the nineteenth century. Book after book, taking the Brigandshaws through their lives in Rhodesia. The last of the true colonials. The Brigandshaws, the Oosthuizens and the Crookshanks. Despite the cold east wind Randall became excited. The floodgate had opened. He had something to do. Something to write. He was smiling. A series of novels disguised as history books. Maybe he would have to change the names of the families.

"What you so happy about?"

"A book. A series of books. A chronicle of the English in Africa through the twentieth century. Oh, Meredith. Thank you. I've now got something to write."

"What happened to *Love Song*? I've looked for it many times in the shops."

"Villiers say it's in the pipeline."

"We'd better go inside. It's getting windier by the moment. Lucky we're not seasick."

"Where's the manuscript of your book?"

"In the outside pocket of my suitcase right at your feet."

"Good. I'm going to sit on one of those benches inside and read your book."

"Don't you want to go to the bar?"

"I'm never drinking again. Do you mind?"

"I'm sure you will. I only drink to keep people company. Well, that's not quite true. A bottle of wine in front of a log fire right now would be perfect. Then we'd make love in front of the fire. Do you really want to read my book now?"

"It's the perfect time. You've read my books, now I'm going to read yours. Come on. Oh, for the African sun."

It took Randall two hours to finish her book, putting it down softly on the wooden bench next to him. Meredith had gone off for a walk round the deck, finding the suspense too difficult. Randall kept his left hand on the manuscript, smiling to himself. Nora was going to love Meredith's book. It would probably make a small fortune.

"You finished it, Randall?"

"Half the children in the world are going to love this book."

"You think so?"

"I know so. You can paint with words, Meredith. I can see the pictures as clearly as if they are in front of me."

"You're lying."

"Let's promise each other one thing. That we never lie to each other. That even if it's going to hurt we still tell the truth... Now, look at that. We're coming into port. We've arrived."

"You're not kidding me?"

"Nora will want a hundred thousand dollar advance from Henry Stone. We'll register the second copy to America tomorrow morning. You do have a copy?"

"Of course I do. Oh, Randall. I'm so happy."

"So am I. We're going to love each other. We're going to write. Side by side. But first let's get off this ship, find ourselves a hotel, and go fuck our brains out."

"I couldn't put it better myself. Oh, Randall, we're going to be so damn happy."

"I know we are. Forever. We're going to be happy forever."

3

———————

*T*hey left the small boutique hotel satiated two days later. An estate agent was going to show them round the small island. Randall left his car in the agent's garage. The man was smiling all over his face as he offered them six properties, each farm with its photograph.

"Not often we get a famous author looking for a place on the Isle of Man. What is it? A tax dodge? The island is semi-independent under the crown."

"A place to hide. That third one you showed us looks perfect on paper. Sixty acres of fertile land and a nice old farmhouse."

"Will you require a mortgage?"

"I don't think so." Randall was smiling, thinking of all that royalty money sitting in his bank account. "If I like what I see I'll give you a cash deposit and wait for the transfer. There won't be any trouble with residency. Despite my Zimbabwean accent I'm a British subject. My mother and father were born in England."

"Thrown out, were you? That President Mugabe doesn't like you colonials."

"He threw my father off our farm."

"So you know about farming?"

"Tobacco. They don't grow tobacco in England. Why we were

encouraged to go to Africa, so the British could buy their tobacco with sterling and not in dollars from the Americans."

"The old days of empire are long over."

"Yes they are."

"That mountain you can see is Snaefell. If two thousand feet above sea level is a mountain. In a month's time it will be covered in snow. The farm I'm going to show you is on the other side. Between Snaefell and the sea. Very quiet... What does your wife do?"

"She's a writer. Children's books."

"Sounds a perfect life."

"It's going to be. Why does the owner want to sell?"

"He's dead. The kids live in Australia. Been in the same family for three hundred years. The world's changing, Mr Holiday. Or do I call you Mr Crookshank?"

"It doesn't matter."

"There's an old RAF station not far from the property. The old Nissen huts are still standing. Built during the war as a training camp."

"Why are so many houses derelict? That's the third one I've seen."

"The little people. They leave them standing without roofs for the little people. We Manx people are superstitious. You can't destroy an old building or the little people won't have anywhere to stay."

"Is the farmhouse we're going to see haunted?"

"I doubt it. All that mumbo-jumbo is in the mind."

Meredith was looking out of the window of the backseat of the agent's car smiling to herself when Randall turned round.

"It's such a lovely setting for one of my books." Meredith had a faraway look.

"What kind of books do you write, Mr Holiday? I know the name of course. Don't read much myself. Prefer television."

Randall looked at the man without answering... Ten minutes later they arrived at their destination.

"I've got the keys."

"I rather hoped you would."

"Hasn't been lived in for a while. The windows are small so it's snug in winter. Every room has a fireplace. One nice big bedroom and three little ones for the children."

"Electricity?"

"Oh, yes. All the modern conveniences blending in with the old. I hope you like it. It's furnished. The eldest son who has given me power of attorney to sell the house doesn't want the old family furniture. Says it would be too expensive to ship it all the way to Australia... Come inside... There we are... What do you think, Mr Holiday?"

They went from room to room and out to the sheds. There was no livestock. An old tractor stood in one of the sheds. The place looked derelict.

"How long ago did he die?"

"Two years ago. People don't want to live on farms miles from nowhere. Why the price is so good... You want me to show you the rest?"

"What do you think, Meredith? Two of the small bedrooms will make writing rooms. One for each of us."

"It's perfect. Dusty but perfect. With a fire in each room during the winter it'll be as warm as toast."

"Good, I'll take it. Can I write you a cheque now for the deposit or back in your office?"

"Back in the office. This is the fastest sale I've ever made."

"It works that way sometimes. When can we move in?"

"As soon as you like. I'll have some cleaners go through the house and shine everything up. Remove all the dust sheets. You've made my day."

Randall, holding Meredith's hand, looked around their new home. It wasn't quite a farm in Zimbabwe, but it was going to be home.

"How long will it take to clean up the place?"

"A couple of days. Longer for the garden. Are you going to employ servants?"

"They interrupt our writing. Maybe someone to come in a couple of days a week. We'll see."

"Sold to the man from Zimbabwe. You two look so happy together." The man had spoken to Meredith.

"Oh, we are. You can't believe how happy. It's the only panacea of life that's important. Being happy. With someone you love. With something to do that you love. This is going to be just perfect, don't you think, Randall?"

"Absolutely perfect... Back to the office, Mr Corlett. Let's go sign the papers. On the way can you show us the post office? We have a parcel to register to America. We'll first need to buy one of those stiff envelopes to take the manuscript."

"It will be my pleasure. The stationery shop and then the post office. Then you'll sign the legal papers."

"Then I will sign the papers."

"It's so lucky the wind went down and the sun came out. A perfect day, Mr Holiday. A perfect day."

Two days later with Meredith's manuscript on its way to Nora Stewart with a note from Randall to show it to Henry Stone at Villiers Publishing, they moved into the old farmhouse, a wicker basket on the backseat of Randall's car, Mr Corlett following behind in his car with the keys. When they walked into the house with its beamed ceilings, the beams black with age, everything was spick and span. When Randall looked at the furniture he had bought no longer covered in dust sheets he knew the son in Australia had made a mistake. The furniture was antique. Probably worth more than the house. Old furniture handed down from generation to generation, the family having no idea of its worth. In an alcove in the lounge with its small windows facing the mountain three or four miles away was a grand piano. Someone in the family must have loved music. The cleaners Mr Corlett had sent to the house had lit fires in all the fireplaces to get rid of the last trace of damp. The walls surrounding the fireplaces were nicely warm when Randall put his hand on them.

"What's in the basket you're carrying, Mr Holiday?"

"Pussy cats. Six of them. All kittens. One of the cats at Animal Welfare had had a litter. We took all of them."

"You like cats?"

"We'll have to teach ourselves to play the piano. The double bed in the big bedroom is a bit small but it will do. First thing, Meredith, is making the bed. We bought all our linen from that shop you sent us to, Mr Corlett. You've been more than helpful. Even the fridge is working."

"In the old days people slept comfortably in smaller beds. It was warmer. There you have it. You are now the proud owners of Jurby farm. I'm sure you will both be very happy. Anything you need, you know where to find me. You'll have to put in your own phone. Buy yourself a television. I'll be off. My job is done... May I open the lid and look at the kittens?"

"When we're settled, we're buying a dog. Those writing desks are just perfect. One for each of us."

"How old are they?"

"Six weeks. You can let them out. All we have to do is unload the car, fill up the fridge and I'll make some supper. You want to stay to supper, Mr Corlett? Meredith bought a case of South African red wine. Nederburg. It's the best."

"Oh, no. I couldn't intrude. The light will go soon. Better go. My wife gets nervous when I'm late. Married thirty-one years. Can you believe it?"

"Thank you again."

"My pleasure. I'm going to find one of your books and have a read."

"You don't have to."

"Just look at those kittens. Don't come out. I know my way."

The front door closed. They were on their own. In front of the fire in the lounge, Randall pulled Meredith close. They kissed, a long, slow kiss of contentment. Randall put more coal on the fire from the coal scuttle. The cleaners had left fireguards in front of every fire in the house with a full coal-scuttle next to the grates. Mr Corlett had earned his commission.

"Welcome to your new home, Meredith."

"You think we should open one of those bottles of wine to celebrate?"

"Why not? I'll start the cooking later. Everything out of the car then a glass of wine by the lounge fire. Those old armchairs look so comfortable."

"It's so cosy. Do you even need a phone or a television?"

"Let's wait and see. Fish for supper. Brings back memories. Pity they didn't have any mackerel."

"You think Nora will like my book?"

"Of course. I told her to like it. Just kidding. Your book will speak for itself. Come on. I shouldn't drink but I'm going to. Tonight's a celebration. For us and our new home. Can you play the piano?"

"'Chopsticks'."

"We can learn. This is going to be one big adventure."

"I love you, Randall."

"I love you, Meredith."

For a long, long moment they just looked at each other. Outside the light had almost gone. They could hear Mr Corlett's car now far away on his journey back to his family. Meredith broke the moment they were going to remember for the rest of their lives, and walked across to draw the lounge curtains. Randall went to the kitchen, opened the case of wine and popped the cork of one of the bottles. He had remembered to buy a corkscrew with half a dozen wine glasses. When Randall put his nose down to the top of the bottle, the red wine smelled delicious. By the time he went back into the lounge, Meredith had been into their big new bedroom, made the bed and drawn the curtains.

"It's just so snug. When are you going to start writing?... Do you want a family, Randall? I can stop taking the pill if you want me to. When are we getting a dog? Maybe a couple of horses. Never ridden a horse in my life but I'll easily learn."

"You should sniff the wine before the first sip. We can cook the fish over the fire. Put some potatoes in tin foil. Those hot coals look perfect. Quite like old times. Whoever said you can't have a *braai* inside a house?"

"I remember that word."

"You have a good memory."

"Do you want to have another child?"

"If you get pregnant we will marry."

"So, that's a yes. Oh, Randall."

"How's the wine?"

"Like everything else it's perfect."

"I'm going to buy a big freezer so if we're snowed in we'll have plenty of food. Tomorrow, if the sun is still shining, we'll take a run down to the beach. I'll give you a toast. To the future Mr and Mrs Crookshank and their family."

"Just look at those kittens. They love the place as much as we do."

"First thing tomorrow, before we take a run to the beach, I'm going to start writing my African saga."

"I'm going to start a book about a family of kittens who live on a farm with two nice people. There'll be the dogs and the horses. Very young children. A perfect paradise far away on a farm."

"What about ducks and chickens?"

"Of course. I'd forgotten the ducks and chickens."

"And a goose. Got to have a goose."

"You think they have owls on the Isle of Man?"

"I'm sure they do."

Randall's foot moved out and touched Meredith's, their armchairs across the fire from each other. They both sipped at their wine. The sound of the car was long gone.

"We're alone in paradise, Meredith."

"I know we are. I've never been this happy in my life. How long will it take my book to get to America?"

"A week. Maybe ten days."

"How long will it be before I know?"

"Why we need a phone. I told Nora to phone me when she's read your book. Why we'd better get a phone."

"And a television. Then we can have the world, but only when we want them. Do you want a boy or a girl?"

"It doesn't matter."

"Then I'll have twins. One of each. Let's make love on the carpet."

Both of them laughed. Two of the kittens came and sat in front of the fire.

"You want me to turn on the light?"

"Whatever for? There's nothing more comforting than firelight."

THE NEXT DAY Randall went to his desk. The fire was low, the room still warm. Randall put more coal on the fire and settled down. Outside the small window in front of the desk it was raining. The wind had come up. Far away he could hear the waves of the sea crashing on the shore. The sheaf of clean pages was in front of him. Randall began writing. It was 1887 in the bushveld of Africa soon after the arrival of Sebastian Brigandshaw from England. Sebastian was riding a horse, looking out over the savannah. There were animals as far as he could see. A herd of elephant. A family of giraffe. Small buck, their heads and shoulders visible above the dry, waving grass. It was the dry season, barely a cloud in the sky. A few, small motionless white clouds smiling down on Sebastian. As far as Sebastian could see in any direction there was no sign of humanity. No people. No huts. Just the bush and the wild animals... Within a minute Randall lost touch with reality. He was back in his Africa. Back where he wanted to be, the words flowing onto the blank pages as Randall reached into the mind of Sebastian. When Randall came out of his trance two hours later six of the pages were covered with words. He was back in a book. He was writing. He was happy. It was enough for one day. The story would stay in his thoughts and subconscious, the story building until he sat at his desk the next day.

When Randall got up to stretch, the coals in the fire were glowing, the room as warm as toast. Randall could again hear the sound of the sea. They had drunk one bottle of wine before making love on the carpet in front of the fire. There was no trace of a hangover. Randall felt good. In the lounge, in front of the fire, he found Meredith. She was curled up in the chair reading a book.

"You didn't have any breakfast. How did it go?"

"I'm in. I'm in his head... I never eat before I write."

"You want some toast? You bought a toasting fork, remember?"

"I'd love some buttered toast. A little marmalade."

"I'm going to start writing tomorrow. I've been making up the story in my head. If Nora gets me a publisher I want to do my own illustrations. I've fed the kittens twice. Those cats can drink milk. Why don't we bring that big settee in front of the fire and we can curl up together? Do we have to go outside?"

"I don't think so. We have everything we need."

"Tea and toast round the fire. Help me with the settee. I could do some scrambled eggs to put on the toast. We need some chickens in that old henhouse. Do you want me to read what you've written?"

"I reread three times until I'm satisfied. Let me finish a chapter."

"I'll go put on the kettle."

NORA STEWART PHONED three weeks later after Randall had finished the first chapter. Meredith had started her book and gone off the pill. It was all happening.

"Where are you, Nora?"

"I'm in New York. Villiers are launching *Love Song* in the spring. You'll have to come over."

Randall said nothing, waiting. Meredith was looking at him, her eyes full of expectation, mingled with the fear of rejection.

"Is she there?"

"Right in front of me."

"Let me speak to Meredith."

Randall handed Meredith the phone and watched.

"Hello. This is Meredith Harding."

For what seemed like forever to Randall, Meredith listened, at first a frown on her face. Randall, the tension physically hurting him, watched the panic on Meredith's face subside into a smile.

"Thank you, Nora. I'll tell Randall."

The phone went back on the hook. One of the kittens got up on the table next to the telephone and rubbed its back on the phone.

"What's the story?"

"She loved it. So does someone called MaryJane at Villiers Publishing. Oh, Randall. I'm going to be published. That old saying is so true. It's not what you know but who you know. Without you, my darling, none of this would have happened."

"There's another true saying: 'if the book sucks it won't publish'."

"You made that up."

"But it's true... They are launching *Love Song* in the spring. You can meet everyone when we go over. It takes a good six months to put a book together after it has been accepted. Did Nora mention an advance?"

"She's asking for fifty thousand dollars. They'll come back to her with the contract. I'm not sure whether to whoop and sing or pass out with excitement."

"The sun's shining in paradise. Let's go to the sea in the car and walk down the beach. The dogs will love a walk along the shore. I'm so happy for you, Meredith. How was the book going when the phone rang?"

"My heart stopped. I knew the call was from America. I had that feeling. Let's go to the beach and walk off some of my excitement. I feel like I'm bursting."

"Before we go, you'd better phone your mother. Give her the news. They need a bit of excitement. She'll be so proud of you. Just maybe, maybe only, your father will stop watching the sports channel."

"Not a chance."

"I'll go make us some lunch while you talk to your mother."

As Randall went to the kitchen he was smiling. There was no hurry to make the lunch. Mother and daughter would be talking the best part of an hour. The puppies, both of them Collies, one male and one female, followed him into the kitchen. Randall took sausages out of the freezer and put them in the oven, away from the cats. He let the dogs out of the backdoor from the kitchen and followed them. From the lounge he could hear Meredith talking on the phone to her mother. There was plenty of time for a walk.

RANDALL AND MEREDITH were married in Liverpool six months later. Meredith was five months pregnant. Both families, including Randall's brother Phillip, who had flown over from Zimbabwe, were at the family wedding. They were married in church unlike his registry office marriage to Amanda. The church of England ceremony in the old Norman church made Randall hope his new marriage would be forever. Among the guests were Mr Corlett and his wife of many years. The church bells rang out to celebrate their union. The first book in Randall's African chronicles was halfway finished. The names in the book were now fictional. Mr Corlett, always helpful, had found a house-sitter to look after the farm and the animals, an old couple, friends of Mrs Corlett. Myra had come up with her three-month-old daughter from London with her parents, having flown over from America to show her mother and father the healthy baby girl. Myra was radiant. Julian, in the middle of making a new film, had stayed in America. Randall and Meredith were due to meet up with Julian at the launch of *Love Song*, all part of their honeymoon. With the help of artists at Villiers Publishing, Meredith would complete the illustrations of *Talking to the Animals* and read through the edited book before its June publication. In December, the fifty thousand dollars had been transferred to her bank account in Douglas by Villiers. They were due to sail by ship from Liverpool to New York at the start of their honeymoon.

When Randall walked from the churchyard to his car, to drive to the reception at the Hardings' home, the press were waiting. Randall was back in the spotlight, his privacy broken. Meredith smiled and waved. She too was about to be famous. The reception was a blur of congratulations, Randall managed to make a speech and keep himself sober. And then, like so many times in Randall's life, the expectations were over. He was married. Soon to be a father for the second time. The only person missing in the family wedding was his son, James Oliver. One day, hopefully, they would get to know each other.

"You two have a good boat-trip. Give my love to America."

"You and Oliver look after yourselves. Thanks for coming up."

"You can't make new old friends, Randall."

"Are you two going to be all right financially?"

"Of course we are. We didn't want to take anything from your wedding. It's yours and Meredith's day. Our good news is we are back in the theatre. A new repertory company has employed both of us. Who knows? One day we both might be famous."

"Careful what you wish for. Julian hates it. I'm so glad for you."

"One day soon we'll be touring to Liverpool and you can come and see the play."

"I'll look forward to it."

One after the other, Randall hugged his friends. They were all emotional. Of all the wonderful things in Randall's life there was nothing better than true old friends.

JUST THE GAME OF LIFE (BOOK THIRTEEN)

CONTINUE YOUR JOURNEY WITH THE BRIGANDSHAWS

The Brigandshaw Chronicles will return in late 2021 with *Just the Game of Life*. To ensure you don't miss any updates on this release, please like Peter Rimmer's Facebook Page or alternatively follow Peter on his Amazon's Author Page.

PRINCIPAL CHARACTERS

❧

The Crookshanks

Amanda — Randall's ex-wife
Bergit — Randall and Phillip's stepmother
Beth — Harry Brigandshaw's daughter and married to Paul Crookshank
Craig — Randall's half-brother
Myra — Randall's half-sister
Randall — Central character in *Look Before You Leap*
James Oliver — Randall and Amanda's son
Jeremy — Randall's father
Mrs Crookshank — Randall and Phillip's paternal grandmother
Paul — Randall and Phillip's uncle and brother to Jeremy
Phillip — Randall's elder brother

Other Principal Characters

Alison — A girlfriend of Phillip's safari operator friend
Ben Crossley — Randall and Phillip's maternal grandfather

Brenda Foster — A London manager at Villiers Publishing

Ernest Bligh — A London private detective

Felix Kranskie — A Hollywood film producer

Florence — An old friend of Nora Stewart

Harry Wakefield — Journalist at the *Daily Mirror* and central character of *The Best of Times*

Henrietta — Julian Becker's New York travel agent

Henry Stone — Randall's editor at Villiers Publishing

Holly — Julian's girlfriend at drama school

Ivey Conway — James Tomlin's girlfriend

James Tomlin — Randall's friend and roommate at Mrs Salter's

Jensen Sandler — Film producer whose wife was caught in bed with Julian

Jocelyn Graham — An intern at the *Daily Mirror*

Johnny Stiglitz — Henry Stone's assistant

Jojo — Craig Crookshank's girlfriend

Julian Becker — An out-of-work actor in Los Angeles

Kaitlyn Harvey — A girl Randall meets at his book launch

Keith Fortescue — Felix's lawyer

Lucy Haynes — A girl Randall meets in the Rising Sun pub

Manfred Lewis — Randall's American agent

Meredith Harding — A girl Randall meets in the Rising Sun pub

Mr Corlett — Randall's estate agent on the Isle of Man

Mrs Salter — Longstanding landlady of Randall, Oliver and James

Nora Stewart — Randall's American independent publicist appointed by Villiers Publishing

Oliver Manningford — Randall's friend and roommate at Mrs Salter's

Romano — Felix Kranskie's manservant

Sedgewick — Phillip's safari driver and assistant

Silas — Long-standing house servant on World's View

Susan — Henry Stone's third wife

Timothy Wendel — An aspiring actor and companion of Nora Stewart

Trent — Felix Kranskie's chauffeur

Wanda Worthington — An actress in *Masters of Vanity*

Willard — Farm worker on World's View

DEAR READER

∾

Reviews are the most powerful tools in our kitty when it comes to getting attention for Peter's books. This is where you can come in, as by providing an honest review you will help bring them to the attention of other readers.

If you enjoyed reading *Look Before You Leap*, and have five minutes to spare, we would really appreciate a review (it can be as short as you like). Your help in spreading the word and keeping Peter's work alive is gratefully received.

Please post your review on the retailer site where you purchased this book.

Thank you so much.
Heather Stretch (Peter's daughter)

ACKNOWLEDGEMENTS

~

With grateful thanks to our *VIP First Readers* for reading *Look Before You Leap* prior to its official launch date. They have been fabulous in picking up errors and typos helping us to ensure that your own reading experience of *Look Before You Leap* has been the best possible. Their time and commitment is particularly appreciated.

Hilary Jenkins (South Africa)
Agnes Mihalyfy (United Kingdom)
Daphne Rieck (Australia)

Thank you.
Kamba Publishing

www.ingramcontent.com/pod-product-compliance
Ingram Content Group UK Ltd.
Pitfield, Milton Keynes, MK11 3LW, UK
UKHW040715150725
6897UKWH00028B/370